M000216956

POISON

Cambridge Murder Mysteries

by Charlot King

The Cambridge Murder Mysteries Series:

Book 1: *POISON*

Book 2: *CURSED*

Book 3: *BLOOD MOON*

Book 4: *A CHRISTMAS MYSTERY*

Book 5: *VALENTINE'S DAY – KISS OF DEATH*

Book 6: *COMING SOON*

Copyright © 2015 Charlot King

All rights reserved.

All rights belong to the author
First published as an ebook 2015
Published by: Beautiful Day Cambridge Ltd
ISBN: 978-0-9934083-0-4

Illustration: Robin Howlett
All Rights Reserved

All Rights Reserved by Beautiful Day Cambridge Ltd

The moral right of Charlot King to be identified as the author of
this work has been asserted by her in accordance with the
Copyright, Designs and Patents Act 1988.

No part of this publication may be reproduced, stored in a
retrieval system or transmitted in any form or by any means,
without the prior permission in writing of the publisher, nor to
be otherwise circulated in any form of binding or cover other
than that in which it is published without a similar condition,
including this condition, being imposed on the subsequent
purchaser.

Disclaimer: This is a work of fiction. Names, characters,
businesses, places, events and incidents are either the products
of the author's imagination or used in a fictitious manner. Any
resemblance to actual persons, living or dead, or actual events is
purely coincidental.

DEDICATION AND THANKS

Thanks to Katie, Penny, John, Jo, Lindsay, and my father, John, for all your support. To Robin Howlett who is a supremely talented illustrator. I would especially like to thank my son, for all his encouragement and belief in me. Finally, I wrote this novel while my mother, Cassie, was ill. She has now sadly passed away. I dedicate this book to her.

PREFACE

If you visit Cambridge, do remember to walk along The Backs, wander along King's Parade, take in the magnificence of the colleges, and punt out to Grantchester for tea in the orchards. You won't be disappointed.

PROLOGUE

There's a reason we say 'mad as a hatter'. In the 1800s, many hatters were poisoned by mercuric nitrate, used to remove fur from animal skin to make hat felt. Poisoning symptoms included tremors, pathological shyness, timidity and erratic behaviour. Some might say a fair price for animal cruelty.

My hat hits the water, drifting away like a little boat, oblivious to splash and panic. My nemesis, peering over the bridge above like their plan has come together. Everything's happening at once. I can't feel my feet. My hands are stiff; I can taste my chest bleeding, fluid running down inside my torso. My stomach's burning; I'm vomiting and just emptied my bowels into my trousers. The river's carrying me away to my death. I know it, but is this just a dream? The pain has taken over my brain. I want to sleep... water under Magdalene Bridge is eerie, the dark current moving faster towards Jesus Weir. Everything's growing fuzzy like I'm dissolving as the blood runs out of me. Here come the low banks, the poppies, the gardens. Me, a petrified buoy, I watch them as I float by. Oh, Elizabeth Green's. How could I forget? I can see it. I can see her light on. Oh my, that's her. That's her. Help.

1

1
QUIET MONDAY

'All things are poison, and nothing is without poison; only the dose permits something not to be poisonous.' Paracelsus

It is not so late that only foxes are crossing Cambridge streets, but an echoey Monday nevertheless. Laughter all trickled into drains along with kisses from weekend revelry. The metre-wide Corpus gold clock on the corner wall of Bene't and Trumpington Street ticks erratically, deliberately only accurate once every five minutes; its black chronophage grasping at the seconds as they try to escape its metal claws. Faded glows from the neo-gothic gatehouse Porters' Lodge at Bene't's College cast insignificant shadows towards the Chapel on King's Parade, standing firm on its own chessboard lawn, defying anyone to take this most important piece in the city.

Within arm's reach, just along a squeezable alley, emerald glints exude from The Green Magician. Aromas of basil, tomatoes and red wine escape up steps, luring naive nostrils down into the dark cavernous hole. Laid out for lovers, poets, accidental tourists; anybody who will sit quietly and part with currency to lazy waiters, still musing over last night's satellite football results. This small corner of Cambridge is only just still open for business this early in the week.

At the far end of The Green Magician, a man and his dog slurp spaghetti meatballs, sitting opposite one another across a table like an old married couple. In the next alcove, photographs litter a wall with faces of bemused looking celebrities, who once took a wrong turn and have now been captured forever in frame, tonight forced to peep down on an elderly lady, busy with a crossword over her tiramisu. Bang in the middle of the gloom at a central table, two fresh-faced kids in a state of virginal romance hog the limelight as they pour sugar in the salt and stuff breadsticks up their nostrils in an attempt to make each other titter at first love ingeniousness; then post everything on their social media sites.

Nearer the door, and tucked under the stairs, the shadow of a woman leans heavily over a table grabbing at the face of a man she tries to kiss. Edward Wiley maintains an air of dignity only a Don might, leans backwards, an eyebrow raised. An odd pairing, him with his sleek, chiselled good looks and calm decorum, and her, pug heavy fattened skin, ruby wine moustache and odour of desperation. The elderly lady on the table adjacent peers at Edward as he brushes under his plate wiping away crumbs, then beckons his date to sit down.

"Really, cease this darling." Edward's mellow evocative tone reveals a charmed background, mirrored by the first gentle crow's feet around kind eyes. Edward rubs at his nose and runs his tongue across his front teeth. Susan Bunt replies a little too loudly.

"You used to friggin' want to. You're no fun anymore. Come on." Her words cut into his ears like pins into a cushion, as she implores him to let her nuzzle. But Edward holds her gaze, causing her to sit back in her seat, and with an ease which takes the sting out of it, his words drift effortlessly across the table.

"Come off it, Poppet, I still want to, always," breaking a smile, "I just couldn't possibly risk it in here. I mean, gracious, you know I'm not one for public sharing of bodily fluids and all that jazz. I'm also beginning to feel a little off colour tonight."

"Behind doors, curtains, locked key, and no lights on these days," Susan retorts huffily, "I haven't seen you in ages. You know you've been away too long on that bloody field trip." She takes a big gulp of wine, adding, "You've hardly eaten anything. This was supposed to be a romantic dinner."

Edward rubs his nose again and sniffs.

"My chest's a bit tight, maybe a cold. Be better tomorrow, probably caught a bug from the flight home. You know what the air is like in the cabin — another reason not to go near you. You don't want to catch anything. And please don't drink so much." He grimaces a little in pain, perhaps indigestion. Edward picks out from his pocket a packet tied up with a bow and hands it to Susan. Opening it, she gasps at a bright red and black necklace.

"It's beautiful."

"I saw them and thought of you. Here." Edward helps Susan tie the clasp of the necklace around her neck. "It looks lovely, Suse. But not as lovely as you." Edward reaches into his coat and brings out another present. This time unwrapped. It is a small wooden face mask, grimacing with a tongue lolling to one side. "Supposed to ward off evil spirits," he says. Susan pulls an 'Oh my' face, a little unsure about this second generous offering, but still with hope for the evening. Edward reaches again into his pocket, this time pulling out a wallet.

"You can't be leaving already?"

"You know what I want. But I have to talk to Rebecca if you haven't forgotten that minor detail. I only saw her briefly this morning before I went to the department. I'll call you. I promise. I need to lie down now. I'm exhausted."

"What do I care. Go, don't go." Susan leans back in her chair.

"Believe me, though I'm relieved to be back my family are the last people I'd like to be spending time with right now."

As Susan then slumps forward, putting her head in her hands and exhaling loudly, Edward calmly puts money on the table and gets up, wiping his mouth with a napkin. He shakes a grey duffel coat over his shoulders, checks his watch, puts on his fedora and makes one final plea to Susan.

"I'll see you tomorrow. Can't we leave it until then? Oh, and do wear something more cheery. That cloak has something of the night about it." Edward looks at her cloak, draped over the back of her chair.

Tipsy and somewhat melancholy, Susan Bunt lifts her head and watches Edward climb the stairs out of the basement restaurant.

"That's it. Go on, desert me. Run back to wifey," she curses up at him, immediately angry at herself for her caustic tone.

"Goodnight Susan. Don't be cross. Get home safe. We'll talk in the morning. I promise it will be better tomorrow. I'm going to sort this."

Any impartial observer couldn't miss the whiff of rejection, the lingering rosy Merlot being the only kiss of departure on Susan's lips. What is Edward doing, going back to that waif? Running the whole thing through her mind, brushing tears from her clammy cheeks she imagines every detail of her abandonment. It almost comes spewing out of her. Edward can be so callous, so cold, so bloody English. She hates him. Hates him for rejecting her again tonight. He's never going to leave his wife. Never. How could he have made promises before he went away? Just to get her hopes up? That was cruel. She was not going to have it. She was going to sort him out. Susan gets up, swaying a little as she puts on her cloak, and leaves more determined than ever.

*

Less than a mile away, an Edwardian house backing onto the River Cam, named Foxes' Haven, enjoys the silence of its only occupant. Wearing a man's midnight blue fine cotton cardigan over a cream loose linen dress with artisan pockets, fifty-something Elizabeth Green pushes her dinner around delicate porcelain. Much too late for any digestive routine, Elizabeth's stomach aches with emptiness, yet nourishment is too hard to swallow. Elizabeth looks at her copy of Much Obliged Jeeves. Even Wodehouse can't bring her cheer tonight.

A grandfather clock ticks over family photographs, which all stand to attention on the sideboard in this elegant home; smiling faces, in mist on mountain peaks, under blue sky at seaside landscapes, on snow-covered walks with ruddy cheeks, in front of cars at classic motor gatherings, revealing Elizabeth Green's life to anyone who cares to glance. In one picture her tiny bones with slightly pulled up shoulders lean into a very tall man – giving the impression of an anxious person when in fact it is just the result of congenital poor posture. Her big brown curls squashed up against his shoulders. Elizabeth stares at the photograph and slowly picks it up: her sweet pixie face, intelligent yet vulnerable green eyes, completely masking her sharp tongue and short attention span for fools. She stares at her husband's strong jaw, mop of straw hair and focuses on the tiny glint the camera has caught in his right eye, his crooked smile exposing irregular teeth, as well as his double chins. He is perfect – was perfect – and now he's gone, taken in his late prime before he got a chance to enjoy more time with Elizabeth. She knows she's now lost the best side of herself, the side only he saw. Such thoughts haunt her. Clasping the photograph she stops breathing, her emptiness pervasive, the pointlessness of continuing reverberating.

Outside the frame, Elizabeth feels time frozen in her veins. Knows she can't tell anyone how she feels, it isn't like her to burden anyone. She just moves from one thing to another, using this to try to get through that. Maintaining a positive outward front at all times, just brought up that way. But she can't ever let herself feel love again, for when the loss comes, it is just too much. It spills out only when she talks to Gerald, even though he doesn't answer back. Both of them made a pact that whoever died first, they'd send a sign to the one remaining who was to use all five senses to be alert for such a message. But there have been no signs. She puts the frame back on the sideboard and listens to the silence. Would anyone notice if she were gone? Elizabeth's face is etched with fine lines from a life she didn't choose, haunted by happier memories.

Bertie returns from somewhere and stands for a moment by the door. He moves a little, maybe five feet to the lit fire where he pauses again, sits and cleans his chest, with one eye on Elizabeth sitting at the table. He knows her face like the creases in his paw. Her cheeks, once full have lost a little lustre. Her lacquered curls a little more dishevelled. Her smile not making such a regular appearance. But Elizabeth's eyes still adore him. Bertie walks over and brushes his leg against hers. Tears spike as she leans down to stroke his soft fur. Her fingers sweep through Bertie's hair, brushing against her skin like a hundred kisses — Elizabeth booms at Bertie.

"Bertie. Muddy paws on my rug. What shall we do? Digging up my flowers isn't gentlemanly either. We need to have a little chat about that at some point. Let's book an appointment in the diary shall we?"

Elizabeth picks up Bertie and gives him the biggest hug. Bertie obliges and lies still in her arms.

CHARLOT KING

2
RIVER CAM

Susan flicks up her floppy hood, cloaking herself in black velvet as she clumps across cobbles heading away from The Green Magician and down King's Parade towards All Saints' College, boiling at Edward's decision to return to his wife. A couple of late opening cafes reflect silhouettes of people nursing nightcaps. Teddy bears in brightly lit shop windows eagerly wait tourists return in the morning. Susan scowls past a handsome young man ambling back to his digs after discussions on Plato and Aristotle at a Fellow's rooms. A beautiful couple snuggle into each other as they giggle, beaming at Susan seemingly just to rub her nose in it as they walk by. Susan's temperature rises, grinding her teeth her footsteps grow more determined to have it out with Edward if she can just catch up with him.

A fit looking man on a bicycle in black leggings and purple racing vest glides past Great St Mary's Church on the Parade towards Susan, then slows down and starts to circle her. Susan watches him, and for a moment thinks perhaps she knows his face? But in no time, and with exaggerated gesture, he points and glares at Susan, while cycling towards her at increasing speed. Putting her hand to her face, and just when she thinks she should scream, an elderly man steps out from around the corner of St Mary's Street disturbing the cyclist, who whizzes past and cycles off. Hairs prickle down Susan's spine, the gentleman smiles, lifts his hat and is immediately gone. All of a sudden no one else is about, and Susan feels completely sober. Left wondering about the altercation she heads towards the river.

*

Having left a little time ahead of Susan so as not to be spotted together, and now some way from the cafe, Edward walks along Trinity Street, enclosed by looming walls of darkened college brick. Cutting a fine figure in his fitted spring duffel, his chinos brush against chestnut leather brogues squeaking slightly from their newness, his footsteps echoing on the walls around him. Edward's eyes sparkle in the inky night, his golden skin with tinges of sunburn picked out by each streetlight under the brim of his hat. Air flows through his nostrils, clean and fresh. But it hurts his chest, and an intense pain rushes up his throat. He uncontrollably vomits into the side of the wall, causing him to pause with surprise and more pain.

He knows it is summer here but now back from his trip and all that equatorial heat he feels shivers and thinks perhaps he has flu after all. A window of the oldest bookshop in all of England lights up an 1859 first edition of Darwin's Origin of the Species, inviting passers-by to reflect on the impressive shift such a small tome had on their understanding of their place in the world. Edward doesn't notice. He's just heaved up again. He heads down Garret Hostel Lane to cross the River Cam, mulling over the evening's proceedings.

Despite the friction with Susan, his increasingly poor stomach and painful lungs, he feels relieved to be back in

England. He likes England very much. It is his favourite place in the world. With the summer stretching ahead of him, and students soon all gone down after examinations, Cambridge academia will be quiet, and he can finish his research in peace, enjoy balmy nights the city brings, and spend time with those close to him. He'll see Susan again after he's spoken to his wife, Rebecca, in the morning. Susan has to learn that she can't just snap her fingers. He loves her madly, yes. But she rejected him when they were both young, and now she wants him to end it with his wife immediately? Not asking for much, yet he loves being in love. He can't deny it. He wants to shout it from the rooftops. It's like something he's been waiting for all his life, and now he's found it. And what with the great news too. It's all so exciting and scary.

He just hadn't felt like staying with her tonight, he is feeling really ropey, maybe severely jet-lagged and needs his bed, perhaps he's going to be sick again, and his chest feels full of fluid. Edward throws up against a wall and looks at blood in the mucus on the stones. He staggers on, wishing he had taken the straight route back to Bene't's College front Gate, instead of choosing the longer route to come round The Backs, so as to look like he'd returned from his department rather than his lover.

*

Elizabeth leaves Bertie on the table licking her plate clean of juices and walks across the room to where a grand piano stands by French windows which are wide open to the night. Ready to be played, its keys shine with polish and love. She lifts the lid on an old teak stool, immediately releasing a redolence of well worn, loved old books, containing memories to transport her away. Picking out her choice she then sits, pulling up long sleeves of the poorly fitting man's cardigan and begins to play 'Cheek to Cheek', by Irvin Berlin. Closing her eyes, there in front of her is Sir Gerald Green, his rough roguish smile, his bellowing laugh, which makes his belly wobble. Together with her he sits on a picnic blanket by the River Cam at Fen Ditton, points out swallows up on the warm drifts and creates imaginary pirate ships from the shapes of small white puffy clouds. Throwing bread for the ducks, he quacks back. Silly old fool. Gerald raises his eyebrows as a bee feeds on his jam scone, knowing she would reprimand him should he brush the bee away. She holds a picture of him in her mind so real, for that moment, her heart jumps. The summer air catches Elizabeth's breath, and he is gone. She opens her eyes and stops playing. The room now deathly quiet. Gerald's departure leaving the bitter reality that she has lost the only person who really understood her.

*

Susan feels uneasy after her encounter with the cyclist moments ago, yet remains cross at Edward. She is going to make him pay for putting her second. He can't treat her like this! Hurrying through centuries-old alleyways between high college walls she takes a short cut to the river, near where she knows Edward will be just ahead, sneaking in the back way to College, as if from the department if she can just catch up and have it out with him.

Turning a corner in a narrow passage, she stumbles into someone but doesn't see their face. In the commotion Susan is grabbed around the neck, she can feel the grubby, sweaty hands tightening. Her body sways, buckling under the knee as her neck is stretched like a saveloy against the wall. In the silvery black air, the alley is deathly quiet, all but her choking croak as Susan is violently pushed down towards the pavement. She begins to pick out tiny brickwork against her face, moss clinging on for dear life between the cracks, trying to make a go of things in this lightless alley. Her eyes bulge as her cheek presses deep into damp stone as if it will be her final resting place. But then she feels the constricted arteries in her neck begin to flow, as the grip loosens and the assailant turns then runs. The alley is empty again.

There is no one to cry out to, though Susan has no voice left in her. She takes a moment before fear grips her with thoughts of her attacker's return and so she rushes on, her legs carrying her though buckling under each step, while her throat is still gasping for breath. Looking back, Susan checks to see if she is being followed, before disappearing around a corner. Maybe it is time to go home.

A short while later, from either side of the River Cam, two people walk onto an arched bridge. They meet on the steep brow, stop next to each other against the glinting bronze rail. One of them is Edward. His face in the moonlight looks fraught against the willows. The other in complete silhouette, a crow-black figure.

"Hello. I thought we'd sorted it? I'm feeling dreadful. I need to lie down." Edward says, not expecting this chance encounter. No response is returned from the dark shape. A cloud covers the moon, and for a few short moments, all is enveloped in utter darkness. Those moments linger like empty blackness, which blocks out everything. A scuffle and then a splash echoes under the bridge, and another as hands clap on the water's surface like swan's wings. The cloud passes, and moonlight shines back onto the bridge. Only one person remains. That person hesitates for a moment, looks down at the figure now in the water, but makes no effort to help.

*

Not far away, Elizabeth Green flicks through the same piano book and comes to 'Blue Skies'. Taking a long determined breath, she bows her head to the keys and starts to play. Sentimental paintings of Wicken Fen, the line of London Plane trees on Jesus Green, add colour to the wall behind her. Her music flows out of the windows, carrying some distance up into the night and drifting across the ink-black river, until finally merging with disturbingly violent splashes in the water from underneath the arch of the Bridge of Sorrows. A person's hands groping, flailing, a lolling head panic-stricken. Ducks disturbed from a hole in the wall plop down and obliviously pass the person now struggling for breath, as they glide away in the opposite direction to find a quieter patch for the night. In the distance and now out of sight, a person still standing on the arch of the bridge morbidly stares at the dark spectre, then, convinced of the finality of their actions, hurries away in slate silhouette, not looking back with any change of heart for the body fighting the water below.

The waters flow around a bend in the river, carrying the sodden casualty further down towards Jesus Weir and Lock. Two lovers amble over Magdalene Bridge some way in the distance and, unaware, blissfully kiss in the moonlight. Windows in an illegally moored narrow boat glow with orange light, as smoke plumes out from a cosy wood burner chimney. All doors shut up tight, making it impossible to hear the terror cries bumping across the ripples onto the bow and back again against college walls, eventually, each single note evaporating into the night air.

Struggling past high walled river banks, slipping under and resurfacing, someone is losing their battle for life, as Elizabeth's playing is interrupted by the grandfather clock chiming, or was it a banging door from somewhere? Elizabeth's fingers retreat back into the large cardigan sleeves as she glances at the hands on the brass face resolutely staring back midnight in concert with a strong dong, dong, dong. She gets up to leave the drawing room, anxiously unsure as if she has remembered something, but then forgotten what it was. Bertie rushes out.

The watery figure's last chance lures them into false hope, as they are taken past a low bank edge, now nearing the weir. Gliding towards someone's garden. With all willpower of a drowning person, they cling onto the grass on the very edge, too weak to do any more. Elizabeth steps out into her garden; illuminated from kitchen light she carries leftovers from her dinner for any interested wildlife. She taps the side and starts to chatter to her regular evening visitors yet to make an appearance.

"Delicious. Potatoes and peas. Hedgiepogs! Come, come, come!" Her ample garden rambles down to meet the River Cam. A wide and sloping lawn squeezes against narrow borders on either side, full of lavender, rosemary, roses. Eighty feet away at the bottom, the drowning shadow has noticed her and calls up the lawn, gasping for breath, choking to death. Elizabeth, on hearing a noise and thinking it may be a hedgehog replies, "What's the matter with you tonight? Got a cold? Well, don't pass it to me, or Bertie. I've had enough colds to last me until winter. Thank you very much."

Buoyed by the hope of a human voice, the person pulls at the grass and lifts their arms to hold a lavender stump, vomiting, convulsing, taking last breaths. Elizabeth can hear, but not see properly through the silver birch trees.

"Who's there?" She walks towards the noise, now just making out a man in the moonlight. Her footsteps tread the grass more quickly, and she throws herself into a run. The person is screaming with every ounce of life left.

'Serve us', or is it 'Served us tips!' Elizabeth can't quite make it out. She sees a man struggling in the water. Bending down, she grabs his coat and pulls at the heavy material. Together they get him half out of the water. Choking, and finding it hard to breathe, he clutches Elizabeth's hand. Doubled up in pain, like some wild animal caught in a trap, his body convulsing, his eyes wild and rolling. His arm badly cut, as she holds him tight.

"Edward? Edward. What on earth. Come here, come on. We'll get you out. Stretch."

"Serve us tips," he gurgles. Elizabeth can't quite

understand him. Edward convulses, his head lolling up close to her face, and stares at her intently, but then his mouth twists in utter horror as he takes in the breath of death. The pain has gone, and he is no more. She cannot hold him and slowly he falls back into the water.

Elizabeth, lying flat out on her stomach on the damp grass, watches with desperation as he slips under the murky water and seems to catch on something, suspended like a merman, he moves with the ebb and flow of the slow-moving current. His eyes stare back at her in shock, his arms higher than his head as if reaching back up for her to help. A shiver runs down Elizabeth's spine, and she withdraws a little, but then spots a hat floating down the Cam and straight towards her, bobbing behind the ghoulish figure. It hits the edge of her garden bank, and she leans in and picks it out. In the moonlight, Elizabeth can see the name, Edward Wiley, clearly written on the inside lining of the fedora. She shakes the hat, still dripping with water, and as she does a small plastic bag falls out having been tucked in the inside rim. The bag, smaller than the size of her hand, has a tiny seal zip. It is empty but for a whiff of white powder. Elizabeth looks at Edward, still holding the hat, her breathing growing evermore shallow, the wet lawn soaking her clothes. She feels a strong sense of disquiet that this was meant to happen in front of her.

3
POWER

The sun rises, and the sky changes from black to reds. The latest model executive car drives up a fairly deserted motorway in the fast lane, breaking all speed laws. Inside, a man is listening to BBC Radio 4, the familiar pips signal six o'clock. Headlines chirp 'Today the prime minister will announce that he's preparing for a Cabinet reshuffle later this week after the recent election victory. Some unexpected names have been mentioned to replace a few of his most loyal hands. And we will be speaking with the deputy prime minister before seven, about who he believes are the most desired colleagues to make their debuts off the back benches'.

Inside the car, on a heated seat, a man dressed in a bespoke pinstripe suit turns off the radio and picks up an electric razor. He starts to shave one side of his face, then the curve of his chin. His briefcase on the passenger seat is open, with the word 'Westminster' on headed paper inside. Jonathan Smythe-Jones, Member of Parliament for Ely, a barrister with ambition emblazoned on his cuff, and with a life full of appointments and schedules, finishes shaving his other cheek as his phone rings. He answers, picking up the small hands-free earphones, squeezing them in a little too deep. His gravelly voice replies to the caller.

"What?" Jonathan takes a sharp intake of breath. "Look, calm down. I've told you I'm coming." He pauses to listen, picking at the white cord running from his phone to his ears, then interrupts impatiently. "Please don't lecture me. I know how serious this is. If you hadn't quite forgotten, I'm waiting to hear from the PM. Yes, driving to meet you now, all right? I'm not about to let this, or anything else ruin my chances." Another pause to listen, then he replies, "Are you not even there yet? What the bloody hell have you been doing? You're going to make me crash at this rate. Well, don't tell the police anything until we've spoken. Let me manage Rebecca. I'll have to put a lid on this. Just get there, quick smart." He listens again, then angrily replies, "Why do you think they need to know that? Look, I'll be there in an hour. Hell on a stick, say nothing."

As he cuts the call, veins protrude in Jonathan's neck. He rubs at his collar and emits the deepest of sighs, then studies his reflection in the driver's mirror. He raises his jet-black eyebrows deliberately at the tips and pulls back the skin on his face, narrows his eyes and focuses back on the road. This isn't going to be a good day. There is nothing about recent events which will allow it.

There is something about hitting forty that sharpens focus towards pessimism. The last-ditch run for success, with a head firmly looking behind for younger contenders, Jonathan is feeling remarkably queasy as he drives towards Cambridge, a journey he seems to be doing all the time at the moment. As he stares into the middle distance, he spots a crow on the tarmac ahead, picking at road kill. The crow continues to hold his ground, despite the car drawing nearer. He is half tempted to run the thing over, but at the last moment violently swerves. Unblemished, the crow nonchalantly hops away in the opposite direction, as

Jonathan   Smythe-Jones   tries   to   regain   control.

4

THE AMIABLE MAN

The sun pushes through darkness as the police forensics team combs the area near the dead body, which has now been pulled up out of the dark water onto the grass at the end of Elizabeth's garden.

A police officer tapes off the garden at the water's edge, stopping any intentional mooring or entry. Towards the house, past a large Victorian pale brick, wood framed greenhouse, Inspector Abley stands under a parasol with Elizabeth, accepting a cup of tea in fine bone china, plopping in a lump of sugar then stirring with a spoon far too tiny for his meaty hands.

A tall, well-fed amiable man, Bob Abley is easy in his own golf-course preserved skin, the creases around his eyes hiding well any look of an overworked copper. Dressed in an off-the-peg suit, open to reveal a golf shirt, and wearing his favourite well-worn moccasins, his attire sets him apart from the uniformed and forensic officers. His light brown messy hair and kind chocolate colour eyes that tilt upwards towards the brow of his nose, and two fawn caterpillar eyebrows walking down towards his ears, give him a compassionate edge, so often lacking among his hard-nosed colleagues. Some say he has been promoted as much for being liked as being able to crack a case.

"Do your officers always arrive before you these days, Inspector?" Elizabeth booms, adjusting cups on the tea tray on a garden table beneath the parasol, from which Bertie studies proceedings. Bertie sees his opportunity and dips a paw straight into the milk she brought out for the Inspector. Elizabeth ignores this and takes a sip of her own peppermint tea, but Inspector Abley raises his eyebrows and thinks twice about drinking his own milky tea, placing his cup back down on the tray and choosing to ignore Elizabeth's barbed comment, familiar with them as he is.

"I never thought I'd be standing with you this morning. That's for sure. It's good to see you, Liz." Elizabeth watches Inspector Abley give her a big grin, but chooses to maintain stern eye contact, as she wants him to spill what he knows about Edward. Abley continues, "You know when you've been in this game as long as I have, you're never surprised by deaths in the river. Calm on the surface, but the weeds, oh my. They should be pulled up."

Elizabeth plays like a cat with a mouse. "Inspector, would you like to join our group to stop the ecological destruction by pennywort and other invasive species along this stretch? You'd be most welcome. Many hands make light work."

Inspector Abley takes a moment to process the entrapment. "What? Er, no. I'm just saying. I must see more deaths than most because of the green stuff and all the rest of it. Nothing more. I'm a busy man. Look, fetch yourself back indoors. I'll let you know when we're leaving."

Elizabeth knows Inspector Abley always solves a case more quickly when she lends a hand.

"Our paths have not crossed all year, and now here you are on my path."

"Looks like grass to me." The Inspector looks down at his feet, standing on the grass. Elizabeth can't believe the simplicity of Abley's thoughts, so explains.

"I was speaking metaphorically. But my path over there was clean before your colleagues arrived." Elizabeth points to her neatly swept path, now with muddy boot marks up and down the cobbles. She narrows her eyes at the mess then looks to the sky. "I think we both agree that we work so well together, Inspector. That I complement the talent you have for–" Elizabeth searches for any words to describe Abley's talent, "people skills, with my sharp investigative mind. This doesn't look like an accident to me. Ask me back, and I'll solve it for you. You always do better with me, you know it." She knows she's too pushy, almost too mean, but she can't help it.

Inspector Abley's eyes widen at Elizabeth's dig at his abilities, choosing not to remind her that he is the full-time Inspector, not her. She's just someone he chooses to hire every now and then as a consultant when relevant, not on the police staff payroll. Other people at the station think she's far too interfering and prickly and should stick to academic life, her full-time job as a Senior Lecturer and Fellow at the University of Cambridge. He knows she is very good at this, and been doing it for years. A memory returns of all those times before, when she treated him like her assistant. But it makes him smile, as he didn't really mind. He knows she is a good woman, and despite what other people say, he actually likes her. Then he looks to the grass, admiring the neat short cut of the blades, and takes a swing of an imaginary golf club before delivering the blow he knows will hurt.

"A person needs time to recover from grieving. You're not ready, not for all this." Abley pauses and watches Elizabeth's face turn to disappointment, so he continues to try to gently explain. "I can't ask for your help, not yet. Not under the circumstances. And you know we'll manage, not as well of course, but we've been managing without you, Liz. And anyway, it still might be an accident, you know." Inspector Abley looks around at the commotion of the men in white forensic suits, and a police photographer snapping away, not believing his own words.

Elizabeth feels stomach punched. It has been a year, surely an acceptable gap before she returns to help? Just for a bit, and on some cases. He doesn't mean to upset her. He's one of the kindest men she knows if a little simple. Both qualities she finds unusual for an Inspector, but surprisingly comforting. She wants to scream at him, but can't find her voice, can't get any words to come out right. Inspector Abley clumsily changes the subject.

"Is that blood?" Abley looks at the cardigan Elizabeth is wearing. There are tiny patches and a scattering of specks of dark red blood down the side of the sleeve and by the pocket. For a moment, both wonder if it might be hers. Elizabeth gathers her composure.

"I tried to pull him out of the water, but men are always much heavier than they look, aren't they? It must be the beer they drink or the steak they ravage."

"I am sure you tried your best. We have people for that. It's all okay now." The Inspector looks at the cardigan. "May we take this for evidence? It might be useful, along with the hat. Thank you for retrieving that from the river."

Elizabeth reluctantly takes off the cardigan and hands it to the Inspector, who holds the neck with a pen so as not to get his own DNA on the garment, while at the same time rummaging in his jacket for an evidence bag.

"Careful. You'll stretch it. It's, it was, his favourite."
Inspector Abley looks confused, so Elizabeth finishes the sentence to help him out.

"It's Gerald's."
Abley feels wretched; he is a bloody detective. How could he be so stupid? He tries to rectify his gaffe but doesn't know what to say.

"Of course." Abley places the cardigan now gently in the bag. "You'll get it back, once we've done the necessary."

"Nothing comes back. Even you can't bring him back, Bob. He's gone." Elizabeth stares at the cardigan, then at a crow in the Beech tree, bouncing on a twig far too small to carry its weight.

For all its not bringing people back, death certainly has a habit of bringing back memories. Despite the brisk air of the morning and the fresh blood on her lawn, with difficulty, Elizabeth lets go of any thoughts of Gerald for now and switches her attention to Edward.

"And now he's gone too. What's to become of this place? Perhaps I'm jinxed?" She asks, half to herself. Inspector Abley shakes his head.

"I'm sorry Liz. I do, you know, want you consulting for me. It's, well, it's just too early, isn't it? I think you know I'm only doing this for you." Abley bites his bottom lip, then turns and sees a Constable and passes him the bag with Sir Gerald's cardigan trapped inside the clear plastic.

"Look after that, will you, son?" The Constable nods and walks off. Abley turns to Elizabeth. "You know the SOCO just told me there are no stab wounds, just a cut on his wrist perhaps from the fall into the water. This might be a tragedy. That river takes as many as it chooses. Excuse me for a minute, will you?"

"What about your tea?" Elizabeth asks.

"Oh, I'll be back for that." Inspector Abley looks at his tea, at Bertie licking milk off his paw then smiles at Elizabeth, then turns and walks away to talk to another uniformed police officer, who is pointing at the river. The frogman has just found a shoe and is placing it on the bank.

Elizabeth can't take her eye off the transparent bag containing one of her most precious belongings, as the young Constable continues up the garden and without care throws it onto the back seat of a squad car. She is stuck to the spot. She knows everything is too early. What did the Inspector mean not ready for all this? How presumptuous people are. What could he know anyway about her being ready?

Then Elizabeth's eyes are drawn to splashing in the river. The frogman surfaces with another watery exhumation, this time trousers, then spits in his goggles before taking another dive to see what else is down below. Two men in white forensic suits measure, mark out and sift through topsoil by the bank. A police photographer takes grim shots, close-ups of the fear and shock in Edward's face. Clicking at hands, feet, neck, hair. Why so many photographs? The photographer doesn't see Edward, just a dead body. His job to collect the evidence, the voyeur, no matter how morbid. Elizabeth looks at the terribly contorted face of Edward staring back at her. The pain reflecting all his dreams cut short, the lack of proper goodbyes, unfinished business. If she could have just told him that everything would be okay. But as she held Edward in her arms in the dark, half-in, half out of the water, she hadn't been able to do anything. Bloody useless, and now what?

Elizabeth absentmindedly wanders over to the greenhouse and twists shut the brass doorknob, looking at the huge grapevine behind the panes. Frustrated with how things have been left with the Inspector, unable to make things better, to tell him the truth, to trust him with her true feelings. Not even the affable Inspector can see how she needs this, needs to be useful to someone.

Elizabeth is going out of her mind at home, with little to do but her department research, and looking after her grandson, Godric Cartwright-Green, who's staying with her right now and is far from a model pupil. She is not even sure whether he will be here for long. The university may well send him down. Her selfish daughter has brought up Godric to be quite the cocky young man, with a higher opinion of himself than the Eiffel Tower. But less thought about her the better. And no matter how hard she tries to distract herself with work, or grandmother duties, there is still something missing, more than just the gaping hole of losing Gerald. Elizabeth cannot seem to grapple with a constant   uneasy   feeling.

5

THE HEDONIST

Elizabeth's grandson, Godric, saunters towards her. Snake hips in flannels, lithe body in floppy white shirt. At just nineteen, his large eyes, lips and blond curls give him the look of other worldliness. Just a boy in a man's vessel, his skin so peachy the glow leaves you in awe and jealousy. Grey eyes flecked with diamonds so sharp they could pierce your heart, and a look so innocent. Looks are often deceptive, particularly in the case of her grandson, Elizabeth thinks. Of course, she loves him, but she wishes he'd be just a little less flippant and a tad more honest.

"Bunny, good morning." Godric kisses his grandmother on both cheeks, his screechy voice not matching the rest of him, and also at odds with her own booming tones. She shuts her eyes to hold the sensation of his love for a moment. Like butterflies on a Buddleia, her heart dances, this boy can charm the birds. When she opens them Godric's eyes are glued to his mobile. She cautions him.

"You'll gamble everything away."

"Up two hundred this week, Nanna. Told you, only penny shares." Godric squeals, cutting slices into the air, glancing up at the police and then back at his phone. "Blue lights woke me up. Should be illegal."

"Where are your slippers?" Elizabeth asks.

Godric winces dramatically.

"Slippers won't sort a bad gene pool and this leg. Has there been a massacre here, or what?"

Elizabeth thinks there certainly has in her petunias. She's not about to fill in Godric too quickly on the details. Let him wake up a bit first. She looks down at Godric's bare feet and guides him into a chair under the parasol facing away from the commotion, puts his mobile on the table and pours a cup of tea. Godric pets Bertie under the chin and around the ears.

"Hello Bertie, old bean. You been killing the blackbirds again? Told you those coppers would come after you in the end." Bertie's ears pull back at the shrieking pitch of Godric's voice.

"Don't tarnish Bertie with your own bad habits."

"Killing blackbirds?"

"You having been up to no good, that's what." Elizabeth hands Godric his tea. "You could do with a bit more work for your exams. I don't see much evidence of revision."

"Ugh. Geniuses don't revise. I have a reputation to think of."

Elizabeth thinks perhaps a close fail this year might give Godric the kick he needs to enter the real world, after having been spoilt by public school and a guilty absent mother. She never had such privilege. Elizabeth is also slightly perturbed that he doesn't look in the slightest bit bothered by what is going on around him. Perhaps he should know what happened after all.

"I couldn't do anything Godric. I was utterly useless."

"What are you talking about?"

"I was feeding the hedgehogs. I wasn't really that

hungry last night, so there was a lot left, you know."

Godric, still stroking Bertie, looks at his nanna, now quite red-eyed.

"I heard you playing the piano. Poked my head in, but I didn't want to disturb. I was zonked. College dinner followed by Granta bar. D'you need a hug from handsome Godric?"

"If you avoided that place you'd probably still have two good legs."

"When they have a different type of whisky for every night of the year, I'm afraid that's just not possible."

"How did you sleep through all the commotion? There must have been six or seven police cars outside since just gone midnight."

"Single malt. Does the trick every time. Out like a baby. Until they woke me up this morning, that is. Why are they still here?" Godric turns his chair to face the activity and spots the body. "What happened to him? You didn't cook him one of your breakfasts, did you?" Godric's eyes linger on the partially closed body bag behind the peonies, and two SOCO officers now erecting a white tent. He is shocked by his own flippancy and makes a mental note to be a better person. Inspector Abley walks back up the garden towards them.

"Who's that dreamboat heading our way?"

"Inspector Abley, dear. Best behaviour."

"Not that chap you go on about, who doesn't know his thieves from his own belly button."

"Shh, Godric."

"Hello, son." Abley greets Godric and nods to Elizabeth.

"Inspector Abley, this is my grandson, Godric. He's staying here during term time and some of the holidays. He's an undergraduate at the university."

Godric stands up and holds out a hand for the Inspector, and slightly bows his head in an overly pretentious way.

"It's my first year, Sir. What's not to love?"

Inspector Abley stands back a little, ears ringing from Godric's piercing voice. Elizabeth looks at her grandson with beady eyes and says sarcastically.

"He's a genius, Inspector. Study doesn't come into it. He has a good gene pool. Sit down Godric. The Inspector can see you have a bad leg." But Godric remains standing, wobbling on his leg for her benefit, holding onto the table, causing Bertie to jump down. Inspector Abley looks at Godric in the peak of health. Elizabeth also wonders why Godric is overplaying it. Perhaps he's had one too many drama lessons. He's always singing, dancing or acting in some play or show. Anything rather than working, it would appear.

Bertie wanders over to where the photographer is chatting to a SOCO and rubs his legs against them both. The photographer bends down to stroke Bertie under the chin. Elizabeth has a slight pang of jealousy every time Bertie seems to treat complete strangers with the same regard he treats her.

"How is it that Bertie may be allowed to walk freely in my garden, but I may not, Inspector?"

"Come now. You know the rules of contamination."

Godric puts a hand on the Inspector's shoulder, being quite over-familiar and insubordinate.

"Bunny says you're the best crim' catcher in the whole of…" Godric pauses for the right insult, "why East Anglia!" then looks at Elizabeth knowingly. He has indeed heard about Inspector Abley, but more for his bumbling efforts and propensity to be elsewhere when things hit the fan. Inspector Abley nevertheless puffs out his chest.

"I'm afraid there's been an incident here. Your nanna found a dead body last night. This river claims too many victims. There are always those who think they're invincible when under the influence."

Elizabeth turns and raises her eyebrows at Godric, for doing exactly that last night. Inspector Abley reluctantly fills Godric in as to the victim. "A Mr Edward Wiley. Your nanna identified him, and we appear to have retrieved his hat."

"Not Edward Wiley from Bene't's College?" Godric looks across the garden to the early dog walkers on Jesus Green on the other side of the river, processing Inspector Abley's words, then at Edward Wiley now zipped up tight beside officers setting up the tent, and back at Elizabeth now realising that she was trying to shield him from the news.

"We are pretty sure, yes. Did you know him?" Abley asks Godric. Godric looks up at the Inspector, the sun now rising higher, bright in his eyes.

"If it's the same Dr Wiley, he's my rowing coach. Quite a good one at that. A bit soft, you know. Doesn't punch. But on the skills side, pretty darn useful."
The Inspector wasn't expecting this, as Elizabeth had omitted to tell him earlier. He flicks her a glance, then asks Godric another question.

"Right. How well did you know Mr Wiley?"
Godric feels his heart drop but knows he must answer, yet he's unsure what to say.

"I spent a lot of time with him on the water, Inspector. He helped me sharpen my oar entry skills. They needed a little polish. Although Toby Pinkham is always ribbing me for bent curve entry and I think that's unfair, to put it mildly. He's the one who has a bent, you know, hoohar. Anyway, Dr Wiley did a lot to help increase my lung capacity on the machines too."
The Inspector is unsure of Godric's train of thought, so Godric continues.

"We're not similar, Inspector. Edward, earnest chap, maybe a pint or two. Me? Self-confessed bacchanalian."
Inspector Abley leans into Godric, still a little confused.

"When was the last time you saw him?"

"For goodness' sake, Inspector. Is this really necessary? Godric doesn't have anything to do with this, now does he?" Elizabeth tries to shut down this intrusion into

Godric's morning. Godric shakes his head, knowing the Inspector is only doing his job.

"No, it's all right Bunny. I'm trying to think. Um." Godric puts his hand on his head and scratches.

"Take your time. I know it is a big shock," Abley says.

Godric obliges Abley's curiosity, although doesn't feel as much in shock as he knows they think he does.

"Haven't been rowing for a week. Hurt my knee. Fell off a scooter, doing tricks with Perry Sidcup on Parker's. Nothing broken. Ruined my favourite suit trousers. Bought them in San Gimignano last summer and whatnot." Godric bends his knee, remembering the injury, disappointed that the no-hander-flip could have incapacitated him like that. Elizabeth passes a blanket to Godric who sits then covers his knees like an elderly invalid enjoying the attention, wincing for effect and letting his nanna fuss.

"You should have warmer clothes on. Where's your vest? That knee will go stiff."

"How will a vest make my knee better, Bunny dearest?"

"You're the scientist," she replies.

Godric screws up his face, what does that mean? Abley smiles at Elizabeth, pleased the attention is not directed at him this time, then continues.

"Right, well, thank you. I hope the knee gets better. Actually, you have to keep using it, don't they say these days? Gentle walks, light pressure."

"Definitely not. Rest first." Elizabeth insists she knows best. Godric interrupts all knee talk.

"I was going to say that they all go past here in the morning and sometimes in the evening, depending how keen. I'm sure I've not seen Edward rowing on the river for ages. Maybe for over a month? I think it could even been more. Last time I saw him, he was coaching some first timers, you know, with a megaphone and a bicycle, riding alongside. A softer voice than most who bark orders. They were a shoddy bunch, kept knocking into narrow boats. That's why I remember. There were these baby ducklings he was trying to protect. He told them the boatmen would shout if they hit the boats again, but he'd kill them if they hit the ducklings. Nice chap." Godric smiles at Elizabeth, who returns the smile. Abley is bemused by Godric's seeming awareness of Edward's voice and yet the lack of his own screeching. Elizabeth supports Edward's concern for wildlife, booming,

"Quite right too. Those rowers kill ducklings and goslings every year. It's carnage out there. But do the police do anything about it? No, they do not. Apparently, animals don't count. We must talk about this further, Inspector. Treating sentient creatures with respect is just as important as any human being. As Mahatma Gandhi said, 'the greatness of a nation can be judged by–"

The Inspector interrupts.

"I think I might need to get back to my Sergeant in a minute, so if I may just finish asking Godric a couple of questions."

Elizabeth gives Inspector Abley a steely glare. Inspector Abley acknowledges Elizabeth's point but is here to try to find out why he has a dead body on his hands. And quite frankly knows he'll lose the animal discussion again if he dares respond. Grateful for the lead, Abley looks at Godric.

"Would you happen to know, Godric, which boathouse Edward belonged to?"

Godric obliges the Inspector.

"He was in the CUBC. That was a while ago. He switched to row for Bene't's when his lectureship began. Something about wanting to focus on grown-up things. Books, he said, and just dabble with the oars."

"Was he good?"

Godric sips his tea and smirks as he replies,

"Books? I have no idea. Rowing? Was in the Boat Race twice. Lost both times. Rowing is a serious sport, Inspector. Can take your life if you let it."

Elizabeth thinks of how many hours Abley spends on the golf course.

"The Inspector would know all about sport taking over."

"What? Oh." Abley takes another swing with an imaginary iron. Godric looks at Elizabeth.

"I have a grandfather who was on the winning side, Inspector."

Abley acknowledges this.

"Good to win, but it's how you play that counts."

Elizabeth explains the Inspector's comment to Godric.

"Inspector Abley is a very modest golfer. His handicap is–"

Abley puts a hand to Elizabeth's mouth before she can reveal it.

"I've been working on it for far too long. It's nothing to be proud of," Abley shuts down talk of his performance. Godric, meanwhile, can't resist. He gets up and puts the blanket around his shoulders and takes an imaginary swing, mimicking the Inspector.

Elizabeth is aghast at both of their attitudes in this grave time, with a body not twenty feet away. She can understand her grandson, who seems to have no proper emotions that she can fathom, and in this instance appears to be merely copying Abley for his own childish amusement, but as for the Inspector? Perhaps they are not right for each other. Godric, still swinging, talks to the Inspector.

"I don't have any sticks here in Cambridge, left them at home, but I'd love to play a round some time."

"I am sure the Gog Magog can find you some clubs if you'd like a game," Abley offers.

"Thank you. I used to tee off a handicap of–"

Abley interrupts Godric. To brag about one's handicap to a fellow golfer before a game is poor form.

"Keep a man guessing. More fun as we go round, don't you think?"

"Of course. I was going to say abysmal, just to warn you that you might want to bring a newspaper or something, while you wait for me to hack it out of the rough." Godric smirks. Abley smiles back then looks Godric straight in the eye.

"Just one more thing, did Mr Wiley know you lived here, with your grandmother? As if he did, that would be a strange coincidence, don't you think?"

Elizabeth places a hand over Godric's mouth, in a pointed manner to copy the Inspector's previous silencing of her own.

"I'm glad we are back to talking about the tragic news at hand, Inspector. Edward knew I lived here. And Godric, your leg, you can't play golf yet. Biscuit, Inspector?" Elizabeth picks up a plate of home-made biscuits from the tea tray and offers them to Inspector Abley, in an attempt to divert his questioning from how well they knew Edward, as for now, she is keen to keep something back. Abley looks at the plate and turns pale, knowing how inedible such treats are likely to be.

"Thank you, Liz, but I shouldn't ruin the cooked breakfast with my name on it back at the station. And Mrs Abley is making steak pie for tea, must pace myself today."

"Breakfast sounds like a jolly good idea, Inspector. I'm starving for something savoury." Godric swerves the biscuit issue himself. Elizabeth maintains a stare straight at the Inspector with beady eyes, waiting expectantly for him to try one of her baked offerings.

"Oh, go on then." Inspector Abley picks up a biscuit and takes a bite. Elizabeth watches him. She appears to have little idea of her lack of culinary skills. Godric tries not to smirk as Abley attempts an 'Mmm'.

Elizabeth half frowns as she watches him chew the biscuit too many times, masticating like a cow, and taking a rather unusually long time to swallow. Then she remembers something and holds up a necklace made up of pillar-box red and black beads, which she had brought out from the kitchen on the tea tray, temporarily hiding between the flaps of a tea towel.

"Oh yes, before I forget, I found this on the lawn, right on the edge, almost in the water." The beads glisten with the fresh morning dew as the long necklace wiggles like a snake below Elizabeth's hand. Inspector Abley leans in to scrutinise the necklace.

"Could a friend of yours have dropped these at a different time perhaps? They don't look like anything Edward would have worn."

Elizabeth can't entirely be sure if Abley is being serious or sarcastic, and is affronted he doubts her.

"I'd have noticed these beads on my lawn if they'd been here a while. The grass is cut twice a week. They're so bright, like little fires each one. Maybe he threw them on the lawn before he died?" Elizabeth is overwhelmed by a wave of sadness for Edward and looks down to the water. "It was there all right, and not before."

Inspector Abley reaches into his pocket for an evidence bag and opens it for Elizabeth to drop in the necklace, as he lightly reprimands her.

"You shouldn't have picked this up then. It will have fingerprints on it, now mixed up with yours."

Elizabeth places the necklace carefully in the bag, looking at the almost too red little beads glint back through the transparent covering. Godric doesn't like Inspector Abley's tone.

"I expect in the heat of the moment, Inspector, that is the last thing Bunny would have been thinking about. Too upset about finding a dead body. Don't you think?"

Elizabeth is indignant at the Inspector's audacity and doesn't need Godric to fight her battles.

"Listen to me. You wouldn't have found this had I not picked it up. It was on the lawn under my lavender right by the water. You were grateful I picked out the hat, isn't that a little hypocritical? And you shouldn't have disturbed my ducks and hedgehogs with all these men trampling about

everywhere. Look, they haven't touched their supper."
Elizabeth points at the leftovers she put out last night for
the wildlife, which are now surrounding an overturned
bowl, all squashed beneath the Inspector's feet. Abley pulls
a face, trying to brush off all the squashed peas from the
sides of his moccasins. Elizabeth holds up the biscuits.

"Have you any more bags Inspector?" As Abley puts
the necklace in his pocket he gets out another bag, and
Elizabeth drops in the remaining biscuits, forcing him to
take them. "For your coffee time. They're good for you.
Ginger and Lemongrass."

Hiding his distaste for the biscuits, Inspector Abley
knows precisely what he will do with them when he gets
back to the station.

"Marvellous. Thank you."

Elizabeth squints her eyes with suspicion at the way the
Inspector manhandles her biscuits, smashing them down
into his pocket. Abley looks up and then at Elizabeth.

"Well, I'd better get on, Liz. Came up to tell you that
we will need to keep the cordon on your garden from the
river for now. Stop any trespassers. Once we've cordoned
off this bit, you can use the terrace and to the right of your
garden, but will need to leave the rest undisturbed."

A Constable calls Inspector Abley away to discuss the
case. Godric moves closer to Elizabeth and looks down to
the river, his next words almost to himself.

"Edward was a strong swimmer, Bunny."

Elizabeth pulls Goldric's shoulder round to catch his
eye.

"And he swam to me. I'm sure he was trying to tell me
something, just before he died. I didn't understand it. He
was choking, but he said something like 'Tis', 'tibs', or
'tips'. 'Serve us Tibs', 'serve us tips', something like that?
What do you think it means? What is tips? Is it a drug of
some kind?"

Godric glares at his grandmother for suggesting he'd
know the names of all the drugs, even though he does.

Not that he regularly imbibes, just the odd bit of opium now and then at Freddo Morrison's. Just sends him to sleep. Much prefers whisky.

"Hang on, Buns, you mean he wasn't dead when you found him?"

"He died in my arms," Elizabeth says.

"Oh my, oh come here, Bunny." Godric hugs Elizabeth. "You poor thing. And you've been bottling that up." Then Godric pieces things together further. "Hang on again, have you told the Inspector?"

Elizabeth shakes her head. "Not yet."

"How exciting." It is not clear why Edward died on their lawn, but neither can deny that it isn't more than a little strange. Godric thinks how particularly shaken his nanna looks by this death. He has heard her talk of her adventures, as she calls them, with her Inspector. But he didn't expect to see her quite so anxious now Inspector Bob Abley is back in her life.

6
THE MYSTERY IS INSIDE

Politician Jonathan Smythe-Jones has made it to Cambridge, found a parking spot just outside Bene't's College gatehouse on King's Parade, and now crunches across Ramn's Court. He looks up and sees Rebecca Wiley, his sister, peering from her college room window. Beautiful and frail, she smiles back at him then disappears from view.

Ignoring the 'Keep off' sign, Jonathan walks on the tightly mown grass, takes out a cigarette case from his jacket pocket, opens it, places one between his lips, flicks open a silver lighter, and draws in heavily. His manicure and cufflinks, as well as pinstripe suit reek 'old money'. Hair lightly greased, thick, black, and brushed up and away from his face, just the front rebelling and falling into his steely eyes. As he exhales he wafts smoke, blinks shut his long lashes as he fails to stop some drifting back into his face. Handsome from centuries of good breeding, Jonathan stands confidently in his six feet two inches. As he inhales, he hears little feet patter behind him and turns to see that Rebecca has rushed down to greet him. A plainclothes policewoman, who is, in fact, a family liaison officer, as well as an officer in uniform appear with Rebecca and respectfully stay some distance away.

Rebecca, in a delicate dress covered with tiny rosebuds, her strawberry blonde hair cut sharply into a bob pinned with a silver butterfly, a face free from make-up and open with innocence, hurls herself into his arms. Jonathan flicks his ash on a pigeon picking at the lawn beneath his feet.

"What a mess, Sis." Taking another long drag from his menthol cigarette, Jonathan rubs her back.

"Did you have important meetings?" Rebecca asks, burying her face into his chest.

"No. Don't worry about me. Anyway, I asked Kat to come and stay with you until I arrived. Where the hell is she?" Jonathan's phone goes off in his pocket. He takes it out and cuts the call. Tearily and a little hysterical, Rebecca looks to her brother.

"What am I going to do? They came here and woke me up to tell me my husband is dead. Edward can't be dead. Of course, he isn't. He did everything for me."

"I'm here Bex. You've got me now. I'm struggling with this situation as much as you. I have some papers for Edward, in the car. Very important. Are they sure it's him?" Jonathan takes out a handkerchief from his top pocket and gives it to Rebecca, then takes another drag on his cigarette and exhales sharply. She notices the knuckles on his right hand have cuts on them, and there are scratches on the back of his hand. What would a lawyer be doing with a fresh injury this time of the morning? Rebecca doesn't know what to think. She's just glad he's here to go with her to identify the body.

*

Back at Foxes' Haven, Elizabeth pours flour over egg and milk, whisking pancake batter by hand, as Godric stands eating a piece of slightly burnt toast. They both watch the Inspector through the window coming towards the house and then heading up through the side alley, which passes by her kitchen door. Irritated by the large presence of police, she shouts at him through the open window.

"I was going to cut the grass today. The bottom needs doing!"

"I rather like daisies and clover, common, but pretty. Everywhere needs a bit of rough," the Inspector shouts back as he goes past. Elizabeth and Godric then peer through the window and watch the men carrying Edward's body away on a stretcher, the body bag now covered with a green blanket. Elizabeth shouts to the rest of the police officers walking up the garden.

"Use the path!" Then she turns to Godric. "Ruddy policemen won't solve it in a hurry. Time for breakfast now at the station I don't doubt. My taxes paying for their time sitting about, nattering. And they say men don't gossip. That place is full of it." Elizabeth continues to stir the pancake mix, thinking about what Inspector Abley said earlier. "He was wrong, you know, not to hire me back on the spot. I bet I could solve this quicker than any uniformed or otherwise."

Godric echoes what his nanna is thinking.

"When you say solve it, you mean you think this is a suspicious death?"

Elizabeth pours the pancake batter into the pan, swirling the mixture to the edges, on top of the oil.

"You said it yourself. He was a strong swimmer."

"He'd beat us all. Can I help then, I mean, if this is one of your adventures? Can we solve it together? Revision is such a bore, Bunny."

"Can you get rid of the mud they've traipsed through the back path please, dear? How is one supposed to maintain standards, when people take so little care over them in today's world?"

"My leg, it's too hurty. I mustn't do manual things. And

41

isn't it a crime scene?"

"What did your mother teach you? Honestly, you can help out now and then on household chores. They aren't going to kill you."

Godric hugs Elizabeth, who is now watching the pancake fry. He can see in the background the last police officer putting a cordon over the back garden, preventing entry from the back alley or house, and then remaining to watch over the garden against intruders.

"Well that's that then, I can't sweep up. We mustn't go out the back door. But I tell you what. I'll sample this pancake for poison, to check it's safe," he suggests.

Elizabeth sighs; at least her grandson keeps things cheery around the place. "This is all a bit irregular. Don't think you are going to get this much excitement each time you stay with me, Goddy." She flips the pancake and then looks out the kitchen window and continues, "D'you know what's really bugging me. Someone or something is eating my grapes in the greenhouse, and I'm buggered if I know who."

"Shouldn't grapes be eaten?" questions Godric.

"Not from my greenhouse. I was in there yesterday, just soaking up the wonderful aromas, and two more bunches have all but been picked clean off."

"Are you sure you haven't taken them for something? Jam?" Godric rules out the obvious.

"Jam? Yes, I'm quite sure. Don't question me or you won't get this." She prods the pancake, "No, there's no mistake. They're nearly ripe, but I want to leave them for my wine chap. He's coming next week, and I'll have nothing to give him at this rate. Whoever's stealing them has gone through a lot. I'm lecturing in half an hour in the department, but first I'm going to lock that greenhouse door. See how the thief gets in that way."

"Good idea. I'll keep an eye on it with my binoculars."

"While you are revising? Please, just get on." Elizabeth prods at the pancake, her thoughts turning to Edward. "I might go and speak to Mrs Wiley."

"Ah Rebecca, of course." It dawns on Godric about Rebecca. "Sometimes I look at her at choir practice and think she's so delicate that she might sing out her last breath, like a little bird. And the way she looks at me. As if she needs saving. Not sure she knows she's barking up the wrong tree with me, Bunny."

Elizabeth cuts him off. "Oh, is she in your choir? I must come and hear you," then adds tersely, "Rebecca Wiley will just have to be strong like the rest of us."

Godric knows how his nanna had to be strong when his grandpa died. Elizabeth slips the pancake on a plate and places it on the kitchen table, which she has laid for Godric, full of jams, cream, chocolate spread. Even in a crisis, Godric can rely on his nanna to maintain good culinary standards, even if the results aren't always a great eat.

"Eat. Let's keep our normal routine. It's all too much. A dead body in my garden."

"Are you okay Bunny? Don't you need some sleep? Let me make you a hotty botty."

All of a sudden a burst of emotion rises from Elizabeth. How the hell does she know if she's okay? This is not normal circumstance. It has been a long night, and she is feeling quite light-headed indeed. But there are things to do, and anyway, she is still too shocked to sleep. The finality of death again has come hurtling back towards her, crashing into her life, attempting to knock her off her feet. But she won't let it.

"Edward swam to me, Goddy. To me. He died in my arms. It looked like he had made a gargantuan struggle. Why? Don't tell me that it was for no reason."

"I'll do nothing of the sort. But what about you, Bunnykins?"

For all his arrogance, Godric loves his nanna dearly and feels so protective. She's the only one in the family with manners and decorum. The only one who doesn't crudely raise her voice in the house, or scream at him like a fishwife. He couldn't wait to get away from his mother after he finished boarding school. Besides, there is always afternoon tea available at Bunny's with a box of cakes from the patisserie, her little traditions of eating at the table with napkins, and a little bell she rings to alert him to luncheon. He likes all these things, the style, elegance. At last, he is with a kindred spirit, the epitome of cultured and civilised lifestyle. A most agreeable predicament in which to find himself. He places his napkin on his lap and squirts golden syrup over his slightly overcooked pancake and spots the blueberries his nanna has put in a pretty porcelain bowl, the fresh tea in a pot with milk in a jug adjacent, and fruit juice in a pitcher.

Elizabeth, lifting her loose leaf peppermint, is still ruminating about why Edward came to her, what was he doing in the water so late, and at all? And what had happened to him? Too many questions, and no sleep to boot.

"Grandpa died a pointless and tragic death. But it was an accident. There is not a day goes by... Edward's death... feels like something entirely different."

A little concerned, Godric watches his favourite nanna as she walks out of the room. He mouths a 'Thank you for breakfast' towards the door, disappointed she won't hear.

Elizabeth's mind is swirling with too much information. She thinks again how Inspector Abley would not let her help with this case. This was no accident, of that she is sure. Whether the Inspector wants it or not, she's bally well going to find who killed Edward. There is something about being alive that makes you feel guilty around the dead. If she could find the killer and bring them to justice, well, that must make things a little better, mustn't it? It's wrong to kill. Though if she could kill whoever is stealing her grapes, that would be a different thing altogether. Elizabeth climbs the stairs and looks out of a window at the top of the landing. From it, she can see her garden and the river. There, in the right-hand corner of the garden stands her beautiful greenhouse, gravel surround, water butt and a collection of terracotta pots scattered with seeds, all framing the view. A crow perches on the tree beside, standing guard.

"That's it my beauty, sound your caw when you see anyone, and I'll come running. And if I catch them stealing anymore, I'll skin them like a grape!" Elizabeth knows she now has two cases to solve, the murder of Edward Wiley, and the theft of her prize grapes from her very own greenhouse.

*

In the grounds of Bene't's College, life is waking up. Students meander to breakfast. Others return from showers, crossing the paths of disapproving Fellows already up two hours previous, who tut at their idleness. A gardener and his wheelbarrow are halfway to cutting a sharp border into the lawn along the Chapel side of Bene't's Ramn's Court, as Jonathan and Rebecca walk past on their way to his car, just through the gatehouse on King's Parade. Directly beside Jonathan's is a police car, with officers already sat inside, waiting to accompany Rebecca to the station to identify her husband's body.

Jonathan opens the passenger door, leans in and chucks all his work papers aside to make space. Rebecca watches as Jonathan's briefcase flies on top of a garden shovel, half covered with a blanket on the back seat. He guides his sister into the front, passes a seatbelt across her lap and clicks it locked then kneels outside the car by the passenger door, so his face is level to hers and he's out of view of the police.

"They will want to formally question you shortly. Is there anything you should tell me now, darling, before we do this?" He looks into her eyes, but Rebecca averts her gaze.

"Like what?"

"They're bound to ask you quite personal things. That's their job."

"What things?" She thinks, like why you have a shovel in the back of your car?

Jonathan looks up at the sky and moves his head from side to side, not quite believing he is here rather than in Westminster, waiting to hear from the Chief Whip if he has a place in the Cabinet. He prays to himself that this doesn't mess the whole thing up, but his heart knows it might. This makes him more short-tempered than usual, more irritable with his sister, whom he loves and is probably the most patient with than any other.

"I don't know, do I? Like, if you loved him. Were you happy? Was everything rosy in the garden of marriage? Bex, I can't protect you if you won't let me. You need to open up. What has happened here? You haven't been the happiest pair have you?"

Without moving his head he rolls his eyes straight down at his sister, waiting for her response.

Rebecca feels like she's been stung by a swarm of bees. Her own brother, accusing her of practically being responsible. "How can you even think that now? What if the police are right? What if it is him lying on that cold slab?" She wonders what he means about getting her story straight. Does she need to make up a story? Rebecca feels drained like a wilting flower and shuts her eyes.

"I'm just warning you, be careful what you say. Blurt everything out to me, but not to the police. They're not your friends, that's all." Jonathan stands up. He turns and looks towards the tourists who have begun to appear on the street. With an angry face Rebecca doesn't see, he inadvertently glares at them, hoping that Edward hasn't left all his worldly possessions to the starving Africans, so in love with that continent he was. And hopes that he has made provision for his sister, as Edward came from a wealthy family. Jonathan is only thinking what everyone else would be thinking, he tells himself. He also wonders if he'll be able to have Edward's tennis racket, as he's had his eye on it for the past year. Perhaps Rebecca wouldn't mind as it was far too heavy for her. Rebecca's eyes remain shut as she speaks softly to Jonathan, who doesn't hear.

"I think I will die. Curl up into a tiny crumpled ball. I was not supposed to live as a widow."

Jonathan slams her door shut and walks around to the driver's side. The police officer in the car beside, impatient, watches his every move as Jonathan gets in the car, turns the key and starts the engine. The police car starts to pull away, and Jonathan's car begins to follow down King's Parade. Rebecca panics, this is not the reality she is willing to accept.

"I can't be in here." She starts to rattle at the seat belt hysterically to try to get out. "I hate being in the passenger seat. You know I can't travel unless I've had my pills. I feel claustrophobic. I want to go back!"

Rebecca starts to scream, so Jonathan slaps his sister on the cheek.

"Calm down. I'll open a window, see look. Fresh air. There you are."

"I can't breathe. Turn off the heat."

"Okay. There, it's off. What Rebecca wants today Rebecca gets, and no questions."

"You'll be married to Kat soon. You don't care about me. You're never here when I need you."

"I'm here now, darling. My fiancée said she would be too. Where is she? Be strong Bex. You didn't love him, truly love him, did you?"

"Stop it. Stop it!" She hits her brother's arms, but her punches are so pathetic that he remains unmoved in his seat. "He's not dead. Don't let him be dead, Jonathan. Don't let him be dead."

Rebecca reclines her seat and lies with her eyes closed. She puts a scarf over her face to block out the world. Jonathan's car turns into Lensfield Road, with a police car in front, the convoy heads towards the police station, as Jonathan plays over the logistics in his head. Edward was dead. He knew it. So what did they need to do to keep a lid on things? What objects always turned up when someone was dead, to reveal the truth, to blow things up in the press? CCTV, the bank details of what had last been spent, and the phone. He couldn't do anything about CCTV, but if he could find the wallet, the phone. Try to sort this himself. Anything else? He ran this over as quick as he could in his head. He needed as few repercussions as possible.

"Did you find his phone upstairs, Bex?" Rebecca's eyes remain closed, her head dipped.

"No."

"His passport?"

"No. Only his wallet."

Jonathan thinks about asking Rebecca to lie to the police about the wallet. It makes sense. What will the wallet do other than make this into a bigger story than it is, with all its clues? She removes the scarf, opens her eyes and feels the wallet in her pocket.

"You know, I never really thought he liked you. But he had your number in it, so he must have." She takes out the wallet from her pocket and shows Jonathan the piece of paper, which has a number on it. Rebecca knows this is her brother's by heart.

"Shall I take that?"

"No. The police have already asked me to give it to the Constable who was with me. I forgot, but he knows I have it. What do you want it for?"

"Oh, nothing. Great minds think alike, that's all. I was going to do the same thing." Jonathan covers his thoughts.

Rebecca is angry at Edward still, especially as the wallet also has Susan's phone number in it, clearly written on the back of a photo of Susan. This makes her blood boil.

"Susan is so ugly."

"But no phone?" Jonathan digs again as he knows he

heard Rebecca say there was no phone, but pushes to see if there is more information about where it is.

"No."

Jonathan realises this is not good news. It will track where Edward was that night. It will have evidence of his calls, where he went. This will be enough for the police to find a story, for the media to tease it out day by day. It will be enough to ruin his chances of the Cabinet. This is the worst day for him. He'd better get that tennis racket.

The police car comes to a halt on Gonville Place, realising Jonathan is not following at the Hills Road lights. They hit their horn to encourage him to move. He puts the car in gear and slowly pulls away, unsure of what both he and Rebecca will face at Parkside Police Station.

"You look exhausted, my tiny mouse. I'm sorry for hitting you."

"My cheek hurts. Maybe you killed Edward. You've always had a violent temper."

Jonathan looks at his sister with derision and drives on past Parker's Piece, full of happy people sitting eating sandwiches, chatting, and playing football.

7

A FINE MIND

Wearing a light fawn linen jacket and cream trousers, Elizabeth peers over the top of her spectacles and lifts her head from her notes as she delivers her lecture to a packed auditorium of undergraduates on the topic of UK non-native invasive poisonous plants. Perched on their wooden seats that steep up high to the back of the room, not a whisper is heard, only scribbles and concentration fill the centuries-old hall.

This is the esteemed Cambridge Department of Plant Sciences on Downing Street, a street lined with buildings so tall they block out the sun on the pavements below, leaving a whistle and whip of the wind through innocent pedestrians travelling its length. Buildings so austere and full of such intelligence they might melt the brains of lesser mortals who take a wrong turn. Downing Street is the preserve of the elite, rushing to and fro, with their important thoughts and discoveries. Plant Sciences holds botanical collections of global significance, houses experts with knowledge spanning from rainforest ecosystems to molecular genetics, is highly selective, highly exclusive and only admits the cream of the country.

Elizabeth's students have worked hard to earn the right to hang on her every word as she clicks through slides on an old fashioned roller projector, revealing plants from around the world, and recites with enthusiasm and passion the detail of their specific attributes. Like for no other lecturer in the department, all the spotty, lanky youths never miss the opportunity to hear Professor Green tell stories of imaginary triffids and real-life murderous individuals in the kingdom Plantae. Little do they know that Elizabeth, with her thirty years of experience, can easily multi-task and while taking a lecture can also be thinking about things she has to do in the day, whether it be shopping for food, or gardening jobs when she gets home.

Today Elizabeth thinks about Edward. Since she left home, his grisly death has brought a trail of questions. Nothing adds up. Where had he come from? Jesus Green, or further up river? It must have been further up, or his hat wouldn't have drifted past her lawn. If it was further up, then why hadn't he got out earlier? He could swim well, he could have swum to the side, or got out at Sandymee's punts by Castlebridge College. Maybe he'd been pushed over the boards further down, had a fight. Maybe he'd been walking. But to where? He lived in College. She knew that. So where was he going which would have taken him further away? And at that time of night? It wasn't the water that caused him to die. It wasn't polluted, it was clean. She knew that too, being a keen and active member of the local river conservation group. And whose was the bright red and black beaded necklace, and why did Edward have it? It seemed as puzzling as the little empty bag in his hat and the last words he uttered, 'Serve us tip'. Elizabeth clicks to a slide of the hemlock plant. She's more sure than ever that he had meant to come to her. Meant to find her.

If she could just think... think woman. It was all in

front of her.

"As you will know, hemlock is also known as conium maculatum. The whole plant is poisonous. Anyone tell me more?"

A boy puts his hand up in the front row: Mr Jenkins, a cocky lad Elizabeth rather likes for his 'have a go' optimism. She walks right up to him and almost leans over him.

"Well, if you eat it you puke, dribble, seize up and snuff it," he says. There is a ripple of giggles.

"Thank you, Jenkins. Yes, as Mr Jenkins so eloquently put it, this is not a plant to be trifled with, and can, on the rare occasion, be fatal. As you should know, hemlock contains piperidine, alkaloids, coniine, N-methylconiine, conhydrine and pseudo-conhydrine, which attack the central nervous system. Hemlock can be found as far back in records as Socrates, who was poisoned with it, and of course, it was mentioned in King Lear and Hamlet."

Mr Jenkins then fiddles about in his pocket and pulls out a brown paper bag, very crinkled and old. He holds it up for many to see and asks Elizabeth a question.

"Professor Green, what are these?" Mr Jenkins then hurriedly takes out a dried mushroom for Elizabeth and the lecture hall to see. He twirls it in his fingers, as there are some 'ohs' and scuffling in the auditorium, as students strain to look at what he has in his hands. Elizabeth snatches the mushroom and holds it up for everyone and responds to his question.

"You tell me? A rather shrivelled specimen now, but in its glory, a shiny prolific wonder."

Mr Jenkins stands up and coyly builds his part, looking forward to the reaction he'll get from the room with his next words.

"A good friend of mine told me," the young man sniggers, "they're shroomies, Professor." There is a small round of tittering in the room as Elizabeth takes a better look.

"You mean, you think these are Psilocybe semilanceata or the liberty cap as it is more commonly known, Jenkins? The little beauties containing compounds called psilocybin and psilocin. Of the world's psilocybin mushrooms, the most common in nature and one of the most potent. It has a bell-shaped cap and a small nipple-like protrusion on the top, though these must have lost that through age. I'm sure you were just testing me, Jenkins, to see if I'd mention how if ingested they give you a mild hallucinogenic trip, some say psychedelic, where you hear colour and see sounds and all the rest of it."

"Really Professor. I'd no idea they did that." More laughter from the room as Jenkins smiles, faking innocence and then wiggling his eyebrows up and down to reveal he knew exactly the effect.

"I will take those, thank you. Because now I must ring the police as you have a Class A drug in your bag."

"What?"

Elizabeth takes the paper bag with the dried fungi from Jenkins's hand, much too quickly for him to stop her. She walks back up on stage.

"Did you not know that the 2005 Drugs Act amended the Misuse of Drugs Act of 1971 to clarify that fresh, dried or stewed magic mushrooms that contain psilocybin are Class A, under clause 21? I guess not. Has anyone got a phone?" A number of gasps in the audience at the implications of what has happened and a couple of Jenkin's enemies hold up their phones. Elizabeth pauses. "No, in fact, we don't need to phone the police on this occasion, but perhaps suggest you lay off picking fungi for a hobby, as you're not very good at it. These are not psilocybe semilanceata, Jenkins. No, that would have been slightly less of a worry. They are dried Amanita phalloides, the deadly death cap."

There are a number of gasps from the more intelligent in the hall, who realise Jenkins's error and the dangerous implications.

"This particular fungus has been the cause of most mushroom poisonings, possibly including the death of Roman Emperor, Claudius," Elizabeth continues, "The principal toxic constituent is a-amanitin, which damages the liver and kidneys, often fatally. Just half a mushroom is enough to kill you, and there is very little anyone can do once you've ingested it. The death cap grows fresh from August to November usually, but drying mushrooms like this can sometimes also concentrate the poison and certainly make them harder to identify. So, you have escaped possible death today, Jenkins. Let's be thankful for that. Where on earth did you pick them, and where have you been storing them?"

"In the woods behind my lodgings and in the fridge with my sausages," says a worried Jenkins.

"A seven-year stretch in prison for magic mushrooms, or death. I'd stick to the grocers for your fungi in future." Elizabeth raises her eyebrows at him. There are more gasps and gossiping in the room.

"Are you keeping those then?" asks Jenkins.

"That might be a good idea."

"My flatmate was going to make mushroom pasta tonight. Thanks, Professor." Jenkins looks as white as a sheet and returns to his seat.

Suddenly Elizabeth thinks whether it was something Edward ate? He had all the classic symptoms of poison. Vomiting. Spasms. It was staring at her in the face. Why the hell not? Omphalotus olearius, jack-o'-lantern, might have been used in place of chanterelle mushrooms, had he eaten suchlike. Yet could this have been enough to kill him? There were no news reports of accidental poisonings in restaurants of Cambridge last night. What if it hadn't been accidental? Any attempt on a person's life would have to assume the victim was going to eat the mushrooms, and liked mushrooms in the first place. Elizabeth thinks perhaps he'd eaten dinner with someone he knew well, someone who wished him harm. Someone who knew his tastes. What had happened to them?

She realised Godric had mentioned Rebecca, but she didn't know her, nor did she know the rest of Edward's family. For a colleague she admired, she realised she didn't know much about Edward outside of work. Then there was still the question of how he ended up in the river. If he'd been poisoned, surely there would be no need to push him in as well, unless to confuse matters. Perhaps he staggered and slipped in the dark? Elizabeth's mind cannot stop racing over the 'what ifs'. She has to get to the police station to talk to Inspector Abley about the post-mortem report. Elizabeth feels a sudden wave of urgency to find out what happened to Edward.

"Professor?" Jenkins looks at Elizabeth, who appears now miles away in her thoughts.

"Serve us tips," she mutters. How Inspector Abley expected her to stay off the case was ludicrous. It happened right under her nose.

"Professor?" Jenkins raises his voice, which snaps Elizabeth out of her thoughts.

"Thank you, Jenkins. Thank you all. So, next week, we will go back to plant adaptation and environmental change, looking at the rhododendron in Snowdonia. Read up, read on."

Elizabeth leaves the stage and rushes out, fifteen minutes early, as the students start putting their notebooks away and stand up to go, not thinking anything of the abrupt departure by this particular eccentric tutor. More chatting about the deadly death cap rumbles through the hall. Professor Elizabeth Green stuffs the bag of fungi into her briefcase. She will dispose of it later.

8
A LOVING BROTHER

At Parkside Police Station Rebecca and Jonathan are guided into a rather sterile room, adjacent to where bodies are stored in preparation for post-mortems. A police liaison officer hands Rebecca some photographs of distinguishing marks on Edward's body. A mole above the right cheek of his buttock, a scar on the left side of his neck where he had an infection once, and it had to be drained. Photographs supposed to make it easier for Rebecca to be sure it is Edward, but making it ten times worse as she can already see him, knows the man in front of her. Rebecca throws herself on the viewing window, behind which Edward's body rests on a display table, for identification purposes. Uncontrollable guttural moans bellow from Rebecca. Jonathan stands beside her, staring at Edward through the glass. Jonathan's voice resonates like a hiss around the deathly silent walls in which they are presently trapped.

"I've just told the office, Sis, that I'm going to stay up here with you. I can't leave you now." Rebecca's tears stream down her nose and attach themselves to the glass, bereft now that an identification has been made.

"He looks so small." She stares at Edward, adding, "He's very tanned, isn't he? I didn't notice before."

Jonathan doesn't take his eyes off Edward. "Well, he was in Nakuru, it's hot there."

"How did you know where he was?" she asks her brother.

Jonathan comes across all guilty. "He told me before he went away. Why?"

Rebecca looks at Jonathan and can't work out why then Jonathan's phone starts to ring, and he picks it up.

"Yes, hello Katie. No, I can't. I can't come back now. What is it, ten o'clock? Haven't you heard? Okay. Yes it's bad news. Very bad." From the corner of his eye Jonathan notices Rebecca flinch, so he moves away to the furthest corner of the room and turns his back for the remainder of the call, muttering quietly into his mobile phone. Rebecca, still leaning on the glass, leaves a fingerprint trail on the window as she presses both hands against it, talking to Edward.

"I loved you the most you know. Why did you go and do this to me? Leave me like this. Who am I going to talk to? I was always here for you. Remember that. Remember that I sacrificed everything for you, for your career, for your life, to be by your side. I wanted to do that. I love you. I love you, Edward. What have you done?" Rebecca starts to wail more angrily. "You've abandoned me when I need you most. You've left me alone in this nightmare world. I'm not ready. I didn't want you to go. What were you thinking? You must have wanted to win bad." Rebecca loses any puff left and feebly lets herself drift down the window. "Oh Edward, I'm sorry. You have to believe me. I didn't want this to happen."

Two assistants in forensics wheel Edward out of the room and the police liaison officer inside says they have to continue now with the post-mortem, as they have already started and can't delay. Rebecca hasn't eaten this morning, and neither has she had anything to drink. The stillness in the air and the reality of the situation cause her knees to buckle, and she starts to fall. The police liaison officer catches Rebecca, Jonathan still completely engrossed with his phone.

"I will see you tomorrow. I can't wait to be honest. This is madness." He pauses as Katie speaks on the other end of the line, then replies, "I'm not sure I can go through with it now anyway. Yes, if Edward's dead, doesn't that put a whole new light on South Africa? We knew it would be difficult. I think the opportunity has gone. Katie, you're my angel in the darkness, let's have a bottle tomorrow. Yes, bring them to sample at the flat."

"Water. I need water," Rebecca cries.

"Let's sit you down, Miss, and I'll get some from the corridor. Just wait here." Rebecca is helped by the police liaison officer into a hard plastic seat at the back of the room, and she immediately drops her head between her legs.

"I need to lie down, now. I think I'm going to faint." Rebecca drops to the floor and all but passes out. The police liaison officer rushes back in and gives Rebecca some water, holding Rebecca's back for support, kneeling beside Rebecca who sips the water then lies down. The police liaison officer shouts over to Jonathan in disbelief.

"Sir, I think your sister needs you?"

Jonathan hangs up.

"What happened?"

"She feels a little unwell. I'll see if I can get the doctor, if you can stay with her please, and give her your full attention."

Jonathan nods and bends down beside his sister. He takes a cigarette out of his pocket and goes to light it. The police liaison officer points to the 'No smoking' sign. Jonathan rolls his eyes and puts the cigarette back in the case and tersely replies.

"Even now?"

The police liaison officer speaks to Rebecca before she leaves for the doctor.

"Miss, you know that the police would like a statement, once you are feeling up to it."

"But I wasn't with him. He came home and went back out again. I didn't see him after that."

The police liaison officer replies,

"That's fine, then tell them that. You too, Sir."

"Yes, but I hadn't seen him in ages," says Jonathan.

"They will want a statement from you as well." The police liaison officer raises her eyebrows at him and then leaves for the doctor.

9

THE LOVER

Susan Bunt is on her mobile, pacing her living room in a manky dressing gown and scuffed green slippers. Built in the 1970s, the house directly overlooks the river at Chesterton, a once pretty village on the edge of Cambridge, now a sprawling conurbation. Inside, poorly hung curtains cling to rusty poles, blocking out the impressive view. Papers pile high on every table, marking out two decades of inhabitance like rings of a tree. A desk lamp burns dust in a dark corner over an idle computer, a lit cigarette leans into a reclaimed pub ashtray, and a coffee cup emits vapours.

"Yes, flight EA627B to Cape Town. That's right. You're sure there are no delays? Perfect. Upgrade everything, please. Yes, First Class. At the check in? Thank you."

Susan hangs up, catching a glimpse of herself in the mirror, which is hung next to a photograph on the wall of a neighing horse looking straight into the camera lens, showing a gap in his front teeth. In the gloom she leans in to examine the bright red, small dots, neatly peppering her blotchy skin where her necklace was last night. She's sure it will be long gone from the alley now, someone will have picked it up. She's sad as she liked it, as she liked all of Edward's thoughtful gifts. She was just unlucky to have been in the wrong place, she thinks. At least they didn't steal her wallet or mobile. Thank goodness for her cloak with so many hidden pockets. What did her attacker want, she wonders for the umpteenth time?

Susan picks up her cigarette and coffee, peels back a front curtain and peers through the nets out across to Stourbridge Common. Cattle graze in the distance on the rough grass and pick at the trees as rowers steam past at full speed. Susan finishes her coffee and searches in the pockets of the cloak hanging on the door. Finding what she's looking for she visibly relaxes, taking out her passport and Edward's beneath it. Excitedly she stuffs both into a travel bag on the table and continues to collect things to shove inside, some clean laundry from a clothes horse, a pair of trainers by the sofa. She shuts down her computer and walks out of the room to get more things to pack.

10
BENE'T'S COLLEGE

Head Porter, Sidney Carter, dressed in a smart suit, stands in the Porters' Lodge at Bene't's College this morning. Bene't's don't require porters to wear bowler hats or tails these days like other more traditional colleges. His silver handlebar moustache, however, is still the highlight of many a tourist photograph. Sometimes when he wears it straight, his colleagues make their disappointment known. Little do they know the time it takes to wax and tease into the stiff curls on display. Right now, Carter is the only person in the lodge. A radio blares out cricket from the Oval. Neat rows of pigeonholes line half the room. The other half has paintings of the Chapel shown at differing angles, and a year planner with many pins stuck to the dates in red and green. Carter has been at Bene't's for thirty-four years and sixteen days. Every year, since hitting thirty years' service, he has been given one more week of leave, which he finds most dull and comes in anyway. Ordinarily, at this time he would be on patrol, checking up on undergraduates who often like to pull the odd prank in

Easter term to relieve the stress of examinations. But at the moment his head is down as he sifts through envelopes which arrived in the morning post, methodically assigning each piece into the rightful pigeon hole. A collection of parcels sit on the counter, waiting for him to sort.

Sir Percival Flint, the Dean of the college, enters. Dressed in a dark navy suit, light blue shirt, bow tie and slicked back hair, the fifty-six-year-old Don has the look of someone carrying the weight of the world on his shoulders and is ready for early retirement. Spending most of his life in college, Percival grows increasingly lonely without his wife and teenage children who reside in Dorset, though he hides it well, until he's imbibed in a bit too much port after dinner, then will tell you everything about his dog, Rufus, and show you pictures of the walks he has along Brownsea Island when he manages to get down for the weekend. Carter has heard this story many times.

"Morning Carter." The Dean picks up some keys hanging on a hook behind the counter.

"Morning Dean."

"Just popping to the Archives if anyone needs me. Got to check something in the estate papers for the bursar. Why the man can't do his job, I'll never know."

"Right ho. I'll ring down if anything's urgent. The police were here earlier, Sir. Looking for Mrs Wiley. Thought you should know."

"Yes, thank you, Carter. They telephoned they were coming earlier — dreadful business. We've lost a good man. I'll be saying a few words at dinner. Will you inform those Fellows dining to get there ten minutes early?"

"Poor Mrs Wiley. She'll take it bad, no doubt."

"Quite, I'll go and see her shortly. We must do everything we can to protect her in this most difficult time. Perhaps you can arrange for her meals to be taken to her rooms?"

"Of course, Dean. And I will tell the Fellows about

your words before dinner, to be prompt."

"Wonderful."

"Talking of protecting Mrs Wiley from outside forces, Professor Green just swept in like a bat, and has already gone up to see her."

"Really? What for?" the Dean asks.

"I tried to inquire as to the purpose of her visit, but she just told me not to fuss and to stick to my job. I told her that was part of my job then she poked her tongue out at me, Dean, and smiled." Carter says, smirking.

"That blessed woman. God, make speed to save us all." The Dean strides out, off on the course of his day.

"Often brings me a bottle of brandy at Christmas, she does," Carter continues to talk to himself, then turns to the parcels on the counter. He sees one addressed to Rebecca Wiley. He's about to call after the Dean, but spots he is already halfway across Ramn's court. Carter puts it into Mr Edward Wiley's pigeon hole. He'll take that to the lady later, as he's sure she won't want to be disturbed anymore this morning. An old Bakelite art deco telephone trills in the lodge. There is no answerphone or telephonist here. Just the random efforts of porters, who take turns in deciding if they'd like to help the prospective caller. Carter hears the noise in his sleep, and has grown used to ignoring its first rings, allowing the faint-hearted enquirer to give up their efforts and leave things be. Finally, he walks across and picks up the receiver.

"Lodge."

"Mr Idiot here."

"Mr Idiot? Who's this?"

"Iman."

"Iman Idiot? Peterson, I know that's you."

Carter hangs up the receiver and chuckles to himself. The students have grown so tame. Although he was too young to deal with the prank when students put an Austin Healy on the Senate roof back in 1958, he did have to organise the far less glamorous removal of a toilet seat from a Chapel spire later in 2002, at great expense to the college. Yes, that was stuff and nonsense. Scaffolders erected almost all the scaffolding to retrieve the seat, only to find that overnight the prankster had moved the toilet seat to a different spire. So they had to move the scaffolding to the new spire and start all over again.

Carter couldn't wait for a bit of peace when the students would go down this summer, though secretly he did look forward to their return in September. The Fellows were getting old, like him, and were a much less exciting bunch.

11
THE WIFE

Elizabeth catches her breath after climbing the rickety stairs to the third floor of Edward and Rebecca Wiley's Bene't's College rooms. She feels rather light-headed, not having slept last night or touched much food to speak of. Rebecca Wiley has only just returned from identifying Edward's body and tells Elizabeth to make herself comfortable while she temporarily retires to her dressing room to splash water on her face.

Elizabeth perches uncomfortably on an oversized worn bottle green Chesterfield, which stands like an island in the grand drawing room. She looks around the centuries' old uneven-walled, wonky wooden-doored room, caught in the darkness. Only little windows look out to the sky, which for an early summer's day is looking a little too overcast for Elizabeth's liking. An open fire crackles and spits, having been lit by the bedder to take the chill out of the morning. Two browning spider plants trail down the mantelpiece. It strikes Elizabeth how remarkably empty the room is of personal belongings, thinking how many things of Gerald's she retains, just to keep him close. Where is the evidence of Edward? An old book chest stands under a window, a woman's floppy hat resting on top. A corner table carries a small radio. No television, no ornaments. She notices a pair of Wellington boots by the door, caked in mud. Above them hangs a photograph of a neighing horse looking straight into the camera lens, showing a gap in his front teeth.

Elizabeth had liked Edward for his generosity, his positive spirit and sense of humour. But she was also particularly fond of his loyalty to her. Just weeks into his post he had come to her defence in a rather bitter row in the staff room between herself and the then head of department who thankfully has now retired, but at the time was criticising Elizabeth's views on plants and animals, saying they compromised the department. Elizabeth had told the then head that he might fairly be accused of being very dull indeed as well as ignorant. Just as the head was about to explode Edward had jumped in and said what Elizabeth meant to say was that diversity makes the world go around, and he for one applauded Elizabeth's determination and convictions, and even if he didn't always agree with them that the department would be a poorer place without Professor Green.

As Elizabeth is remembering Edward and his kind support, an ethereal Rebecca returns, followed by Jonathan who takes Rebecca's jacket and hangs it up by the door. Elizabeth politely stands.

"Thank you for seeing me, Mrs Wiley."

"Rebecca, please." Rebecca smiles, but Jonathan is unhappy with the intrusion.

"I really don't think this is an appropriate time, do you? I've already had to turn away the local papers. I thought the porters are supposed to stop unwelcome visitors?"

Rebecca gestures for Elizabeth to sit back down.

Elizabeth smiles at Rebecca.

"Thank you." She perches again uncomfortably, and now quite thirsty.

"Ignore him, Professor Green. He's just overly protective," Rebecca says.

Jonathan huffs and walks to the window, replying to his sister,

"You should be resting. Not answering yet more questions. The police kept you far too long. I shall have to talk to the Chief Inspector. Does he know who I am?"

Rebecca ignores her brother and turns to Elizabeth.

"He looked so cold and still, not like my Ed. Hair stuck to his head. He always has such bouncy hair." Rebecca pauses then looks into Elizabeth's eyes. "He's gone, hasn't he?" Not so much asking the question anymore, just saying it out loud in case someone can tell her she's wrong.

"I'm sorry." Elizabeth looks to the floor out of respect and then back up at Rebecca.

"Your message said they found him in your garden?" Rebecca asks.

Elizabeth wipes her brow with a handkerchief. Sleep deprivation catching up with her.

"Yes. I tried to help him, but there was nothing I could do."

"Wait, what? He was still alive?" Rebecca is visibly shocked.

Elizabeth replies hurriedly,

"Yes, but only for a moment. Just seconds."

"The police didn't say that. Why didn't they tell me? That changes everything."

Elizabeth realises she still hasn't told the police that minor but important detail, and backtracks as much as she can. She's not thinking straight. No sleep. She must find out what Rebecca knows before she leaves.

"He passed away very quickly by the time I got to him. As I say, it was seconds."

Jonathan walks over and leans on Elizabeth.

"What did he say?"

Elizabeth ignores Jonathan Smythe-Jones' question. She doesn't like his tone, thinking him self-righteous, which grates on her nerves tremendously, and she always trusts her first impressions, unlikely to change her opinion of this rebarbative man. Rebecca presses Elizabeth into the Chesterfield and sits beside her.

"Was he scared? Did he say anything about me?"

"He couldn't speak very easily, Rebecca. He was in pain. I'm very sorry."

"He spoke! What did he say?" Rebecca looks very anxious.

"He just mumbled. He lost his breath and passed away. You have to understand. It's been a long night. I watched him die. He drifted away looking at me. That's all. Then he was... just like the police told you," Elizabeth says, then shuts her eyes. Rebecca leans into her face a little.

"Most people, before they die, call out for their loved ones, don't they? I thought he might have said 'Tell Rebecca I love her'. That's the kind of man that he—" Rebecca struggles to say the word 'was'. "He isn't like most men."

Elizabeth can agree on that.

"He was a good man."

"He loves me, really loves me like no other. He has a big heart."

Jonathan Smythe-Jones presses Elizabeth for information.

"What did he say, exactly?"

Elizabeth opens her eyes and sees this unpleasant man snarling at her.

"He just mumbled. I couldn't make it out, seriously. Serve us something. It made no sense. Serve us tibs. He passed away straight after. Please." Elizabeth feels she's being interrogated rather than the interrogator. What is she doing here? Why is she putting herself through this when she could be at home in her garden? But she can't, she can't sit with the sun on her face, watching the river, as a man died last night. This woman's husband, this man's brother-in-law. It's all tangled, and she can't see the clues.

Jonathan walks back over to the window and spots something outside.

"My cue for a cigarette I think. Shan't be long."

Jonathan strides across the room opens the door and walks through. He pokes his head back in.

"Shout if you need me, Bex, I'm just below the window."

"You're not supposed to smoke in the court. They'll tell me off." Rebecca glances at her brother.

"Not today they won't." Jonathan glares at Elizabeth, then disappears. Elizabeth waits until she can't hear any more footsteps on the stairs and then leans into Rebecca.

"When did you see Edward last? I wondered if you'd eaten with him last night? Perhaps shared a meal?"

Rebecca turns back to Elizabeth.

"He'd just got back from Africa. I saw him in the morning, perhaps for half an hour, and then he rushed off to work, to the lab. That's it. He never came back."

Elizabeth wonders whether to believe Rebecca.

"So where did he eat?"

"I don't know."

"What did you do after you saw him?"

Rebecca fiddles with a string of pearls around her neck.

"I had a sleep. I hadn't slept much the night before. Probably because I knew Edward was coming back. Then Kat rang, offered to take me out to lunch."

"Kat?"

"My brother's fiancée."

"So you didn't see Edward at lunchtime?"

"No, although he must have popped back while I was out, as some of his stuff had moved." Rebecca can see Elizabeth doesn't know what she means. "He'd put things in the linen wash basket, emptied some of the things out of his case. That's all."

"So why not have lunch with you? Surely he missed you?"

"He often stays, late at the lab after a trip. Things fresh in his mind, he'd say." Then Rebecca realises she is using the wrong tense, adding, "Stayed late." She looks at Elizabeth for answers. "What was it again that he mumbled? Are you sure he didn't call my name?"

"He said something about a serve us tea, tibs, tips? That mean anything to you?"

Rebecca shakes her head. A woodpigeon 'coo coo-coo's outside the window. Elizabeth is thirsty but knows that she may be close to opening up with Rebecca so with a dry mouth and perspiration on her forehead she continues.

"I haven't come to cause you any more distress. But would you mind telling me what state Edward was in before he died? Was he worried about anything? It might just help work out what happened."

But Rebecca doesn't like this shift in questioning.

"I've told the police all this."

"Rebecca, my garden is not easy to climb into. Next door is much easier; it has a lower lawn to a slipway. I know, I've fallen in before myself and had to traipse through Mrs Cloud's kitchen after being mightily grateful for it. She wasn't happy, but her husband built it you see. He likes to scull in the morning."

"What has this got to do with Edward?"

"He came to me."

"I don't understand."

"Why take the more difficult route?"

"Maybe he knew you lived there. That you'd help?"

"Maybe he knew I'd find his killer."

"What?" Rebecca gets up and walks to the fire and leans on the mantelpiece. Elizabeth maintains an uncomfortable perch on the sofa.

"I don't think this was an accident. I don't think he drowned and I think he was very agitated. Like he was running or swimming away from something, or someone."

Rebecca replies, "But the police haven't said anything about any of this? I think they would know if anyone knows. I have just identified my poor–" Rebecca takes a sharp breath, she is beginning to well up again, "my poor husband. And I thought you wanted to talk to me as a friend. But instead, you're inventing lies. My husband was a good man. He had no enemies."

"He was a strong swimmer. It was a calm night. The water is not toxic. He appeared to have a severe reaction to something," Elizabeth replies.

"How would you know?"

Elizabeth is uncomfortable about sharing her expertise. "I work in the Department of Plant Sciences. With Edward."

"Yes, Edward talked about you before, which is why I agreed to see you. Though I haven't seen you in college."

"I find that Bene't's doesn't have the menu which quite fits my palate, their thirst for dead animal is quite depressing. Roast pig here, pheasant there. I'm sure they'd serve swan if they could."

"I ate swan once. At one of Kat's dinner parties."

"That's illegal."

"And so is not telling the police that someone wasn't dead when you found them."

Elizabeth can't argue with that. She is cross at herself that she has failed to keep control of this conversation. She knows people are her weakness, or rather talking to them, reacting with them. She wonders how Godric manages it better than she, even though behind the skin he's much less thoughtful. She looks at Rebecca who is waiting for an explanation.

"I just wondered if you knew if he'd fallen out with anyone?"

"No."

"Did he know anyone who might want him hurt? I feel there is something gravely wrong here."

"He drowned," Rebecca replies.

"No, he was in pain Rebecca. I could see it in his face. His expression."

"I think you should leave."

"I just want to help. Tell me if he had any enemies. That's all, and I promise to leave."

Rebecca puts her head down, shuts her eyes, then slowly lifts her head and looks out of the window.

"I saw the devil outside college the other day. She was just standing there, below our window, looking up."

"The devil?"

"Edward's ex. She never forgave him for marrying me. Spurned Susan."

Rebecca walks to the window.

"People have pasts, why do you call her the devil?" Elizabeth is curious.

"She was jealous. Wouldn't let go," Rebecca replies bitterly.

"What did she do? Outside the college?"

"That's what love can do. Eat you up from the inside, until you're full of acid. She was always around, in our face. Once, we came home, Edward and I, only to find someone had been in our rooms. Nothing was taken, only a dress of mine. Cut up into tiny pieces."

"You think it was her?"

"She'd cut it up, and put it out on the bed, all in tiny shreds. It was expensive, silk. Stupid cow. Cut up the wrong dress though. It was one my brother had bought me, not Edward. Didn't have the result she'd wanted."

"Well, that's very interesting indeed. One more question, was Edward happy?"

"Of course, we're in love, a very happy marriage. We can't be separated, which..." Rebecca stumbles over her words, again realizing she is talking about Edward as if he is still here, "which is why I need to lie down. I am desperately tired, and I think I've answered as many questions as I am able."

"Of course." Elizabeth stands, relieved to leave the leathery sofa, walks over to the window of the Wiley's rooms and sees Jonathan shouting at a woman. Absent-minded, she strokes a dead campanula on the windowsill.

"I will see myself out, and you are right to get some rest now. You have been most helpful."

12
THE FIANCÉE

Elizabeth steps out into the hallway and shuts the door behind her, wondering when she will allow herself to rest. Not now. Not yet. She hears silence behind the door. She stops for a moment in case anything happens from the other side. But there's nothing. She nods to herself and then makes her way down the communal spiral staircase. For the first time in ages Elizabeth feels completely occupied, doing something which stops her from thinking, from remembering, from being emotional. She is aware this feels like a natural fit and wonders if she should have been a detective rather than an academic. Elizabeth catches a glance of herself in a wall mirror. Her eyes ablaze, her cheeks red, and right now she feels alive and can feel her heart beating fast in her chest.

Kara Anderson, known by her friends and family as Kat, stands elegantly on the court lawn below Rebecca's rooms. Still in a silver ball gown, sky-high heels and aquamarine pashmina, Kara is a little dishevelled having not yet gone to bed. Her face rosy, her porcelain teeth slightly too white, her long, blonde wavy hair clipped into place by many decorative flowers. A strikingly long-limbed woman, as tall as Jonathan. She hugs Jonathan, who is too cross to hug back.

"Why didn't you come over when I called?"

"I couldn't drive, I had to wait. I'd had a few. I tried to get here as soon as I heard, but the Cambridgeshire taxis all go to beddy-byes as soon as the clock strikes twelve as far as I can tell. The taxi took ages to come, by which time I'd already sobered up. I counted the units and hours."

Kara was disappointed by Cambridgeshire. Expecting the high life and glamour, she had learnt to her cost that drive more than a mile out of the city of Cambridge and you are into a fenland of empty fields, big skies and quiet so strong that you can hear a pin drop, and have all the time in the world to find a needle in the umpteen haystacks propped up across the land, because there is bugger all else to do.

"Bloody typical. Who've you been with?"

"Just a few friends. It's not my fault you moved us to a backward constituency where it takes ten times longer to do anything, or get anywhere. Parochial purgatory."

"I haven't got time for this."

"Neither have I. I gave up London for you. You leave me alone up here, while you have a ball. Do I complain?"

Jonathan is incredulous and gesticulates at Kara.

"All the time. You don't stop thinking about yourself. My sister has been going through hell the past eight hours. Edward is dead, and what do you do? Go out and drink champagne with your hooray friends."

"I'm sorry, all right?"

"If you hadn't been out with that motley crew you would've been here much quicker."

"Can you stop going on, I've got a headache." Kara storms off, too upset to continue the fight.

Elizabeth walks across the court to Jonathan, who remains on the grass. The college grounds are not busy as it is lesson time, and they are the only souls about apart from a solitary young man walking across the court in the distance.

"Perhaps she's in shock."

"She's fine. Gone off in some strop, as per usual. Oh, I'll never understand the opposite sex. Anyway, really, what business is this of yours?"

"I was talking about Rebecca, your sister?"

Elizabeth watches the leggy blonde striding away, and is hit by a wave of sympathy for this woman, apparently wasting her life on such an unpleasant man.

"So you thought you'd have a poke about, eh? Women of a certain age always know best, don't they?"

"Hmm, how remarkably astute you are." Elizabeth is affronted at the age remark. Who is this no-man? Irritated by him, she wants to say something cutting. And boy does she know how. But she wants to find Edward's killer more, so she keeps it reigned in. The irritating man continues to speak.

"Forgive me. I'm tired. I'm supposed to meet the prime minister this week. A Cabinet matter and all the rest of it."

"Ah, a politician. That makes sense."

"What do you mean by that?"

Elizabeth wonders whether to take him down with a cutting comment but decides against it this time, not feeling great herself, instead plumps for false flattery.

"You look very smart, natty dresser. You're paternal towards your sister, protective."

"I can't help protecting my sister." Jonathan huffs.

"Don't worry. I'm no threat either to her or your career, whichever party you represent."

Jonathan defrosts a little.

"Don't normally insult constituents with ageist remarks, forgive me. Hope we may count on your vote at the next election? A while off now though, eh." Jonathan takes a peek at Elizabeth, whose eyes burn into his.

"I believe I have the right to keep secret who gets my

support," she replies.

"Quite right. You stick to your guns."

"I don't care for wings left or right, or indeed clubs, or people telling me what to think. Wings should remain the possession of birds. Being a professional politician, I suppose you are used to toeing the party line."

"Oh, I'm a lawyer by trade. Had been in the office when I got the call. Usually, start work at five in the city. Early. Merchant, not criminal. Not much use here with Edward and all."

Calling his bluff Elizabeth probes.

"Who said anything about a crime here?"

"No one. Who'd want to kill Edward? Harmless as a fly, wet as a baby's blanket," replies Jonathan.

"I'm quite surprised you brought up the idea."

"Well it runs through your mind, doesn't it? I mean that's why you came to speak with Rebecca, isn't it?"

"Yes."

"Then I'm just saying what you're thinking."

Elizabeth can't argue with that. She watches Jonathan leave to follow Kara, throwing his cigarette butt onto the gravel. She is slightly puzzled by how different his attitude is to his own sister's. Was her dislike of him clouding her judgement? Probably, but she enjoyed finding an enemy, and Jonathan Smythe-Jones could be it this morning. Male, upper-middle-class elite politician, neither seemingly interested in true dialectic nor democratic ends, rather more of a Machiavellian intern.

As Elizabeth turns on her heels toward the main gate, she glances up at Rebecca's window. But Rebecca isn't there. She can just see the tip of the dead campanula. Elizabeth wonders about this dysfunctional family. The brother-in-law who appears to have an overprotective streak. Could Jonathan have killed Edward if Edward was upsetting his sister? She ponders on that. Certainly, it seems that Jonathan had been in London, but maybe he could have still made it up here and gone back to work afterwards; who would have noticed at that time of the morning? But what could Edward have possibly done to incur the wrath of his brother-in-law? And surely Jonathan would not do anything to upset Rebecca, much less kill her husband. It was clear Rebecca loved Edward in some way. Could it have been Rebecca? She was a little woman in frame and disposition but could have got someone else to do her dirty work. Though where was the motive?

*

Kara plonks herself in the passenger seat of Jonathan's car and bursts into tears. She's not sure if this is because she hasn't had any sleep, or perhaps because she hasn't eaten, but when Jonathan is grumpy, she does wonder what she's letting herself in for, wanting to become Mrs Smythe-Jones. She loves this life, wants to keep her diamonds, balls and champagne, wants it all, his life too with all its pomp and ruddy English traditions, and she knows Jonathan loves her deep down. Yes, it is probably the fatigue setting in. She had been rushing about last night after all. She wonders if Jonathan has any water in the car. Water will make her feel better. She opens the glove compartment, but there isn't any in there. She spots some tissues and pulls out the box. Behind it, she can't miss a letter, which doesn't look like Westminster business. Something about the size and type of envelope, about the handwritten 'Jonathan' on the front and the South African postage stamps. Curious, she pulls out the letter and opens it. The quality paper is stiff and has just one crease across it. She opens the fold and reads the contents.

Jonathan,
I can give you this much for now.
You'll have to wait for the rest until I get back from Cape Town.
There is a cheque for £40,000 enclosed.
Leave it. I'll sort it.

Edward.'

There is no cheque with the letter, although a paper clip is still attached, hinting at one before. That is not an insubstantial sum. Kara can't believe that Edward is dead and on the same day she finds that he's paid her husband-to-be £40,000. What was going on between them? Kara never much liked Edward, too earnest, too pleased with himself, yet in a humble way if that was possible. That passive aggressive thing that comes with good education, good schooling, from being forced through years of tuition, ending up confident but not a show-off, reticent yet opinionated, self-aware but not self-obsessed. To be a leader, but quietly stoic. It drove her nuts, so no, she isn't as upset about Edward as she ought to be.

Kara panics as she sees Jonathan's silhouette walking around to the driver's door. She stuffs the letter in her purse as Jonathan slumps into the car.

"What a morning. I'm not leaving Rebecca. So we'll have to swap roles. You take the car, go home get some rest. You look like you could do with it. Get some clothes for me will you please, and I'll meet you back here later, around lunchtime? We can all have lunch together and be a normal, grieving family. At least for the outside world." Jonathan lights yet another cigarette. It is a chain-smoking day.

"Sorry I was late. I don't know where the time went."

"Those people you hang out with." Jonathan shakes his head.

"Yes, they're no good, I know. I'll try to cut down."

"Tell me that you're legal to drive, at least."

Kara nods. She definitely isn't, but daren't risk him knowing with his temper. She'll just leave college and go and get a coffee somewhere. What he doesn't know won't hurt him. He's clearly holding secrets of his own.

13
A FRIEND

Inspector Abley arrives at the black iron gates of the University Botanic Garden. The lush, peaceful greenery enticing you in, at odds with the street outside and the cars rushing into the city, honking horns and revving their engines. Just inside, standing on the entrance pavement, Abley overhears a group listening to their guided talk about how the gardens were set up by John Henslow back in the nineteenth century and now span a forty-acre oasis in the heart of the city. He smiles, knowing Elizabeth would prefer to keep casual garden visitors to as few as possible. He is suddenly surrounded, this time by local wildlife enthusiasts meeting this morning to spot badger latrines in the herbaceous beds, after having earlier examined a new sett in the pine tree nursery.

Abley flashes his detective badge at the ticket collector inside the payment booth and is soon alone again as the gaggle of animal spotters, clutching notepads and binoculars, dissipate along West Walk towards the lake, while he opts for the opposite path which heads directly to the glasshouses. On his way, he notices two young children exploring the rock gardens, pretending they are pirates; a mother sitting on a bench having got them out early in the hope they'll run out their energy. It fleetingly transports him to a time when he came with his own mother. She would bring him with his younger brother when they were small to feed the ducks and sometimes have a picnic. From across the gardens, he can see the tall black pines and giant redwoods and smell the cedar drifting across the path where he used to play hide and seek with Derek.

More recent memories of meetings with Elizabeth, arguing about a case in the garden cafe or popping up to the laboratories to ask her opinion about something or other also start to resonate. All that had stopped when Sir Gerald died, when that private tragedy came tumbling down on his friend. He had not meant to seem so heartless earlier. He knew Elizabeth wanted to come back and get involved, but if he did not look out for her now, who would? She needed a break. Anyone could see that. Abley had known Elizabeth for many years now. Some think her a cold fish – and he would not want to be on the wrong side of her tongue – but more than most he knew how she could hide her emotions, her feelings, that she was a kind woman, and always on the right side of right. Now as he walks towards her, he begins to feel a little guilty. She is still clearly in no fit state, but he knows how much she is addicted, just like him.

Abley reaches the first of the tall brick-bottomed sloping-roof glasshouses. To get to the smaller houses in the middle, you have to enter a side door, which leads you down a warm internal atrium, opening into smaller individual framed glasshouses within the beautiful huge structure. He can't see Elizabeth yet, and hot humidity hits him like a wall through the first door. From dainty alpines to tropical climbers, the glasshouse collection is packed with exotic and rare species. As he walks, poking his head in each separate door behind which is a different collection, he finally spots Elizabeth in the meadow house. In her pretty green gardening apron, she is counting small plants, inspecting them for vigour. The stronger ones she's removing, and replacing on another tray. Inspector Abley comes in and watches her for a moment and smiles. Unsure of how to strike up conversation he begins instead to stroke a plant.

"Hello, Liz."

Elizabeth looks up, unsure why the Inspector has made such a trek to see her, but wondering if it is to ask her back to work.

"I have left you a number of messages at the station, Inspector. You haven't been here in ages now, have you?"

"No, I don't suppose I have."

The Inspector looks around the glasshouse. Its fine timber frame is laced with the cleanest, most delicate panes, making any man think of golf, cricket or footballs smashing through making a hellish noise, disrupting the work inside.

"Missing it? Everyone misses the Botanic Gardens after a while. Isn't it just the best place in Cambridge? Always quiet in the week too. No one here bothering the plants with their litter, or their poking and prodding. I really think they should ban young children."

"Surely they're future botanists, aren't they? Toddlers love nature, before all those time-wasting gadgets set in."

"A little tinker was picking flowers in here at the weekend. Father apparently defended him, saying he was being creative and was going to make his mummy a pretty picture when he got home. I could draw a picture of what I'd do to him." Elizabeth looks affronted at the audacity.

"Good job for everyone by the sounds of it that you didn't catch him." Inspector Abley raises his eyebrows. Elizabeth crosses her arms and stops what she's doing, so he tries to undo his veiled insult by moving the conversation on a little, talking about his own children.

"Thank goodness my two are ploughing their own furrows. Just come to check that you're doing okay? You know, after last night. I shouldn't wonder if it was all a bit of a shock?"

Elizabeth recognises Abley's bumbling attempts to find out how she is and shakes her head.

"I'm perfectly fine. If that's all you wanted you'd have sent a junior along, or perhaps the police doctor. How is Mr Simpkins?"

"It takes such a long time to get into a normal surgery appointment these days. I haven't time to sit in a GP waiting room with everyone coughing and spluttering. Simpkins is a fine doctor, would you like to see him?" Inspector Abley is feeling his way with Elizabeth, trying to read her mood.

"Oh really. Will you come to the point? And did you listen to my messages about food poisoning as a possibility?"

"It looks like we have to keep the cordon in your garden for a while longer. It does look suspicious."

"Someone died there last night. I don't expect any less. But get those Neanderthals to be more careful with my lawn."

"They should be gone by the end of the week."

"Tell me what you know. Then I can offer my theories and run some tests for you. That's why you're really here again, isn't it?"

The Inspector pauses, still frustrated by what he has to tell her, "No, it isn't actually."

"Then what?"

"The pathologist wants more time if you must know. He's working on it." Abley replies.

"Why? What have they found? Who's doing it, is it Leedham? Leedham is always so slow, so pernickety."

Abley doesn't want to be drawn, especially as she is right. Leedham is slow. So again he tries to change the subject.

"These are lovely plants."

"Tell me." Elizabeth is having none of his prevarications.

"Deep red flowers. What are they? Mrs Abley would love some of these in her conservatory. She still has that wisteria you bought her all those years ago. It's growing up the entire side of our west wall now. Pretty lilac flowers."

Elizabeth starts to walk away from the Inspector. She waves her hand, so Abley relents and offers up the information she requests.

"It's Leedham, yes. He told me that Mr Wiley had a cardiac arrest, but he's found traces of toxalbumin, so there is toxicology now to consider." Abley immediately regrets revealing the unknowns to Elizabeth.

"Well, I can completely help with that," she says eagerly.

"And by the way, you were breaking the law by not telling us that Edward wasn't already dead, for chrissake Elizabeth. How on earth am I going to square that peg?"

Elizabeth knows she's in trouble.

"Didn't I? I thought I had."

"Oh no, you didn't. It's not in any part of your statement."

"It must have been the shock." Elizabeth is telling the truth, she thinks. She must have just forgotten to tell them. Was that it?

"We'll have to get an additional statement from you, so I think you'd better start thinking how you can justify having left out that minor detail."

"All right," Elizabeth gets defensive.

"It changes everything. You know that technically makes you a potential suspect now, the last person to see Mr Wiley alive." Abley rocks on his toes. Elizabeth tugs at her hair in exasperation.

"Don't be ridiculous. I just forgot. I forgot, all right? He died so quickly. He only uttered a couple of words, and then he was gone. Did you say a suspect? So you think it wasn't a normal drowning after all?"

"He only uttered a couple of words? Elizabeth, you can't withhold evidence from the police when there is a death in suspicious circumstances, or I shall end up having to arrest you. What were the words?" Inspector Abley nervously rubs a plant as they stand and talk. Elizabeth notices and goes to draw his hand away, relieved for the change of subject.

"Inspector. You shouldn't have touched that. Here." Elizabeth wipes his hands with a cloth, smirking at him for jumping back in fear. "Ranunculaceae family. More commonly known as monkshood," Elizabeth wipes between his fingers, "or wolfsbane, soldier's cap, devil's helmet."

"All right, I didn't touch it for long." Abley pulls his hand away from Elizabeth.

"Wouldn't lick your fingers. Know how you like your food," she says, enjoying winding him up.

"Why? I only touched it."

Elizabeth wants to remind Abley just how smart she is, and how he needs her on the case.

"Pretty bit like a delphinium. If you were to eat it, you'd get a transient burning in the mouth, followed by several hours of vomiting, diarrhoea, severe blood pressure abnormalities, slip into a coma, have convulsions. Without treatment, could quite possibly die. If you touch it, the poison is absorbed through the skin. You won't feel any problems in your stomach, but your hand and then arm will start to feel numb as the poison heads for the heart. This is the queen of poisons, Inspector."

"Eh?" The Inspector looks at his hand and goes to a water tap in the glasshouse.

"Some florists have reported feeling unwell just from working with it. You have to be unlucky though. I think small contact would probably be fine." Elizabeth feels a little guilty now as Abley washes his hands vigorously, so much that the tap water spills over the tray catch, onto the concrete floor.

"Probably? Why are you growing it here? Children come in, don't they?"

"This particular glasshouse is not open to the public, because it houses very poisonous plants. It remains locked. It is one of the deep ironies of the Botanic Garden, as you will find this plant in many gardens anyway and growing wild. We live in a culture of health and safety and insurance claims gone mad."

"Insurance claims? Bit hard if you're dead."

"Calm down, Bob. You'll be fine."

The Inspector puts more soap from the dispenser on his hands and washes them again.

"You're safe now," she continues to try to calm him.

"Really, if it is that poisonous?" Abley tries to change the subject and directs his questions back at Elizabeth. "What words did Edward say before he died?"

"Serve us tea, or serve us tips. It was hard to tell. I don't know."

"That's three words."

"Two or three words. He repeated them actually if you must know. Could he have been talking about the restaurant? They served him, and then he gave a tip? He could likely have been hallucinating by that point."

"You must tell me these things in future, or we're going to fall out." The Inspector continues to wash his hands. Elizabeth does not like Abley's reprimand.

"It was once used to kill wolves, you know, that particular poison. Arrowheads dipped in it, as the effects are quick."

"Bloody hell, Liz. What are you like?"

"You only touched it." She smiles.

"You grow it," Abley huffs.

"It can be found in many places in meadows. Hence it's in the meadow garden glasshouse. It's a native species. How many people do you know who have died from monkshood poisoning?"

"How would we know?"

"Really, calm down. Look. See?"

Elizabeth goes over and touches the plant with her hand having taken off her glove to illustrate it is okay. She wants to calm Inspector Abley down.

"You'd have to touch it more than that. Not just for a few seconds like you did. You'll be fine."

"Aren't you going to wash your hands?" Abley shows concern for Elizabeth, moving to provide space by the tap. Elizabeth puts her glove back on and tries to find out again if Abley is asking her back to work on the Wiley case.

"So he had a cardiac arrest? You stopped by to tell me that? The toxalbumin though. That could have come from so many things."

The Inspector turns off the tap and wipes his hands dry with a paper towel.

"No. What I came to say," the Inspector has calmed down and speaks quietly, "was make sure you share all information in future and please leave the case to us. I heard you were at Rebecca Wiley's first thing this morning, telling her he was still alive when you found him, telling her it could be murder when we're still doing the post-mortem. I thought you had a lecture to give?"

Elizabeth raises her eyebrows and corrects Abley.

"I just said that something about this is odd because it is. And I can't say I much took to Jonathan Smythe-Jones. An oily character if ever there was. He looked as guilty as hell. Chain smoking menthol cigarettes."

"We found a packet in Edward's jacket. But according to his wife he doesn't smoke."

"See how useful my visit was this morning, Bob?"

Inspector Abley realises he is unfairly drawing Elizabeth into the case again.

"Look Liz, your expertise has always been relied upon, and you have helped solve some of our toughest cases. How can I put this politely? Stop interfering." Abley tries to temper the blow with a softer tone. "I'm just saying that you've crossed the line into police work. Please stay clear of it."

Elizabeth can't look at Inspector Abley. "Just make sure you don't touch anything else on the way out."

The Inspector is used to Elizabeth's abrupt demeanour and tries to smile at her, at least to show no hard feelings. He gets no response from her in return, no flicker of vulnerability, so decides to turn on his heel and leave the glasshouse, shutting the door behind him. As soon as he has gone, Elizabeth removes her gloves and walks over to wash her hands with soap. She wanted to make a point to Abley, but she doesn't want to feel under the weather later. She rubs her hands under the water to make sure the poison is off.

14
GRANDSON

Elizabeth starts back on her earlier task of identifying stronger seedlings from the weak. There is a flicker of hurt in the corner of her eye, but she won't let it build. She knows she's stronger than the Inspector. She also knows she'll crack this case before he does – with or without him. She bends down to dig the soil before planting out one of the stronger seedlings and hears the door creak open again.

"Look, Inspector, I hear you loud and clear. You've drummed the message home. No need to twist the knife–"

It's Godric worried about his favourite nanna, and just has time to check all is well before his next lecture.

"Hello Bun'. What did he want?"

Elizabeth shrugs so Godric continues.

"You swooped out of the house this morning like a carrier pigeon with a message from God."

"More to the point, what do you want, Godric?"

Elizabeth knows that when Godric wants something he inevitably seeks her out and acts overly nice. Godric takes hold of his nanna's hand. Now she knows for sure.

"I wanted to check you're okay because you've been through it. You haven't had any sleep. So if there's anything you need, or if you'd like to have lunch together later, just say the word. Nothing's too small."

"I wish everyone would stop fussing. Don't I look okay?" Elizabeth is having none of his concern.

"Actually, you look," Godric thinks twice about what he was going to say, that she looks shattered, "you look radiant, as ever. Just a tad tired around the tiniest of edges, but other than that, you have a glow which would rival any nuclear power station, Bunny."

Elizabeth has had enough of this.

"If you're not going to revise, that's your funeral. But I need to work, Godric. Sorry for snapping. And I'm having lunch with Emily today. Aren't there things you can be getting on with?"

Godric puts his head to one side and limps a little towards the window to look out into the far distance as he screeches his next words.

"I feel so tired, from having woken so early. I feel like I need a pick me up."

"That'll be the pickling of your liver, no doubt."

"Touché." Godric smirks at his grandmother's pointed reminder of his hangover.

Frustrated with her work, Elizabeth takes it out on the plants.

"Oh bugger. These won't flower. If they won't flower, then I just can't get them to propagate. We are running low on seeds. Summer lady's tresses. Thought to be extinct in the wild."

Though he already knows far more than the average fellow about them, as a result of living with his nanna, Godric can't think of anything less interesting than plants, unless you can ferment and drink them, or perhaps smoke them. He changes the subject.

"They're still there. At home. I always think frogmen

look a little peculiar. You know, with their faces all steamed up, and their lips stretched apart by breathing apparatus. A bit like Muppets."

"They'll not find anything," Elizabeth states dismissively, getting out a little brush and pollinating some wildflowers.

Godric tries to be super agreeable. He has something on his mind.

"I half wondered if there was anyone left at the Parkside Police Station with all the forensics going on at ours."

But Elizabeth is off in her own thoughts, trying to piece together the last twenty-four hours of Edward's life.

"So the police clearly suspect malice. They found traces of toxalbumin for goodness' sake. What more do they need? You don't find it naturally in high doses like that," Elizabeth says, having worked herself up into a fervour. Godric again, with ulterior motives, agrees with everything Elizabeth says but is also worried about his nanna doing too much.

"Well, that sniffs of something odd indeed. But I'm sure the Inspector can handle it, don't you think? You look like you have your hands full here."

Elizabeth isn't grateful for her grandson's advice.

"Haven't you got lectures to go to?"

"Well, funny you should say that. Yes, and with my leg, it is proving rather tricky. I mean I want to revise at the library. Then I have evensong." Godric looks through his long eyelashes at Elizabeth. "You know what would help? The Talbot. You did say to rest my knee." Godric could not look more puppy-eyed if he tried. But Elizabeth is having none of it.

"You don't need a car for that. We live in the centre."

Godric tries one more tactic.

"I'm sure I could hear it speaking to me this morning, saying 'summer is here. I need a drive. Let me out.'"

Godric is not helping Elizabeth's mood.

"Perhaps the Inspector was talking some sense earlier. A bit of exercise might do you good. And as far as I can remember, the Talbot is not a talking car, Goddy."

"Okay." Godric puts on a limp as he walks away from Elizabeth and stands looking out of the glasshouse across the grass. "Did you see Rebecca by the way? She might be at evensong tonight, though with all the circumstances I doubt it."

All at once Elizabeth, able to talk about the case again, stops what she's doing.

"Yes, as a matter of fact, I did. She was very teary, as one would expect. Though also very jumpy when I told her I thought Edward didn't die from drowning. Even a tad argumentative. Pointed the finger at a woman who used to date Edward. As much as accused her of having the motive. Bit quick, don't you think? To process everything. Most people would still be in shock, not thinking straight." Elizabeth looks at Godric who nods, then continues, "Phoned the police afterwards. Something's not right there. Maybe not right with their marriage that she's not letting on. And if you're someone who wants to stay around you use poison on your victim and not use a gun or knife, with all that traceable blood and weapon hiding issues. Poison is the sneaky way to kill someone right under peoples' noses. It also works if you're too small to kill your victim." Elizabeth looks at Godric again for his agreement. Godric, however, has other news.

"You know what's really weird? When I was upstairs in my bedroom I saw this person, standing watching the frogmen from the other side of the river for a bit, you know by the tennis courts on Jesus Green. I couldn't see their face, as they were just that bit too far away. But I could tell they were watching. They stood there for ages. Perhaps twenty minutes, not moving, just facing the house."

"People are nosey, Godric. There is nothing strange about that. That child in the fountain, however, that is not on. I will have to let the park keeper know. Oh dear, what is he doing now?" Elizabeth bangs on the window at the parents who have let their little toddler son climb into the garden fountain, disturbing all the lilies and frogs. But they don't hear. Godric is not content to leave his own story there, however, as he wants his nanna's opinion, having been a trifle spooked.

"Yes, but they were taking photographs. They had their camera. It was a long lens. I could see the size of it from my window. I think it was a man."

Elizabeth answers Godric, but her attention is still on the little boy splashing about in the fountain.

"Bit morbid I suppose. All those men in the water could have brought something up at any moment. Perhaps a newspaper photographer?"

"No, not photos of the frogmen. Photos of me. They were pointing the camera into my bedroom. I was looking at them, and they were looking at me. It gave me the heebie-jeebies. The lens kept reflecting against our window."

Elizabeth agrees this is a little odd and turns to look at Godric. But Godric is already leaving the glasshouse, disappointed he hasn't been given permission to drive the family car, but at least reassured that Elizabeth is okay for now.

Shortly after, Elizabeth packs up what she is doing as she knows she is getting nowhere in the glasshouse this morning. She hangs up her apron, then talking to the plants, she tells them, "You'll have to wait." She is more determined to find Edward's killer, even if she has to go behind Abley's back. He'll thank her for it later. He always does. Why can't it be easier, why can't he need her? Why can't anyone need her? It would appear this morning that even Godric is only after the car. But before she leaves, she goes outside, walks over to the fountain and has strong words with the parents, whose toddler is promptly lifted out of the fountain and starts to cry.

15
CHESTERTON

Elizabeth has left the glasshouses in the Botanic Garden and is cycling across Jesus Green, past the huge lines of tall London Planes, tennis courts and outdoor swimming pool. She crosses Victoria Avenue, heads towards the Fort St. George pub and out onto Midsummer Common, backing down as it does to the river, lined with rowing clubs and boathouses. This is Elizabeth's most favourite common, open to the sky, surrounded by trees. She soon leaves it behind, however, and heads for Chesterton on a mission, her curls spewing out the sides of her bright yellow cycle helmet, her linen coat flapping. She whisks past people eating lunches on the riverbank, solitary scullers working their way down to Fen Ditton, and an industrial-sized lawn mower wafting summer smells of cut grass.

Elizabeth wants to pay a visit to the spurned ex-girlfriend, Susan Bunt, of whom Rebecca Wiley spoke earlier. Even if it was a ruse to deflect attention from herself, it worked, as Rebecca has pricked Elizabeth's interest. Susan may know something. What if she isn't friendly? What if she is actually the murderer? Should Elizabeth have told Godric where she is going? No, it will be fine. She can handle herself, and after all, anyone who is an ex-girlfriend of Edward can't be that hard to deal with. Edward was one of the gentlest of spirits in her whole department.

Elizabeth reflects back on her conversation with Godric. He was really only coming to see if she was okay this morning. Had she been too mean about the Talbot? She knows Gerald would have wanted him to use it, but somehow Elizabeth still can't bear to see the car on the road without Gerald in it, as this would be another glaring fact that he is gone. Gerald has started to drift away from her, and now the only thing that remains are fading memories. She senses she is getting something wrong about Edward's death, feels she is missing a clue. If only Gerald was here. Elizabeth starts to talk to him.

"Rebecca was so bitter about Susan. I feel like I'm being set up, coming to see Susan like this." Elizabeth passes a couple of lovers holding hands who have been watching her talk to herself as she cycles towards them on the river path. Unperturbed, Elizabeth smiles and carries on talking. "On the other hand, Jonathan is a classic murderer. Arrogant, angry, with such narcissistic qualities. And this murder feels planned, Gerald, don't you think?"

Elizabeth continues along Riverside, leaving the centre now, passing moored canal boats, rusty houseboats, scattered recycled debris, dogs barking. On the top deck of an old lifeboat stands an impromptu work of art. Two Barbie dolls sitting on miniature deck chairs under a toy-sized parasol, all propped up on a makeshift toy bath boat on top of a houseboat deck. At the start of Stourbridge Common, trees begin to take hold of the view, met by tall grasses, as this stretch of the river is left for the cattle, whose heads dip almost permanently grazing, save for the odd check for stranger danger.

Elizabeth gets off her bicycle and walks over the Green

Dragon Bridge by the public house of the same name. She stops at the top of the brow to look up and down the river, bemused more people don't do the same, instead choosing to hurry past, not noticing the willow trees kissing the water and river banks touching the horizon. She used to sit and drink cold cider with Gerald sometimes on The Green Dragon's riverfront when they were younger. These days you're hard pressed to find a table, it is so popular. She doesn't go anymore, though is reliably informed the beer is still cold, the service warm, and there are always swans up on the bank to hiss at you for your ploughman's.

A little further down the river, overlooking Stourbridge Common is a pub, The Pike & Eel, so close to Elizabeth's heart that it aches with hurt to see it now closed and derelict. She remembers taking this route to Fen Road so many times and many moons ago, to take a break from her doctorate. She'd step out onto the grass and sit on benches to eat her supper, sharing it with the ducks and sunset. Now forlorn, with its fate unknown, just a shell of a building holding the conversations of people and memories past. When all that goes, only the echoes of a disappearing community will hang in the air where the penny ferry slopes hint at past trips to the largest common in Cambridge.

Elizabeth feels the chill of Edward's death on the water below. The cries carried on the ripples having swept past this stretch. Not twenty-four hours have passed, and the water looks darker below her feet as it runs at a pace on its long journey to the sea. She can hear 'serve us tip' in her ears, and Edward's urgent voice to communicate this message. If only she could have understood better what he was trying to convey.

Elizabeth continues down Water Street, to Fen View Court and is soon locking her bicycle to the front garden railings of a red-bricked house in a cul-de-sac, overlooking the River Cam. She walks up the garden path to the front door and rings the bell. Ivy has grown around the porch, and a spider guards a corner, keenly observing Elizabeth's attempted entry. Frosted glass of the front door reflects a quiet hallway. 'Ding dong', there is a pause and then to her left Elizabeth notices the curtains twitch.

"Hello, Miss Bunt?" Elizabeth stands back from the porch to be seen from the front window. "May I have a quick word?"

Susan opens the window a crack. She is at least three feet higher from the ground outside than Elizabeth, so feels at a safe advantage.

"Who wants to talk?"

"Elizabeth Green. Hello. May we speak? About Edward Wiley, Miss Bunt?"

Susan disappears from the window, and through the frosted glass in the front door Elizabeth sees a shadowy figure moving towards her. Susan opens the door a crack. Dressed in a black trouser suit and a blue scarf covered in Scotty dogs, Susan flicks her ash out towards Elizabeth then inhales a long drag of her cigarette as she scrutinises this serious-looking lady in linen and a cycle helmet.

"What do you want? And it's Doctor Bunt."

"I've come to talk to you about Edward Wiley. I've just been with Mrs Wiley, and she said you knew her husband, that you were once close, Dr Bunt." Elizabeth takes off her cycle helmet and tries to tidy her unruly curls. Susan thinks angrily of Rebecca.

"That scrawny cow? I've never been close to her in my life. What's it to you, who are you?"

Elizabeth looks at Susan while clipping her cycle helmet to her linen jacket pocket.

"I'm a colleague of Edward Wiley, I knew him from the department. May I come in a minute to talk to you about—"

Susan is having none of it. Anyone who knows Rebecca is bad news.

"No, you bloody can't, now piss off."

Elizabeth persists, trying to work out if Susan knows about Edward.

"Have the police not been in touch?"

"Police?"

Elizabeth thinks perhaps Susan knows nothing.

"About Edward Wiley."

Susan is curious.

"What about Edward? What's happened?"

Elizabeth pauses and looks at Susan. How is she going to break it?

"Dr Bunt, have you not seen or heard the news?"

Susan now opens the door wider and leans against the door frame with her arms defensively crossed.

"No, I haven't seen the ruddy news. What are you on about? Do I know you?"

Elizabeth pauses at the gravity of having to break it to Susan.

"May I come in?"

Susan finishes her cigarette, stubbing it out on the wall.

"No, you bloody can't. I haven't got time for chats with any old stranger. Just say what you've got to say, then do one."

There is a long pause as Elizabeth looks at Susan and away again.

"I think we should do this indoors."

Susan blows the last smoke from her lungs out towards Elizabeth, who winces somewhat at the stench.

"Just tell me, or sod off."

"Edward is dead, Dr Bunt."

Susan stares at Elizabeth, then looks across the river at the cattle.

"Dead?" Susan can almost hear the cattle chewing from where they stand, in spite of the river separating them. "The heifers are through the gate again." Susan's voice wavers.

Elizabeth can see the colour drain from Susan.

"I think you'd better sit down. Please, let me help you

inside."

They wander into the hallway, Susan no longer objecting, instead in a daze, talks only of the mundane.

"Excuse the mess. I was going to clean up today. Been a bit distracted."

Elizabeth is still unsure whether Susan already knew of the death and is putting on an act, or is genuinely shocked, as she strikes her as a rather dark horse.

"It's a terrible shock, a dreadful thing. I'm sorry you had to hear it from me. Let me get you a glass of water, is your kitchen through here?"

Elizabeth spots the kitchen off the living room and pops in to grab a glass of water and have a bit of a snoop. The kitchen is messy, and the cupboards reveal sparse contents, Elizabeth thinks, as if this rather large lady deliberately keeps no food in the house in case she eats it. She looks in the fridge, again, quite empty. Perhaps Susan is planning to go shopping soon.

In less than a few seconds Elizabeth brings out the only clean mug full of water and returns to Susan's side. Susan has slumped down onto the sofa, with her head tipped back she stares at the smoke-stained ceiling. Elizabeth hands her the water and looks about the cluttered room. A momentary lull in conversation leads Elizabeth's eyes to wander to the bookcase full of Yeats, Dylan Thomas, Virginia Woolf, Aldous Huxley, a candle half burnt, a box with Rizlas and some fruit jellies the only ornaments. She spots a computer at a desk, and a full ashtray beside which an Anglepoise burns, causing yet more cigarette stench to rise. Susan clocks Elizabeth's disdain at the mess.

"I've been working on a paper. Don't tend to make contact with the outside world until I've finished."

Elizabeth wonders if Susan is just making excuses for why she may not have heard the news about Edward, though the computer work looks genuine, judging from all the butts and coffee rings.

"I'm sorry. May I?"

Elizabeth points at a chair covered in jumpers and socks, for her to sit on. Susan makes no reply, so she takes that as a yes and places the clothes on the floor then eases herself down.

"Are you sure it's Edward who's dead?" Susan asks, adding, "I was only with him, what–" Susan stops herself from saying what she was going to reveal. "Why have you come here? I mean to tell me? What are you doing?"

Elizabeth thinks this a fair question, though Susan seems to have recovered from her shock rather quickly in her opinion. If she had just heard someone close had died, she would be unable to talk, think, see.

"I found him," Elizabeth replies.

Susan sits forward and stares at Elizabeth.

"Where, where did you find him?"

Elizabeth isn't sure if she is being played now. But goes along with the questioning.

"Near Jesus Lock. I live up there, Dr Bunt."

Susan continues to question.

"What, in the Lock House?"

Elizabeth wonders if she can test Susan, just to see if she is the killer.

"No, further up. My garden backs onto the river near Castlebridge College. Do you know that route?"

Susan doesn't answer Elizabeth's question, instead asking her own.

"Did he drown?"

Elizabeth wonders how Susan could have known that he'd been in the water if she knew nothing and was innocent. She decides not to answer the question, but reply with a question.

"I'm sorry to ask you this, as I say I've spoken to Rebecca Wiley this morning and she told me that you and Edward were close. He was very popular in the department, and I'm at a loss as to who might want to kill him?"

"Kill him?"

Elizabeth stares at Susan. She does seem to look shaken. Perhaps she's a good actress. There are a lot of poetry and literature books on the shelves. Elizabeth thinks of herself as a scientist and as such leaves all that drama to the creative, artsy people. Even if Godric says she is dramatic, and come to think of it, Gerald used to tell her how flamboyant she could be when out enjoying herself, she knows she has a logical, rational mind. Elizabeth wants to find out more about this enigmatic woman.

"You're in shock. Is there anyone I can contact? Family?"

Susan shakes her head. Her family is not from around here, and her friends are scattered all around the world now. She used to have more, but years of neglect and throwing her life into her research put paid to that.

"I can't believe it. When?"

"Last night."

Elizabeth wanders over to the laptop on the table and searches for the news. She tilts the screen and shows it to Susan. The headline reads 'Don dies in tragedy on river'. Next to the photo of Edward is a photo of his famous politician brother-in-law. Susan points at Jonathan.

"He threatened me to stay away from Edward, because of his beloved sister."

"So you know Jonathan Smythe-Jones?"

"We both studied English, though he was an All Saints' man, always more acerbic than most, both in the Footlights," Susan smirks. "Why join if you're not funny? He directed some revues. Bossy as hell, didn't last long. They kicked him out. I guess that's when he chose politics. Those who can't, and all that."

"You were in the Footlights?"

"Wrote a few sketches, performed a bit of comedy, yeah. I saw him last week in college. He was always visiting his sister. Obsessed, Edward thought. The two of them went everywhere."

Elizabeth observes Susan's jokey mood and brings it back to Rebecca.

"So you also saw Rebecca then?"

Susan glares at Elizabeth, drinks the water down in one and reaches for another cigarette from the packet on the table, offering Elizabeth one.

"No, I believe it was you who spoke to the skinny bint. She said I'd know something? Full of poison she is, face like butter wouldn't, you know. What would I know?" Tears start to fall on Susan's cheeks. "I can't talk now." Elizabeth politely declines the cigarette and gently presses Susan. Less certain she's read the situation right.

"It's widely known that people remember important facts immediately after an event, and by talking about it that we manage to capture all the pieces of the puzzle. Otherwise, the memory fades. Just one more question, why would Rebecca Wiley mention your affair to me do you think?"

Susan, now irritated by Elizabeth, picks up a lighter.

"How the hell do I know, are you a bleeding detective or something?"

"No, I'm just trying to find out what happened."

"You ask too many questions."

Elizabeth shuffles, still standing. She knows it won't be long before she's asked to leave.

"But Mrs Wiley was quite vocal about an incident where she described seeing you outside their rooms at Bene't's, just watching their windows?"

Susan is growing more agitated, scowling at Elizabeth.

"I'm a Fellow at Bene't's for chrissake. I stand all over the place in the grounds, talking to people. You think I'd waste my time staring up at her window? If anyone hangs about, it's that stick insect. She has no profession other than shopping and pure idleness. This conversation is irritating, especially under the circumstances."

Elizabeth shuts her eyes for a moment and holds her

breath from Susan's smoke wafting over in her direction. Then continues,

"It's the circumstances that made me inclined to pay you a visit."

Susan fires off another insult at Rebecca Wiley.

"Anyway, that scrawny vulture. Got her talons into Ed. She wanted his money. He doesn't love her." Susan pauses and then corrects herself. "Didn't."

"He married her?" says Elizabeth. Susan starts to usher Elizabeth out.

"Before he knew what an intense suicidal vacuum she is. I think you should go."

Elizabeth continues to press for as many answers as she can get.

"You weren't jealous of them then?"

This rattles Susan hugely, her tone growing with impatience.

"Yeah, I think you're going now."

But Elizabeth turns her back to the door and faces Susan in the hall.

"Rebecca said you wouldn't leave them alone."

"Ha! I saw him last night." She stops herself, realising she's said something she shouldn't, nervously loosening her scarf. Elizabeth can't refrain from pushing further.

"You may have been the last person—"

Susan interrupts.

"He was fine. He was going to talk to Rebecca."

"He lives with Rebecca," Elizabeth replies.

"He was going to tell her that he was leaving her. For me. Now get out!"

Susan holds the front door open now, for Elizabeth to leave.

"Just one thing, Dr Bunt. If Edward was going to leave Rebecca when was he going to tell her? Was it definitely last night?"

Susan snarls. "Yes. Maybe he told her, and she got angry. I don't know."

Elizabeth is not sure she believes Susan is being honest.

"What if he changed his mind and told you over dinner that he wasn't going to leave her after all. Maybe you got angry?"

Susan spits with anger, "You have the gall to come in here and tell me Edward is dead and in the same breath accuse me of his murder? Just go, before I do something I regret!"

Elizabeth trips on a packed bag in the hallway by her feet, along with a big cloak. She looks at the bag and up at Susan.

"Are you going somewhere?"

"You are!" Susan forcibly pushes Elizabeth out the door. Elizabeth stumbles and falls backwards onto the garden path, her cycle helmet pinging off her jacket and rolling into a patch of garden border.

As the door slams, Elizabeth lies for a moment looking back at the house and can see Susan's retreat through the frosted glass in the front door. She tries to remember everything Susan just said, but her heart is beating fast from the altercation. Elizabeth calms herself down with a few deep breaths and looks out at the cattle who unsurprisingly haven't been disturbed at all and are still chewing. Elizabeth pulls herself up, brushes down her clothes and wanders over to her bicycle. She thinks on the mysteries of the human heart, which keep us in a quandary over the choices we make. If Susan really didn't know Edward was dead, and she thought he was leaving Rebecca, then why was Susan packed? But if Susan did know he was dead, then she was a very good actress and could even be the murderer. She certainly had a temper. Also, Susan was clearly planning to leave for a while, as Elizabeth had noticed plants in the kitchen sink, soaking in water.

As Elizabeth pulls her bicycle to the path, she observes Susan looking back at her, net curtains pulled up, the window open a crack to give the house a little respite from yet another cigarette. It makes Elizabeth cough, the smell of ash still lingering on her lovely linen coat. The little spider above the door in the ivy peeps at Elizabeth, warning her off. She mounts her bicycle and joins the gravelly path along the river, passing a dog walker with a Bloodhound, stopping to say hello. Back at the house, Susan is now shaking with anxiety, watching Elizabeth stop to stroke the dog, talk to the woman and then cycle off into the distance and around the corner until she disappears. She tightens her scarf and flinches a little, then walks over to the packet of cigarettes. She has an excellent excuse for chain-smoking today.

16
THE GREEN MAGICIAN

A uniformed police officer, followed by Inspector Abley, walks down into the now fairly quiet Green Magician restaurant. The officer turns over the closed sign on the front door as he crosses the entrance. Someone takes out a mobile phone to take a picture of the policeman, making Abley both amused and concerned at what the young do with their gadgets and time these days.

Despite the day having brightened up, the gloom of the basement hits Abley like a wall. The smell of different foods mix in the air, of pasta, tomatoes, spinach, fried vegetables and the taint of red wine. He can see steam rising from the open hatch through to the kitchens, and hear pots clanging. Those sitting around him look a little like the undead, pale and stationary, their eyes wide staring at him in unison, aware of the blue stripes behind him. Abley has been here before. Previous owners had been involved in money laundering. Then before that, about ten years ago, he remembers when a fight kicked off, and someone was glassed. Now, he thinks it feels more touristy, less local somehow. More anodyne.

"It's okay everyone. There's nothing to see here."

But the few people eating brunch quietly disagree. Abley walks up to what looks like the man in charge then leans over the counter.

"Hello. Are you the manager?"

"No."

After some seconds of this impasse, Abley replies,

"Well, can you get them, please?"

There is a lull in the room, while everyone waits for the manager to appear. A fork clanks on a plate as someone else tries to chew quietly. Finally, the manager comes out from the kitchens, eating a slice of ciabatta. Dressed in a dark, tightly fitting expensive suit, with a chiselled jaw under a closely shaved beard, he acknowledges Inspector Abley and notices the uniformed officer standing nearby.

"Hello, I'm the manager, is there a problem?"

Abley smiles,

"I'm afraid we're going to have to temporarily close this establishment, Mr er–"

"Stower."

"It may have come to your attention, Mr Stower, that there has been a tragic death in Cambridge last night, of a Mr Edward Wiley. While investigations continue, we need to search the premises as we understand he ate here before his death." Abley hears a gasp from the restaurant as more knives and forks clank down. "I hope this isn't going to cause you too much inconvenience. We will conduct our search as quickly as possible."

"Do I have a choice?"

Abley shakes his head and shrugs his shoulders. The manager nods, reluctantly, which gives Abley his cue to turn to those still eating inside.

"Shall I?" The manager nods again, this time rolling his eyes. Abley addresses the diners. "Sorry folks, we are going to have to ask you to leave, as we must temporarily close The Green Magician. Nothing to worry about, they are just helping us with routine enquiries."

The uniformed police officer returns up the stairs to get his forensics team waiting outside in a van. One diner protests that he hasn't finished his pizza and has just ordered a lemon mousse.

"Sorry for the inconvenience," Abley replies, but in reality couldn't give a hoot about the man's pizza or lemon mousse, as he watches an overlarge belly wobble as the man stands up to leave. Clientele start to put on their jackets and pick up their bags, with half-eaten meals left on the tables. The manager placates them with offers of free food next time they come in.

"No need to settle up. Come back when we're open, and you'll get a complimentary meal as well, care of Cambridgeshire police." He looks hopefully at Inspector Abley, knowing full well that the police don't compensate. "Just give your name outside to the waiter." The manager orders a waiter up to the top of the stairs by the door to take names.

The uniformed police officer is now joined by two SOCO officers wearing white suits, who have to push past people on the stairs leaving in the opposite direction, now gossiping to one another. The SOCOs walk into the kitchen and start opening fridges and cupboards, taking out all the ingredients, much to the chagrin of the chef who – still wearing hat and apron – demonstratively waves his arms in the air until he is also ushered out up onto the pavement outside. The manager turns his attention back to Inspector Abley, who offers acknowledgement of the minor commotion.

"Please accept my apologies. Might I ask, were you working last night?"

Flatly and without hesitation, the laconic manager replies,

"When am I not working?"

Abley pulls an envelope from his jacket and draws out a photograph.

"Do you recognise this man?" Abley holds up a photo of Edward Wiley.

The manager does and nods sadly.

"Yes, I saw it on the news this morning. And you're right. He was here last night, dreadful business. Out of curiosity, how d'you know he ate here?"

"A lady who was dining here alone called us this morning. He also had one of your paper napkins in his pocket." Abley pulls out the napkin in a police forensics bag. It is broken up by the river, but the words The Green Magician are still visible.

"Ah, must be Mrs Humble. She sits alone, does the crossword while she eats. Every night. I would've got round to telling you myself. Just been too knackered."

Abley is not impressed but can understand as this looks like one of those places likely to wear a man out.

"Is there a way of finding out what he ate?" Abley asks.

"We should be able to find out the orders from the bills and work backwards from what we used in the kitchen. Let me have a look. Ordinarily, it would be a lengthy process, but Monday's are always quiet. There weren't too many in."

"Were there any unusual dishes on that night? Specials?"

"No, the normal menu. As I say, Monday. It's too quiet to do anything fancy." Mr Stower lifts out a hand-held gadget and scrolls down to Monday, clicks again on a table number.

"Here we are. Mr Wiley paid cash. I know it was him, as we number the tables. He was in for a long time. You can see that the first order put through the till was a 7.00pm and the last order was at 11.30pm. Everything's electronic now. We keep a tab. Helps us know when people are not spending enough, and when it's time to go over and ask them if they want more, it flashes and everything. Though I would have remembered him. Well dressed, not our typical punter."

Abley looks at the high-tech gadget, which does indeed look very snazzy.

"He spent £128.45 and left a £24 tip. Mainly on alcohol. A couple of Manhattans early on with some cashews, two whisky shots then a gap before buying a bottle of the good Wolf Blass. One had the sea bass the other the mushroom risotto. A chocolate mousse and the cheese board. Then another glass of red."

Abley is curious about the food.

"We'll need more information on the sea bass and the mushrooms, and such like."

"Most of what was left in the fridges chef's already thrown out. Should be in the bins though, out the back. Everything's fresh, but we can trace back to our suppliers and see if anyone else has had problems. We have a local chap who brings fish in from the Norfolk coast. Fresh caught. We use him a lot and freeze a bit. It lasts us the week, and then he comes again. He's got excellent produce, that's why we use him."

Abley digs to find out more, glad that he's got this far with the manager, but curious for that clue to help him solve this so he can maybe squeeze in nine holes this afternoon.

"That would be very helpful. Very helpful indeed. We can talk to your suppliers if you just give us the details. You said 'they' ate and drank. Do you happen to remember who Mr Wiley was dining with? Man, woman, young, old?"

"I wasn't out here all the time, but I saw a woman, about his age. Such an odd pair. She didn't look his type."

Abley looks at the manager a little quizzically, not entirely sure how helpful that is.

"All right, bluntly he was immaculately dressed, looked a class apart and she, well, she didn't."

Abley shakes his head a little, indicating that's still not much help.

"It's all I remember. They were sitting in the corner,

and it is quite dark in here at night."

"Right. Thank you. If you remember anything else, would you get in touch?" The Inspector hands the manager a card, who takes it and nods.

"Do I get any compensation for this?" The manager watches the final straggler client leaving his near empty restaurant.

"Helping to solve a case of a suspicious death in Cambridge? We shouldn't need to close you for more than twenty-four hours. I'll give you a photo of me if you like for your wall?" Abley smiles up at the celebrity photos in the alcove.

"Great." The manager realises there is nothing he can do.

Abley nods and smiles and then walks up the stairs. As he leaves he passes a police officer carrying out food.

"Would you take statements off any staff working here last night please?" The officer nods and holds the door for Abley.

Abley stands outside for a moment. Not sure of his next move. Just a few yards away he can see Bene't's College and the sky above. A man with a camera stops to take a picture, probably just of the Chapel, like hundreds that day. Abley sees the man drop a chocolate bar wrapper from his pocket into the alley. This infuriates Abley, but he can't be sidetracked now. He needs to focus on the case. He wants to solve this. He thinks about what the manager said: a woman who doesn't fit with Wiley, an odd pair. Well, that wasn't Rebecca. She looked like just the type of young lady a fellow might have on his arm.

The police tape over the entrance of the restaurant at street level. Abley walks back up the alley, picking up the chocolate wrapper and depositing it in a bin then clicks open the locks of his BMW 4-series coupe, double-parked on King's Parade. As he gets in, he looks at the increasingly busy pavements, people perched like pigeons along Bene't's College wall, drinking their coffees, licking ice creams, fiddling with cameras or just looking about. It is beginning to look like a great day to play golf. Much to his annoyance, he knows that this case is nowhere near finished. He starts the engine and heads back to the station.

17
PARKER'S PIECE

'Good people do not need laws to tell them to act responsibly,
while bad people will find a way around the laws.'
Plato

Elizabeth makes her way to the Cambridge Police HQ
across the green expanse of Parker's Piece. She walks past
the tall central lamppost, known to locals as 'Reality
Checkpoint', so called because it is where you leave the
bubble of the university for the real world where locals live
down the Mill Road. The police station is directly next to
the Cambridge Fire Station, the two buildings imposing
themselves upon the lower corner of this twenty-five acre
square of mown grass common, cut by two diagonal paths.
Less visible are its cricket field and white racing track
markings used by the local school. Not ten minutes from
most of the colleges in the centre, and equidistant to the
railway station, Parker's Piece often has people playing
Frisbee, football or generally chatting and watching the

world go by with impromptu picnics. But Elizabeth has no time for this today as she marches on, determined to discuss this case.

She finds Inspector Abley in the police canteen, finishing a very late breakfast. Police officers crowd the hall, grabbing snacks after a night shift or early lunches before the start of their beat. It has the air of a school canteen, with wafts of bacon mixed with pizza and sticky toffee pudding, chairs scratching across hard floors, tables creaking under the weight of elbows and some rather large officers devouring apple crumble puddings.

Most have noticed Elizabeth, aware of her reputation for helping the force solve cases, though few have ever spoken to her. Some show surprise to see her after such a long absence. She receives smiles and a nod in acknowledgement as she walks to the far table and comes to a standstill over Inspector Abley's chair. Abley shovels food as Elizabeth raises her eyebrows and coughs. Finally aware, he continues to do the crossword in his 'red top' paper, which also covers the death on the front cover with the word 'suspicious'. Stabbing at a few chips, he dips them in egg. Elizabeth breaks the silence.

"Haven't you solved it yet?" This falls on deaf ears, so she continues, "All right, what leads do you have? Maybe we should swap information?"

"Hello to you too."

Elizabeth finds this blanking of her request nauseating.

"Look, wasting time, stuffing your face, reading rot isn't going to help."

The Inspector doesn't rise to Elizabeth's rudeness. He knows her too well.

"My mother always said you can't do a day's work on an empty tum. Who am I to argue with a good woman?" Abley nods at his paper. "I'm doing the crossword while I eat, that's all. To what do I owe the pleasure?"

Elizabeth picks up the paper and reads out one of the clues.

"A sport with time for tea. Hmm. You'll be here all day with these."

The Inspector grabs his paper back.

"Hey. Don't knock it. It helps me relax, and stops the onset of... you know..." Abley pauses. Elizabeth helps him out.

"Dementia?" She perches uncomfortably on the chair opposite, desperate for the Inspector to crack on with the investigation, drums her fingers on the table and stares directly at him. Again, Inspector Abley knows the signs, so doesn't rise to them.

"Cuppa?" Abley offers, as he plops two sugars into his own.

Elizabeth frowns and continues to try to get Abley to sit up and listen to her.

"I came to tell you I've spoken to Susan Bunt, Edward's ex-lover?"

Abley, irritated replies,

"What? I thought we'd agreed that you were not getting involved?" Abley doesn't want to let her blind refusal to ignore his request rile him. Instead decides to share that he knows a thing or two about Susan Bunt too. "I think she may have eaten with him last night at The Green Magician. I've just got back from there."

Elizabeth maintains the drumming of her fingertips, still wanting Abley to crack on.

"Yes, she was with him last night. She admitted that to me. There is something which doesn't make sense about it. She felt, fake. Don't leave it too long. She looked like she was about to leave Cambridge."

Inspector Abley raises his eyebrows. She's telling him how to do his job. This time he can't help show his irritation.

"I wish you hadn't called on her." Abley puts on his most forceful voice, but Elizabeth knows he's soft underneath. "You're crossing the line again, Liz. Why are you doing this?"

They both know.

"Dr Bunt said she didn't know about the death. Can you believe that?"

Elizabeth picks up a chip, looks at it and puts it back down.

"Hey! I had my eye on that one." Abley stabs the chip with a fork and bites it in half, chewing. "And you broke it to her?" He shakes his head at her again. "How did she react?"

Elizabeth wants him to get up off the chair and race out to talk to Susan Bunt now and can't hide her impatience.

"She seemed genuinely surprised, but as I said, she had bags in the hallway, so I'm not sure I believed her. And she pushed me over as I left, desperate to get me out. I think you should visit her sooner than later. Otherwise what if she leaves?"

Inspector Abley is now worried about Elizabeth.

"What do you mean she pushed you? Are you okay? That's assault."

"No, not really. I suppose I may have provoked her." Elizabeth looks sheepish.

"Elizabeth."

Elizabeth knows Abley is both worried and cross at the same time. He always calls her Elizabeth when he's irritated. Just like her father used to do.

"I was seeing if she killed him."

Abley replies, "We will pay her a visit, but I have to interview the Dean of Bene't's College, as well as talk to Edward's brother-in-law. I hear he's tipped to join the Cabinet from the back benches."

Elizabeth doesn't want to hear about that annoying man, replying,

"Dr Bunt knows him. Warned her off Edward, apparently. Oily bunch, politicians. Power hungry, that's all they're in it for." Elizabeth dismisses them, taking the pen from Abley and filling in five down in the crossword.

Watercress.

"We live in a democracy, Liz. That means whatever you think of them, we need politicians."

Elizabeth fills in another clue, six across. Skirt.

"We do no such thing. We live in a media run society. Decisions made on a whim. They suppress us with gossip and trifle, so we don't wake up to see what the establishment is doing. They're the pigs in Animal Farm. And that is being mean about pigs, who are much nicer."

"I'm sure the pigs don't mind." Abley looks at his bacon, which he prongs on his fork. Elizabeth eyes the bacon.

"What have they ever done to us? They are gracious, intelligent and compassionate creatures. And we factory farm them and submit them to torture and worse at the slaughterhouse where you can hear their screams for miles." Elizabeth fills in another clue. Retirement.

Abley, who was about to put a slice of bacon in his mouth, suddenly loses his appetite and clanks down his fork, wiping his mouth with a serviette.

"Well, you might be right about that Smythe chappy, but I don't want you putting his back up. He's bound to have friends in high places, and we don't want him to interfere before we find out what happened."

Elizabeth watches Abley sip his tea, hoping he's heard the irony in his own words.

"I should imagine speaking the truth will be something of a quirky rarity to him. If I see him, I can't promise not to put his back up, as you say. He is a most disagreeable fellow. But I will try not to, just for you. His sister, on the other hand, is almost too good to be true. She is yin to his yang."

Abley smirks, knowing Elizabeth has lined up all the suspects already and found them all guilty of something, like she always does.

"So you don't suspect her?"

Elizabeth doesn't like it when Abley twists her words.

She fills in another clue. Pacemaker.

"I didn't say that." Elizabeth picks a mushroom from the Inspector's plate and pops it in her mouth. "There's something about her too. Can anyone be that much of a willow? Anyway, while I have been conducting all these interviews and holding down my academic duties, what have you been doing?"

"Told you, I have just come back from shutting down The Green Magician."

"May I look at the food samples?"

"No. And I was doing that!" Abley says defensively, almost incredulous that she would ask and irritated that she's almost finished his crossword.

Abley gets up and pushes the chair back towards the table and it makes that noise only metal on lino can make. He can see that Elizabeth is disappointed by his continual refusal to let her in on the case, so offers her a crumb of information.

"Before The Green Magician, we also checked out the boathouses. Nothing." Inspector Abley turns to go back to work. Elizabeth follows him out of the canteen, commenting,

"Are you going to waste perfectly good food now?"

Inspector Abley looks at her wryly. They walk out of the police cafe together and head down a long battle-ship grey corridor.

"Did you come in to update your statement? You must do that."

"Yes, I will."

"Make sure you do."

A police officer hands Inspector Abley a letter. Abley strolls into an incident room, places it on the table and Elizabeth follows. He turns to gently ask why she's still on his heels on this case.

"Are you following me?" Abley looks at Elizabeth, but she impatiently waves him further into the room.

"Look, we have our best officers on this case,

Elizabeth."

There are a couple of police officers pinning things on a board. Abley stops trying to dissuade Elizabeth and concentrates on the job at hand. In front of him is a photograph. He points at it for her reaction.

"His shirt has been torn, not hugely, but around the chest area."

Elizabeth observes the image, a close up of the tear. Quite surprised, she replies,

"Goodness. Looks like a struggle occurred."

Abley points to another image.

"We found some of the shirt on the Garret Hostel Lane Bridge as well. Look at the micro-shards of shirt tissue blown up. It's unrecognisable here, but he definitely ripped it on his way into the drink."

Elizabeth is curious.

"How did you know to check?"

"We found a glove on the bridge identical to another in the water for an opposite hand," says Abley

"Does that mean he was pushed? That he struggled not to fall?" Elizabeth replies.

Abley doesn't know but bluffs it out.

"Quite probably. Oh, and you were right about the red and black beaded necklace. It was somehow at one point attached to his jumper, as there were fragments of a bead in the weave of his shirt."

Elizabeth asks fervently,

"What if it was Susan Bunt's? She was hiding her neck, and I definitely saw scratch marks. She was wearing a scarf to try to conceal them. What if he tore it from her trying to get a grip of something in a last attempt to save himself before falling in? I bet that's what happened."

The Inspector raises his eyebrows, giving her a final warning.

"Let's stick to the facts."

At that moment a pathologist, Mr Leedham, walks into the room. A skinny little man with a bald head, dressed in a white coat with a row of biros in the top pocket in four different colours. He places some rather spangly orange glasses from his head down onto his nose and hands Abley a preliminary report.

"Hello Inspector," Mr Leedham says then his eyes narrow. "Elizabeth Green, what a pleasant surprise. What is it, a year? Good to see you, though I'll be honest, we have managed without you. Quite a surprise, no? Though it's been a little quieter, less high drama I suppose."

Abley tries to cut the conversation.

"Never mind all that. What does the post-mortem say?"

Leedham smiles not up to the eyes at Elizabeth and takes her hand to kiss it, but she withdraws it and offers comment back to Leedham.

"Your glasses, they're so bright."

"Yes, you like them? I wanted to find some snazzy ones, you know. There's still life in the old dog yet, and all the rest of it."

Elizabeth takes the glasses.

"They'd be great to find in the dark."

Leedham smiles,

"Exactly. Yes, thank you. Very useful when I'm reading before bed."

"And they're so much better than that toupee you used to wear. It didn't do anything for you. It looked like you were wearing a gerbil on your head. Much better au naturel."

Mr Leedham doesn't know where to look and takes back his glasses.

"The report?" Abley nudges Leedham again to discuss the results.

Leedham, still unsure whether Elizabeth was being nice or nasty, shakes his head and replies,

"The time of death I'd put somewhere between eleven and one a.m."

Inspector Abley looks at Elizabeth knowingly.

"I think Professor Green can help with a more precise time. Elizabeth will be making a new statement very shortly."

Elizabeth looks at Inspector Abley as if butter wouldn't melt. Mr Leedham looks at the Inspector curiously, but Abley brushes over it.

"Go on, Mr Leedham."

"Mr Wiley's heart was slightly larger than normal, but that could have been because he was a bit of a sportsman, allegedly. Something else though, much more interesting. His organs were failing, all at once. There's no doubt about that. From the bile in the liver, the dark colouring in his kidneys and the burning and lacerations in the lungs. Not caused by water."

The room is quiet. This is new information. Elizabeth wastes no time in seeing if Leedham knows what he is dealing with yet.

"What from? I mean, that would have to be either ingested or injected to cause something like that?"

"Not sure. Running more tests. It could be auto-immune, we can't rule that out." Mr Leedham is far less interested in the rest he has to impart. "Apart from that, I found small traces of fish with scumbitoxin–"

Abley interjects.

"We're checking out all the food from The Green Magician, for anything suspicious. Should be able to cross ref that shortly. So that was what he ate last night."

Leedham responds to Abley, keeping it professional.

"Scumbitoxin can sometimes turn you red if eating duff seafood, open all the lesser blood vessels in your body, so you look like a lobster. Not shut down your vitals though, but has sometimes been known to cause a severe change in blood pressure which can be serious. But I don't think there were nearly enough traces of this for it to have caused what happened to the deceased. It wouldn't affect the lungs either. The toxalbumin was there as well, as you know."

Elizabeth then interjects, desperate for more detail.

"Toxalbumin is certainly a fascinating find. Which first? Which organ?"

Leedham raises his eyebrows.

"It was probably the heart which did it for him, but his liver was failing second, after that the kidneys. There would have been a lot of respiratory problems caused by the burning in the lungs. As I said, it wasn't the quality of the water that killed him, nor the amount in his lungs. The water samples tested remarkably clear. It is a good sign for the Cam to be honest. Do you know I saw a heron down on Riverside the other day?"

"No, where?" Abley replies, not himself a birdwatcher, unless they are found on the golf course.

"Closer to the Elizabeth Way Bridge. Just on its own. I watched it catch a fish. Remarkable."

Elizabeth inhales then exhales loudly, as most locals know there are a few herons near where Leedham mentions. Abley looks at her eye rolling and cuts the conversation about wildlife.

"Right, thank you, Mr Leedham."

Elizabeth, keen to get Inspector Abley to make this a murder inquiry, moves the conversation on.

"The symptoms would suggest that this was no accident."

Leedham is quick to clarify.

"All I'm saying is that he died from something other than water, other than drowning. Incidentally, there was cocaine in his bloodstream, though not enough to kill him."

Abley and Elizabeth are surprised but then think back to the little plastic bag in Edward's hat, which the Inspector has already sent off for tests, and which he now confidently guesses will turn up the same substance.

Abley would rather he spoke with Leedham now in private and out of earshot of Elizabeth, so leans in quietly to Leedham, in an attempt to have the final word.

"We spoke to Edward's head of department, and he told me that Mr Wiley had just got back from a field trip to Africa. Could it have been a foreign pathogen?"

Leedham replies to the Inspector louder than Abley had hoped, allowing Elizabeth to hear.

"Yes, it could have been a foreign pathogen. If he'd been feeling rough, with flu type symptoms as well. Yes, quite possibly. We can certainly send off some samples to SOAS."

Elizabeth can see holes in this line of enquiry.

"Mrs Wiley said he seemed perfectly well when she saw him earlier that day at breakfast. No one else has mentioned that he looked pale. Some said how tanned he was."

Leedham defends his last statement.

"Pathogens take different lengths of time to run their course. It's hard to rule out a virus or even a bacteria just because he was feeling fine in the morning. Some are super quick, but then you'd know more about it than I do, Elizabeth, isn't that right?"

Elizabeth tries to turn the sarcasm into a positive.

"Are you asking me back, Mr Leedham?"

Mr Leedham looks at the Inspector and back at Elizabeth.

"Er, it's not my place I don't think, do you? I'm sure I'd love to, but it's up to the Inspector which consultant experts he hires. I think the budgets are quite tight at the moment, aren't they Inspector?"

Elizabeth looks at Abley, but he cuts short the idea.

"Liz, it was you who followed me in here, asking all the questions. No one is asking you back. I know you're interested in the case and you may be of great help to Mr Leedham here, ignoring the personal insults on his appearance of course. But we have things covered, and I'm asking you to go home. We don't need you. That's my final word." Abley looks at Elizabeth hard and does not remove his eyes from hers until it has sunk in. Eventually,

Elizabeth releases her gaze and moves to the door. She can't quite hide the stinging blow dealt by Abley's exclusion. Tears gather, but she stabs her fingers into the palm of her hands to control them and looks away. Abley has seen, however, and is immediately full of remorse by the harshness of his words, and in front of his colleague, and so as she leaves he follows her out. When he gets to the door, she is already halfway up the corridor.

"Liz, I'm sorry. And make a new statement asap, please. Do it with Sergeant Lemon."

But Elizabeth doesn't look back. She holds her left hand up to show no hard feelings. She has also managed to sneak away with the note that the Constable gave to Abley just minutes ago in the corridor. Shocked to read its contents, Inspector Abley's Superintendent is asking Abley to leave Jonathan Smythe-Jones out of this inquiry if possible, for he will soon be appointed either as home secretary or given another Cabinet position. Elizabeth folds over the letter and leaves it at reception, asking them to return it to Inspector Abley, in the same breath as booking an appointment to see Sergeant Lemon.

Before long Elizabeth has made it out of Parkside Police Station and is standing in the middle of Parker's Piece. The sky is overwhelmingly bright, with only puffy clouds drifting by. She sits on a bench to think. What is she doing? Nobody wants her on this case. In fact, she'd guess they are doing everything to keep her off. But it's eating at her. She can't leave it alone. Is it Edward? She liked him very much and is still shaken by his passing. Why couldn't she do anything to help at the end? She feels like she let him down. Or, is it the thrill of the puzzle? She's not addicted to crosswords or sudoku. She doesn't watch game shows. But when it is a matter of life and death, of human nature, Elizabeth can't get enough. It's as if she needs to understand why to find her own peace.

Elizabeth grows more determined while sitting on the bench. How dare people leave her out of things. She knows Edward was murdered now, is convinced of it. And he came to her. Why? Her suspicions are with Susan. Why is she running away? Elizabeth looks up and can see the cafe kiosk in the opposite corner of Parker's Piece, with tables and chairs scattered for people to sit and eat ice creams. Thirsty, she watches the man make someone a noisy coffee. She gets up and heads in the opposite direction.

18
THE BACKS

The Backs this morning, like an impressionist painting all muted greens and yellows, are quiet and still. Curved bridges line up along the river, stretching across like shoelaces. Weeping willows trail their foliage in bottle green waters and rustle in a sheltered breeze. A moorhen glides almost invisible along the bank's edge, bobbing for grasses, while a solitary student sits with his book bag and contemplates next term's courses, already lost in thought and anxiety.

Having unlocked the chain which holds all the punts together, Kara puts the keys to All Saints' College boathouse back on the hook. She's returned from home, changed out of her dinner gown into a softer, summery green dress. She dumps her jacket on a chair, stuffs some dirty clothes of Jonathan's into a bag and watches as he stretches his arms above his head, now dressed in fresh chinos, pink striped shirt and deck shoes.

Kara then places the picnic basket she brought for lunch down by the water's edge. As they all stand on the slip it is evident they are the only souls on this stretch of river. Soon May Balls will replace exams and this spot will be packed with girls in glamorous dresses and boys in their best suits. Rebecca stares at the water gloomily, not having changed from this morning, her hair a little more dishevelled and her eyes puffy.

The weather has brightened up, with more than enough blue sky to share and a temperature warming the day, Kara is ready to try to cheer Rebecca and take her mind off the horror that has just occurred. Her idea hasn't worked on Jonathan, however, who'd rather be anywhere else and is far from convinced about this hare-brained excursion.

"What possessed you?"

"We all need fresh air and sunshine in our lungs, Jonny. We're like flowers, you can't keep us cooped up inside or we'll wilt and—" Kara was going to say die but stops herself, and looks at Jonathan apologetically. He hugs her.

"My career is about to go stratospheric and I should be in London, my brother-in-law is dead in suspicious circumstances and I'm all over the papers. And you say let's go punting."

Kara sighs.

"I just want everyone to relax, find some peace and eat something. Then we can go back and Rebecca can sleep. We'll be away from prying eyes here. It's quiet, Tuesday. Her apartment will remind her of Edward if she stays cooped up there all day." Kara looks over at Rebecca. "Are you okay, darling?"

Rebecca doesn't acknowledge Kara's voice, too far away in her own thoughts, almost oblivious to the fact she is now walking down inside a punt. She plonks herself in the middle seat, puts her head back and dips her fingers in the water under a willow, the punt in danger itself of being eaten up by the dangling lime canopy. A swan glides out, startling Kara. He taps his beak, waiting to be fed and then spots the expensive looking wicker basket on the edge.

"Off you go." Kara pathetically shoos the swan, who

ignores her. Still on the slip, Jonathan's phone starts to ring.

"Hello. What? I can't talk now. No. Listen when I said I couldn't talk I meant it. I don't know. Just look into it. I told you Edward and I were in this together. I don't know what he knew. What? All right, all right. Check it out today and get back to me." Jonathan turns his back, so no one can hear the remainder of his conversation. Kara tries to strike up her own with Rebecca, while continuing to wave her arms at the increasingly inquisitive swan, who continues to ignore her like everybody else.

"Jonathan says you must come and stay with us at the house for a while, Rebecca."

Rebecca is in a state of delirium.

"I'm staying in college. I must be near Edward. Everything's here."

"We'll help you pack your things. You don't have to leave anything behind." Kara tries to calm Rebecca, but is also aware the swan has now lifted the picnic lid and is pecking about inside. Just as Kara wonders if she is going to have to wrestle a large bird while trying to console Rebecca, Jonathan finishes his call, deftly grabs the picnic basket, steps onto the punt, simultaneously shooing the swan away by unwrapping a cucumber sandwich and throwing it ten feet away. The peckish swan glides off after another top snack and Kara looks lovingly for the first time today at her soon to be husband.

"I can't live without Edward." A distraught Rebecca pulls at Jonathan's jacket as he settles into the next row of seats further away from the stern.

"Let's see how good Kat is with a pole shall we?"

Kara secretly likes to punt, as she's very good at it, but replies,

"Are you not doing it?"

"It was your idea, my Dear. I think you should at least do the first stint. I haven't slept." He smiles at her and then leans across and affectionately rubs his sister's leg.

Quietly to herself, Kara says, "Neither have I."

Kara takes the pole at the end of the punt as Jonathan pulls at the willow leaves to nudge them in the right direction. Kara, having done this many times before, expertly pulls up the pole and places it carefully down into the water, hoping for things to return to normal and Jonathan to relax and be back to his loving self. The three of them glide off down the River Cam. Rebecca glaring at Kara as much as watching the scenery go by.

*

Elizabeth, undeterred by her visit to the Parkside police station, has chosen to ignore the Inspector. If he doesn't want her help then she'll solve the case without him. She's back at Bene't's College, and has already checked Rebecca Wiley's rooms but no Rebecca, so has come back out onto the lawns by the river where she bumps into the Dean of Bene't's, Professor Percival Flint, who appears to be entertaining a rather cocky man, black hair and an expensive suit squeezed around his pudgy legs. The Dean greets Elizabeth.

"To what do we owe this pleasure? Thinking of defecting?"

Elizabeth is having none of it.

"Hello Professor Flint, and what a preposterous idea."

The Dean smiles,

"Our rooms are very spacious you know, Professor Green."

Elizabeth looks to her toes and frowns.

"And a little draughty. I do like the Rubens on display, but Granta suits me just fine thank you. I was hoping to catch Edward Wiley's widow. Do you happen to know her whereabouts?"

The Dean shakes his head.

"Dreadful business, isn't it. Carter said you were here earlier. You should have told me you were visiting again.

Twice in the same day, I would have given you a Fellows' prospectus. About time you joined a proper college."

Elizabeth plays along with the Dean's little game.

"I'll inform the Master that you speak so highly of Granta College, shall I?"

"Just teasing. I'm fond of Granta as well you know. Less pretentious than some of our more competitive friends," The Dean nods his head towards the direction of All Saints' and St James' Colleges.

"Where may I find Mrs Wiley?"

"What do you want her for now?"

Elizabeth is not going to reveal the information Professor Flint is hoping for.

"Oh, a private matter."

The Dean knows he could ask that Elizabeth leaves Rebecca alone on the college turf, but he's never won an argument with her yet, and really doesn't have the stomach for a face off in present company.

"She went off with her brother. That lawyer chap turned politician. Nothing like Edward, is he?"

"Dr Wiley was a scientist of whom we could all be proud," Elizabeth replies.

The Dean's guest finally pipes up.

"Ha! The Ed Wiley I knew didn't know when to calm down or when to give up partying, and liked his recreational props too." Dr Eruna sniffs and rubs his nose to indicate exactly the habit he is implying. "Was always last on getting through the gates at night. Gave the porters the right ol' run around. Old habits die hard." He holds out a hand, which Elizabeth refuses to take, instead just smiling with her mouth not her eyes. Dr Eruna is not deterred. "Michael Eruna. I was at college at the same time as Ed. Though I didn't actually study here at Bene't's, but we were both in Plant Sciences. He went one way, I went another."

The Dean feels it is best he introduced with more detail.

"Dr Eruna has interests at the Science Park, Labzuu. You may have heard about some of their innovative medical treatments using genetic modification?"

Elizabeth is unimpressed. She has little trust of those who try to genetically engineer everything to achieve a quick fix. Nature will find a way in the end. It cannot be controlled. And there is definitely something of 'The Day of the Triffids' about this man. She gives him something to think about.

"Dr Eruna, you may like to know that the police are looking into the cause of death of Dr Wiley. It was quite probably murder and they are interviewing everyone who knew him. So, they might be interested to know that you were his peer at university and that you hold such differing views to most who knew him. Suggesting he was some sort of drug addicted, beer swilling hedonist."

"Hey. I didn't mean anything. He may have been a bit of a party boy in his youth, but I can't think of a man less likely to have enemies."

The Dean, shocked by the news, quizzes Elizabeth further.

"Are you saying the police think it's murder? We can't afford for all this unfortunate business to affect the college."

Elizabeth didn't mean to alarm the Dean, whom she knows is not good with stressful situations and worries more than he should. She often wonders why he took the role of Dean in the first place, possessing such qualities.

"Don't worry. Nothing could tarnish this wonderful establishment." Elizabeth gives him a wry smile, but it doesn't allay the Professor's new found anxiety.

"Quite, quite, of course. But we can't have a scandal. I do believe I saw her and her brother and a nice young lady heading towards the punt house come to think of it. All Saints', yes. Perhaps you will find them nearby?"

"Right you are. Thank you, Dean." Elizabeth turns on her heel towards the grounds exit by Christina College and onto All Saints' punts. Before out of earshot, Percival Flint calls to her.

"Can we enjoy your company at dinner any time soon, or perhaps evensong?"

Elizabeth spreads open her arms.

"You know your cook doesn't like my requests, Dean. And being an atheist doesn't really sit well with choral appreciation, now does it."

Elizabeth leaves, crunching her way across the gravel.

The Dean and Dr Eruna walk back up through the college grounds and approach the Porters' Lodge doorway, as Carter talks to a junior porter about an undergraduate using his window ledge as a refrigerator.

"Milk, four cans of bitter, and a kipper, sir."

"Just tell the lad that if we find this hanging outside his rooms again then we will have to find something else to hang outside there in its place."

Dr Eruna stands with the Dean in the lodge doorway, reminding him of an earlier conversation.

"Don't chicken out now Percilicious. You are my cherry on top."

The Dean halts in the door, blocking Dr Eruna's entry and hisses,

"If you think I'm going to lose this chance for the college you've misjudged me. But I don't have to like it. You lied."

Dr Eruna steps back out onto the path, with no desire to make this a long conversation either.

"A cool two million on submission and double on publication of our joint research findings." He winks at Professor Flint. "Just make it clear that Labzuu are the best company in the world, and there will be rewards for the college a plenty."

A young undergraduate has come to pick up his room keys and has to squeeze past the Dean.

"Morning, Sir."

Percival Flint can't remember the name of the lad.

"Morning."

Dr Eruna has had enough. He has to get back to the office.

"Just finish it, and I'll say as many thank you 'Sirs' as you like." Dr Eruna walks towards the gate out to King's Parade. Jokingly he throws a last line to Flint. "And keep that nosey bird away, right? As much as accused me of stirring over Edward. Who does she think she is? Silly old crone."

Dr Eruna walks off, and immediately Professor Flint knows he was right about him. Anyone who thinks Elizabeth is a silly old crone is on the wrong side of right. She's the most intelligent woman he knows. Difficult. But don't they come together? Professor Flint is so repelled by the impression of Dr Eruna that he can't help himself from stepping back into the lodge and physically shuddering. Carter notices the Dean's anxious demeanour.

"A friend of yours, Sir?"

"Carter. Any friend of the college is a friend of mine. Some I hold dear to my heart. Some I should only shake hands with from the safe vantage point of separate continents wearing radioactive protective clothing."

"Quite so, Sir."

"Please. I don't want to be disturbed this afternoon. I have rather a lot of work."

Carter nods and watches Professor Flint walk away. There is something about his step that makes Carter mildly concerned. He's never seen the Dean so preoccupied and clearly distressed. Much changed from earlier this morning. Carter draws his eyes into a squint and thinks. Then decides that perhaps it is just down to this business with Edward Wiley. Carter has himself been busier than ever keeping the press out of college grounds, and has already shut the doors to the public, as he'd caught a couple of journalists pretending to visit the Chapel, and sneaking back to try to rummage through Edward's rooms. Why all the fuss? Was there something more to it? One reporter said as much, mentioning there were far too many frogmen on the river for it to be accidental. The paper printed 'suspicious', yet the police are yet to confirm. Yes, that would be why the Dean looked so pale, Carter had no doubt. After all, there hasn't been a murder associated with the college since that law student murdered his father and buried him in the garden.

19
THERE IS NO ESCAPE

Susan slams the front door and looks up at her home, nestled in this piece of Chesterton along the river, far out from the city. She steps back and picks up her bag while a taxi, churning out exhaust fumes, has crept up to meet her. Susan peers in the front window.

"Station please."

The taxi trundles away, taking its time to clock up more on the meter as Susan sits in the back and ponders on plans made and how things have dramatically changed. She is a survivor. There are many more chapters left in her life. But what does Cambridge have left to offer? An unhappy tenure with colleagues who don't much like her work. She is always the outsider, left out in the cold when it comes to dinner party invites, the last to know college gossip, and never asked for her opinion.

Susan has grown old and more jaded with this esteemed city, which only has time for success and brilliance. She chides herself for falling for the stereotype English gentleman of high intellect. Edward once admitted he'd taken seven 'A' levels, not to brag, just to correct her when she once called him a dumb scientist who wouldn't understand her poetry lectures, telling her that he did actually have an English degree that he'd completed part-time as a hobby while he was studying his post-doc in science. He'd also taken two PhDs, one in science, another in philosophy. Yes, there was no argument, Cambridge knew how to find the smartest. The city had not made her welcome, but perhaps she just tried to fit into a world where she didn't belong.

The taxi makes long work of wending its way out of Chesterton and onto the ring road, heading southwest towards the railway station where it catches the brow of the Elizabeth Way Bridge and meets traffic. Susan glances at the river flowing under the bridge and peers over to watch a few people walking their dogs on Midsummer Common, rowers practising for the May bumps and cyclists passing to and fro along the water's edg past the moored narrow boats and boathouses. Edward would have got a chill in the river she thinks, as it is early summer, but the temperatures are still low.

As they take the East Road towards the station, Susan begins to notice overweight shoppers waddling towards the shops, no doubt the grubbier end of the city and a world apart from college high table. She feels an affinity with these strangers, less than perfect, but still human for chrissake. And for all the high pomp and ceremony, Cambridge is not that far from the gutter after all. It has turned her sour, and she knows she is leaving for a reason.

She thinks of Edward and wonders why he had been so cagey about his last trip to Africa? She was cross at him for keeping secrets, for leaving her. And she deserved the right to know everything. He had messed her about too many times. Well, no more. The taxi gets caught in traffic at the corner of Parker's Piece. A crowd cheers at outdoor comedy performances by the glass-walled swimming pool on the south edge of the Piece. A clown on stilts spills out into the road, and fake falls onto the stationary taxi taking Susan to the station. The driver scowls and points at the paintwork on his bumper. The clown quickly apologises, rubbing the bonnet with his jacket and smiling, then notices Susan's sullen face and pulls comedic faces in her window to try to cheer her up. Susan frowns, so the clown shrugs and goes back to the adoring crowd. Susan has an idea. She gets out her mobile and rings Edward.

"Hello? Hello Edward. Did you tell her? I hope you told her, but I'm sorry. I'm sorry it came to this. You shouldn't have left me." Susan's taxi pulls away, suddenly a bank of lights turn green, and the taxi makes it to the corner and the Catholic church of Our Lady and the English Martyrs before coming to another grinding halt.

*

Kara, Jonathan and Rebecca have punted a little way down the river past the All Saints' Library and lawns of St James'. Unfortunately, Kara's plans for privacy have backfired, the water now crowded with punts loaded with tourists coming from Sandymee's at Magdalene Bridge. Rebecca has worked herself up into a frenzy thinking about Susan and is shouting off vitriol.

"I hate her. The fat slug!"

Jonathan doesn't much like Susan, but aware they are being overheard from all directions would prefer his sister didn't use such a foul turn of phrase.

"C'mon Sis'. Susan is not my favourite cup of tea either, but let's not bring ourselves down to her level, eh?"

"She's a pudgy, slime faced idiot. I hate every inch of her sweaty, smelling flesh."

Kara smiles weakly at Jonathan, what are they going to do?

"Let's talk about something else. How about opening that picnic? I could do with a cold drink up here, punting's thirsty work."

Rebecca flips the wicker basket open and violently throws a glass bottle of lemonade at Kara, which nearly hits her. She wobbles a little on the back of the boat, frowning at Rebecca for a moment as the bottle splashes into the water behind.

"Woah, okay. Thanks, I think."

Jonathan chips in.

"Here, Darling." Jonathan passes Kara a beer then pulls out another for himself, while Rebecca retrieves a bottle of champagne.

"Great, I didn't know we were celebrating. Thanks, Kat, for your sensitivity. But then you always were the party girl."

"Sorry. I just put it in there as I thought it might help us all relax. It wouldn't be me if I hadn't, now would it?"

"How true," Jonathan knows his fiancée so well.

"Well let's celebrate then." Rebecca struggles with the bottle, ripping off the silver foil angrily, then getting frustrated with the metal twist. Jonathan watches and offers to help.

"Give it here."

"I have it!" Rebecca protests then pops the cork, drinking the explosion of foam shooting out the top, some spilling onto her cheeks and dress.

"Go steady. It's not quite lunchtime yet. Want to keep some room for the" Jonathan looks in the picnic, "smoked salmon and quails' eggs." He looks up at Kara. "Nice."

"Cucumber sandwiches. How spiffing." Rebecca continues to drink down champagne like it is water. She pulls out cucumber sandwiches from the container, and with a fling scatters them widely in the water. One lands in another punt.

Jonathan says "Sorry" to adjacent punters as he tries to stop Rebecca. She's having none of it.

Kara tries to explain.

"They're for our picnic. We need them more than the ducks do. Save some for me, Darling."

"Quack, quack, quack." Rebecca stands and continues to throw sandwiches. Kara is concerned the punt is becoming unsteady.

"Rebecca, do sit down. You're making a bit of a scene," Jonathan suggests.

"Oh, so sorry. What am I thinking?"

Rebecca starts to throw sandwiches at an adjacent punt chauffeur, shouting at him.

"Edward hated you lot. Always prancing about like you own the place."

"Rebecca. Stop. Sorry," Jonathan apologises, noticing a sandwich has landed in the rim of a chauffeur's boater. The chauffeur deftly removes it, takes a bite, and shouts back.

"Thank you. No crusts. How delightful." He doffs his hat to Rebecca, smiles to his boat of tourists – who all nod at Rebecca as if this is some ritual on The Backs – and then continues with his tour in mandarin, effortlessly gliding by, making this river pastime look like a walk in the park.

Rebecca, now bored, finds some crisps and opens the bag, which explodes onto Jonathan. She bends down trying to pick them up, putting retrieved crisps back into the bag.

"Can you sit down now. You're going to have us all in." Jonathan tries to get his sister to calm down, while Kara has drunk most of her beer and has bent down and picked up the odd cucumber sandwich from the river. She looks at Rebecca.

"Darling. It's going to be okay."

"How will it? I hate her." Rebecca swigs her champagne and sways in the boat. A few people watch from a bridge, which had been earlier swept for fingerprints.

"Your brother's always bending over backwards for you. He said we should keep you company. He's supposed to be in London."

"Jonathan's only interested in his career. You know that Kat. Does nobody tell you anything? You sad act."

"Thanks! I'm here, you know." Jonathan is exasperated with both of them.

Rebecca looks at Kara.

"How could you bring me onto the river? Today of all days."

Kara is wobbling as a result of Rebecca rocking the punt and makes a last effort to control Rebecca.

"Enough, Rebecca, we're just trying to do our best. We've always just wanted to be a decent family. To be honest and respected. You're part of that."

But Rebecca isn't listening.

"She's ruined my life. I've nothing. No one. Edward. I'm..."

Kara is curious what she is going to say next.

"What?"

"I'm going to get Susan's pug ugly face, and wring her bloody neck!"

People observing from the Wren Bridge raise their eyebrows and walk to the other side as the punt goes underneath like a Pooh stick, keen not to miss any of the action when it reappears. Amongst them is a local newspaper photographer, who, having been kicked out of Bene't's College earlier, has come to take pictures of the river where Edward fell and can't believe his luck.

Kara has punted close to the grassy bank between St James' and All Saints', and Rebecca begins to step out of the punt, putting one foot up on the side, ready to exit and start her attack on Susan.

"Rebecca, sit down." Her brother is now agitated and puts his beer down on the punt floor.

"Don't try to stop me."

"Please." Kara tries to balance the punt with the pole as she walks towards Rebecca, encouraging her to sit down as the punt drifts away from the bank again. Rebecca's arms flail as she resists, brushing Kara's helping hand away, she accidentally hits Kara's face and knocks her into the water.

Jonathan watches as Kara, and the pole fall away from the punt. He picks up his beer and raises a toast, as the people on the bridge cheer. He looks up at them and raises the bottle again in acknowledgement. The local newspaper photographer gratefully snaps this opportunity, unspotted by Jonathan. As she swims to the bank, looking back Kara notices her fiancé's lack of empathy. She then coughs out water as she clings to the edge. Rebecca continues without a flicker of guilt.

"I'm going to kill Susan."

Jonathan takes hold of Rebecca's arms, shakes her and quietly hisses,

"Get a grip. People are listening. You want them to hear you say that?"

Rebecca glances up to see everyone watching her then glimpses at her brother. Jonathan looks up, this time straight into the camera lens. The flash snaps away. He whispers urgently in Rebecca's ear.

"Let's sit down and eat our strawberries. Susan will come a cropper, don't you worry."

Elizabeth has been watching a while, with the other spectators from the bridge. She walks over to meet Kara, offering her a hand to climb out. Jonathan reaches over for the punt paddle. He spots Elizabeth.

"Not you again. Are you following us, or something? You're beginning to grate big time!" he shouts. Elizabeth is now standing next to a dripping Kara.

"Is your husband always this charming?"

Kara smiles, grateful for the help to get out of the river.

"Thanks. He doesn't mean it. And he hasn't made an honest woman of me yet."

"We nearly met before. When you were outside Bene't's in the court earlier this morning. You were wearing such a beautiful dress. Elizabeth Green."

"I suppose I did look better then than I do now. Kara Anderson. Just call me Kat, everyone else does. Are you at

Bene't's?"

"No, but I did know Edward Wiley. He was a colleague of mine. He passed away in my garden last night."

"Oh. Rebecca's been mumbling this morning something about Edward talking before he died. Was that to you? What did he say?"

Jonathan wants rid of Elizabeth and makes no effort to hide it.

"I'm beginning to think this might be a case of harassment you know, Mrs Grain."

Elizabeth shouts to Jonathan in the punt,

"It's Green. I just wanted another quick word with your sister, if I may?"

"My sister needs her privacy and time to grieve, for crying out loud!."

Rebecca ignores her brother and shouts back to Elizabeth, wanting to know more about Elizabeth's investigations.

"You've been to see her, haven't you? See, I told you she was the devil. Did you see it in her eyes?"

Elizabeth wants to know Rebecca's reaction to Susan's accusation she made earlier.

"Susan said that Edward was coming to talk to you. That he was going to leave you."

Jonathan interrupts.

"That's it." He paddles furiously to the side to reach Elizabeth.

Rebecca stands up again in the punt and fizzes at Susan's words.

"I'll kill her!"

It all feels too out of control for Jonathan, and he takes it out on Elizabeth.

"I'm coming over there, and you'd better be gone, Professor Green!"

Kara can see her future husband growing progressively angry so leans into Elizabeth.

"Perhaps you should go. This isn't a great time. I know

what he's like and he means business."

Elizabeth is not deterred by his ridiculous protestations and continues to press Rebecca for a reaction.

"Is it true Rebecca? Was he about to leave you?"

Rebecca's contorted face spits out the words.

"How can you ask me such a thing when my husband has just... the woman is evil. No, of course not. We were going to have a baby together. I'm pregnant."

Jonathan looks at Rebecca completely shocked, temporarily forgetting his anger at Elizabeth. Kara looks floored by the news, asking Rebecca,

"Is this true?"

"Will everyone just leave me alone," Rebecca replies.

Jonathan has managed to row the boat to the bank, and Rebecca jumps out and runs towards St James' College. Kara looks to follow, but Jonathan shouts,

"I'll go. You go watch this ruddy punt." He then looks at Elizabeth. "Leave us alone. This is enough damage now."

Kara defends Elizabeth.

"Jonathan, it's hardly this lady's fault."

"This is a proper stinking mess." Jonathan runs off after Rebecca, who has already made it across St James' lawns heading for New Stone Arches.

The photographer thinks he has enough, chuckles to himself and heads back to the paper, as Elizabeth smiles at Kara.

"I didn't mean for her to run away. Is she always like this?"

"It's unusual circumstances, isn't it?"

"Yes, quite so. Well, then I apologise for aggravating the situation. I just wanted to find out if Edward was just about to leave his wife before he died."

Kara isn't sure where the conversation is going.

"Sorry, you must think this rude. But why are you talking to friends and family of Edward? I mean, you're not a policewoman are you?"

"He was a friend of mine. I'm concerned that something is amiss, that he didn't die by an accident. Did you know Edward?"

Kara shakes her hair, takes off her tiny cardigan and squeezes it out. The spray touches Elizabeth's sandals causing her to step back.

"Not very well to be honest. They hadn't been married long, and he was always abroad on some research trip or other. It is simply awful. I can't believe she's pregnant?"

"Why?"

"Oh, nothing really. I didn't think they were trying I guess. Just a feeling, you know?"

Elizabeth steals a beady look at Kara.

"But you're surprised?"

Kara doesn't answer Elizabeth.

"Quite something to keep to oneself when there has been a death. Well, I guess I should get out of these wet clothes if you'll excuse me?"

"Didn't your fiancé ask you to watch the punt?"

"He's always asking me to do things. If I did all of them I'd never have time to do the things I want to do," Kara smiles. Elizabeth starts to walk away but then finds that Kara is also walking the same way, back to Bene't's.

"My bicycle is at the Porters' Lodge. You parked out front?"

"No, I'm just going to borrow some clothes from Bex's rooms."

"Have you a key?"

Kara thinks the question odd, what business is it of hers?

"She never locks anything. They've had more than one thing stolen over the past year. You'd think she'd take up the college offer to install locks. But they're creaky old doors. Hundreds of years old apparently. Edward didn't want to bastardise them with modern trappings. And now, now we have to stay close, or we fear Rebecca will lose it if we don't. You saw she's not the most balanced of people.

That's why Jonathan cares for her so."

Elizabeth continues to walk alongside Kara, warming to this too beautiful woman.

"Could Rebecca have harmed Edward?"

Kara hesitates on the gravel, pulling at her wet green dress, to separate it from her legs.

"Surely not. You don't think so, do you? Why would she?"

Elizabeth watches the water run down Kara's face from her dripping hair.

"I just wondered what you thought."

"Even if she wanted to, she's hardly strong enough."

"Perhaps. Forgive me, I know it is most rude, but I can't mask my curiosity. Where is your accent in South Africa? Cape Town?"

Kara smiles,

"Yes, I grew up there and in Jo'burg too."

"Is that where your family live?"

"Mum is from England and always had an affinity with the place. She's dead now. Sorry, I really must get changed."

They start to walk again, and Elizabeth has to speed up her pace to keep stride with Kara.

"Is your father still in Africa?"

"Yes, though he travels a lot and is hardly there. I don't have much to do with it now, I never go back, not since I came over to Cambridge for my degree."

"Oh really. When was that?"

"Years ago. Ethics. I met Jonathan at a ball. Here in fact. All Saints' College. Well, bye."

Kara begins to walk away from Elizabeth, towards Rebecca's rooms, but Elizabeth stops dead to try to keep the conversation going for as long as possible. Kara politely halts.

"Oh, you're both alumni? All Saints' punts, a good perk."

"For him, yes. Nothing so grand for me. I just liked the

look of the city. I was at Cambridge polytechnic as it was then. Anglia Ruskin now, still stuck out on the East Road, with its burger bars and pound shops. Jonathan says he has the breeding. I have the money. Nouveau riche."

"I do admire your engagement ring and earrings. They're huge."

"Jonathan spoils me. Well, I think this is me."

"Quite. Nice meeting you Miss Anderson. I hope Jonathan manages to catch up with Rebecca."

"I'm sure he will. Goodbye."

As Elizabeth turns and heads towards the main gate, she wonders about Rebecca, who has just dropped this bombshell on her brother and Kara. Kara, or Kat, seemed like a graceful gazelle from the African plains. Though what she was doing with that awful man she really doesn't know. Good job Rebecca has her family around her. Elizabeth knows more than most how important that is.

20
GERALD

'Death is a fearful thing.'
William Shakespeare

Elizabeth has left Kara at Bene't's, picked up her bicycle and made her way down Trumpington Street. She cycles past college hubbub, and finally the white-pillared front of the Fitzwilliam Museum. She is soon seated at a mezzanine table in a far corner of Browns restaurant, a pile of unmarked essays sitting next to her. Listening to a jazz pianist play Autumn Leaves, Elizabeth surveys the ambient room, full of laughing happy people; it feels like a world away from the past twelve or so hours.

She has come to have lunch with Emily Masters, an esteemed Professor of Classics at the university, and Fellow of St. Andrew's College, who also happens to be her oldest and dearest friend. They often make this their haunt, as it is close enough for them to have a noon-time interlude from never-ending academic responsibilities. Emily enters through wood panelled revolving doors, a little late having played catch up all day. She spots Elizabeth and points to the maître d', who walks her over to the semi-secluded vantage point. Thin as a pencil, Emily wears a very expensive deep grey jacket and skirt, hugging her frame, and a ruffled cream blouse. With grey stockings and black suede high heels, she looks much younger than her fifty-seven years.

Emily kisses the maître d', one on each cheek. The maître d' knows her well and asks if she'd like 'the usual?' and if Professor Green would like 'a top up?' To which she nods and Elizabeth gratefully thanks him. The maître d' promptly walks off in the direction of an art deco bar, and Emily sits down. She removes fitted gloves to reveal immaculately painted nude nails and a huge diamond ring. Reeking haute couture, with freshly blow-dried auburn hair set this morning, she is the most elegant woman in the room.

"I must apologise for being late. I was kept back by the Master."

"Have you been naughty again Emily?"

"If only. I don't know how he expects us to tutor the freshers and final years this term with less of us now. My one-on-ones are banked up until the fourth of July."

"You're their favourite Professor."

"I mustn't grumble. Oh, how the charmed live. Talking of charm, how is my favourite person in the whole world?"

"You must mean Pepper?"

"No, Elizabeth, though Pepper and I had a lovely walk on Jesus Green this morning. He was playing ball with me for a change and not trying to worry the canal boat cats, the cheeky mutt. He was off the lead yesterday and ran straight into the Jesus Green Lido. D'you know they've opened it now, for the summer?"

"Is it really that time of year already?"

"Anyway, I was talking about you." Emily rubs Elizabeth's arm.

"I'm okay." Elizabeth smiles and sighs.

Emily then remembers.

"Did I tell you that I've managed to get those tickets for us to see Carmen at the ENO?"

"A treat. Thank you. What are you eating?"

Emily picks up the menu, looks up and notices the pianist.

"This chap is good, isn't he? I think he's studying for his doctorate at St James' you know. I'm sure I've heard him play at a recital there. I suppose this is pocket money."

"It's good to see you, Emily."

"Let me look quickly and get something ordered. I have just an hour, and then I have to give a lecture at two this afternoon on Greek Philosophy, the Socrates years."

"If I weren't so busy I'd sneak in the back."

"Normal busy, or busy on police work? I've been calling you all morning. I saw the news. That golfing policeman waffling on and I recognised your garden. The hundred and one bird tables in those silver birches and Bertie in the background watching them intently."

"The garden is trampled like the playground of a herd of elephants."

"So is it true?"

"What do you mean? Is death true? Yes, it comes and comes. You should've been on my lawn at midnight last night. Poor, poor Edward."

"Why didn't you ring me this morning? I could have come over to be with you."

"Funnily enough I had a lecture this morning, and I'm behind in the meadow glasshouse. And what's worse, the police are entirely clueless as to the cause of death. I've been trying to work it out all morning."

"Isn't it too early to be stepping back into those shoes?"

"It's been a year. It's still too early for everything. Eating. Laughing. But this, I'm simply needed."

"Has Lazy Abley asked you to get involved then?"

Elizabeth pauses and looks down at the table.

"Not exactly. And, he's not lazy, he was there, early hours."

"You mean you're meddling Liz. Where have I heard that before?" Emily smiles wryly, "And what about Godric? Without your watchful eye, he'll get up to all sorts of mischief. And don't tell me you haven't got enough college and departmental work?" Emily looks at the essays next to Elizabeth.

Elizabeth's beady green eyes narrow. "You know there was an odd man with Professor Flint today, Eruna? Some company he owns and runs, called Labzuu. You heard of them?"

"No, I can't say I have. Why?"

"His eyes were too close together. Something about him. Why did he tell me he knew Edward? It felt like a subliminal confession. But then again, maybe the lover did do it? She's acting hysterical."

"Oh really, Bunny. If you're going to talk murder over a perfectly innocent meal, then can you start at the beginning."

"They took his cardigan away."

"Whose cardigan? What are you talking about?"

"Gerald's. There was blood all over it. I think Edward's been murdered. I can feel it. His wrist had cuts. Why?"

Emily is upset for Elizabeth.

"He'll always be with you." Emily pauses, knowing the words won't make anything better but needing to try to help heal the wound. "I can talk to the police. Get it back for you, if you like?"

"Nothing comes back Emily. We're on a carousel, spinning around at five hundred miles an hour. We cling on or fall off. Some of us, like Edward, are pushed."

"Well, I wish you wouldn't get involved with that Inspector. He gets you to do all the work then he takes all the glory. Spends half his time on the nineteenth hole that one. That's what Cuthbert says, wearing some loud golf

151

sweater."

"Don't be too hard. He's just a man. He's agreed to take Godric for a round as his guest."

"I bet his report card at school always said 'could do better'."

"All the more reason to help him do better."

"Don't get wrapped up in all this again. As your friend, I say stay out."

"I'm fine."

"We all know what stress can do."

"I'm fine. I'll tell you what is stressing me out though. My greenhouse thief. They've been at it again, taken some more of my grapes. But they won't get away with it. I set my Dictaphone up in a corner this morning. If they come in again, I'll catch them on a recording."

"But that won't last the whole morning, will it?"

"I've got to try something before I lose all my crop."

At that moment the mâitre d' comes back with a glass of wine for Emily and half a stout for Elizabeth.

"Are you ready to order?"

Emily looks at Elizabeth.

"I'll have the grape salad, please. Have you any fresh in today?" Elizabeth asks.

"Plus a young bean penne pasta, please." Emily looks at Elizabeth who nods. "Make that two, but no pesto on Professor Green's."

The mâitre 'd replies, "It's organic, vegan pesto."

"Then yes, please. I'd like that very much." Elizabeth smiles.

21
PASSPORT TO NOWHERE

Dropped off earlier, Susan stands on what she thinks is a vast ugly concourse outside Cambridge railway station. She remembers the mature trees which once lined the entrance, now chopped down like some Dr Seuss Lorax massacre, and bicycle racks removed to be replaced by stark office buildings, budget hotels and affordable flats. Her eyes can't seem to settle on anything beautiful. This drab picture of a planned future, the first sight any tourist sees of Cambridge is enough to make them jump straight back on the next train to King's Cross.

Susan has had time to drink her second coffee and smoke her third cigarette, having deliberately got here early so as not to miss her train. She watches the queues for tickets spiral round back near the snake of taxis. Glad she pre-booked, she stubs out her cigarette and brushes shoulder deep through tourists staring at the departure board next to Marks & Spencer. Susan carries her tightly packed shoulder bag, walks up over the station bridge to platform seven and begins to relax as she spots a space on a bench in the all-weather shelter to wait for the twelve thirty-five to Stansted.

Unzipping her backpack, she pulls out Edward's passport, looks at the picture in the front then throws it in the bin adjacent to the shelter. Susan hasn't noticed that further down the platform police are waiting, masked by many tourists. She checks her watch. She imagines the hot weather she'll be flying into, and can't wait for the freedom and escape. Perhaps she'll have a drink of Amarula cream for Edward and watch the sunset over Camps Bay beach, just a day away from that picture postcard. Sometimes you can even see dolphins putting on a show.

It is then that Susan sees the reflection of the police in the window of a station platform shelter. As soon as she spots them, they disappear. So jittery, she wonders if she imagined it, hopes she believed it. But then another police officer flashes past as just an image in the glass. Her stomach does a twirl, and she makes her way down the platform and back over the bridge. She looks behind her and can see the police officers following. Her walk turns into a trot and then a canter as she gets to the barriers she can't find her ticket. Where is it? She puts her bag down and shouts at the ticket man to let her out in the panic. He shakes his head.

"Not without a ticket."

She scrambles and finds it in her pocket, and puts it in the barrier which opens. But as she walks through a policeman grips her shoulder and Inspector Abley steps from the entrance and shouts,

"Miss Susan Bunt?" Susan nods, and he continues. "We would like to speak with you about the death of Edward Wiley. We have reason to suspect that someone may have murdered Mr Wiley, and we would like it if you could help us with our enquiries back at the station."

Inspector Abley spots that Susan's scarf has come loose, and he can see red marks around her neck, perhaps from the necklace? Was Elizabeth right? Susan protests, and tries to shake her shoulder free from the officers.

"Oh no. Please, please. This is wrong. I'm going to miss my plane."

"We'd like it if you'd accompany us to the station."

"No!" Susan punches Inspector Abley and runs past him. The police officer who had her by the shoulder chases and catches her, holding her up against a taxi, the same taxi in which she got a lift to the station. The driver winds down his window and speaks to the policeman.

"Serves her right for not tipping me."

Inspector Abley follows, holding his nose from the punch. When he reaches the commotion, he doesn't hesitate to read her rights to her.

"Susan Bunt, I'm arresting you for assaulting a police officer. You do not have to say anything. But, it may harm your defence if you do not mention when questioned something which you later rely on in court. Anything you do say may be given in evidence. And we will also be questioning you over the death of Mr Edward Wiley while we're   at   it."

22
HIDING SOMETHING

Susan sits across a table opposite Inspector Abley in a particularly drab windowless room at Parkside police station. Inspector Abley's nose is still red from where Susan punched him earlier. A police officer guards the door, and a recording device sits on the table, though Inspector Abley still prefers the old cassette system and argued as much when they were phased out. His Sergeant already pushed 'Record' half an hour ago, but they are getting nowhere with this morose woman sitting opposite. She hasn't looked up for the entire interview, just shuffled her feet and clutched at her face occasionally. Abley tries again.

"Perhaps you could help us with this?" The Inspector places a photograph on the table in front of Susan and studies her reaction carefully. The photograph is of the red, and black beaded necklace Elizabeth found in her garden, next to Edward Wiley. Susan glances at it for what seems like half a second and looks away. "It was found close to Mr Edward Wiley on the night of his death."

Susan doesn't even look up to answer but shrugs. "Dr Bunt, it is obvious to all that you have marks on your neck, which look very much like the print such a necklace might make if it were to be pulled against your skin. Given the proximity, this was found to Edward, and the fact that you admit you were with him the night he died, perhaps close to when he died, might we deduce that this is your necklace?" Susan stares at the floor, subdued. She does not answer. "Can you please look at the photograph again Dr Bunt."

Susan then lifts herself on the chair and looks Abley directly in the eye.

"Are you going to charge me? Because it feels like you don't have any evidence and you hope I'll hang myself."

Abley is not deterred.

"I don't want anyone to hang themselves. We can do this forensically. Just look at it please." Susan continues to look down. Abley is used to this. "Listen, Dr Bunt, the quicker you answer our questions, the quicker we can get to the truth. We believe Edward was murdered. We have asked if you wished to have a solicitor present and you declined. I ask again, would you like us to fetch the duty solicitor, as you won't be leaving until you answer our questions. I have to caution you that you have been arrested for assaulting a police officer and will be charged with this offence."

Susan looks up and studies the photograph carefully, then looks at the Inspector from under her fringe and nods.

"For the record, Susan Bunt is nodding, indicating that this is her necklace. What was Edward Wiley doing with your necklace?"

"For God's sake, how do I know? It was taken." Susan hides any expression from Abley by burying her face in her hands.

"Why were you leaving?"

"I was going on holiday."

"Perhaps this time you would care to elaborate, for the tape. What holiday? Where?"

"A safari."

"You like big game? I hear the best place to see them is in the Serengeti or Masai Mara?"

"I've missed my flight now, haven't I?"

Susan feels claustrophobic, trapped. How did they know to catch her at the station? It must have been that woman who came to visit. She'd clocked her bag. Who was she? Now in here, being accused of murder? It was all over now. If she could have just escaped to the big skies of Africa, she would have been able to forget what had happened. It wasn't her fault. She kept telling herself that.

"Why did you run away from us?"

"Like the gazelle runs from the lion."

"This isn't a joke. A man has been found dead, with your necklace in his hand. You are the last person seen with Edward."

"I know my rights. I can say no comment."

"Were you the last person to see Edward?" Abley knows full well that this was Elizabeth, but wants to test Susan's response.

"No."

"All the evidence suggests that you were." Abley knew he shouldn't have said that.

"So prove it." Susan is beginning to look sweaty. "Can I have a cigarette?"

"I'm afraid the station is a no smoking area. You were seen in a restaurant with Mr Wiley the night of his death. Can you confirm this?"

"We're lovers, all right? Worked that out, have you? He'd just got back from Africa, and I hadn't seen him in a while, okay?" Susan pauses, the reality of his death hits home.

Abley continues,

"What did you both do after the meal had finished?"

"Went our separate ways. I was a little narked as he was

going back to his wife. He was always promising he would finish it, but then he'd say he couldn't, for this, that, or the other reason. There'd never be a right time. Last night, he said he was going to do it, and I believed him. But he still made me mad as he said he couldn't come back with me. I couldn't help have a niggling doubt. Anyway, he went home, and so did I."

"You say he made you mad. Yet you don't have anyone who can vouch for what you did next? Did anyone see you?"

Susan hesitates.

"I was on my own."

"So those marks on your neck were not sustained while you were busy pushing Edward into the river from the bridge?"

Susan breathes an impatient sigh.

"Edward left me in the restaurant. Afterwards, I was going to walk along the river path to get home, as the moon was full. It was a beautifully peaceful night. But—" Susan isn't sure how this is going to help matters. It surely will just complicate them, or they won't believe her. "I got roughed up down Blind Man's Alley. There was a kerfuffle."

"A kerfuffle?" Inspector Abley leans back in his chair, feeling like he is finally getting somewhere.

"Someone grabbed me. It felt like they were trying to strangle me for a moment, then they ran off with my necklace. It was bizarre. I was so shaken. The marks are from where they were gripping me."

"All they took was your necklace? That's rather useful. Fits with everything. Why didn't you report this earlier?"

Susan was right. They didn't believe her.

"I don't know why I didn't report it. I knew I had a lot of work to do, to finish my paper before going on holiday. I've been up all night. Look, they're beads. Nothing I could report to the police. Can I have them back?"

"Tell us about the necklace."

There is a lull. Susan is exhausted from the questions, which seem to be going round and round. Her head begins to swirl, and she starts to feel clammy.

"May I have some water, please?"

Inspector Abley nods to the police officer by the door, who in turn disappears to get Susan some water.

"Tell us about the necklace."

"Edward bought it for me on his last trip to Africa. I love black and red, and I guess that's why he chose it?"

Abley presses Susan further.

"So we're meant to believe that you were walking down an alley, and this happened the same night Edward died when someone robbed you of it?"

"If you don't believe me, why don't you have someone look? I am sure they'd find scuffed cobbles and my DNA all over the alley. I got attacked, end of. Surely big brother will have CCTV somewhere. All that college money to protect."

"You were rather close to Edward then? We believe he fell or was pushed from Garret Hostel Bridge."

"I didn't see. I wasn't there. I've already told you. Hundreds of times."

"It all sounds a bit... you're saying that someone tried to strangle you?"

With her head in her hands, Susan hears the police officer come back in the room. She looks up to see him carrying a cup of water. Abley is a little irritated that it has broken his flow of conversation but can see Susan is struggling and so nods for the officer to give Susan the water. He does so and then returns to guard the door. Susan takes a long drink and puts her fingers in the cup and drips the water on her forehead. Abley presses her once more.

"Please continue."

"I've told you. It did feel like they were strangling me for a moment. Then they'd gone. Just like that."

"And what did this person look like? Did you manage

to catch any distinguishing features in their appearance?"

"No, just think, if I had remembered them then I'd have an alibi. Please, can I go or are you going to charge me? I'm beginning to feel unwell."

Inspector Abley puts the passport on the table in front of Susan.

"Why did you throw away Edward Wiley's passport?"

Susan realises they must have seen her do it. Why are they saving it until now to bring out?

"I took it last night in the restaurant from his jacket. I was going to surprise him with a last-minute holiday after he'd told Rebecca he was leaving her. Edward loved Africa. I had it as I was going to leave it at the check-in. But then I panicked. I got rid of it, as I thought you'd wrongly suspect me if you found me with it."

"That makes no sense. So you throw his passport away, you have a last supper with Edward. He is going back to his wife?"

"No, you are getting it all wrong."

Inspector Abley doesn't know what to believe. He decides to gather his thoughts outside and stands up.

"For the record, we're taking a break. It is one thirty-one on the clock." The Inspector gets up from his chair and walks towards the door. He looks back at Susan, who is now sweating and looking very pale.

"May I have some more water?"

He nods and leaves to get himself a coffee, pointing to the Constable at the door to sort out another water for Susan and then shuts it behind him.

At the end of the corridor, Abley waits by the coffee machine for the cup to fill. It just doesn't make sense. Why has Susan made up such a strange tale about being attacked? Who's going to fall for that? For the first time, he begins to think he might be on to something. He could have done all this without Elizabeth, who has just served to put Susan's back up if anything. But then he pulls out Susan's ticket from Stansted airport for a flight to Cape

Town at three o'clock today and also realises that Susan may well have got away if he'd left it much later. Yes, he had Elizabeth to thank for that at least. But he had it covered now. Susan was going to sing.

*

Back at Rebecca's college rooms Jonathan and Kara have started to pack up Rebecca's belongings to take back to their house. Kara, now dressed in one of Rebecca's sweaters and jog pants, has a large plain brown box and is gently placing all of Rebecca's shoes in tissue paper from the shoe rack. Rebecca, upset with the police who have been through everything while she was out says,

"I don't want to leave." Rebecca throws a pretty orange dress from the suitcase to the floor, while Jonathan takes Rebecca's hand and tries to calm her.

"You'll be much better off at our house. We can be there for you. Take care of you at this difficult time. The national press has picked this up. There's no privacy here. And what if the police want to come back again to look through Edward's things and–?"

Kara interjects.

"Are we not taking them too? I think Rebecca might want everything close."

Jonathan walks over and picks up some shoes.

"Hey, you kept the black velvet heels with the straps and bows."

Kara watches Jonathan pick up the shoes and smile, then also tries to make light and walks over to Rebecca to sit down beside her.

"I get lonely in the house, it's so big. I rattle about. It would be lovely to have you keep me company. Jonathan's always in London."

Rebecca resists the invitation.

"This is our home." Rebecca's bottom lip wobbles a little. "If I leave then I'll lose those things that keep me close to Edward."

Kara strokes Rebecca's hair.

"But we're your family. We need to stick together." She stands back up and picks out another pair of shoes from the wardrobe. Jonathan selects half a dozen dresses and puts them in the suitcase.

"Put those down!" Rebecca jumps across the bed and turns over the box of shoes, and all of Kara's carefully packed shoes in tissue paper come spilling out.

Kara throws her hands up and leaves the room for some air. Jonathan follows her out. Kara turns when she hears his steps and walks over to the window.

"I'm tired, look at me." Kara pulls at the sweatshirt. "This is such a mess."

"She's just lost her husband. She's upset." Jonathan puts his arm on Kara's shoulder.

"She's also mad." Kara sighs.

"At Susan Bunt, not at you."

"What is she like, this Bunt woman? I guess you know her?"

Jonathan raises his eyebrows.

"I met her a few times, a long time ago, then when she was with Edward. Was a beast to Sis' when Edward left her. No manners. But murder?" He pauses to think about it and looks out of the window at the now beautifully sunny day. "Maybe."

"Do you think Rebecca is still jealous of her?"

"Quite possibly. Though God knows why. Susan looks like the back end of a—"

"Okay, I get it. Rebecca sounds mad at her. Do you think she—"

Jonathan interrupts Kara, changing the subject.

"I had a call, on the way back with Rebecca. I have a place in the Cabinet. They're not saying what yet. Can I count on you two not to fuck it up? If only Rebecca doesn't run off again, and you can lay off the booze."

"You need to ask?"

Jonathan is suddenly ill at ease with the rooms.

"No course not. What was I thinking?"

Kara knows Jonathan's sarcasm when she hears it.

"I'll lay off the booze."

"It's like living in Dickensian times. I mean look at this place."

Kara agrees, touching the campanula on the windowsill.

"Even the plants die here."

*

Susan is motionless on her chair in the interview room. She sits alone at the table, her water cup empty. She can see the Inspector through a glass circle in the top of the door, talking to another police officer just outside. The Inspector nods, listening, then looks closely at Susan. Then the door opens, and he comes through, returning to his seat. He throws a cigarette and a box of matches to Susan, aware that he is breaking the rules. His fellow officer who has also entered turns on the recorder.

"Are you charging me? Otherwise, I'd like to go now. You've kept me long enough."

"It would appear that the waiter in the restaurant confirmed that you did indeed leave separately. And a couple in the corner seemed to think you both looked very much engrossed in conversation."

Susan raises her eyebrows.

"We are, were, in love."

"Another couple said they saw you alone walking along King's Parade. Thank yourself lucky for wearing such a distinctive cloak. They said you looked a bit like the grim reaper."

"Aren't I the popular one."

"We also have CCTV footage of you stumbling along Fen Road, again alone. There appears to be an African face mask just outside your house, which has Edward's DNA all over it."

"He gave it to me. I must have dropped it. So you can let me go. I mean we did leave separately. That proves I went home."

"I'm just trying to find out why Edward Wiley is dead. There's no proof you didn't catch up with him later. You're not off the hook just yet. You certainly had a motive."

"What motive?"

"You couldn't have the man you loved. He chose Mrs Rebecca Wiley as his wife. That must have stung."

"Listen, Inspector. I know what you're trying to make me do, admit I killed Edward, even though you have no evidence. It would be easy for you. A quick open and shut case. I wouldn't. I couldn't kill Edward. You see, we were expecting a baby and going to start a new life together. My baby is going to have to grow up without a father. I don't think I'm ready to be a single parent mum. What life is that for my baby?"

The news throws Abley. Why had she not mentioned this before? They arrested her and handcuffed her, and he remembers the Sergeant pushing her into the car. Oh my God, and now he's been making her sit here, with cigarettes? Abley was always a big softie about women and babies – even criminals.

"Why didn't you say?"

"You didn't ask."

"Dr Bunt, this is a serious inquiry."

"Don't I know it."

Susan Bunt looks clammy and unwell.

"All right. All right. Sergeant, get Dr Bunt some more water, will you? And a cup of sweet tea and see if you can find a sandwich."

The policeman by the door pops out to do as he's told.

"You are free to go once you have made a statement of the events of the night and what you did, and also please include the alley altercation. If you can do this before you leave that would be beneficial to everyone." Susan nods. "We'd like it if you remain in Cambridge, for the foreseeable future. We won't be keeping your passport, but would urge you to cooperate with us."

"So you don't think I'm guilty of anything?"

"Let's just say that we are letting you go without charge for anything related to Mr Wiley, but don't pop the corks. We may be charging you with assaulting a police officer."

"Why don't we say we're even and call it quits? I could sue for missed holiday expenses. Danger to my baby."

"You don't seem to understand the law. It doesn't work like that, and I'll have that back."

Abley snatches the cigarette from Susan's mouth and stubs it out in the ashtray. He picks up the packet on the table. She sighs, knowing he's right. Inspector Abley gets back up on his feet.

"This interview is terminated at two ten."

The remaining uniformed police officer turns off the recorder, and Abley leaves the room without looking back. Susan leans back in her chair. The police officer gives her paper and a pen to make a statement, and another returns with water, a weak looking tea in a paper cup and a tomato sandwich   in   white   bread.

23
THE RELUCTANT PARTICIPANT

The Dean of Bene't's College, Professor Percival Flint, leans against a cold radiator under a tall bay window. His view spans across to the other side of The Backs and verdant pastures framed by tall beech trees. He watches cattle chomp their way through unmown grass, sharing their field with two goats. Willows hang over punts full of tourists looking at this otherworldly place. A couple point up at the window and wave. Professor Flint, not wanting to appear rude, nods back.

Dr Eruna, meanwhile, is swivelling around in the Dean's chair and kicking his heels against a precious cherry wood desk. The Dean sighs and turns to face his least favourite scientist.

"Can you stop doing that."

"What?"

"It's made for sitting."

"Nonsense. Its destiny was to impart joy for all those who spread their buttocks."

"You're knocking six bells out of my Chippendale."

"This old bit of firewood?"

"That desk alone is worth more than a graduate's yearly fees."

"Okay, I'm stopped, if it will make you more receptive towards the idea."

Professor Flint takes the few steps between window and desk and walks behind Dr Eruna, placing his hands on the chair, warning him.

"I don't want any underhandedness. I've told you I'd write the damn paper."

"Yes, but when? You seem to be getting cold feet."

"I've yet to see a big cheque for the college that you promised."

"I'll make the first donation."

"It's too large a sum for a donation. People will grow suspicious. You'll have to make it out to the college research fund, and we can tie it into future research for the students. Just give me half now, like you said you would."

"Ah."

"What?"

"It's just that I've written to the funds committee already about the best way to donate. I have to have a receipt. I can't just hand over millions in cash."

"You did what? You promised to come through me."

"I thought they'd get excited, that it would be nice. I said that it was as a direct result of the research you have conducted for us."

"Tell me this is a sick joke?" The Dean replies, angry, keen not to make a meal of this.

Dr Eruna, forced to keep still now by the Dean's hands on his chair, starts to play with the Dean's computer keyboard instead. He can see that Flint has the internet open at a news page. He clicks off that and types in 'how to write faster', and thirty-one million searches come up in .32 of a second. Flint shuts the computer down. "They're going to ask for academic rigour now, don't you see? You've made this virtually impossible for me. They'll want to peer review my work."

"I don't see why you're getting jittery. We can find a couple of people in this esteemed university, surely, to review a paper. Everyone has their price."

"I agreed ages ago when you hadn't told me the whole truth. Leave that!"

Professor Flint takes a valuable antique Baccarat paperweight from Dr Eruna's hand, to stop him juggling with it. Flint walks back over to the window.

"I don't feel happy about this. I don't think—"

Dr Eruna starts to tire of Flint's stalling and makes it plain he has no more patience for delays.

"I told you all you need to know. We need that recommendation, so make your pen write sweet compliments. Your reputation is worth more than your personality, Percy."

"I'm not sure I can."

"You need to grow a thicker skin. If you don't, then I'll have no choice but to tell the world that you were trying to get money out of us, and were willing to write anything to do it."

"What?"

"You leave me no option, Percy."

"Oh, right. So we see your true colours, it's blackmail now is it? And who would believe you? I'd say you were lying."

"Well, all those trips. Let me see now, to Paris, to New York, all paid for by Labzuu."

Professor Flint's beetroot face starts to spit at Dr Eruna.

"They were research trips."

"Yeah, yeah. So staying at the Ritz, that's normal is it, for a Don's salary? Listen, don't beat yourself up over it. When this is published, we'll all make millions. It's the credit we need. We deserve. You know we're not the demons as painted. What's wrong with helping us a little?"

Dr Eruna, having the upper hand right now, keeps his

composure, while Professor Flint fumes.

"The expensive PR firm you've hired, and the metres of barbed wire around your offices are just for show, are they? People had warned me about you. I should've listened."

"What I don't understand about you Percy, is why this sudden change of heart? So, don't take our money if you think it's dirty. But you still owe us the paper."

"You know it's not for me. I'm doing this for the college. God help me."

"This college is loaded, come on, don't lie to yourself."

Dr Eruna gets up and wanders over to the window to join Flint. Professor Flint laughs at him, saying,

"You think we're so wealthy. It's all locked up in land, in property. I cannot access that. Not for tuition, for the students. How much do you think it costs to run a college like this?"

Dr Eruna remains as cool as a cucumber and replies,

"We can set up Fellowships. Let us come into bed with you on a large scale. Hey, why not? It's a great idea." Dr Eruna waves to some punters who wave back, giggling thinking they have just waved to a royal or someone famous. Flint sees this and pulls the curtains slightly to obstruct him from view, ashamed to have Dr Eruna in sight.

"No. This is more than enough contact between us."

"But you'll be asked about us. You'll have to defend the company. You can't go back on that, or I would have to admit what you have done. Writing a recommendation about unproven science. Hmm, an end to your career."

"A Fellow of our college is dead. Please don't tempt me to add to the toll. I must ask you to leave now."

"Okay, but let's meet later. I have to do something in the centre but will be back in a while. We need to iron this out."

Dr Eruna leaves, as Percival Flint looks to the ceiling and slumps into his chair. He picks up the phone and speed dials. No one answers, so he starts to leave a message.

"I need you to call me. It's urgent. We need to talk."

Percival hangs up.

*

Not far from the Professor's room, Rebecca is now alone in her married couple's college apartment. Kara and Jonathan have left, taking away the first carload of boxes. She sits on the bed looking at the sky through the tiny leaded window. A blue silk scarf with little Scotty dogs draped over her shoulders, the radio beside her, quietly emitting classical music. After a short time, the piece comes to an end, and a presenter reads the news headlines. 'The brother-in-law of MP Jonathan Smythe-Jones has died after falling into the River Cam last night. Dr Edward Wiley was a Don at the university. Cambridgeshire police have not confirmed the cause of death, but the local MP for Ely, Jonathan Smythe-Jones, released a statement saying the family are devastated and to thank people for their kind thoughts at this unfortunate time.'

Rebecca gets off the bed and starts to go through her jewellery box and stand. She looks at a lot of necklaces. She can't find what she is searching for. Makeup bags, carry purses are emptied, but still nothing. Then she opens the table drawers one by one and tips out all the lingerie: black, pink, green with tiny petals. She can't find it. Rebecca walks across to her bedside table and pulls open the drawer. Nothing. She leans across the bed and opens Edward's bedside table. Rebecca looks panicked. She scrabbles in some final boxes Kara and Jonathan haven't taken yet but still nothing.

"Where is it?"

She hears a knock at the door and walks out into the drawing room. It is Carter, with a parcel and a tray of tea and biscuits. Rebecca carries them into the bedroom. How kind of Carter. Using some scissors from a drawer, she cuts open the wrapping. Inside is a bundle of handwritten letters, tied up with a ribbon. Rebecca recognises the handwriting as she unties them, letting them fall and scatter on the bed around her. There must be two dozen at least, all with foreign stamps. She starts to read the first, and her face begins to change. As she turns the page, she looks at the envelope in disbelief and back again at the words. Her eyes fill with tears until one escapes and runs down her cheek.

24
THREATS ANND ACCUSATIONS

Susan left Parkside Police Station about half an hour ago and has now made it straight to the woman she blames for her arrest. Spoiling for a fight, she storms through the small side entrance on Hills Road to the Botanic Gardens without stopping, only to be chased by the gatekeeper to buy a ticket.

"Er, excuse me, Madam, the gardens have a small entrance fee. Do you have a friends pass, or would you like to purchase one?"

"Where's Elizabeth Green? Her department secretary said she was here."

"That will be five pounds please if you want an 'on the day'."

"Tell me where she is, and I'll pay you."

There is a pause and Susan angrily shouts,

"I'll find her myself then!"

Susan rummages in her purse and pulls out a ten-pound note.

"There we are Madam, you'll find her in the Scented Garden."

Susan rushes along the path. As soon as she gets fifty or so feet along East Walk, she can smell the cedar of Lebanon. It doesn't lift her mood, but she remembers when Edward brought her to an evening tree concert 'Sounds Green in the Garden' last year, where a tour of the trees preceded a jazz band playing by the lake. She was moved to hear that night that a group of badgers had recently taken up residence as could be seen by much scuffing of the lawns. Last year seems long ago.

Now she feels bitter phlegm in her throat, angry as she smells the lavender wafting upon the breeze, followed by aromas of Helichrysum italicum, the curry plant, arousing hunger in her gut. Susan spots Elizabeth leaning over with some secateurs. She grabs her shoulder, twisting her violently around and pushes her right into a bank of rosemary.

"How dare you. You come round asking questions. Poking your nose in. Next thing I know I'm being arrested by the police!"

Elizabeth flounders in the bush but refuses to give Susan any advantage and coolly addresses her as if nothing has happened.

"Hello, Dr Bunt. There's no need to manhandle me."

"It was you who told them I was leaving, wasn't it?"

"If you must know I did mention I thought you might be going somewhere, yes."

"I missed my flight, my holiday. Been accused of all sorts."

"I thought it mildly odd. Your lover is dead, and you are not waiting around for the funeral."

"He's dead! And his family will be all over that. Why are you interfering with my life? You owe me, big time."

Elizabeth pulls herself up and brushes down her clothes.

"A holiday? Where?"

Susan is incredulous. Will Elizabeth not heed her warning?

"I want to know why you're poking your nose in all this and to warn you to stop leading the police to my door, or else!"

"I beg your pardon?"

Susan leans into Elizabeth and pushes her face right up against her nose.

"You're going to repay me, one way or another."

Elizabeth raises her eyebrows but doesn't flinch. She stares at Susan and says,

"Look Dr Bunt. We're both alive. Edward is dead. You say he meant a lot to you. I'm sure he would not want you to fight those who are trying to catch his killer. The police are only doing their job, and I saw your bag, and you were leaving. There is not a hell's bells chance that I'm going to reimburse you for anything. Why you feel the need to come over here and shout the odds, I don't know. It just makes me think that perhaps I was right and you are trying to hide something. Threatening me will get you nowhere."

"If you don't leave me alone and lay off then you'll be sorry. Very sorry. Do I make myself clear?"

"The police would arrest you as quick as you like. Stop shouting at me and start talking. Why here? Why today?"

Susan backs down a little, but there is still venom in her eyes.

"I'm angry with you."

"You're angry, that's for sure."

Susan exhales sharply and then tosses her arms violently in the air and twists around.

Elizabeth, a little disturbed by Susan's aggression, nevertheless goes back to her work of taking small cuttings of some scepter'd isle. Susan's energy trickles out of her, her face falling into a morose resting state. She throws herself down on the timber sleepers of a wooden shelter, sweet lemon of rosa mulligani, trained across its roof and sides.

"They told me you found my necklace in Edward's hands, how did you know it was mine?"

Elizabeth can't read Susan's mood, or what she will do next, so continues to try to treat her normally replying,

"A hunch. You were covering red marks on your neck. Your scarf slipped."

"Yes, well thanks to you it's police evidence now. So I guess you thought you'd stitch me up." Susan bitterly continues, "Maybe you killed Edward. How come they haven't arrested you? He was in your garden."

Susan can't see, but Elizabeth rolls her eyes with tempered derision, then turns to face her.

"I can't help what I found. Have you been eliminated from suspicion? They've presumably released you. You haven't escaped, so..."

"The Inspector was cagey. Says I mustn't go on any travels. Means I lost my whole trip."

"They want to find out what happened. It wasn't an accident, of that they're pretty sure. I'm sure you'll get your necklace back when they find out."

Susan is now utterly dejected, slumping down in her seat.

"He brought the necklace back from his last field trip. He'd had a bad time over there."

"Africa. Why?"

"He wouldn't say. He just said it would all come out in the wash."

"That's a strange thing to say. Did you tell the police?"

"What do they care? Just want someone banged up for it."

Elizabeth continues to cut at a plant and puts the cuttings in a small basket with water in the bottom while talking.

"But you knew him better than most, you may know something which you don't think is important, but pieced together with other information will give the police a clue. What was he doing in Africa, Susan?"

"The department might have thought Edward was just researching the Bilbao tree. Nothing else. But the other night he told me he was repulsed by something he found. And that certain people would never live it down."

"Baobab tree, or Adansonia," Elizabeth corrects Susan's pronunciation of the tree's name. She then stands up straight. "Follow me if you will, Susan. This won't take a minute."

"Why? Where are we going?"

"Just to a glasshouse," Elizabeth replies. "I want to show you something."

The two walk from the Scented Garden up the path past the fountain towards the glasshouses. Susan scuffs her feet along the gravel, making evident her lack of enthusiasm for this detour.

"Plants aren't my bag."

"So, how did you two meet?"

"You ask a lot of questions. Huh, what does it matter now? We met at college, as undergraduates. A group of us used to hang out together, and we took it further." Susan looks at Elizabeth. She might as well tell her too. Perhaps it would elicit sympathy. "I'm carrying his baby."

Elizabeth tries not to overreact.

"You told the police?"

"I'm sure it was the only reason they let me go. Why would a woman who's pregnant kill the father, unless he's some kind of monster? But the Inspector is convinced I have something to do with Edward's death, just the way he spoke. He's wrong."

"You know that Rebecca is also pregnant?"

Susan is completely stunned but tries to hide it. How could she be? She looks at Elizabeth quizzically and laughs.

"What's so funny?" Elizabeth turns to look at Susan as they near the glasshouses.

"If you want to think someone killed him, I'd look at Rebecca. She's the one who had the most to lose. He wasn't feeling well by the time I met up with him. Maybe she poisoned his lunch."

"I thought pregnant women don't kill the fathers. Although one only has to look at the arachnids to see that's entirely inaccurate."

"I told you. He was leaving her."

"According to Rebecca, he didn't eat with her that day at all. He ate with you though."

"Maybe I should go myself and find evidence that it was Rebecca." Susan makes to go. But then Elizabeth stops her and says,

"Just a few more steps inside this first one. Look." Both walk through the first glasshouse and come to a halt near a baobab tree. "Here." Elizabeth points upwards. "Adansonia, or baobab."

"It's upside down?"

"The trunk in a large adult tree can store up to one hundred and twenty thousand litres of water. For much of the year, the leaves are not present, and it just looks like the roots are the wrong way up. This is what Edward was looking at, only in bigger form. They grow up to a hundred feet in native habitat."

Susan doesn't look interested, and just wants to leave, replying,

"Yes, that's quite interesting, as you say."

"D'you know that the large trees when dead are often hollowed out and used as bars to meet? Isn't that simply wonderful?"

They both look at a small version of the tree, warm inside the heated house. Susan pulls out a cigarette and goes to light it.

"No smoking."

"You're as bad as Edward. Hated cigarettes, said I'd have to quit when we got together. No need now. Just stop talking to the police, alright?"

Elizabeth takes a flower label from a plant and writes her telephone number on it. She gives it to Susan.

"He used to come in here to get away, you know. If you think of anything, telephone me. If you don't want to go to the police, tell me."

"Don't hold your breath," says Susan as she walks off to leave. As she joins the exit path, she examines the label Elizabeth has given her. Two landlines; who has a landline, let alone two?

Back in the glasshouse, Elizabeth is glad Susan has gone. Although it's a warm day, a chill has run up her spine. Something about that woman signals terrible news. Elizabeth hopes she's not the one on the end of it next time. And although having indicated the opposite, hopes she won't be hearing from Susan for a long time.

25
LOOKING FOR SOMETHING

Jonathan and Kara are at home in their barn on the edge of Ely, having come back with the first carload of Rebecca's stuff. Jonathan opens the doors onto the garden, outside the swimming pool sparkles in the sun. Both are uncomfortable that Rebecca insisted on staying behind, but aside from throwing her over his shoulder, Jonathan couldn't see how they could force her. Kara tidies away evidence of last night's partying. Magazines strewn, glasses half-drunk, bottles tipped and dribbling their near-empty contents onto glass coffee tables, CDs scattered out of their cases. Jonathan pours himself a whisky. He looks irked. Kara approaches Jonathan, holding half a dozen glasses in her hands.

"Are you going to work from home more, now Rebecca will be living with us?"

Jonathan takes a swig and looks at Kara.

"Sometimes I think you have no idea, Kara. Cabinet is going to be full on."

"So I'm left with nanny duties?" Kara flounces out to

the kitchen with the glasses and two empty bottles of red. Jonathan takes a large gulp of his drink and picks up a magazine to look at the pages full of fluffy bubblegum stories about which celebrity is dating who, and how big is someone's house. He grimaces and drops it down again. Looking around he doesn't know if this is going to work. He's been having doubts, and Kara knows it. She walks back in with a cloth and some salt.

"It's too late for that. You have to do it when it's wet," he says, somewhat half-heartedly.

"Well, I'll give it five minutes, and if it doesn't work, I'll bring in the heavy guys."

"Is this going to work?"

"Salt always works."

"I meant…"

He looks at her again, exhausted. Kara knows what he is talking about.

"We'll more than work. This is just a very stressful day."

Jonathan continues to press.

"Have you any idea what it will be like actually being married to a member of Government? It's not all polo and country club."

"It's what I want for you."

"But you'll have to behave, or you'll end up in one of these magazines in a compromising position." Jonathan glances at the celebrity magazines on the coffee table.

"You know I'm faithful."

"I only meant they'll shoot you drunk, coming out of some club or other. How will that look?"

Kara thinks he sounds more worried about himself.

"And we're back to your career. You promised it would be different if we came up here. Three times I've seen you this month. One meal on our own. One. You're always promising you'll be up and then something comes up. No wonder I end up partying with friends."

"Don't do this. I've told you it won't always be like

this. But, if you can't even help with my sister, what does that say about us?"

Jonathan turns on the TV and flicks to the news channel. He can hear the presenter talk about him. A graphic pops up titled 'winners and losers'. Jonathan is on the graph under winner. This makes him feel good. He sits and takes out some cocaine from his pocket, and with a credit card lines up two hits and snorts them up. Kara continues to clean the carpet as she speaks to him.

"Why do you always make out everything's my fault?"

Jonathan sniffs up a third line and looks at Kara, a little more distant than usual. He steps back from her to talk.

"Life can't just be one big party, one big punt, champagne picnics, ball gown wearing glitter-fest. I'm going to be busy. I'm going to travel. That's not going to change. Be honest, is this what you want?"

Kara looks up from the carpet and shoots a glare at Jonathan.

"All right, if we are talking about honesty. Tell me what the money from Edward was all about?"

"What money?" Jonathan is shocked.

"The cheque. I saw the note in the glove compartment from Edward."

For a moment this floors him. He has been rumbled, and his best defence is attack.

"What are you, spying on me now?"

But Kara is also thrown by his lack of quick explanation. She wanted him to tell her it was nothing. Now she's curious.

"Has it got anything to do with his death?"

Jonathan picks up his drink and strides out onto the terrace by the pool, shouting back,

"How can you even ask me that?" But he isn't waiting for her answer. He walks down the side of the pool and onto the lawn towards the orchard at the bottom of the garden; anything to get away from Kara, his biggest problem right now.

Kara picks up the salt and stares into the garden after Jonathan. She knows best not to follow him. She turns and places the salt on the table and picks up a wedding magazine, looks at the cover and then tosses it back and surveys the mess of the living room. What has she become and how did they get here?

*

Elizabeth is still at work at the Botanic Garden but has moved from the greenhouses up into the Gilmour Suite, one of a number of small laboratories in the grounds, set up to study plant growth and development. All white and steel, clean and sharp edges, she spends hours working here, examining the compounds and molecular structure of plants. However, Elizabeth always feels happiest further along the corridor. For next to the Gilmour, just a stone's throw away is the University Herbarium, which contains over one million pressed and dried plant specimens, including the vast majority of those collected by Charles Darwin on the Beagle voyage. She often spends the night when she cannot sleep poring over one species or another from the drawers that house collections from around the world. And although not in it now, Elizabeth can always feel the herbarium calling, like a beating drum of rustling leaves and seed shakers.

It is gone five thirty in the afternoon. Light still streams in. Elizabeth is alone, with all her colleagues having clocked off. She stands at a workstation peering through a microscope, examining plant chemical traces in a petri dish. Close up she picks out cells being attacked by the chemical molecular composition. Elizabeth looks up as she has just discovered something she expected, but hoped she would be wrong about, as it takes things into an altogether darker twist. Walking over to a shelf, Elizabeth rises up on her toes to reach a book down from the small laboratory library. As she pulls the book off the shelf, she glimpses outside.

Under the pruned lime trees on the cafe terrace, she sees a family with two children, the children running around a table with their mother telling them to stop and how they have to go soon. Elizabeth turns the pages of the book and finds what she wants. Like the family below, Elizabeth knows it is time she should go. She thinks back to when Susan turned up a couple of hours ago. Why come storming over and threaten to do her an injury if she is innocent, but what a crazy thing to do if she is guilty? Elizabeth did not doubt that she may well be pregnant, but does that make it more likely? Was Rebecca right and Susan was just the spurned ex-girlfriend? But, if Susan did not do it, then who did?

She spots the front page of the local paper on the work station below, with a photo of Edward and one of Jonathan. After the mention of Edward's death, it reads that Jonathan is tipped for the Home Office and goes on to quote him talking about family values. The reporter mentions his aristocratic background, a known shooter and hunter with a temper. Once in a physical fight with someone outside a Party conference over fox hunting.

*

Dr Eruna has returned to Bene't's College after his earlier visit to the Dean's rooms. He stands outside the Porters' Lodge. Through the wide arch, his eyes fall on imposing limestone and lawns mown within a millimetre of their lives.

He remembers his short lectureship here, how antiquated, how snobby and so deliciously top-drawer. Landing Professor Flint's paper will be the making of Labzuu. Sure, the company has made him a multi-millionaire, but he wants to reach far higher than that, and have Labzuu become the multinational to rival all others.

The establishment has taught him to think big. He spots Carter coming through from a back room into the lodge.

"I wondered if I could trouble you for a favour, Carter? I have this letter I'd like to give to the funds committee." Carter takes the letter from Dr Eruna and places it on a back bench next to the telephone and a pile of other letters.

Dr Eruna is about to leave when Carter starts a conversation.

"Sir, might I ask, the Dean informed me you are a Fellow alumni. I must apologise, I pride myself on a face."

"I was mostly in the States, only had dinner a few times at college when I was in the UK. But, I'd like to go and try out the Fellow's bar now. Is it open?"

"Fellow's opens at six thirty this evening. Sorry to press you, sir, but were you here as a young lad? I'm sure I would have remembered you?"

"No, at Cranmer College as an undergrad."

"Never mind, Sir. You managed to escape in the end."

"It's a good college, Carter. It suited my needs."

"Perhaps you might like to try the Bene't's Bar?"

"Of course. Have you seen the Dean?"

"Not recently. Would you like me to call his rooms?"

"I'll surprise him. See if he'd like something to help fire inspiration." Dr Eruna leaves the lodge and heads out towards the Dean's rooms before Carter can stop him. But Carter does pick up the phone to announce Dr Eruna's impending arrival, though the Dean does not answer.

26
LABZUU

Godric leans back in the overlarge chair, sitting at Sir Gerald's desk in the study. The computer screen is so close to his face it is almost too large to focus. The room is lined with books on three walls, mainly hardbacks; an eclectic collection of medical, skiing, cloud formations, political biographies, books on art, and so on. On the remaining wall, a large sash window opens out onto a side garden. Two bird feeders hang on an iron pole nearby. A robin is eating food Elizabeth put out earlier while keeping a beady eye on Godric.

Godric can smell his grandpa in things. Propped up on every surface are photographs, old rowing trophies and above Godric's head, suspended from the ceiling, an oar from Sir Gerald's days rowing as a Blue. He hears the front door slam and Elizabeth call.

"Cooee!"

"In here!"

Elizabeth pops her head around the door.

"I thought we could eat supper later. Tea and cake now?" She holds up a box of cakes from the patisserie.

"Ooh, what have you got?"

"Viennese slice, Chelsea bun, cream éclair, and a vegan carrot cake which has my name on it." Elizabeth walks out to the kitchen, fills the kettle, then takes two plates from the cupboard and walks back to Godric, grabbing some napkins from the side.

"Lovely."

Godric takes out a slice.

"I've had a look for you on that chap, Dr Eruna? Quite interesting."

"Most helpful. But this doesn't mean you are on the case. You have your exams, remember."

Elizabeth leans over Godric's chair to see what he's found.

"I damn well am your assistant, and your payment is cream cakes every afternoon, or I strike and will write to the papers."

Elizabeth, eager, waves Godric to get on with it. With a mouthful of éclair he obliges.

"It says here that Labzuu has business interests in the UK, Europe, the Americas and the African continent, including Kenya, Zimbabwe and South Africa."

Godric bites into the cake again and squirts out cream.

"Don't eat and speak at the same time, Goddy."

Godric ignores his nanna.

"Interests in research and development but it doesn't say on their website what in particular they're doing – just the medicines they've already produced. It's just a promotional site really, no news unless it relates to profits and products."

Over Godric's shoulder Elizabeth can see the Labzuu website then Godric clicks to a news article about Labzuu and drops cream into the keyboard. Both of them pull a face, and Godric tries to wipe it off with his fingers, putting the cream in his mouth. Elizabeth can't believe it.

"Eww, dirty. So they're helping people?"

"Not exactly. As you go to news or put in a search to see what other people think of them it's a whole different story. You have to dig a little. There are a few blogs and some claim Labzuu took DNA from Maori people without their permission in the nineties, and have developed their genes and not given a penny back."

"That was where Edward was doing some of his field work. Very interesting, Godric." Elizabeth takes a fork and cuts her vegan carrot cake into pieces.

"A few angry people are writing about Labzuu in general. You know, calling them scum, thieves."

"Gerald went over to work with the Maori and local farmers."

"Really? I didn't know."

"Yes, he was helping them fight to keep some of the land that the government wanted to sign over to big agrochemical companies."

"I had no idea."

"So this means something. It feels like everything is connected. What's the Dean of Bene't's doing with Dr Eruna?"

"Not sure. One blog here says Labzuu is working with a tribe in South Africa, paying for DNA. Quite controversial. I've printed some stuff out, just like a real assistant would."

"Thank you so much for this. Okay, you're my assistant. But that means only assignments given, not original work."

Godric nods excitedly, picks up the keyboard and licks more cream off the keys, then picks up the Viennese slice, takes a big bite and drops jam on the desk. Elizabeth glares at Godric.

"Assistants use plates."

Elizabeth looks at what is on the screen and thinks how Edward had just got back from a round trip in Africa. Kenya and South Africa. He must have found something

Dr Eruna was keen to keep under wraps? Godric is almost at fever pitch with his new role.

"There's not stacks on the news wires, just a small bunch of activists following them. They seem to have a good reputation, because of the degenerative brain disease treatments they've got going. You know, TZ921?"

Godric clicks up a snazzy image of a top-of-the-range branded medical pill.

"Oh, goodness. Maybe that's why the Dean's involved with Dr Eruna. I can't imagine him caught up in anything less worthy."

Godric shows Elizabeth how the web is flooded with positive images and advertorials about how the company is helping people. Elizabeth wonders what she should do next. As if reading her mind Godric speaks.

"I have choir practice, but after that, we can look for more information."

"Thank you. This is most illuminating."

Godric puts the rest of the cake in his mouth all in one go as he stands up from the chair.

"Do assistants get to drive the Talbot?"

"Walk. What shall we do for supper? You coming back?"

"I'll grab something at Bene't's from the bar."

"Make sure it's non-alcoholic."

Godric leaves for evensong and Elizabeth makes herself peppermint tea. When she returns to the desk, Bertie has just started to lick her carrot cake. Elizabeth smiles and sits to read the article about Labzuu that Godric left open.

"Bertie, what is that creep doing with Percival Flint?"

27
THE LETTER

A couple of miles away Susan Bunt walks through her front door holding a shopping bag. Having gone straight home after her encounter with Elizabeth, she's been back out to pick up some food from the local corner shop and is now feeling mellow, having bought a stack of carbohydrates, chocolate and more wine. If she can't go to Africa, she is going to bloody well enjoy herself here.

Susan picks up the post from the front door mat she'd walked over earlier and takes it to the kitchen. As she puts everything down, she notices among the pile an envelope with handwriting she recognises. She pours herself another wine from the fridge, and with one hand holding her glass she reads the letter and becomes increasingly agitated. Taking a large gulp, she fumbles in her pocket and takes out the flower label with Elizabeth's telephone numbers, walks over to the phone and dials. She looks at her watch as the phone continues to ring. Elizabeth must have left the Botanic Gardens. But there is another number. Maybe second time lucky, she dials again. As she continues to hold on the line Susan downs more wine, pulls back her curtains and opens a window to let fresh air into the stuffy house. She hopes the person on the other end will pick up the phone soon.

"Yes. Hello? It's Susan Bunt. Yes, is that Elizabeth? Oh, thank goodness. I know, yes. Well, you said I could call? Yes, no please listen, yes. I will. No, please, I've phoned you because I need to see you again. Today. It's really important." Susan listens to Elizabeth on the other end, then interrupts, "Can we meet as soon as possible then? Bene't's? I need your help. No, I'm going straight there now, to catch Rebecca. I need to go now. I don't have time to explain." Susan listens on the phone again. "Yes, I'll walk down. It's fine. No, no. See you shortly." Susan eyes the wine and looks at the clock. A couple more glasses to steady her nerves first.

28
BERTIE

As soon as Elizabeth rings off from Susan, she picks up her coat and looks for her keys. But Bertie is now rubbing himself against her legs, telling her it is most definitely supper time. Elizabeth has agreed to meet Susan at Bene't's and knows Susan lives further out, so guesses she has time to quickly cook Bertie a little bit of fish for his tea. Elizabeth strokes Bertie and calls to him 'fish fish' and his ears prick up. If only she could understand his language too. He follows her as she walks into the kitchen, opens the fridge, turns on the hob and puts a piece of bass into the frying pan with some oil.

Elizabeth doesn't see why she should force her own vegan diet on Bertie. She's long decided that the best, most sustainable food to buy him is fresh fish. Given their land-locked location, this is more rigmarole than she hoped. None of the fish stalls in the market sell local sustainable produce, though some purport to be organic, and most supermarket fish is not locally sourced either. But after investigation, Elizabeth found a Hunstanton man who fishes out from Brancaster and makes a trip to Cambridge twice weekly to deliver to local restaurants.

Brancaster is one of the little villages on the extreme northern tip of Norfolk, with miles of sandy beach and dunes. If a fish is going to die, then better there than in some fish farm, where the fish can't swim free or see the sun glinting down through the waters. She persuaded him to make a detour to drop off her small order for Bertie. While the proprietor didn't much like Elizabeth, who he found to be brusque and quite demanding, particularly over his punctuality – they had once argued for at least half an hour about him being late, making him an hour late for his next delivery – he did, nevertheless, enjoy telling his other customers and his own small children that he has this mad eccentric Professor who orders his fish for her cat, but is one of those nutty people who only eats nuts and seeds herself. He also felt sorry for the cat. The fish starts to sizzle in the pan, and Bertie jumps up onto the kitchen work surface. If only the fisherman knew that there is no need to worry about the welfare of Bertie Green.

"Get down from there please, Bertie." But Bertie watches the edges of the bass crisp up. He looks at Elizabeth and opens his mouth to reveal his pink quivering tongue. Elizabeth turns over the fish and looks back to Bertie. "Four minutes. Now go and wash your paws."

She picks up Bertie and puts him on her lap, while the fish fries. Stroking Bertie, who is purring very loudly and keeping a beady eye on the cooker, Elizabeth remembers when she first found him on Chesterton Lane one winter day in the snow. She spotted him from her bathroom window. Never mind the cold, he wouldn't have survived long on that busy road, so she ran outside in her slippers and picked him up and took him to the rescue centre to check his chip and find his family. Only he didn't appear to have either, and so they asked if she'd like to foster him for a week in case anyone came forward as there was no space for him at the centre. She said she would most definitely not like to foster him as she was busy and didn't have time to look after a cat. But the lady at the centre gave Elizabeth the most grave of faces and said shame, as older male cats are not desirable, wrongly seen as smelly and with vets bills too, so she wasn't sure what they would do with him as there was no space. Elizabeth did not like the sound of that one bit, so brought him home agreeing that she'd foster him for just a week.

The first day Elizabeth called all the vets, took in photos to pet shops, put up photos on lampposts saying 'Lost cat found' and 'ring this number'. On day two still no one had claimed him and she started to call him Bertie after Wodehouse's Wooster. Bertie wasn't sure how to use her cat flap, would run and hit his head on the window when he saw birds outside in the garden, giving her not much reason to think highly of his cognitive abilities. On day three Bertie sat by the fire and kept as still as a statue until feeding time. Elizabeth wondered if he was just cold to the bone, was ill, or did not want to get in her way in case she chucked him out into the cold. She had a chat with him to tell him that she wouldn't throw him out. It seemed to work as on day four Bertie started to follow Elizabeth about. She would go into the kitchen he would follow, she would go into the study so would Bertie. If she called his name, Bertie would come and brush his body along her leg. By day five, he had somehow managed to push Elizabeth's bedroom door open and was there watching her when she woke. On day six, he was asleep on her pillow as she stirred, leaning into her head. Elizabeth found this most amusing, like wearing a Russian ushanka. Then day seven came, and it was time to take Bertie back to the centre, where there would now be a space for him Elizabeth was told. It was the day he hid under the bed, and when she tried to pull him out, he would lick her hand all over, his tongue like sandpaper and then hide further back and out of reach. So she decided she'd take him later in the afternoon and perhaps mark some essays first until he calmed down. It was then that he came out from the bed, jumped up and curled into her lap, only moving to get up and turn around to sit back down again. She was stuck, so stuck that she missed the time to take him back and the rescue centre closed for the day. She swears that it was then that she saw Bertie smile, up into both cheeks and up to his eyes.

The fish is now ready, but still hot. Elizabeth cuts it open and takes out the bones. She places it on a cold plate, decorated with lots of little tiny kittens in blue porcelain. Then, when she is happy it will not scald her best friend's mouth, she places it carefully on the kitchen floor and pats his head. Bertie tucks into it with gusto and Elizabeth smiles, which is a good job as out of the window she spots the greenhouse door is wide open. Once in the garden, she notices the dictaphone has been knocked over, and the light is not on to show recording. Aha, perhaps she has caught the perpetrator. Looking up there are yet more grapes missing from the vine. Elizabeth pockets the dictaphone and leaves the greenhouse with renewed optimism. The grape thief will be hers.

29
TIME TO SING

Five minutes later and Elizabeth is cycling along Trinity Street, wearing her crash helmet. Peddling at some speed, a Chinese tourist and his lady wife nearly get knocked down by her as they clumsily step out from the kerb. They are carrying a camera and an open map, the man shouts,

"Hey!"

But Elizabeth retorts.

"Ho!" and whizzes past.

*

Percival is in his rooms, scratching his head as he stares at his computer screen. His phone is ringing again, but he is ignoring it. He's been ignoring the knocks on his door as well, especially from Dr Eruna, as he has to start this ruddy paper for Labzuu, but he cannot fool himself. He's hit a wall. He cannot do it. He would be endorsing a very shady product indeed. He has some principles left. He pushes his chair back and gets up, walking towards the bay window. Behind him on the wall is a long photograph of current and past college Fellows. Edward Wiley, Percival Flint and Dr Eruna; Susan Bunt's face next to them, with her arm around Dr Eruna. As he looks out of the window something captures his attention that worries him.

*

Not far from Percival's room, under the fan-sculptured vault ceiling of Bene't's Chapel, sounds of Samuel Barber's 'Agnus Dei' emanate, drifting up from the twenty strong choir standing behind the Rood screen. Siren notes float over pews, striking dumb the college members listening in petrified awe at this otherworldly sound. Godric stands next to Rebecca, amazed to see her still with some life in her bones after the awful news. Just earlier Rebecca wasn't sure she should come, but hearing sounds drifting out towards her room window she was drawn, and with the beautiful Godric she now feels safe. He squeezes her hand as she stands by his side along a finely carved chorister bench.

Susan treads unsteadily across Bene't's Ramn's court from the Parade, heading for the Chapel, having been told by the lodge Porter that's where she will find Rebecca. A college boy notices her walking in a zigzag line but is too polite to interfere, and simply wonders if she's inebriated. She staggers a little onto the grass, leaning momentarily with her hands resting on her knees, and wonders if she should sit here, but is determined to make it to Rebecca. A junior Porter coming back from errands eyes her suspiciously, but as she straightens her spine and walks on, he thinks best not to interfere. Though never having spoken to her, he has seen her photograph on the wall in the lodge and knows she's a Fellow here, and after all, it is past six o'clock. If she wants to take things to make her feel good then what business is it of his? As she turns the corner to get into the North Chapel Gate Susan is increasingly breathless, every step becoming more laboured and heavy than the last. Just one more corner. An American post-doctoral student coming in to listen asks if she is okay. Too weak to speak she nods and frowns, eager for him to leave her alone as she makes a final push up the steps and into the late gothic limestone lobby.

Elizabeth has reached Bene't's gatehouse, having locked her cycle by the college shop, and crosses the street to walk through the lodge, blocked temporarily by a Porter, who has the gates still closed to visitors for the day due to interest over Mr Wiley's death and is now dealing with a group of Chinese tourists asking him what time evensong is, only to be told that they are welcome to come back tomorrow at so and so o'clock. Broken hearted, they will have to wait before they can glimpse the Yángguāng stone nestled in the grass on The Backs. Finally, through the hubbub, Elizabeth spots Susan disappearing inside the Chapel and so decides to follow. Gargoyles above catching the last rays on the roof of this iconic building.

Susan, now pallid, is finding it hard to continue down the aisle. Light streams in through the door behind her and sparkles like a kaleidoscope through stained glass. The choir reaches a crescendo. Susan has now made it to the imposing but completely silent organ and within touching distance of the choirmaster only to collapse at his feet, unable to make that last important part of her journey, Rebecca, not twenty feet away, out of her grasp. The choir continues for not more than a few notes when someone screams.

Elizabeth walks up the steps as the singing ceases and reaches the first line of pews as a few people cluster around in a panic. She rushes towards the commotion and sees Susan, the choirmaster kneeling beside her. Still conscious, Susan looks with horror at Elizabeth and tries to say something, but nothing will come out. She grabs Elizabeth's arm and points at Rebecca. She breathes a sharp intake of air and starts convulsing against the stone floor. Susan slips from Elizabeth's arm, the pain in her stomach excruciating, her neck and head twisting in agony. Beads of sweat on her forehead cover a lobster hue in her cheeks. Her face contorts into a horrific, ugly shape, and she grabs Elizabeth's jaw with a claw-like hand. She won't let go and draws Elizabeth closer to her. She tries to whisper one more time, but again nothing comes out. Elizabeth counter-intuitively leans into Susan's ear and finally hears a whisper.

"Becca," Susan manages to puff out the sound, "Becca."

Elizabeth looks up at Rebecca, who is looking back in horror.

"Has Rebecca done this to you?" Elizabeth looks back down to Susan, but Susan is dead. Petrified, her face shows extreme pain, her eyes pleading for it to stop. Elizabeth covers Susan's eyes. She spots Godric next to Rebecca and wishes he would not get so close to a woman who might be a murderer.

30
WHOSE BABY?

Police tape off a section of Chapel and usher people away from where Susan's dead body has already been covered in a white sheet by a SOCO. Outside, choir members form a line tailing into a hastily erected statement tent on Ramn's court. Inspector Abley walks over to Elizabeth, still in the Chapel.

"Bit of a habit, you being at the scene of a crime, isn't it? Was she alive as well?"

Elizabeth nods, aware of the irony. "Perfect timing, and what are you doing here, really?"

Elizabeth stares appreciatively at the perpendicular architecture and fan vault ceiling, knowing it took over a century to build.

"At last, I hear you admit these deaths are not accidental. I'm here because Godric sings in the choir." Elizabeth is not willing to share information about Susan's call with Abley while he's in this mood.

"I'll hazard a guess there are no stab wounds." Abley is of the opinion that these deaths are both related, and he now has a serious murder inquiry on his hands. One that doesn't come around every day, thankfully. Elizabeth spots Dr Eruna in a pew. She points him out to the Inspector.

"Do you know who that is?"

"Should I?"

"Dr Eruna."

"Dr Eruna?"

"Labzuu. Knew Edward. I did tell you. There's something not right there. He's not in the choir, not at this college currently. So you should be more interested in what he's doing here, sitting there." Elizabeth thinks it very odd. Dr Eruna isn't even in the queue to give a statement but seems lost in his thoughts, fiddling with a prayer book.

"Let's arrest him too then," Inspector Abley sarcastically retorts.

"I'm just saying, I think he's always in the wrong place at the wrong time."

"Bit like you, you mean? Look Elizabeth. Please stay out of this."

Elizabeth can't articulate her frustration with Inspector Abley right now, as she can't bring herself to share her concerns over what Susan was going to tell her, but instead is letting her mind try to connect Susan to Dr Eruna. Could it be Bene't's, were they both students together? What vendetta does Dr Eruna possibly have over Edward and now Susan? She ends her conversation with Inspector Abley.

"Haven't you got people you should be questioning? I think you should add him to the list. That's all I'm saying."

Abley knows she's not telling him everything, and he doesn't like it, but is interrupted by Godric joining them, having been one of the first ushered through police questioning.

"Are you okay Bunny? I didn't know you were coming."

"Ahem, she was watching you sing, apparently."

Abley looks at Elizabeth, so she hasn't told him what she was really doing here. He'll deal with her later. Unconvincingly, Elizabeth tries to cover her tracks.

"Yes, you know how I like to listen to you, Goddy." Godric's reaction gives her away to the Inspector.

"Just mind you go home safely now. Excuse me." Abley walks back to his pathologist, who has arrived to join the existing SOCO investigations.

Elizabeth looks over to Susan's dead body and confesses to Godric, her new assistant.

"She called me. Just before this. She was hurried, rushed, not finishing her sentences, but adamant that I must meet her here."

"Crumbs, that's awful. Why did she want to meet you?"

"I don't know. She didn't say. She was going to tell Rebecca something as well, she said. And she suggested here at Bene't's. Maybe she thought it would be easy for Rebecca to meet here?"

"But Susan and Rebecca hated each other, you said."

"Apparently they did. As Susan was dying, she pointed at Rebecca and whispered her name. Did you see Rebecca's face? Terrified. Like someone about to be found out."

"What?"

Godric tries to process Rebecca being guilty of anything. She's such a frail and delicate creature. Godric then spots Dr Eruna and pulls at his nanna's cuff.

"Look, there's that man from Labzuu."

Elizabeth and Godric head for Dr Eruna but spot the Dean looking flustered walking towards him too. Elizabeth pulls Godric into a pew to get closer to Dr Eruna, to see if she can hear what they say. Godric is bemused.

"Ooh, cloak and dagger, I like it. Are we going to jump him?"

"Shh. Just pretend to talk to me, quietly."

Professor Flint is not pleased to see Dr Eruna here.

"When are you going to give me the space to write this thing?"

Dr Eruna smiles and stares at the stained glass windows.

"I heard the singing and popped in. You were unavailable, even though I could hear you behind your door. Isn't the light pouring in from these windows just magnificent?"

Flint won't be drawn by Dr Eruna's false pleasantries.

"You should go."

"You have to get the report out now. Finish it." Eruna insists, then more thoughtful, adds, "I kissed her once you know, after a common room bash. Something about her poetic melancholy. Made me feel sorry for her. Not afterwards though. She was a terrible kisser, and like a lost puppy always following me everywhere, until she started seeing old Eddie boy. Why do you think she died? Murder?"

Professor Flint's vein throbs in his forehead as the pressure is too much.

"How the hell do I know?"

"I'm paying you a fortune, and you're dragging your heels. We had an agreement, and I don't want to be disappointed."

Elizabeth gets up, encouraging Godric to leave with her, but Godric is still too interested and won't budge. Out of the corner of his eye, Dr Eruna is thrown as he sees Elizabeth Green pulling at a young man, clearly both having been eavesdropping. Elizabeth shrugs, acknowledging she heard everything. Godric gets up and then stops to talk to some of his friends in the choir, while still keeping one eye on Dr Eruna, as Elizabeth heads for the door.

Outside people are still milling. The queue has gone down by the incident tent. Two police cars are parked on Ramn's court gravel. Jonathan stands in the middle of the lawn, stroking Rebecca's hair and hugging her tightly as

203

she clings to his arms.

"I'm glad she's dead," Rebecca confesses to her brother.

"Rebecca darling. It's okay. Oh God, what now?" Jonathan has seen Elizabeth appear from the Chapel door and head in their direction. Rebecca looks around and smiles a little as Elizabeth approaches across the path.

"Hello, Rebecca."

"Hello."

Jonathan tries to stop the conversation.

"Whatever it is, we don't want to talk. Thank you."

But Elizabeth is undeterred.

"I just wanted to ask you, Rebecca, did Susan call you earlier by any chance?"

Jonathan answers for his sister.

"Of course not. What are you thinking? She was a hateful woman. And now she's dead. Good riddance I say. She gave Rebecca nothing but grief."

Elizabeth thinks this is a bit strong, wishing someone dead. Surely he doesn't mean to have gone so far. What is he hiding? Is it that he's just protecting his sister? And how does that relate to Dr Eruna? Elizabeth is sure he has something to do with all of this. Kara comes to join Rebecca and Jonathan.

"Where have you been?" Jonathan fusses.

"Just parking the car, Darling."

Elizabeth ignores Jonathan and continues.

"Rebecca, Susan telephoned me and told me she wanted to meet us both here – to tell us something."

Jonathan's hackles are up.

"Will you–"

But Rebecca interrupts her brother.

"No, I didn't hear from her. She didn't call me." Rebecca genuinely looks surprised at Elizabeth. Then nodding towards her brother and Kara says, "They wanted to take me back to their house. But I heard the music and simply had to sing. Godric held my hand, Elizabeth. I had no idea he was your grandson. We have been singing together now for two whole terms. He's very talented."

"He shares your opinion, Rebecca. I'm just wondering why she told me that she wanted to catch you and have me here too?"

Elizabeth searches Rebecca's face. Either she is a terrific actress or Rebecca doesn't know what Susan wanted to talk about. This reminds her of someone else she doubted, and now she's dead. Jonathan steps in again to protect his sister.

"Can't you see she's in shock? Do you have to hound us all the time?"

Elizabeth is curious. How come Jonathan is here now, just after the death? He doesn't sing and had left Rebecca in college.

"Odd coincidence that you're here straight after Susan dies. I didn't see you in the Chapel."

"What are you insinuating? We came back for my sister. I told you. That woman was nothing but trouble and nothing to do with my sister or Edward."

"No. It's all right Jonathan. Why lie about it anymore?" Rebecca is keen to unburden herself.

"Lie?" asks Elizabeth.

"I know what she was going to say. That he was going to leave me. I knew that already."

Jonathan turns to his sister and holds her hand.

"Rebecca."

"No, it's okay. Why keep it a secret anymore. He's dead and now so is she. Susan sent me Edward's love letters to her. She'd hand delivered them to the college. The Porter brought them up to me, all tied in a bow."

"When?"

"Earlier today I think. He swore undying love to her in them that it had always been her," Rebecca pauses, "that he never loved me, but married me when she had rejected him. That he'd always wanted children and so he thought he was doing the right thing marrying me."

205

Elizabeth looks at the anguish on Rebecca's face, at the sympathy and shock in both Kara's and Jonathan's eyes, but can't help herself and pushes a little for more facts.

"And they definitely came after he died?"

"Yes, wrapped up in a box. Not sure when they had been delivered though, they might have been at the Porters' Lodge for a bit I guess. He'd written to her on every trip he'd taken... even his last. But there was one missing, number thirteen."

Elizabeth ponders.

"Perhaps he was superstitious. You really didn't know before, about the two of them?"

"No. He seemed okay in the morning. Kissed me, told me he loved me. I didn't have a clue."

Rebecca's face creases. "Probably for the best or I would have killed them both."

The comment lingers in all their minds. Kara interrupts.

"Come on. Let's get you home, to rest. Out of this dreadful college."

"The police want me to make a statement." Rebecca resists Kara's arm.

"They can come to us at the house. You need to lie down. You're shivering." Kara continues to coax Rebecca to move. Jonathan agrees, looking earnestly at Rebecca.

"I will be back tonight, I promise. Kat will stay with you until then." He kisses his sister and looks at Kara to take control.

The three of them watch Jonathan leave the court as Godric walks up to them and smiles at Rebecca.

"I'm so sorry, Rebecca," he says, touching her arm.

"I'm not. I hated her."

"I'm sure you didn't hate her."

"I'm really sure, and I'm pleased she's dead."

Even Godric, who isn't easily phased, is shocked by Rebecca's words.

"Will you drive me to Kat's? She's driving me crazy with her sympathy."

Godric looks at his nanna, and she nods. He smiles awkwardly at Kara who is still standing next to Rebecca. Elizabeth spots an opportunity.

"You can pop back for the Talbot if Rebecca doesn't mind waiting here with me for a few minutes?"

"Don't you have your bike?" Then Godric realises that Elizabeth wants to come to Kara's.

"Oh, yes good idea." And then to Kara, "Shall we see you there, Kara? Or do you need a lift too?"

Kara smiles,

"That's okay. I'd better take our car back. But thank you. And just call me Kat, everyone else does."

"We'll take good care of Rebecca, Kat. Pleased to meet you. I'm Godric."

Kara smiles and heads off as Godric looks at his nanna.

"What are you waiting for, Godric?"

"Oh, yes, right. Back in a tick."

31
THE GARDEN

"Just try to keep my name out of the papers, if they call. She may well have been an ex-lover, but what has that got to do with my sister? And tell the Chief Whip, yes, I'll be able to keep a lid on it. It won't get any bigger. How can it? No, don't tell him that." Jonathan Smythe-Jones kills the call to his assistant at Westminster, as he sits on a London King's Cross direct train in the First Class carriage waiting for it to leave the Cambridge railway station. It will get him into his office quicker than the car, and for once he is grateful for the time to shut his eyes.

A strong coffee and a flapjack perch on the carriage table. He faces an elderly woman, who smiles at him and says his flapjack looks nice. What is it about women? Why can't they keep their thoughts to themselves? He has a nightmarish thought where there is just him and millions of Professor Green's in the world, all interfering and bickering, poking and prodding him. He opens his eyes and looks out the window as the train starts to move. He wonders if Kara knows about the money from Edward what else might she know? It was hard to keep everything from her, and he worried now that this marriage might be spoiled from the start. Jonathan decides to make another call.

"Hello, Katie?" Jonathan listens for some time, then replies, "I need some fun back in my life. It's all work, work, work. Yes, let's meet later. I can't wait to see everything you've got to show me. Ha, ha. Yes. Bring the expensive champagne, let's have some fun. Don't tell my fiancée. Ta, ta for now."

The elderly lady now glares at Jonathan, disapproving of his liberal ways.

*

Everything was lush in the hedgerows on the drive to Ely and Kara's house. Having back seat driven Godric all the way in Gerald's Talbot Lago T150C Cabriolet, the three of them all squished in the front, Elizabeth has now left him to stretch his legs with Rebecca down the bottom of Kara's orchard. Elizabeth is observing the pretty borders packed with hollyhocks, foxgloves, roses and daisies. Swifts are on the wing and bees still out searching for an evening drink. Rebecca and Godric share glances at each other over the shock of what has just happened at choir practice.

"Oh, Godric. This is all... I'm not sure I have the strength for it."

Godric smiles, entirely out of his depth with Rebecca.

"It's all very sad."

Rebecca continues, wanting to share with him the feelings building up inside her, of hurt, of anger and now shock.

"I did want her dead, the viper. And now she's gone. She can't hurt me anymore. Does that make me a bad person?"

Godric wonders what is behind her watery eyes.

"You could never be a bad person, Rebecca. You're

too pretty. Pretty people are immune to horridness. I love your dress." He touches the delicate fabric, wondering what it feels like against her body.

"You won't let anyone hurt me, will you, Godric? You will protect me."

Godric is finding this all a bit odd. They know each other from choir, but she is being overly familiar in a most unwelcome way. He puts it down to grief. Then again, maybe he encourages it too. He's always friendly to strangers and still gets himself into corners he can't get out of.

"Who's going to hurt you?"

Rebecca looks around then kisses Godric on the lips, and they stare at each other. Godric is horrified and gently holds her arms to stop her doing it again. She pulls back and starts walking away.

"Rebecca."

Rebecca stops when she gets to Elizabeth, who notices some beautiful hollyhocks and starts a conversation.

"Super flowers. It must be lovely out here in the country. You can't hear all the traffic. I wouldn't swap my garden for the world, but the city does intrude somewhat. And the police haven't helped, traipsing all their muddy boots up and down my lawn. They're still there you know. I can't fault them on thoroughness. But they haven't caught the thief of my grapes either. Still being taken right under their noses."

"I hate gardens." Rebecca isn't sure she wants to stay with Elizabeth, but Elizabeth holds the conversation.

"Flowers are so cheering though. The vivid poppies, their petals like paper. This one, called Lady Diana, isn't easy to grow. How beautifully delicate and fragile it is."

Rebecca picks the poppy and then pulls out the petals and crushes them in her hands.

"Susan has a lot to answer for." Rebecca scrunches up her face.

Elizabeth tries hard to ignore the plant vandalism she

has just witnessed, yet can't help herself think a little less of Rebecca for it.

"It must have been a shock to learn that Susan was also carrying Edward's baby?" Elizabeth pauses. She can see that this information has knocked Rebecca for six, and feels just a little bit less empathy due to the poppy massacre. Elizabeth continues, "That must have come as some surprise?"

Rebecca starts to visibly shake, then feels her knees go and reaches for a garden chair and falls back into it.

Kara arrives with refreshments, and Godric joins them, nervously perching on a chair a little way back from the table. Both he and Kara have heard Elizabeth's question and are looking at Rebecca for a response. But it doesn't come. Rebecca stares wide-eyed into the distance, not listening to a word anyone else is saying. She then slowly closes her eyes, trying to block out the truth. Kara tries to continue as if nothing is happening.

"Let's drink tea. Godric, I have a beer for you. I love how the English always drink tea when there is a stressful situation. I do believe it works. Professor Green, do you take sugar?"

Then suddenly, Rebecca opens her eyes and blurts out,

"Did you know I can't have children, did my brother tell you that?"

There is a momentary pause around the table. Kara, Godric and Elizabeth all digest Rebecca's words. Elizabeth is quite surprised, replying,

"But your pregnancy?"

Rebecca remains silent, as before she continues to stare into the distance, seemingly at nothing.

Kara speaks on behalf of Rebecca.

"There is no baby, Professor. Rebecca and Edward have tried since before they were married. The doctor confirmed that they are unable to conceive."

There is a pause. Godric looks most awkward and tries to change the subject.

"This beer is lovely. Bunny, would you like to split it?"

Elizabeth nods and takes Godric's glass, while Godric keeps the remains in the bottle. He knows she doesn't drink ordinary tea, just peppermint. Rebecca turns to Elizabeth, with utter horror on her face.

"I bet you have lots of children. I bet you're a good mother. You look like a good mother. Kind eyes. Good family, handsome grandson." Godric blushes and now truly wishes he was elsewhere. Rebecca continues, "I would've been a good mother. That bitch would have been a slutty mother. But her poor baby. Edward's baby. I could have looked after the baby. Did it die with Susan?" Slowly tears start to fall on Rebecca's cheek, joined by quiet sobs. Kara makes to hold Rebecca's hand.

"Come on Rebecca, darling. Don't upset yourself. There, there, darling. No use crying over that now. Try to put it out of your mind."

Then as if a wind crosses Rebecca's face, her soft tears are replaced by a hardened scowl.

"Dirty, slutty bitch. She would never have been a good mother. But, my Edward. He's not a bad man for being duped by her. Vixen."

Kara becomes apologetic to Godric and Elizabeth, perturbed by Rebecca's honesty.

"Rebecca doesn't mean it, do you? It's the shock." Kara smiles at Elizabeth, who raises her eyebrows and looks at the flowers in a nearby border.

Elizabeth is running over in her mind whether Rebecca could have killed Susan. She had the motive, but surely that would have meant killing her own husband and Elizabeth didn't think she was capable of that, though a woman scorned. Maybe she was wrong. While Elizabeth had waited for Godric and the Talbot to pick her up earlier to bring her here with Rebecca, she had popped into the Porters' Lodge to see if Susan had contacted Rebecca and if Rebecca had been lying. There was a recorded call from Susan to Rebecca's rooms before the Chapel, and the porter remembered telling Susan that Rebecca was at choir. She had left a message, and it was in Rebecca's pigeon hole. It just said 'Call me'.

Kara gets up to fetch some cakes, fussing that sugar might be good for everyone. Elizabeth stands and offers to help. As she walks into the house, Elizabeth spots an ornate box, quite large, open on the sofa with bits and pieces in white and creams, flowers and cards. Kara sees her looking.

"My plans. They have taken a bit of a backseat over the past couple of days. We're supposed to marry soon. But Jonathan won't let me plan the wedding, just some party favours and the dresses. He's taking care of the rest."

Elizabeth thinks the murders might put a damp feeling on anyone's wedding, and can't believe how stoic Kara is being.

"What do you think it was that Susan Bunt wanted to tell Rebecca, Kara?"

Kara replies to Elizabeth.

"I didn't know Susan, so I don't know, I'm sure. Sorry."

Godric glances back up at the house and can see his nanna coming back out. He picks up a croquet mallet.

"Come on Rebecca. I'll give you a game."

Having given a plate of cakes to Elizabeth to take to the table, Kara starts to walk away from Elizabeth and back towards Godric and the croquet.

"Wait for me. I love this. Such an English game, isn't it?"

Elizabeth is weary of these companions, who have no idea how to host tea. How can she be carrying the cakes right now? That is not a guest's job.

"Croquet may have come over from France with Charles II, or indeed from Ireland," Elizabeth says to herself huffily, as she watches Rebecca in a tizzy throw a ball into the flower borders, knocking out some more beautiful blooms.

*

Elizabeth arrives home later that evening, and is greeted by piles of cat sick everywhere and a sorry looking Bertie. It appears he has thrown up his entire dinner. Poor Bertie. She puts down fresh water, and he sits over it, like an individual deeply regretting having eaten so ravenously. The smell is so strong that Elizabeth opens the French terrace doors. The police tape is still over the garden but – aside from the police officer parked up in a car in front of her house – the garden is now empty of SOCOs. She notices her greenhouse and wanders over to take a look. The door remains locked, so she turns the key, which she took care to remove last time and add to her back door key chain, something she has never had to do in the past.

Curiously, despite the lock, more grapes are missing. She must find time to listen to the tape recording from the Dictaphone, to hear who is stealing them. Elizabeth walks around the front of the house and taps on the window of the police car.

"You say you are a policeman, and this is the scene of a crime, yes?"

"Er, yes Madam."

"Then what are you going to do about the theft of my prize grapes?"

The police officer looks bemused as Elizabeth's beady eyes stare back at him.

32
BACK IN THE GAME

'There is no great genius without a mixture of madness.'
Aristotle

Beside the River Cam, the first punts are being untied from their shackles at Mill Pond on this fine Wednesday morning. Nonchalant chauffeurs chatting with cappuccinos in hand, wipe down the seats before placing cushions and blankets back aboard. At The Anchor pub, the landlord steps out from French doors to hang beer mats over chairs and open parasols to burn off dew. Up on Queen's Bridge, a sweeper vehicle does a doughnut around an old telephone box, catching last night's takeaway polystyrene and cola bottles. Cyclists shoot along Silver Street, dicing with death against the snake of commuter cars to make it to their departments for first lectures.

A young graduate is sprawled out on her coat on the grass at Sheep's Green, reading the morning newspaper. From her vantage point, if she had looked up at Granta

College directly in front of the river, instead of being absorbed by the headlines of death and destruction, she would have noticed a window with light flooding in, illuminating an early supervision taking place. She would also have spotted a tall man with a friendly manner closing Granta College gate behind him, crunching over gravel and across a small garden to climb outside steps to reach the same rooms. But she continues to read, turning the page in her paper to page two, as the headline has made her want to read on. It is about a politician's personal grief following the possible murder of his brother-in-law, and how despite this he feels it is his public duty to continue to toil for Queen and country, should he be picked in the upcoming Cabinet reshuffle. There is a photo of him looking sad and next to it he is quoted as saying that death comes to us all and when it does it is tragic, and he thanks everyone for their support. The graduate thinks how sad it is the academic died, but what a slimy right-wing wanker he had as a relative, then turns the page to read a fashion article about how yellow is the new black this summer.

In the meantime, the tall man with a friendly manner has made it up the steps to the college rooms which overlook the river. He stops at a door then knocks for Elizabeth.

"Come in."

Poking his head around the door, he says,

"Sorry. I was hoping to have a word."

"That's fine. We're just finishing, Inspector." Elizabeth turns to the student who is just getting up from a chair, having finished his tutorial. "I want you to have another stab at that essay. By next week, okay? And when I mean stab I don't mean with a javelin, I mean with those things inside your head called neurons, brain cells, grey matter. Capeesh?" The student nods, a bit disappointed in having to repeat the work. "Come on MacKenzie, think about the exotic species transfer in ship ballast water, and other avenues you've completely overlooked. What about small-island hopping through tourism?" Putting a finger to her head. "Try this time. I know it's in there."

Elizabeth ushers Mackenzie out as Inspector Abley walks past him and enters Elizabeth's college rooms. He hasn't been here for over a year and has missed the view from the window. A profusion of trees and long lawns backing down to the river, with a cluster of college punts chained up by a small bridge.

"See Inspector. I'm resting, just as you advised."

Elizabeth plonks herself down on one of two substantial comfy sofas facing each other, between them a low coffee table, with pretty photography hardback books of plants, piled up like Jenga. Abley sits opposite Elizabeth, on the other sofa and leans back, relaxing. A large bay window is wide open as Elizabeth always prefers a fresh, cold room to a stuffy, warm one. Most noticeably, the jungle of plants he remembers from before has increased in size. Tall ones, fat ones, thick ones, thin ones, ones with scary looking spikes, others with leaves like petals, on every table, on every spare space of floor. So much so that Inspector Abley feels like he's just walked into an oxygen bar.

He looks at Elizabeth's face closely. She's thinner than he remembers. A little more grey, perhaps a few more wrinkles. With all the rushing about over the past day he hasn't been able to observe her so carefully, but in this light, he also thinks how frail she looks. Yet, her piercing impatient eyes are staring straight at him. There is no mistaking that nothing has changed on the inside.

"Are you enjoying taking it easy, Liz?"

"Whatever gave you that impression?"

"There have been no fresh complaints about you. I wondered if you really have been leaving the case alone this morning for a change?"

Elizabeth knows Abley doesn't think for a minute that she has.

"I have just been quicker and smarter than my accusers.

More nimble on my feet," she smiles at him.

"Well, I have to admit, we're struggling. Despite Leedham's best efforts, he can't find what poisoned Edward. And as for Susan, she was asphyxiating, but it appears to be a symptom not the cause of death. He's saying he needs more time and wants to run more tests. But I know how this goes. We end up waiting ages for a result."

Elizabeth watches a swift build a nest in the eaves of her window.

"Leedham is thorough, Bob. You'll get the right result in the end. Better than convicting an innocent person." Elizabeth wonders what Abley wants. This isn't usual, for him to admit they are 'struggling'.

Abley replies,

"Yes, but we don't have time. This is a big case. The press are on our backs. My Superintendent is getting grief from his Chief Super."

"And you came just to tell me, after making me feel this big." Elizabeth holds her finger and thumb an inch apart. "No look, Inspector, this big." Elizabeth holds her fingers even closer and smaller, to make her point.

"Not to beat about the bush, I wondered if you'd consider coming back."

Elizabeth is stunned but doesn't move a muscle apart from shift her eyes from the window to the Inspector. Of course, she wants to come back. Of course! This is her dream, to be useful again, to be needed. But after the fuss of telling her she wasn't ready she isn't going to make this easy for Abley, and she knows he would not expect her to. One needs to maintain standards.

"You were adamant you didn't want me."

"Look, if you are going to be like that. You're all over this case, and you know it."

"You said, if I remember correctly 'it's too soon', and to 'leave the case alone'. You said it to me in my own garden and then in front of Leedham, no less. I think I can recall at least two other times where you have told me to 'butt out.'"

"Elizabeth, don't do this. I've come over here with an olive branch, and you're choosing to make it difficult."

"Ask me."

"I just did."

"Ask me properly. In fact, beg me."

"What? No, I'm not going to beg you. This isn't some weird test. This is real, Elizabeth. We have two people murdered, and we don't even know how I mean with what."

Elizabeth returns her gaze outside and sighs. She is silent and won't make eye contact with the Inspector. She's not going to ask him again, and she knows, as does he, that she holds all the cards. What a refreshing change, Elizabeth thinks to herself. She picks up a journal from the table and casually starts to leaf through it. Inspector Abley leans over, to be closer to Elizabeth's face.

"Elizabeth. Professor Green, Liz, my most annoying, most infuriating, most talented of friends," Abley smiles, "would you do me the great honour of coming back to work as an" Abley labours the word 'expert', "expert consultant on poisons for the Cambridgeshire police force?"

Elizabeth doesn't bat an eyelid, but immediately gets up from her sofa and goes to the bookshelf. She takes down an old tome, with painted illustrations of plants. She looks in the index and opens the book to a specific page.

"Abrus precatorius. The Leguminosae family. Poisoned with rosary peas, also known as bead vine, crab's eyes, love bead or," Liz pauses, "black-eyed Susan."

"What, what is it?"

"Found abrin in some remains of his vomit on the lawn. Abrin, Inspector, is a plant lectin, toxalbumin, related to ricin. Very toxic."

"So this isn't Susan we're talking about?"

"I'm talking about what killed Edward. Abrin, a

powerful toxin, Inspector."

"Did you say rosary peas, aren't they religious? What have they got to do with abrin?"

"Rosary peas have the abrin in. They are used in jewellery among other things. Look like beads? What did we find on my lawn?"

Inspector Abley puts two and two together.

"The necklace! Made of rosary peas?"

"Exactly, Bob. As you say, a necklace. They're okay if not broken, the seeds that is. The poison is inside the seed or beads in this case. Of course, idiotically, tourists wear the poison around their necks as necklaces, and indeed the beads are broken when they are threaded into a necklace as the string goes right through the centre of each seedy bead, you see?"

"I see. So Edward had bought Susan a necklace made of these scarlet poisonous beads and then was poisoned with them?"

"Exactly, Inspector. They are often woven together by locals to sell to tourists, especially in parts of Africa."

"Yes! That's what Susan said. She'd got the necklace from him that night as a present."

"They have other uses. It has been reported that the rosary pea is used by witch doctors in Africa as a poison, to leave the dead with a scared face."

The Inspector leans back in his seat and touches one of Elizabeth's plants, then thinks twice about it and pulls his hand away, wiping it on his trousers. "

So, Susan's necklace was stolen on the night of Edward's death. The necklace you gave me from your lawn by Edward was the murder weapon."

Elizabeth smiles, realising this next bit might confuse Abley, as it took her a while to work out. But before she can explain, the Inspector has run away with his thoughts and is getting it all wrong.

"So Susan poisoned Edward after he'd given her the necklace? We have the case wrapped up in five minutes after I ask you back. That must be a record! Susan murdered Edward out of some jealousy as his mistress. Then she killed herself, dramatically in the Chapel, trying to implicate Rebecca for the whole thing by pointing at her with her last breath. So we'd all think Rebecca did it, to frame her. Thank goodness you solved it. It was all getting a bit complicated."

Elizabeth has thought it all through and what he's just said makes no sense to her whatsoever. How can she correct him without revealing him for the shallow thinker he is, she wonders?

"Not so fast, Inspector. It has been niggling away at me. If Susan had poisoned Edward with the rosary peas from her necklace, what about the red marks around her neck? Why would she make such a fuss to draw our attention to the murder weapon if she did it? It doesn't make sense." The Inspector watches the punts below on the river, still confused. Elizabeth continues to explain. "It couldn't have been beads from Susan's necklace either. The poison is not that quick acting. If he'd given her the beads that night as a present, she would have had to think very quickly to put some in his food, and he would probably have started to feel ill when back at college, not before.

No, the poison didn't come from her necklace."

Abley leans back in the sofa and accepts he is as confused as ever about the beads on the necklace.

"I don't understand. You mean Susan's necklace isn't the murder weapon?"

"That's exactly what I'm saying. The necklace I found in my garden, Inspector, the one you have at the station as evidence, I am sure it had no beads missing. When I gave it to you, it was really tight. There were no gaps in the string. You'd need a few beads to poison Edward. The abrin must have been ground up in something he ate or drank, may be injected to cause multiple organ failure and in high concentrations to speed things along."

Inspector Abley thinks about The Green Magician.

"We've searched the whole of The Green Magician with a fine-toothed comb. Still shut with our men there. They've found nothing."

"You can open it right back up. You won't find anything. Anything the killer used will be long thrown away. Abrin gets you by inhibiting cellular protein synthesis, which would explain the multiple organ failure."

Abley looks a little blank, not understanding how the poison works, but not wanting to admit it. Elizabeth knows him so well, so explains it more simply.

"It stops cells from being able to make the proteins they need. Without proteins, the cells eventually die."

Abley puts on his most intelligent face.

"Of course. Makes sense."

Elizabeth continues,

"We need to find something else with abrin in."

"What if he had them in his pocket and accidentally ate them?"

"Unlikely. They don't look like food. I'll get you the report first thing tomorrow."

Abley stands up, very pleased with how things are moving apace now Elizabeth is back.

"Good to have you back on board."

Elizabeth nods the slightest acknowledgement, but cannot be doing with any sickly gratitude. They both know Elizabeth will solve this now, and he can get back to playing golf.

"I have to go and teach later, and before that I have to go back this lunchtime to see if my poor Bertie is up to eating anything. He's been right off his food. He had fresh sea bass from a chap who delivers Brancaster caught fish."

Abley realises he may be able to do something for Elizabeth.

"Does he happen to deliver to local restaurants as well as to you?"

"Yes. How do you know?"

"Because if it's the same bloke, we contacted him. He was one of the suppliers at The Green Magician. And as it turns out they had some fresh fish with signs of scumbitoxin, the stuff Leedham found in Edward's stomach."

Elizabeth is grateful for the tip. Her heart sinks though, as she'll have to throw the rest of the fish away and find a new supplier. It makes her think of home and something else on her mind.

"Well if you can solve that so quickly, can you at least find my greenhouse burglar?"

"What?"

"Someone has been stealing my grapes. I can't for the life of me catch the perpetrator. And they have been taking them from right under my nose, and the noses of your police officers who are supposed to be guarding my garden. Yet someone is coming in and taking grapes willy nilly."

"Sand, leave sand on the floor. You'll catch the prints, and it will lead you to the thief."

"Sand, hmm. I'm going to try that. At lunch. I listened to the tape recording I made to try to catch them in the crime, but all I heard was hissing, the odd boat noise on the river and a few crows cawing to each other."

Elizabeth looks at Inspector Abley and wonders if he's still unsure of her return.

"What's the matter?"

"Rebecca Wiley told me you mentioned Susan wanted to meet you both?"

"Yes. Most odd. I wonder as I said before if we shouldn't look more closely at Dr Eruna? He was in the Chapel when Susan collapsed, wasn't he."

"You really must keep me abreast of these developments. Can you assure me you will in future, now that you're part of my team?"

"Of course, Bob." Elizabeth sees the Inspector relax a little, but not completely. "Come on, was that it?"

"I'm supposed to be playing today. Captain's competition."

"Ah. What time?"

"Three o'clock. I really don't want to miss it. I could use it to work through all the clues while I play, don't you think?"

"I completely agree." Elizabeth breaks the tiniest of smiles.

"I need to get my head around the case."

"Do that. Work through until two forty-five, and then go and play. No one will complain."

"I'll be back later."

"I'm here. Lemon can call you if something happens."

"If I get a buggy I can be at the Gog clubhouse in ten, from the furthest bit of the course. It's just like a long lunch break."

Elizabeth smiles to herself. Old times.

Abley gets up, with renewed energy.

"Right, good. And as for this Dr Eruna chappy, there were a lot of people in the Chapel."

"Yes, but they were singing. I met him before; he was saying how he knew Edward at college. He was less than sympathetic about his death."

"Perhaps we should pay him a visit. See what he says to us."

"I think that would be a good idea, Bob. Do you think Rebecca and Kara need police protection?"

"We offered a man on the house, but they refused."

"And Mr Smythe-Jones?"

"Oh, I think he can protect himself. You know, he has a motive. Inherits Edward's estate apparently. Edward didn't trust Rebecca to look after herself. With Susan out of the way and no heir – we're talking millions. Do you know, Jonathan said he hadn't seen Edward in ages, but Edward called his landline the morning he got back from Africa from the department?" Elizabeth listens to the Inspector intently as he starts to walk towards the door,

"It's good to have you back. I'll wait for your toxicology report with bated breath. See you later at the station?"

Elizabeth nods. The Inspector smiles and leaves.

Elizabeth puts the book back on the shelf. Relieved at being at a college of only graduates, she builds herself up to see her next Masters' student.

"Next. Come in." A young man pokes his head around the door. Elizabeth picks up his essay and waves in the young lad.

"So, Mr Gimson, making it up again? I can sniff out a fake story at fifty paces." The student comes in and sheepishly sits down.

"I liked your essay about Heracleum mantagazzianum, giant hogweed, Gimson. Indeed now classed as an invasive species. I think perhaps a little too much fuss has been made of this particular invasive. I agree with your conclusions on management. I was particularly interested to read the part you wrote about habitat preferences and your comments that it can be found more commonly along old canal 'toad paths'. Did you study much history at school before coming to Cambridge? I wondered if you'd read about horse-drawn canal boats being pulled along towpaths pre and through the industrial revolution?" As Gimson's face sinks with shame, Elizabeth smiles a little. If Susan did not kill Edward and did not kill herself, Elizabeth must catch the person she thinks really committed the double murder before they strike again.

33
WON'T STAY A SECRET

Jonathan Smythe-Jones is in the Stranger's Bar at Westminster with the Chief Whip Jonathan's party. The Whip, a typical aristocratic politician, is so well dressed he makes Jonathan look a little shabby. Jonathan has the cheque from Edward in his hand.

"I don't think I should cash this, but d'you think he wrote a stub in his cheque book? It could look really bad for me."

The Whip, with a cut glass voice, leans into Jonathan's ear.

"The more you can keep your distance from your brother-in-law right now the better, without of course giving off an impression of coldness to the family. Do you need to spend so much time with your sister? I think your quota for the week has expired."

The Whip looks down at his phone, and hurriedly checks his emails. Jonathan stands up and paces.

"I inherit everything, you know. I just found out. Edward left it all to me. Didn't trust poor Rebecca to look after herself."

The Whip's face moves into a hard glare.

"You need to create some distance, you hear? We need to talk about the country, not your ruddy private life."

*

Kara leans over on the bed and strokes Rebecca's hair. Rebecca flinches. They have been together for a couple of hours, and no matter what Kara does to try to settle Rebecca, Rebecca is having none of it. Exasperated, Kara gives up trying to be a good relative-to-be, opens the curtains and looks out onto her garden, pleased with what she has done with it. Rebecca throws her head back down on the pillow, lost in misery. Kara, on the other hand, takes a deep breath of fresh air from the window.

"It's sunny outside. Your British weather. Make hay while the sun shines, isn't it? Why don't we go and sit on the lawn? I can make you more tea?" But Kara just watches as Rebecca grabs a pillow to mask the ache in her stomach. Kara picks up some perfume and sprays some on her chest and around the room. "You would have been a great mother. You may still. Hey, why don't you help me sort the party favours?"

Rebecca looks at Kara and sighs. Is this what it has come to, the back bedroom of her brother's house, being fussed over by Kara? Does Kara really think she wants to help with wedding details when she has just become a widow? Can she get anymore thoughtless, Rebecca wonders?

"Susan ruddy Bunt. I can't believe it."

Kara opens her wedding box and takes out a couple of sample choices, holding up two small liqueur bottles. She is much too excited about her wedding to continue to discuss Susan Bunt in some downward spiral to hell.

"Come on. I need to place an order today for either four hundred of these, or these almond and chocolate flags. Or should I get both? I can't give young people these. What do you think? Here try one. Might be a better idea than tea."

Rebecca looks at the bottles, which say 'drink me', like Alice in Wonderland, and the bags of sweets.

"Give me one of those." Rebecca opens a bottle and drinks the blackberry whisky inside. She opens Kara's box and takes out another three and puts them on her lap, opening their lids. "Are your family coming? I've not met them before."

Kara shuts the lid on the box, to stop Rebecca drinking anymore as she watches Rebecca down the three little bottles, spilling some on her chin and the duvet.

"Mum died." Kara sips her party favour.

"What about your father?" Rebecca opens the lid to the box to pull out more bottles.

Kara sneers at the thought of her father.

"Not bloody likely. I keep my distance."

Rebecca finds this puzzling. She always thought Kara must have had a good upbringing. She certainly has not ever wanted for anything.

"Isn't he supposed to give you away? I thought you wanted a traditional wedding?"

"I'd prefer absolutely anyone else to give me away. I don't need that pond life to do it."

Rebecca thinks of the perfect person.

"Edward would have given you away. He would have been perfect at that. Not for buying the party favours though. These are nice. He bought loads of toot back from Africa. I expect it included your wedding present. Had dreadful taste in gifts, didn't he? I remember that little mauve gonk he bought me back from Austria. He thought it was the best thing. It was hideous."

Kara picks up the almost empty bottles Rebecca has tossed on the duvet, which are now leaking out blackcurrant stains.

"I don't need gifts. You know me well enough for that.

All I need is your brother, Rebecca. Just a simple wedding, marrying the man I love."

Rebecca half smiles.

"And four hundred people. Get the liqueurs."

*

Mr Leedham drops his orange glasses onto the end of his nose and starts to read aloud.

"She could have committed suicide, but if she'd wanted to there are much quicker and easier ways than poisoning yourself with this concoction."

Abley chips in.

"Her house was burgled." Abley looks at Elizabeth. This is new information since this morning. Abley walks over to the whiteboard and starts writing the words 'double murder?' Elizabeth looks closely at the board and starts stating the facts.

"Susan was all set to go on holiday without Edward. She'd upgraded to First Class. Put her plants in the sink at home, ready to be there when she got back. She was pregnant and at ease with the fact. Not a woman willing to take her own life."

Abley wonders about the murderer.

"Rebecca Wiley. Surely she has a motive?"

But Elizabeth looks to Leedham for him to continue to read his report.

"Mr Leedham, if we go back to the start and retrace what you've found. Then perhaps hear me out? I have a theory."

Mr Leedham starts to read.

"It looks like Susan Bunt lost extensive fluid and there are signs of peripheral neuropathy."

Elizabeth interjects.

"And we agree that Susan Bunt died of a cardiac arrest, but she was a very fit young woman, wasn't she?"

Leedham nods.

"Yes, that truly stumped me. Despite smoking, she had a strong cardiovascular system. The symptoms don't match any one cause."

Elizabeth draws Mr Leedham to look through his orange spectacles at the microscope on the desk. Mr Leedham gazes down the eyepiece as Elizabeth speaks.

"Look at the bone marrow. I found high traces of an alkaloid," Elizabeth says. Then as Mr Leedham lifts his head, Elizabeth holds up a leaf in front of them both, from a plant she has brought in. "Would you like to check through these chemicals with me, Mr Leedham? See if we can't find traces of any?" As Abley takes a peek through the microscope himself, unsure of what he's looking at, a Sergeant pops his head through the door.

"Inspector, there has been an incident at Bene't's College. Another break in."

Abley looks at his watch. It's already eleven. Elizabeth gives Mr Leedham the leaf, as the Inspector takes hold of her shoulders and whispers.

"Glad to have you back. So she was poisoned? Is that what you are saying?"

Elizabeth nods and replies,

"If you're out looking for burglars, catch my grape thief. I can't lose any more. It's going to be a good year."

Mr Leedham is confused, but Abley shakes his head at him to ignore Elizabeth on this occasion. He wants to get this case off his desk quickly, and yet it keeps growing.

*

Jonathan is still with the Whip. They have left the Stranger's Bar and are now walking across the House of Westminster lobby. The two are very close and take a seat at the edge of the wide open room. Jonathan talks first.

"I'm going to deal with this. Make no mistake. This ends now."

"This won't stay secret forever, I agree, and I can't see

you have any choice, but don't do anything stupid."

Jonathan looks angry.

"She's driven me nuts from day one. She hangs around, turning over stones. I won't take it anymore. No, you have my word that I will put an end to it, discreetly but finally. Tonight."

Jonathan knows exactly what he has to do. He wishes there were more hours in the day, the amount of times he has been back and forth from Cambridge to London over the past days. The Whip has no sympathy for Jonathan, only interested in ensuring full party support for Government.

"Yes, well the world can be a harsh place. You know we will back you. We can't afford to lose you. But the fewer people know the truth the better. How can you join the front benches with this hanging over the party, we need your assurance you cut it out and do it quick. Do you need any help? We have people for this kind of thing."

"No, I will enjoy doing this myself, I'm a big boy. That way it can't be traced back to the party."

34
BLACK VELVET SHOES

Inspector Abley dislikes the drive from Parker's Piece and Parkside Police Station to Bene't's College. It is such a short distance as the crow flies, but with the centre of Cambridge pedestrianised many years ago, the car's not a useful mode of transport in this city anymore. His Superintendent has told him to join the twenty-first century and get a bicycle, that it has improved the city centre no end, with no pollution, peace and a more relaxed feel. Abley can't disagree. He remembers the snarl-ups from the old days, but a bicycle is not something he will entertain. He won't admit it, but he never had a bicycle as a lad, so wouldn't know where to start. Now if they brought in golf buggies that would be different. He has suggested it to one or two people, but they look at him with derision, though Mrs Abley thought it inspired and said he could run her into the shops more often.

Abley now drives up onto the forecourt at the front of Bene't's and places police ID in the car window. He turns off Radio 2, his seat vibrator and pops a mint in his mouth. The sun is shining brightly, and already after having turned off the air conditioning, he can feel it warming up. A uniformed officer comes out from the lodge entrance to meet him. Abley opens his door, and the familiar bustle of King's Parade invades his ears. A punt tout doffs his cap at Abley; they all know him well.

"What have we got here this time, Lemon?"

Lemon, a tall, lanky, young-looking Sergeant with a crooked mouth smiles at the boss he admires so much, hoping to be of assistance.

"Sir, it was reported by a Kara Anderson. She's up there now. Member of the family apparently. I can't get her to leave the scene. She's, she's very upset, sir."

Abley pats Lemon on the back and beckons him to follow. They nod at the porter dealing with a bunch of tourists, as they brush past and into the quiet calm of the court inside. Abley breathes again and looks up at the sky. He should be on his way to Gog Magog soon, and it is looking less likely. He exhales disappointment.

"Lemon, this is one of those days."

"Sir?"

"One of those days where things keep getting messier."

Lemon looks at his boss, wondering if he should reply, not knowing what to say.

Edward and Rebecca's rooms have been ransacked. Police tape is across the open door. Abley ducks underneath, along with Lemon, having put on forensic shoe guards. A uniformed SOCO is dusting the room for prints. A table overturned, paintings slashed, drawers open, sofa cushions torn, a plant from the windowsill smashed and on the floor, all the soil spilt. In the bedroom, Kara sits on the floor, a bit flustered, picking up letters as Inspector Abley walks in, followed by Lemon.

"I'm sure my Sergeant has already asked you not to touch anything, miss." Abley goes over to Kara to help her up and remove her from the room. "Might I inquire as to the nature of your being here?"

Kara drops a letter but still holds a black shoe.

"Oh, yes. Sorry. I didn't think. It's just, just so awful. I didn't want Rebecca to see all this."

"It's Miss Anderson, isn't it?"

"Just Kat. Rebecca's soon to be sister-in-law."

Kara goes to shake the Inspector's hand, but he doesn't take up her offer, not shaking hands with anyone involved in a murder inquiry. Instead, to avoid making her feel embarrassed, and already having put on a plastic glove on his way up, he reaches out for the shoe Kara is holding and takes it from her.

"Thank you. I'll take that. Soon to be Mrs Smythe-Jones?"

"We haven't quite walked down the aisle yet. You know how it is?"

"I can't say that I do. Mrs Abley, well, patience isn't her strongest quality. But then not all women are like my wife."

Kara smiles at the Inspector's transgression into his own personal domestic circumstances.

"So, might I ask the nature of your visit, Miss Anderson?"

Kara pauses, smiles then gives the Inspector the rather dull response.

"I was coming to get some more of Rebecca's clothes, and all this. I saw a man running down the stairs as I came up."

Kara wipes away a tear from her cheek, looking strained. Abley smiles at her and then puts the shoe down on the bed.

"Would you be able to describe this man? He might match the description of a spate of burglaries we have had recently."

Kara looks surprised and stares at the shoe.

"The man, Miss Anderson?"

"Oh, yes. I didn't see much of him. He was young, longish hair. Quite an athletic build."

Abley looks at Kara straight in the eye and smiles again.

"Perhaps you can come down to the station when you get the chance to give us some more details."

"Yes, of course. But I don't remember anything else. It's just so upsetting for poor Rebecca. Do we have to tell her? I think it will positively tip her over the edge, Inspector."

"Yes, we'll have to tell her. Are you two close?" Abley asks Kara.

"Very. She sees this place as all that is keeping her near to Edward. Feels like she's being made to move on too quickly, coming to stay with us." Kara picks up the other black velvet shoe from the pair, the bows have been torn, and a buckle is broken. "Luckily we'd taken most of her things over to our house already. Most of this is just Edward's belongings and a few items of Rebecca's she would no doubt have brought over in time."

"Please don't touch anything else, miss. Have you been with Rebecca at all today?" Abley takes the other shoe.

"Yes."

"So you left her at your house while you came over here. She couldn't have come over here herself?"

Kara sees what the Inspector is getting at. Could Rebecca have made it over here to even do this herself?

"I don't think she would have had time, Inspector, do you?"

Abley places the other shoe on the bed.

"Were these her favourites?"

"No, I don't think so. Jonathan bought them for her actually, but she never wore them much. I think they are rather pretty, don't you? Don't worry. I'm not about to touch them again. Just if someone had bought me shoes like this, I think I would have worn them."

Abley thinks Kara looks far too sad to continue the conversation and anyway he wants to get out of here to play his round at the Gog-Magog golf course. He hasn't got time to be talking about shoes.

"Right, well. Thank you, Miss Anderson. If you can see yourself out, I need to talk to my Sergeant."

Kara nods looks around and then leaves. Abley returns to Lemon, who is talking to the SOCO in the drawing room.

"Lemon, let me know if you find anything interesting. Can you brush a pair of black velvet shoes for prints and do a DNA? They were broken. Who burgles a flat and breaks shoes?"

"I know sir, you're right. It's a bit iffy." Lemon looks at the shoes.

"Iffy?" Abley looks at Lemon, who shrugs. Abley then watches Kara leave the court from the window, sighs and then starts to walk down the steps himself.

35
PLANT SCIENCE

Elizabeth enters the Downing Site of the university. The pseudo rhombicuboctahedron shaped sundial casts shadows in the courtyard. Edwardian architecture looms down on Elizabeth's pinched frame while she climbs the steps to the imposing double oak doors, which allow entry to the Botany Building. At the Department of Plant Sciences reception, the office secretary is eating sandwiches at her desk.

"Hello, Professor Green. Not seen much of you this week."

Elizabeth has known the receptionist for many years.

"Hello, Mrs Howcroft. How are we today?"

"Mustn't grumble, Professor Green. Mustn't grumble, although my leg is playing up something rotten this morning. This damp weather."

"Damp?"

Elizabeth looks out the window onto the pure blue sky.

"Yes, the late spring fen mists play havoc with me hip." Mrs Howcroft says. Elizabeth smiles inwardly at this hypochondriac. She is as regular as the sundial outside. Glass always half empty, always with a tale of woe.

"The south of France we are not, though we can't complain, Mrs Howcroft."

"Eh? I think you're the only one here now. Don't forget. It's Dr Grant's fiftieth birthday lunch today."

"Yes, I was coming in for—"

Not listening, Mrs Howcroft interrupts.

"They've taken him for an Italian in that new trattoria on St Andrew's Street, The San Gimignano, supposed to be nice. Left me handling the phones in the department. I don't mind. Not with my intolerances. I couldn't have eaten anything on the menu. It's all wheat and dairy, isn't it? I'm more of your raw macrobiotic. You could catch them if you hurry."

"Thank you. I may give it a swerve today. I have rather a lot on."

Elizabeth notices Edward's keys are back in their place in the key cupboard behind Mrs Howcroft's left shoulder.

"Are those Dr Wiley's keys? Have the police gone?"

Elizabeth looks at the name below the keys. Searching his room might turn up something. Mrs Howcroft glances at the keys then back at her computer.

"Yes, they were in again this morning. They've taken his computer but came back to go through his papers, looking for clues one of them said. I don't know what they were expecting to find. Hardly James Bond in here, is it Professor? Terrible thing though. Such a nice young man."

Mrs Howcroft adjusts her collection of free toys from insurance companies, which are lined up beside her computer. Elizabeth thinks on her feet.

"You know, Dr Wiley borrowed a book of mine, Poisonous legumes of the British Isles, and now I need it. I don't suppose for a minute he'd mind me... I'll take these and have a quick look if it is up in his room."

Elizabeth goes through the door into the little office cubicle, reaches behind Mrs Howcroft's head to take

Edward's keys.

"I'm not sure the police would approve of you doing that."

Elizabeth has an effective rebuff to Mrs Howcroft's concerns.

"As a matter of fact, I'm working as a consultant for the police again, Mrs Howcroft. That's where I've been this morning. Working on this case. Very interesting. Very exciting indeed. I wasn't going to tell anyone, so I know you can keep a secret. I shouldn't suppose they'd mind one of their own popping over the boundary, would you?"

Mrs Howcroft's face lights up, excited to be in on this new development, ahead of anyone else in the department. Wait until she tells the others.

"Oh, well. I suppose that's all right then. Things will get a little more lively around here again. How lovely!" Mrs Howcroft smiles at Elizabeth as she watches her lift the keys off an old wooden fob from their hook. Elizabeth knows that by telling Mrs Howcroft, the whole department will find out about her fresh new reappointment by afternoon break, but she didn't care. Coming back to the force as an expert advisor was still buzzing around in her head, even if her head felt like cotton wool from lack of sleep. She feels smug and is pleased with Mrs Howcroft's reaction. It would indeed get lively again.

"Like you say, Edward was such a nice man. I'm sure he would've wanted to return the book to me. I'll bring the keys down on the way out, Mrs Howcroft."

Elizabeth smiles and walks out through the old hall and up the stairs. Mrs Howcroft goes back to eating her sandwich and reading the local paper. The headline reads 'Second Don dies in Cambridge choral calamity'. She begins to cut out the news and pin it to her collection board, full of Cambridge trivia, next to an article about bat punting tours run by a local firm, with pictures of bats flying over a crowd of tourists drinking champagne and laughing.

Elizabeth peers into Edward's modest departmental study, now devoid of life and ambition. A square line of dust and just a stray mouse mat where the computer once sat. Drawers now emptied, a couple left hanging open in the age-old wooden desk. She casts her eye along packed shelves covering two walls and brushes her fingertips along the rows of books. It doesn't take long to find what she said he had borrowed. She wasn't lying, but it was a handy excuse.

Then she notices a section on the shelf on Kenya, and a book poking out a little more than the others. It is on the anthropological history of plants. Opening it, she finds an envelope between the pages and takes out a letter. Paper-clipped to the pages inside are a few creased pieces of coloured A4 paper and photographs of local people, walking out of what looks like a large white marquee in the middle of nowhere. She flicks through them quickly to see graphs and spreadsheets. Using a tissue she wipes the dust as best she can from the desk where the computer must have been resting, and then sits down to read the letter. Facing the window, she reads on.

"Dear Percival,

I trust this letter finds you in good health. It has been sweltering this past week, hitting the high forties on occasion, making field work quite a trial if near impossible. Although I feel like a fairly fit man, it has been a bit of an ordeal. It still surprises me how night falls so quickly and without there seeming to be any dusk? As if a light is just switched off, and we are left in utter darkness all but for the stars. I digress.

You'll be relieved to know this has not inhibited me in my quest to find the materials you need to make up your mind, and I do have information about Labzuu. Take a deep breath dear fellow; it would appear your instincts were correct. No one wanted to talk about it at first. But then my travails led me to someone just outside of Nakuru, on the outskirts of Njoro. He showed me to a Kenyan research station with the Labzuu name attached.

It all looked above board until he pointed out how they were very actively conducting illegal experiments on people in the community. More specifically, on the tribesmen, women and indigenous population, as opposed to those who have relocated because of the agricultural research and industry. People have been coming and going throughout the day with many different family groups, from elderly, to the young. It would appear that they are all receiving treatment, as many have cotton wool attached to their arms with plasters if you care to observe in the photographs I attach. It is so hot that most are not wearing tops, so this is easily spotted. If you wonder whether it could just be that they are receiving HIV or Flu jabs or something useful, let me tell you I thought the same, so I did a bit more digging.

It turns out, and I saw with my own eyes, they are responding to an advertisement in a local village offering nominal sums in exchange for small blood samples. I can only imagine that this is for DNA samples, as I saw another poster in a cyber cafe in Njoro with 'Give DNA samples for a Kenyan shilling' (less than one pound sterling if you were wondering). I thought it might be that there are scientists at the Egerton University in Njoro working on this with Labzuu, but I couldn't find a link, and I doubt it. There was nothing at the university itself. I had a good look without drawing attention to it.

I have attached some evidence to substantiate. I hope this will find you and help you to make all the necessary decisions you have concerning Dr Eruna.

Your friend and faithful servant,
Ed
Dr Edward Wiley"

As Elizabeth finishes the letter, she is not surprised, but quite pleased she has the evidence she needs to take to Inspector Abley. Perhaps now he will believe her that not all is right about that man, Dr Eruna. Elizabeth begins to stand up from the chair but hasn't heard someone come into the room. They hit her full on the head. She slumps onto the desk, unconscious.

36
NO COUCH POTATO

Elizabeth rests on the sofa as Emily fusses around while a doctor quietly feels her pulse.

"I'll get too hot."

"Nonsense. If you're tucked in you can't go anywhere. Why don't you buy a decent sofa blanket? What did you do with that nice one I got for you, for picnics and things?"

"I'm not about to cover myself in wool, am I?"

"Okay, okay. Static acrylic it is then."

Inspector Abley has a bunch of flowers and is hovering behind the doctor.

"Liz, hello." The Inspector edges into the room and closer to Elizabeth. His guilt is palpable. "I can't help but feel responsible. As soon as I ask you to come back to work, this happens. I knew I shouldn't have–"

Elizabeth is having none of it. She's perfectly capable of looking after herself.

"Nonsense. This was nothing to do you with you. I was in my department for goodness' sake. Everyone else was at a birthday lunch. There was no one there. It should have been safe as houses." Elizabeth takes the flowers and rests them on Godric's back, as Godric is currently whimpering like a dog and on his knees with his arms draped around Elizabeth's legs in a completely over the top outburst of emotion.

"You could have died, Bunny."

Elizabeth rolls her eyes and pats him on the head.

"Put these in a vase, will you Goddy? They're beautiful Inspector but don't buy me flowers from the shop again. They're grown in countries which should be growing food for the local populations, and then flown thousands of air miles. A very dirty product all round."

Abley can't do right for doing wrong. He is disappointed she doesn't like them, as he spent a while choosing. How do you choose for a botanist?

"Okey-doke."

Godric sits up, and the flowers drop on the floor. There are a few minutes of commotion as he swings his torso round trying to grab at the flowers in their plastic wrap, while the Inspector bends down to retrieve them and their heads knock. Emily gives the Inspector a sympathetic look as Elizabeth busily untucks herself from the blanket. The doctor stands up, having finished putting his medical bag back together following Elizabeth's blood pressure and pulse examination. He knows Elizabeth well and speaks frankly.

"You need to go to the hospital to get a scan. I don't have the equipment here to tell you that you'll be okay. The bump looks nasty."

Elizabeth brushes aside his concerns.

"I'll do nothing of the sort. Look, I can sit up without feeling dizzy."

"Well, I have to leave. Call me if you feel sick, light-headed, or you get a pain in your head. Just call me, you stubborn thing." The doctor knows he cannot make Elizabeth do anything. She raises her eyebrows at him, but then this hurts. The doctor smiles and makes to leave. "You should go to the hospital. That's all I'm saying." The front doorbell goes, and Godric moves to answer it, while the doctor follows him out, turning for a last word before he disappears. "Call me if you need me. Goodbye." And Godric and the doctor are gone.

"You hear him, Liz? You could have concussion. He told you to go and get it checked out."

Elizabeth is impatient with everyone, including herself. She does not want all the fussing. She wishes everyone would go, apart from Godric. But even he is getting on her nerves with all his willowy behaviour.

"A lot of fuss for nothing."

"Well if you're not going to the hospital, which is silly, then you need to rest. Lie there and stay put. I can come and look after you. Cuthbert will have to fend for himself," Emily says.

Elizabeth rolls her eyes at Emily and allows her to plump her pillow and pour fresh water.

"When you hit your head, why do doctors always ask you who's the prime minister, as if you're not feeling bad enough already?"

Inspector Abley has been keeping a little distance, but now moves closer to Elizabeth.

"No point in asking if you saw anything, Liz?"

Emily is terse.

"You can ask questions later. You shouldn't have got her mixed up in all this. We all need her here and well."

Elizabeth ignores Emily entirely as if she hasn't even spoken.

"No, Bob, I don't think I saw anything. I was sitting at the desk, with my back to the door when whoever came in and did this to me."

"You shouldn't let her go off on her own. Don't you police always work in pairs?" Emily is cross at the Inspector and Elizabeth for putting herself into dangerous predicaments.

"Have you ever tried to stop her do anything? Good luck with that," Abley responds.

Elizabeth throws herself back into the sofa and puts her arm over her eyes.

"I can still hear you both."

The Inspector defends himself to Emily, now ignoring Elizabeth.

"I think Liz is more than capable of looking after herself, Emily. I do think this was a stroke of bad luck. Being in the wrong place at the wrong time."

Emily points a sharp finger at Abley.

"I blame you. I do. I'm sorry, but she is not in a proper state to be racing about."

As Elizabeth listens to Emily, she begins to realise this could make Abley change his mind over letting her help. All of a sudden she is desperate for Emily not to ruin her return to the police force.

"Emily, leave him alone won't you, for goodness sake. Be a friend and respect my wishes. I know you mean well, but I know what I'm doing, and nothing you say will stop me working again and helping Bob. It's what I want." Elizabeth then gives Inspector Abley a beady stare. "And yes, I agree. I was hit over the head because of where I was I'm sure. There must have been something in that room that the assailant wanted, and thought I was getting close."

Abley is still curious as to what the attacker must have wanted.

"But we went through all his things, twice." Inspector Abley looks at Elizabeth, but she is not about to reveal the letter just yet. She'd like to digest it first for herself. Little does he know, as he continues, "I'm asking you point blank, did you find anything, Elizabeth?"

Elizabeth looks blank, to which Emily stops the conversation in favour of rest.

"I think you should go. I don't think all this excitement is a good idea."

Elizabeth wants to make it very clear she has no

intention of resting for long.

"I'll be buggered if I'm going back to sitting and waiting for something exciting to happen in my life. I'm ruddy well involved, and it makes me feel alive. You take me off this case, and I'll hunt you down."

Inspector Abley is surprised but pleased by Elizabeth's adamant stance. He nods and smiles.

"Of course. I'll call you later to see how you're doing. Get some rest, and we can compare notes tomorrow. As for me, the first tee beckons, I'm late."

Emily rolls her eyes at Elizabeth, what did she tell her friend? As Abley leaves, Godric comes in still holding the Inspector's flowers and now also a huge lavender plant, behind which has snuck Rebecca. Abley is intrigued as to why Rebecca is here, but not enough to stop and miss his game. Emily, meanwhile, is exasperated.

"What is this, spaghetti junction?"

Elizabeth sits up again. What news does Rebecca have?

"It's all right, Emily."

Rebecca comes close to Elizabeth.

"Hello. Sorry for the intrusion, I had to come. I just wanted to ask you if you thought someone had tried to–" Rebecca doesn't know how to finish her sentence as she stares at Elizabeth.

"Kill me?"

"Was trying to stop you–"

"... from interfering?"

Rebecca leans in quite seriously, nods, and makes even Elizabeth flinch back a little. Rebecca's eyes are wide open.

"You must be more careful. And leave police work to the police. It's not safe. That's what my brother told you." Rebecca lifts her serious air. "You must come round and see me at Kat's some time. Come and sit in the garden you like so much."

Elizabeth is bewildered at how mercurial Rebecca seems.

"Thank you. We'd love to, wouldn't we Godric?"

Godric frowns at Elizabeth. He cannot think of anything he would like less. Rebecca has got the complete wrong end of the stick with him. How could she be so blind? Elizabeth raises her eyebrows at Godric, but again it hurts, and she pulls a face. Emily takes control of the new guest and ushers Rebecca out of the drawing room towards the kitchen.

"Come on. Let's put these in water and your lavender out on the terrace. You can help me put the kettle on." Godric is now alone with Elizabeth and itching to talk to her.

"What did the Inspector say about Labzuu?"

"I didn't tell him."

Godric is shocked.

"What? Why?"

Elizabeth is convinced as to the merit of her actions.

"What is there to tell? There's still no evidence. I don't have the letter, whoever hit me took it. I'm not pointing the finger. Look at what happened when I casually mentioned Susan Bunt to Abley. She's dead. I'm not bothering him anymore on Dr Eruna until I've got something."

Godric ponders whether to say the next thing, but cannot help himself.

"Did the Inspector hire you to be a detective? I thought he'd asked you back to write a report on the poisons used to kill Edward and Dr Bunt?"

Elizabeth forgives her grandson for asking a pertinent question, as she knows she is pushing it, but also knows this was always the way she worked with Abley. She would solve the puzzle. He'd get the glory. The more glory he got, the more he let her in on the process of policing and turn a blind eye. It is a grey area she has to admit, but only to herself. She is not going to admit it to Godric, that is for sure. If it got back to his mother, she would not hear the last of it.

"He's off doing what he enjoys. Everyone's happy.

Don't forget, Godric. This isn't a normal case. Edward was a colleague. So I want to do as much as I can. I think Dr Eruna is hiding something."

Godric nods, he also agrees with his nanna, after having found all those protest voices on the internet.

"Okay. Need me to drive you to Labzuu HQ up at the Science Park?"

Elizabeth is tempted. It is good having an assistant like Godric, who is so keen and quite sly. But she remembers why he is staying.

"Do you want to pass your freshman year?"

Godric is resigned to Elizabeth's words. He wants to stay in Cambridge too, it fits him like a glove, and does not want to fail, but can't face revision today.

"You know I do."

Elizabeth pulls off her blanket and drinks some water.

"Then do some revision, Godric. I see young men like you every day of the week. You can't survive on your imagination alone."

Godric though has a genius idea to avoid revision, his least favourite thing in the world.

"Someone has to take Rebecca home?"

Elizabeth thinks it a bit odd that Rebecca even knows that she has been injured. Then thinks perhaps Rebecca called for her at the department and they told her. She guesses there are reasonable explanations.

"Okay, I am going to let you take the Talbot. But only if you're very careful. And if there is a scratch on it when you get back, I will kill you myself."

Godric's eyes light up. This was more like it! He leaves Elizabeth to look for Rebecca who he finds in the kitchen making tea with Emily.

"Is your nanna okay?"

Godric grabs Rebecca.

"Let's get out of here before she changes her mind." He pulls Rebecca into the garage to the Talbot.

"I love this car. It was such a smooth ride before."

Rebecca strokes the side.

Godric grins and opens the door, ignoring her last comment.

"I didn't say, but it's my Grandpa's. He used to take it to shows up and down the country." Godric is sad for his nanna. "He died last year. Bunny stopped using it. It's, well, it's part of him. You know? That was the first time it's been out since, before, when we drove to yours."

"Kara and Jonathan's, not mine," Rebecca is quick to point out.

They get in the car, and Godric pushes a button to open the remote control garage doors. They sit waiting, so Rebecca tries to make conversation.

"What happened?"

"He was on his bicycle. So... Bunny has never forgiven this. Says it was the worst toy in the world. If he'd bought a normal car he probably would've driven to work, but this was his pride and joy, so he would use his push bike. And he was hit."

"I'm sorry."

Godric understands all too well the resonance of what he is saying, but he is not going to let it spoil the trip.

"Put this on." Godric hands Rebecca a headscarf left on the seat. Rebecca accidentally lets go of the scarf, which blows into the driveway.

Elizabeth has gotten up off the sofa and is watching them drive away. Emily comes back in from the kitchen with the flowers in a vase.

"What did I tell you? If you're not going to the hospital, then don't move."

"I'll be fine. But I feel a bit tired. Go on. You go home. I'll take a sleep. You can come back later, to check up on me before bedtime." Elizabeth smiles, she loves her friend dearly but is not about to tell her that right now she has more desire to solve this case than sit about drinking tea with her.

"If you promise to stay put. Here's the phone." Emily

ushers Elizabeth back on the sofa. "Call me if you need anything. I'm going to pop home and put on Cuthbert's dinner. Then I'm right back here. I'll bring you some. We could have it here later."

"Thank you, no. I'm fine. I'm not very hungry. Now go, go on."

Emily replies pointedly,

"I'm coming back later."

Elizabeth looks up and smiles. Emily can be pretty forceful, but she knows she can be more so. They eyeball each other as Emily drums home her concern. Elizabeth rolls her eyes.

"Why does that sound like a threat?"

As Elizabeth hears the front door bang shut and Emily's car engine startup on the road outside, she gets back up from the sofa and walks upstairs to get dressed.

37
WE NEED TO TALK

Kara pours Jonathan a glass of wine as he loosens his tie.

"I thought you were not coming back until tonight? You're much earlier than you said. I would've picked you up from the station."

"I got a cab. Those ruddy trains are packed full of arguing kids, people eating fast food, sprawling into the so-called First Class because of blinking over-crowding. I thought it would be a good idea. Never again."

Kara empties nuts into a bowl and strokes Jonathan's forehead. She is glad he is back and looks at him adoringly. Trying to soothe him after his journey, she says,

"Why don't I buy another car for us? We can have two. It makes sense. What about a fast sports car for you, so you can bomb up the M11?"

But Jonathan is having none of it. He can't decide if it is his journey or seeing Kara that has put him in a bad mood. He removes her fingers from stroking his brow and looks away at the garden through the open patio doors. He settles on the fact that it is the past three days that have made him agitated, not Kara. He can't believe the bad luck he's having. His career is about to take off, and there is a murder in the family. Tabloid heaven. It's all about damage limitation now.

"Let's not jump the gun just yet. I came up earlier than I should because I wanted to talk to you about the wedding."

Kara misunderstands. Her body noticeably relaxes, and she strokes the back of a nearby chair excitedly.

"At last. Good." She takes a large gulp of wine.

Jonathan's face does not convey a man who's excited at the prospect of getting married.

"All this noise up here isn't going unnoticed down in Westminster, Kat. There is stuff we need to talk about which changes things."

Kara pours herself another glass of wine from the pool bar. Just these last words from Jonathan have stolen her cheer.

"That sounds ominous."

Jonathan shakes his head, where to start.

"Where's Rebecca by the way?"

"I don't know. She went out."

"What?" Jonathan is furious and starts pacing. His thoughts of wedding discussions have disappeared. "I can't believe it. Can I trust you to do anything?"

The temperature rises in the room as Kara tries to defend herself.

"She insisted on going to Edward's rooms. The police told her about a break-in. I don't know where she went. I phoned the Porters' Lodge, and apparently, she left college a while ago."

Jonathan clenches his fists and screams to the ceiling,

"Aargh! Why didn't you tell me about this break-in earlier?"

"I didn't want to keep bothering you at work. I thought you'd appreciate me waiting until you got back. I was hoping the police wouldn't tell Rebecca if I'm honest, as all it did was upset her."

Jonathan glares at Kara.

"Well, that's the rest of my day gone. I'll have to go and look for her."

Kara drinks her wine far too quickly and breaks yet more bad news.

"There was a radio report about Elizabeth Green being attacked. You know, that woman you don't like?"

Jonathan laughs out loud. He can't imagine the day getting any worse for him.

"My sister is out there, and you're drinking wine?"

Kara sees Jonathan's red knuckles as he slams down his wine.

"Your hands still hurt from moving those pots?"

"Well, if you will sack the gardener. Have you found a replacement yet?"

Kara moves to sit on a sun lounger by the pool and lifts a 'weddings' magazine to read.

"Have you spoken to the wedding planner?"

"Katie? I'm not getting into all that. We need to talk first. But not before I find my sister."

Jonathan slams out of the house as Kara sips her wine, flicking through the magazine, unhappier than before.

*

Godric and Rebecca edge their way along St John's Street in slow moving traffic. Some are taking photographs of the car against the backdrop of the colleges as Godric plays up to the crowd, raising his nose in the air and tightening his white scarf, which he grabbed just before he left the house, just for show. Although he's not into Rebecca, and acutely aware she has just lost her husband – so it being wrong on all counts – he does rather like driving a pretty woman while being observed by strangers. It's so easy and yet so glamorous.

"Why did you come and see my nanna, Bex?"

"I heard she'd been hurt."

Godric doesn't believe Rebecca but lets it go.

"What do you need to pick up from college?"

"I want to go and rest there. I can't go back to Kat and Jonathan's. They're always arguing, and I don't feel safe." Rebecca looks Godric in the eye. But Godric is curious. Safe? What does she mean? It is probably the safest place for her right now, staying out of Cambridge. She can see he needs more of an explanation, so continues, "Maybe it's because I don't have Edward. I've got nowhere else to go that's close to him."

"I'm going to ask you a personal question, Bex. And you're going to answer, because you have only Godric listening, and he is positively useless at remembering things like this, so will immediately forget anyway."

"I probably won't answer." Rebecca smiles at Godric.

"How long have you known about Susan?"

"Proper chip off the old block aren't we?" Rebecca turns away in her seat and folds her arms. A couple of people walking along the pavement stroke the side of the Talbot as it sits in stationary traffic. Godric waves them away, enjoying the attention, but shouts,

"You can look but please don't touch!" then, turning to Rebecca, "why are there so many tourists? Listen, you're quite a delight. I'm sure you could have your choice of men." He notices the mildly provocative way Rebecca turns to glance at him, and this makes him wince. "Most men, I mean." He qualifies his answer. "So why didn't you leave Edward when you found out they were still together?"

"That's two questions," she replies, turning away from Godric again, this time looking ahead towards Trinity Street, careful not to make eye contact with the increasing number of people admiring the sight of them in the Talbot. Godric starts to push his foot down gently on the accelerator and they begin to move again.

"I just wondered, that's all. Women are not the only

curious creatures you know. Us men have our antenna. I don't understand it."

Rebecca continues to look straight ahead, avoiding Godric's stare.

"Have you ever been in love, Godric?"

"Only a million times a day, darling. In love with being in love. I love everything and everyone, things, inanimate objects. You name it. Not these people though. Will they stop ruddy staring. I think a few minutes of looking at us is more than enough don't you?"

As the car has had to slow again, Godric is now irritated by the tourists and shows them an arched brow. Rebecca, on the other hand, seems oblivious, wrapped up instead in thoughts of Edward.

"You can't control love. You're a slave to it. Makes everything... brighter, more sparkly. But it can destroy you. Make you do really stupid things."

Godric's interest is piqued. What does she mean... what stupid things?

"Like?" Godric asks, while moving the car off again in the stop-start traffic.

"Like murder, of course."

Godric takes his eyes off the road and studies Rebecca. Has she just admitted to killing Edward?

"Not me. Susan. I know it."

Godric then looks at the road and has to shove his foot hard on the brake, as a delivery lorry suddenly stops right in front of them. His brain processes the possible damage he could have done to the car, and what Rebecca has just said.

"But she's dead?"

Rebecca replies, "I guess she wanted to be a tragic figure. Anyway, maybe someone got her back for everything?"

"Susan was murdered, and the person is still out there. It's not her fault. Maybe we thought it was at one time. Why did you lie about the baby, sweetie pops? What's that all about?" Godric stops again behind the lorry which has decided to park up to unload, and Rebecca jumps out. She runs down the street.

"Hey! Rebecca! Rebecca!"

Godric is torn, he wants to chase her, but cannot leave the Talbot. He stays with the car as he knows what would happen if he lost it. Rebecca runs through the streets, banging into people until she gets to the corner of Silver Street and he watches her disappear behind the college walls.

"Oops," Godric says out loud. A couple of tourists smirk at his visible abandonment, and he nods an acknowledgement. "Never understood women, but cars... now that's a different matter, eh?"

38
DR ERUNA

Expecting to see his Nanna at home, Godric arrives back to a quieter than usual house. No radio, no television and Elizabeth gone.

"Bunny?"

He sees the empty sofa, blanket neatly folded, and the internet up on a laptop. Godric looks carefully at the website page left open; it is Labzuu's. He feels sick, where is she? He walks into the kitchen and then runs up the stairs, but no Elizabeth. Godric then heads out into the garden, lifting the police tape. Where has she gone? He is truly worried she left her best assistant behind, to protect her. He said he'd be on hand to help with her investigations. He also not to secretly fancies himself as a bit of a sleuth and wants to be her Watson, albeit a younger, better-looking version. Godric walks back into the kitchen. By the kettle is a note. 'Please, can you put more sand down on the floor of the greenhouse path. Don't ask why. I'll explain later. Now revise. Bunny x'. Godric smiles.

*

Elizabeth left the sofa, despite Emily's instructions, and now pedals her bicycle along Milton Road, towards the Science Park. The road is horrendously busy, and she is continuously overtaken by huge lorries, their drag wind causing her bicycle to wobble. For a moment she worries she will suffer the same fate as Gerald.

Not long after, Elizabeth walks into the glass reception of the Science Park offices of Labzuu still pushing her bicycle. A receptionist shouts,

"You can't bring that in here! You'll have to leave it outside."

"I'll do no such thing. I've had this Ridgeway for twenty years. I'm not about to let some ragamuffin steal it away from me."

"Have you got an appointment?"

"I've come to see Dr Eruna. Floor three?"

"Four. But you need an appointment."

"Thank you."

Elizabeth wheels her bicycle into the lift.

"Excuse me. You can't do that!"

Elizabeth looks up at the receptionist bemused.

"But I am doing that."

Elizabeth ascends in the lift while down in the lobby the receptionist picks up the phone. Elizabeth steps out into a huge open-plan office, with floor to ceiling windows overlooking large trees framing the border between laboratories and farmers' fields beyond. In the corner, a glass room separates Dr Eruna's office from the rest of the workers. Dr Eruna sits at a desk, just having taken a call from reception. The room is remarkably empty, just a couple of people down the far end sitting at computers with their backs to Elizabeth.

"Hello again. Professor Green, isn't it?"

Elizabeth notices how expensively Dr Eruna is dressed

and manicured. He holds out a hand for her to shake, but instead, she takes off her cycle helmet.

"You have a good memory."

Elizabeth balances her bicycle against a coat stand, which wobbles slightly.

"Are you well enough to be riding that? I heard you were hit on the head?"

Elizabeth is surprised the news has spread and perturbed by the sarcasm in Dr Eruna's voice.

"Oh that? It was nothing really."

"Would you like a drink of water?" Dr Eruna smiles creepily. Elizabeth does feel a little dizzy, probably that lift she thinks.

"Well, perhaps I could trouble you."

"You have to be careful with concussion."

The two workers at their computers turn and look at Dr Eruna, who signals for them to leave. They quietly glide out of the space so now Elizabeth and he are alone. Elizabeth's head is fuzzy. She wonders if Dr Eruna caused it.

"Sorry, how did you know again exactly?"

Dr Eruna points to the television in the corner, silent but with subtitles playing rolling news.

"Let's get you that water."

Elizabeth takes the cup and likes how it feels in her hand, so cold. As she sips, it winds her a little, and she doesn't feel herself. Dr Eruna picks up the silence.

"I'm quite surprised to see you. If it's a department visit, we don't have money to invest in botany. Priorities and all that." His ignorance riles Elizabeth.

"With millions of plants still undiscovered, Dr Eruna, where would we be without people researching this important subject?"

Dr Eruna sits back in his chair behind a huge desk.

"You're right. We must be thankful for the study of plant collecting."

Elizabeth walks towards Dr Eruna's desk. She sees a

double helix model and picks it up.

"Like playing God do you, Dr Eruna? Does it come naturally? Any exciting research in Africa?"

Dr Eruna's mood grows darker.

"When has anything we do in Africa been any of your business?"

Elizabeth manages to crush the paper double helix by accident, and puts it carefully back down, now broken.

"I find it peculiar that one man is dead after finding information about your company and trying to warn the Dean."

"Now hang on a minute. I don't like your accusation."

Elizabeth ignores him and continues, now picking up a photograph Dr Eruna has of himself on his desk, which looks like he's giving a speech.

"Edward visited Njoro. I believe you have a research station there? Does this ring any bells?"

Elizabeth stares at him, waiting for the guard to drop, for him to come clean that he knows something about Edward's death, but instead, he grabs the model from the desk that Elizabeth has accidentally broken, gets up and walks to the window.

"People are dying in illegal experiments every day. What safeguards did you put in place, and why are you not conducting them in the UK? Too dangerous?" She asks. Dr Eruna doesn't answer so she continues, walking close to him, to try to see the whites of his eyes. "Edward was concerned, wasn't he? But why was he warning the Dean about you. Why was Professor Flint so interested in your underhand activities?" She watches as Dr Eruna exhales sharply, so Elizabeth steps right up to his face. "You're not going to answer me? Simple as that? Then I'll go and talk to Professor Flint. See what he has to say."

Dr Eruna turns, his manner icy cold, throws the DNA model across the room, and in a fit of anger warns Elizabeth.

"Someone should tell you that accusing someone of

being involved in a murder has serious consequences."

Elizabeth, quite shocked by his reaction, tries to feign being unflustered.

"Well now I'm here I would appreciate you answering my question. What are you doing in Kenya?"

Dr Eruna looks straight into Elizabeth's eyes. His pupils warn her to back off.

"Be very careful about talking about what you think we may or may not be doing. Someone like yourself could easily be seen as an emotional, frail, meddling woman. Wouldn't be difficult to persuade people how you've lost your marbles and should be retired from college duties."

But Elizabeth won't be stopped. She feels a zeal rise in her against this horrid man.

"It's the things you're doing to the future we should worry about."

Dr Eruna is a little menacing and grabs her arm to try to make her sit in a chair in his office, but she pulls away.

"Someone who's had a knock on the head should be careful. Internal bleeding can start sometime after an event like that. At any moment. I think you should take a seat."

Elizabeth's heart starts to race. This was a mistake. She's in the room with a killer. She has to get out.

"No thank you. I think I'll be going if you're not going to answer me. It's a waste of my time." Elizabeth takes her bicycle and starts to head towards the lift. Dr Eruna gets hold of her arm again, and threatens,

"Don't be silly. You're looking most unwell. You need to rest for a bit. I have some medicine for that somewhere."

Elizabeth breaks free from his arm, now pressing the lift button too many times. He can see her panic.

"I'm fine. I don't need a rest, thank you, if you can just let go of me."

Elizabeth keeps hold of her bicycle. As the lift door opens, she starts to move. Dr Eruna blocks her way.

"No more questions, or trips to Bene't's. You have no

reason to go there. You have no reason to come here. Just keep away. Got it?" Dr Eruna glares firmly at Elizabeth. Elizabeth looks into Dr Eruna's angry eyes and then pushes past his arm. "Safe journey home, Professor Green, don't fall under any lorries." Dr Eruna lets go of the lift door, and it slams shut. Elizabeth takes a sharp intake of breath and keeps her nerve. She feels sick, and her heart is racing. How does he know about Gerald? Or is his threat just an unhappy coincidence?

Outside, Elizabeth looks up and can see Dr Eruna looking down at her from behind his huge floor to ceiling office window. She is about to leave the premises when she notices a supercar daubed in something, so wheels her bicycle over to take a closer look. Dr Eruna's eyes follow her to the car and he now also notices red paint still dripping down the windscreen of his Aston Martin. She looks back up at the window and sees Dr Eruna has disappeared. Elizabeth decides not to stick around.

Sometime later, by Viking's Chip Shop on Milton Road, Elizabeth is sitting under a tree, having found a safe place to rest. Her trousers torn, she's upset and tired. Emily pulls up in her Volvo estate, gets out and rushes over.

"Oh Elizabeth, are you okay? What've you been doing?" Emily finds Elizabeth with a small bag of chips and a cola drink beside her. Elizabeth has never been more pleased to see her friend and tears spike in her eyes. She pinches her hand to stop them flowing, unwilling to let Emily see her so upset.

"It was nothing. The nice man in the chip shop let me call you, and offered me a portion on the house. They're quite delicious. The chain is broken, and the nearest bike shop is a way. I hope you don't mind." Elizabeth's bravado does not convince Emily, who can see how flustered she is and wonders what on earth made Elizabeth leave home?

"Looks worse than that. You're all muddy. Your arm, is

that blood? What have you been doing? Didn't you hear a word the doctor said?"

"It's red paint, and I'm fine. I was bored. I thought some fresh air would sort me out."

With some difficulty, and moving golf clubs to make space, Emily lifts Elizabeth's bicycle into the back of her car.

"So why are you so scuffed up? And where did the paint come from?"

Elizabeth knows full well that it came from when Dr Eruna pushed her against his vandalised car.

"Oh, my trousers just got caught in the spokes as I fell. I must have brushed across some paint in the road?"

Emily now offers Elizabeth a hand and lifts her friend up.

"That's not what happened, is it."

Emily knows Elizabeth is lying and this worries her. Elizabeth is not going to bother her friend with what has just happened; she'll never be allowed to leave the house. Elizabeth is also concerned Emily could jeopardise her relationship with Abley.

"Thank you. I've never come off on this road before. It's hairy. The cars don't stop. They just drove past me."

"You could have been killed out there." Emily realises what she has said and feels mortified. Elizabeth assures her.

"Don't worry. You're right. I'm beginning to think I can't do everything myself."

Emily walks Elizabeth slowly to the car passenger door.

"Exactly. Lean on your friends and family. That's what we're here for. It's just… it will take as long as it takes to come to terms with Gerald's accident on the road. Rushing around trying to solve crimes is not doing you any good."

Emily has hit a nerve, but Elizabeth wanted to see into the black of Dr Eruna's eyes. She was right about him. He is most definitely hiding something about Africa. But Elizabeth can not afford to let Dr Eruna upset her, even if just temporarily. Rushing out of his office like that and pushing her against the paint on his car and accusing her of vandalism. It must have been what caused her to lose control of her bicycle, the shock – that and not having slept for two days, and a hit on the head perhaps. But she must get on with her investigations. She would do as Emily says and start to lean on her friends and family more.

"Emily, I need a favour."

Emily pulls out of the lay-by.

"What's this, if it's not a favour? Especially bringing the stink of those chips into my car. Couldn't you have put the leftovers outside?"

"They were very generous with the portion. You know I can't throw food away, the birds will have them. I mean another favour."

"Do I get to know what the favour is before I say yes?" Emily glances at her friend. Elizabeth flinches, exaggerating a pain in her arm. Emily sighs, jokingly, as she continues along. "Of course I'll help you. Don't I always?"

"Can you help tonight? Only I'm itching to find something out about Africa."

"If you let me drive you to the hospital first before we do whatever it is. And we must tell Godric you're okay. Here, use my mobile. You do need to get one of these."

Elizabeth nods and dials, having no intention of getting a mobile herself and never being free from the demands of other people.

"Godric? Yes, never mind all that. Yes, Emily's. I'm fine. Yes. That Dr Eruna's definitely hiding more about Africa. Can you do a bit more digging? Yes, you are officially my assistant. Thank you. Find out how Professor Flint fits into it? Yes, they're doing something in Njoro, search for that connection. What if Professor Flint's in on it? It will cause such a scandal at the college. If he knows nothing, we must warn him. See what you can find out first before we talk to him. Yes, you are the best assistant in the world." Elizabeth cuts the call to Godric. Emily drives off towards the hospital, wanting to ask Elizabeth about everything she's just said, but wanting more for her friend just to rest.

Cambridge and its inhabitants are busily going about their business. On the brow of the road, Elizabeth catches a glimpse of Midsummer Common, looking lush in the warmth of the early evening sun through the car window. Spires in the distance pierce the skyline above the flat land. A boy with a kite runs backwards across the grass, in an attempt to lift it higher into the air.

39
TWO NECKLACES

When Jonathan finally finds Rebecca, she's standing on Garret Hostel Bridge looking through the railings, in the exact spot where Edward dropped into the river. The willows kiss the river on The Backs as punts glide underneath into congested waters, full of more tourists. The sun shines into the library at Christina College and below into the Fellow's Sun Garden. Rebecca looks down at the water, the mirror reflecting back puffy clouds and sunshine as Jonathan leans over the bridge beside her and watches a swan glide underneath. Rebecca talks, almost as if to herself.

"This is our special meeting place. We had our first kiss here. I was walking towards the library for our first date. All the firsts. We were supposed to meet at the ice cream parlour further up for a walk along The Backs, only I was running late, and he'd already left the library and was a little early. Too excited to see me, he said. So we met here by accident. Edward always said it was the best view of The Backs, as you couldn't see the eyesore as you were standing on it. Maybe if we'd met at the ice cream parlour, he wouldn't be dead? He wouldn't have liked me. Seen I'm too fussy about ice cream, or something."

Jonathan interrupts and rubs her back, pulling her into him.

"I was worried sick about you. You'll put me into an early grave. Let's go and have a stiff drink." Jonathan thinks it might help numb her pain, but Rebecca isn't listening.

"He was murdered here. Someone pushed him off this bridge."

Jonathan feels nervous of what Rebecca will say next, as this is a bustling spot and people are passing continuously, stopping to take photographs with those selfie sticks he hates so much. He puts his arm around Rebecca's shoulders.

"Hey, come on now, how do you know that?"

Rebecca stops dead and looks at her brother straight in the eye.

"Didn't you know? The police found some of his shirt on these railings. They told me."

"That's not something you should dwell on now. Leave all that to their investigations. Why did they tell you that, for chrissakes? We need to think about looking after Rebecca. When was the last time you ate? We could go and get a nice pizza somewhere." Jonathan says, but Rebecca is undeterred, with madness in her eyes she is rooted to the spot.

"And a necklace, just like mine."

"A necklace? What do you mean a necklace? What necklace?" Jonathan is uneasy, where is this going? Rebecca takes out her necklace, a red and black beaded necklace. It looks identical to Susan's, identical to the one found by Elizabeth on the grass of her garden, the same one that was being kept at the police station as evidence. Rebecca holds up her necklace in front of Jonathan, perhaps a little too close to his face. This makes him frown and lean back from the swaying beads. There are only half the number of beads left on the necklace, as there is much string showing underneath.

"He gave this to me the morning he died. Then when the police asked if I had lost any jewellery in the break-in, I forgot to tell them about this."

"Oh."

"They told me they found a necklace by Edward, with red beads. Asked me if it was mine. Showed me it in a bag at the station. I wasn't registering. I'd just seen Edward's body. It didn't occur to me. He'd only given me this the morning he came back, and I didn't really look at it properly. I didn't like it. I left it on my dressing table and forgot all about it. He was always bringing me back rubbish presents from his travels. Most of them went in the bin."

"How come you've still got it? Haven't you told the police yet?" Jonathan asks. But Rebecca says nothing, so he continues with his questions. "If they found one by his body, does that mean there are two identical necklaces? And what's that got to do with his death? It must be a coincidence, surely?" But Rebecca isn't listening to her brother. She wants to tell him what is on her mind, instead.

"It took a while, but I remembered I had something with red and black beads. Then I remembered this tacky little present afterwards. Later, when I looked for it on my dresser and in all my jewellery boxes, even the locked ones with my real jewellery, it wasn't there. It was missing. I looked everywhere, and it was gone. But I just looked again today in college, and it was back, after the burglary. And it looks a little tattier, wouldn't you say? Look at all the missing beads."

Jonathan holds the necklace up to his eye.

"Maybe that's how it's supposed to look."

"No, it was definitely all beads when he gave it to me. No string showing. I haven't told the police yet. Do you think I should tell them I found it? I mean, if they have another one, that's probably important?"

Jonathan looks worried by the necklace.

"Maybe you missed it when looking the first time. Maybe it has been there all the time?"

"You can't miss this. It's so loud and garish. I looked in all the drawers. Everywhere. But it came back. Don't you think that's weird?"

"Would you like me to look after it?"

Jonathan reaches for the necklace.

"No, why would I like that?"

"Oh for goodness' sake, Rebecca, you're exasperating. I don't know. I'm trying to be a good brother. What do you want? I've come to find you, to check you're okay. You start on about necklaces. And you don't want my help!"

40
A WARNING

Inspector Abley sits on the Dean's sofa. The large window in the Professor's rooms open to The Backs, wafting in echoes of the day that reverberate gently below.

"Sherry, Inspector?"

"No thank you, Dean. I'm more of a beer man myself. I'm looking forward to a nice cold one with supper. Mrs Abley is cooking my favourite tonight, stargazy pie. Herring, cod, bass all melting into the buttery mash potato and pastry crust. It does things to me. My wife sure knows how to cook."

"That does indeed sound rather good." The Dean doesn't want to hear Abley talk of domestic bliss. It makes him homesick.

The Inspector stretches out his arms on the sofa, happy with his game this afternoon, though he did not win the cup.

"Thought I'd make a detour here on my way home you see, when I got the call, rather than let it wait until morning. My Sergeant said it sounded urgent? I was off duty, but…" The Inspector tries to cover for the fact that he's now in his golfing shorts and shirt and has a tan line across his forehead and looks a little sweaty.

"Thank you. It's quite a delicate matter. It involves someone close to you, of whom I'm also quite fond. Different colleges and all the rest of it." Professor Flint pauses, not sure where to begin. Abley can sense this and tries to put the Dean at ease.

"I'm not shy, just hit the ball and see where it lands." Inspector Abley frowns, more to himself, as he can see that the Professor seems to have the weight of the world on his shoulders, and looks particularly tired. What can be so important?

"It's just, I've, well, had a complaint made against Professor Green in college business, Inspector. Apparently, she's been," the Dean searches for the right word, "interfering with an alumni of our college, in Dr Eruna's private matters. And she has been walking through our college quite a bit, disturbing Rebecca Wiley."

Abley can't believe what he's hearing from the Dean.

"I thought Mrs Wiley had moved out to live with her brother, Dean?"

Professor Flint picks up an apple and fiddles with it, pulling off the stalk.

"Maybe so, I think she still comes and goes. But one has to ask oneself, what is Professor Green doing here?"

Abley is concerned where this conversation is going. He adjusts his shorts a little and coughs.

"What has this to do with me? And she's a Don at this university, is she not? Giving her access for 'walking through', as you put it, any college."

Professor Flint looks edgy, perspiring. Abley tries not to stare, but can't help himself. He notices beads of sweat clinging to Flint's cheeks.

"Well, yes. But, well, Dr Eruna said she has been bothering him at his offices, and didn't have an appointment. Just barged up to see him apparently. He is up at the Science Park, not a public right of way, is it."

The Inspector is less than happy with the progression of this conversation and chooses to stand up and walk nearer to the door.

"I'm sorry Professor Flint, but I can't for the life of me work out why you're telling me this? If Dr Eruna has a problem, why doesn't he go to the station? This is a serious allegation, you know.

You can't call me over here to do the dirty on someone you say you like but don't appear to show much respect for. Have you actually spoken to Professor Green?"

Flint was not expecting this. He has known the Inspector for some years now. He knows private words happen all the time. Why is Abley being so difficult?

Abley watches as Flint's eyes narrow, then listens as he tries to excuse his earlier comments.

"No. I don't have anything against the woman per se, and it may not come as a surprise, but Professor Green doesn't listen to me, Inspector. I thought she'd listen to you."

Inspector Abley smiles inside. She doesn't listen to him either. But this is more serious than that.

The Dean is accusing Elizabeth of something.

"I fail to see how this is college business at all? And Dean, I would be careful before you accuse someone of harassment, whether on behalf of someone else or not."

Professor Flint walks towards the Inspector and leans close to him.

"All right, cards on the table. Dr Eruna told me he was trying to avoid having to make an official complaint at the police station. He found paint splattered all over his car after the Professor had gone to visit him. Bright red paint. It is quite an expensive model though I know nothing about cars, and he said she was scoffing about it, gloating. And I wondered if, well, you could talk to her about it. He knows that you know her very well, and thought a quiet word might do the trick."

Abley is going to get this whole thing checked out. Tomorrow. Flint has irritated him though, and he feels a sudden urge to protect Elizabeth.

"Right, right. Well. Was that it? Accusing Professor Green of criminal damage?"

"Yes, er. Sorry. I know it is very delicate."

Abley is angry, though he tries to remain measured in speech.

"I shall have to write a report."

This makes the Dean panic. It has all gotten out of control. He thinks of the wretched paper he still has to write for Dr Eruna. Will the favours never stop?

"No, please no. Just a quiet word."

"I always find that a quiet word often does the trick too. I would, if I may, return the favour, to you, Sir." Inspector Abley leans into Percival Flint's face. "Professor Green is, as you say, a friend of mine. But she's also an associate working on a murder case. She has just told me that she did indeed visit Dr Eruna. Just before this occasion, she was hit over the head by someone."

Professor Flint had no idea, not having listened to the news, and can't hide his shock.

"Is Professor Green okay?"

Inspector Abley has had enough and opens the door, looking back around it.

"I'm not sure if you are aware of this, but despite knowing she had had a nasty blow, Dr Eruna still made threatening remarks to Professor Green this afternoon. Professor Flint, upon my word, I would seriously consider your motives reporting her to me. I shall certainly be investigating Dr Eruna's conduct. I wish you a good evening."

The Inspector leaves and his words hang heavy in Percival Flint's ears. He realises he is in too deep. Outside in the college court, the Inspector puts a call into the station.

"Is that Lemon? Lemon, can you have a dig to see what

you can find on a Dr Eruna? Yes. Dr Michael Eruna of Labzuu. Yes, the company. And let me know as well, any connections between him and the Dean of Bene't's College. Yes, you heard right. This one may go all the way to the top, son. So be careful who you speak to. Discretion please."

41
AFRICA IS WHERE IT STARTED

Emily is rather tired and not too sure about this wild goose chase. She has bowed again to her friend's dogged determination and found herself at the University Library on West Road. Recognised by its 'dark tower' and infamous and inaccurate myths of housing all the pornography in the country, it contains over seven million titles, acquiring almost every book published in the UK.

While Elizabeth nestles down at a desk poised with a reading lamp for her return, Emily walks with the librarian, who takes down a tome titled Families in Africa in 20th Century Power and Tradition. Emily blows out air at the sight of the size, before watching the librarian disappear off, light as a feather to the stairs, leaving her with this brick to carry back.

"What took you so long?"

Emily drops the book on the desk, causing it to reverberate, and ignores Elizabeth's impatience, instead dutifully reminding her friend of their promise.

"Afterwards, we go to the hospital."

"Shhh." Elizabeth points to the sign to keep quiet, as she opens the book Emily has fetched. Emily plonks herself down next to Elizabeth and whispers,

"What are we looking for?"

Elizabeth whispers back,

"Gerald always used to say Africa was where it all started."

"What started?"

"Everything. Look to plains and the huge skies as they hold the secrets of the stars."

Unsure what Elizabeth is talking about, Emily feigns interest. Elizabeth is so absorbed in the book, peering at the families and faces of those making their billions from steel, diamonds, and tantalum for electronic gadgets and mobiles. Emily meanwhile studies her friend's face. There is a depressing transparency to her obsessiveness that Emily has seen before, which makes the veins in her neck stick out and her eyes look ghost-like. Emily worries that Elizabeth hasn't had much sustenance apart from one or two chips, as she can hear her tummy rumbling. What is keeping her going, what is driving her like this? She doesn't understand it and is more than concerned. She must get her to hospital.

"How long do you think we'll be here, Elizabeth? Should I ring home again to tell Cuthbert I'll be a while, as we'll be off to the hospital after this too?"

"Good idea. I also want to see if they have anything on preventing greenhouse thefts."

*

What Percival Flint failed to tell the Inspector just an hour before is that Dr Eruna is his guest at high table at dinner this evening, and this is making him more than a little uncomfortable with proceedings. The Fellows' anteroom is filling up, with its wall-to-wall wood panelling, chandeliers and paintings of cherubs and horses. Formal hall is always popular with Fellows, who often prefer the company of colleagues to their wives, and the opportunity to over-eat and drink, whilst telling tales of hapless undergraduates who don't know their Sao Paulo from their Sacramento, while how funny it is how the smart ones can recount complex algebra and string theory but don't know how to boil an egg.

At one end of the hall, a number of Fellows congregate around a couple of crystal decanters of sherry on a long oak side table. With the Inspector's words still ringing in his ears, the Dean listens to college Fellows congratulating him on raising so much money with a gift from Labzuu, bringing new investment possibilities. Now categorically out in the open, Dr Eruna has seen to that, ensnaring the Dean before he lay all his cards on the table. New levels of deception are making Flint feel more than a little queasy, whereas Dr Eruna, on the other hand – bang in the middle of the room – is relishing this opportunity to embellish anecdotes about their special relationship to anyone who will listen.

"When I met Professor Flint, I knew that we were going to forge a lasting friendship, as he is such an inspiring and generous man. But little could I have dreamt that out of that friendship Labzuu would have been given the honour to contribute – albeit in a humble way – to the college's future." A few 'marvellous' and 'wonderfuls' from the Fellows as Dr Eruna continues, "For it is by working together on such ground-breaking research with the Dean – and I know we have a partnership which is first-rate, one which will make history in Cambridge, not just for the Science Park, but in the very bones of learning – that these new drugs will be closer to the market and able to save lives in the future." Fellows say 'hear hear' and 'two million', 'wonderful', 'top man' at this news. Professor Flint tries to hide his edginess as he feels all eyes on him from his peers. He appreciates that the drugs of which Dr Eruna speaks will probably make history, but not in the way the Fellows think. Professor Flint has a pain in his stomach and excuses himself with a white lie.

"Do go ahead without me. I'll follow along shortly. I need to attend to something." That something involves a trip to the gentleman's room, and it feels like strong bile wanting to escape from both orifices all too soon for his legs to carry him. He has no intention of making it back to dinner, deciding to check into the Garden House Hotel for some privacy instead.

42
POISONOUS

Inspector Abley walks into the Growth Facility at the Department of Plant Sciences on Downing Street and finds Elizabeth at the microscope.

"Good morning, heard you were here. Emily told me you wouldn't be taken to the hospital last night. How's your head?" The Inspector is munching on an almond-filled croissant and holding a steaming coffee for his breakfast. Elizabeth looks up at him excitedly. She has discovered something.

"Susan was poisoned with an oenanthotoxin. This is an unsaturated aliphatic compound, similar to cicutoxin. So that's a double murder confirmed."

"Why didn't Leedham spot that?"

"This particular plant is not European, and the traces don't have to be very high. You'd need to know what you're looking for. I'm taking samples to him so he can examine them, for a second opinion. But I'm as sure as I'll ever be." Elizabeth is so happy with her discovery that she even smiles at Abley.

"Oh good. So we know it is as you say, double murder. Anything else?"

Elizabeth has been holding back, but now hits the Inspector with more, pulling her glasses off the end of her nose and sitting back down on a work stool.

"Well yes, the plant I'm thinking about is native to Africa. If Leedham confirms my research, then we have it. You see, with this poison the onset of the symptoms are rapid, usually within an hour of ingesting it, sometimes sooner. They include nausea and trismus. Once seizures start, if not treated they can kill rapidly."

"You know the Dean of Bene't's requested I ask you to keep your distance from the college and Dr Eruna." Inspector Abley smirks. Elizabeth is disappointed by Percival Flint's actions. How sad, she thought they respected one another. She is also less inclined to like him now she realises what he'd do for Dr Eruna. Elizabeth realises she may need Bob to protect her as this is getting dangerous. She'd better come clean about the letter.

"I didn't want to point the finger again until I was sure."

Abley knows Elizabeth's tone. He immediately looks straight at her.

"Elizabeth, what have you done?"

Elizabeth tries to look humble. It doesn't work.

"I was going to tell you... I found a letter in Edward's room. It was addressed to the Dean. Edward was warning him to stay away from Labzuu, as they were involved in illegal testing experiments in Kenya. Whoever hit me must have taken it."

Abley coughs out some croissant, after everything he has said. Elizabeth hands him a muslin, which he refuses, as it looks like it has seen better days.

"When were you going to tell me this?"

"I thought you'd think I was exaggerating. I wanted proof first. I think Dr Eruna has something to do with the murders. Edward starts digging about the company, and then winds up dead. But why is the Dean defending Dr Eruna? Do you think he could be tied up in all of this?"

"That might explain something we found when going through files on Edward's computer. An email from the Dean to Edward. Flint was inviting Edward Wiley to dinner and thanked him for the information." Inspector Abley replies, continuing, "But we didn't know what information. It must be the letter you found. Edward must have kept a copy of the letter he sent to the Dean in his rooms. The Dean must have received the information from Edward, though where that is, I don't know, as his reply went on to say Edward Wiley should talk to Professor Prins about the other matter. Didn't say what the other matter was. And I'm not sure if they ever met. Haven't followed that lead up yet. What's Prins's field?"

"The economic dynamics of the African continent, been Prins's favourite topic on the lecture circuit for years. What that has to do with it I'm not sure. But one thing is clear. The Dean is trying to hide shady deals in Africa that would bring the college into disrepute. Edward was warning the Dean in that letter... so someone kills him before he can tell all?" Elizabeth says.

The pieces are falling together. Elizabeth clenches her fist and waves her pen about. Abley is excited and grabs Elizabeth by both arms and pulls her face up to look at his. There is a moment between them, two friends, intimate. Elizabeth feels vulnerable in his arms like someone is looking after her, on her side. She breaks eye contact and raises her shoulders for Abley to let go, which he does. Abley coughs, aware how close they just got.

"I shall make another visit to the Dean, and leave Dr Eruna to me, Liz."

Elizabeth smiles at Abley, a little more relaxed after their contact, and says,

"An ill woman of a certain age, with concussion, can't get up to much. So d'you think we've found our killers? They have motive."

Abley reminds Elizabeth there are still things missing in their deductions.

"We need proof."

The Inspector leaves, raising his eyebrows as he goes. Elizabeth has not felt this alive in ages.

*

Rebecca is standing in the Dean's rooms with Jonathan. The Dean is now keen to distance the college from Edward and Susan's deaths as much as possible.

"I know it's sudden, and I'm very sorry. But we're so limited for space. The new Fellow is moving in on Monday, Mrs Wiley."

Rebecca drops to the Dean's couch.

"He's not even cold in the ground, how can you do this? My life is here."

Professor Flint tries his best understanding voice.

"Unfortunately we need to replace Dr Wiley's lecturing and teaching duties immediately. Someone must take his place by Monday, or we'll have a riot. The chap we've found, good fellow, has nowhere to live. We have packing facilities here if you would like us to help. Carter will arrange for everything to be boxed up? If you had nowhere to go, it would be different, but clearly, you have loving family around you."

Jonathan chips in, trying to help.

"We've said Rebecca can stay with us, for as long as she wants."

Rebecca is having none of it and pulls her face into a scowl.

"Why are you both so keen to organise me? I want to stay in college."

"I'm sorry Mrs Wiley, but that is no longer possible."

Then an idea strikes Jonathan.

"How about if I rent a flat here for double the price?"

"It's not a question of money, though we do need to charge. It's the fact that Rebecca is not associated with college, I mean with any duties here."

Jonathan makes a last effort to assuage the Dean.

"What if I make a generous donation. A truly generous donation?"

The Dean sighs,

"Don't get me started on generous donations. They always come with strings which I don't have the taste for."

Jonathan knows that's the end of it. He sits with Rebecca and takes her hand.

"I could buy you a flat on the Parade, Rebecca. Overlooking the college, so you still feel near."

Rebecca pulls her hand from her brother's and rushes out. Jonathan glares at Percival and then rushes after Rebecca.

Outside Rebecca and Jonathan stand in the sun as Rebecca cries.

"What a beastly man, so stiff about the whole thing. You know, Edward liked him a lot. Always said he was a good man. Didn't see any of that, did you? I can't believe he's doing this."

Jonathan replies while rubbing Rebecca's back,

"Maybe he didn't like Edward as much as he let on? I have to put in a few hours at the constituency surgery in Ely, but Kat is coming to take you to get some food. Let's get a coffee while we wait for her."

43
PROTEST

A forty strong group of protestors are gathered in a field directly next to the Science Park campus just a hundred yards away from the offices of Labzuu. Bobble hats, dreadlocks, purple-haired youths mix in with bespectacled middle-aged, middle-class folk in their luminous cycle jackets, with placards leaning against bags and a loudhailer propped up against an angry looking man's boots.

Elizabeth and Godric are among them, trying to integrate with their new 'best friends', as the group sip their last drinks from flasks of hot chocolate and read their leaflets and smile and chatter to each other nervously. This protest has been advertised on a social media site Godric found, and Elizabeth thought by joining the protest they might get some more information about Labzuu. Godric sticks out wildly from the others, in his plimsolls, flannels, white shirt and floppy fringe, while Elizabeth in trousers with a green and black stripy jumper and pink scarf blends in perfectly with the eccentrics and vibrantly dressed activists.

The placards are handed out, reading 'Eruna is unethical', 'Labzuu-PIRATES' and 'Ovakin kills'. The angry looking man has now picked up the loudhailer and starts to rally everyone to begin walking and chanting as they head towards the offices, 'Stop illegal experiments!' and 'Shut down Labzuu!' Another man has more placards he got out of his car and walks over to the group handing out a few. Some distance away a bored cameraman, reporter and producer are standing about smoking and chatting, wondering if this is too dull for the lunchtime news later. Godric is handed a placard which reads 'Stop Tests Now', and he effeminately starts to wave it about. Someone hands Elizabeth a placard which reads 'Eruna is an Egit'. Godric smirks and shakes his placard at Elizabeth encouragingly, and Elizabeth shakes hers back. The protestors have now all reached the lawn in front of the Labzuu buildings and are gathering in a circle, moving round anti-clockwise.

An employee tries to leave the offices without being noticed, but the crowd spot him and immediately cheer 'go on you traitor', and 'do you sleep all right at night?'

Godric, in the crowd, shouts across to Elizabeth,

"Remind me why we are doing this again?"

Elizabeth is determined.

"One chap I just spoke to said they are testing in Namibia, despite Europe banning the particular drug tests here last year. These people think they shouldn't be allowed to get away with it."

There's a surge in the crowd as a female Labzuu employee tries to enter the offices. She's pushed and jostled as she walks by, and trips a little. A bit of a foray starts as she shouts at the protestors, and two security guards move in on her behalf and begin pushing the demonstrators back. A police van and squad car bellow around the corner and screech to a halt. The doors on the car fly open and two armed police, with batons, still pocketed and protective vests, rush out towards the crowd, entirely overboard, to support the security guards. The camera crew perks up and starts filming, the reporter now trying to mingle in the crowd to get the best piece-to-camera, but is accidentally hit on the head by a placard, yet regains composure and still says her lines perfectly. A policeman gets out his loudhailer.

"No permission has been sought for this protest! You must disperse and leave! If you continue, then we will have no alternative but to arrest you for breach of the peace!" The crowd starts to surge and jeer at the police. This is enough of a signal for the police rear van doors to fling open, and twelve police in armed gear rush the crowd, this time with batons in their hands. Elizabeth and Godric are separated, and Elizabeth finds herself thrown to the front of the crowd. There is much jostling, with fists flying and protestors pushing against the police, who are now also clearly making arrests. As Elizabeth is grabbed by a large policeman and led towards another police van that has just turned up, she looks up and sees Dr Eruna looking down out of the window. She sees Godric stuck right in the middle of a mosh of police and protestors, who are jostling and using batons and placards each trying to try to stop the other side. Godric waves her that he's picked up the scarf she dropped. The reporter continues to do her piece to camera and tries to interview Godric as he is being pushed about.

"Why are you here?"

Godric is gratefully pushed away from the microphone as an angry man leaps forward to answer for him.

"Labzuu are criminals. They've been conducting illegal experiments out of the public eye in places like Africa and Latin America, experiments that are banned in Europe. We're here to bring this to the attention of everybody. They try to keep it secret. They've also been taking DNA from indigenous people and ripping them off. Just practically stealing it."

"Do you know this for a fact? And please remember

we are now reporting live."

"Yes, we have evidence. They're criminals."

The protestor is grabbed by the police and led away to the van mid-interview. Godric takes this as his cue to quietly walk away from the protest unnoticed. He walks towards the company building and gets out his mobile, trying to look busy. A police officer eyes him suspiciously, as Godric wraps the pink scarf around his neck and with a flourish says,

"I'm a reporter, caught up in it. Sorry, have to file a story. Excuse me please," and turns his back on the policeman, who carries on pushing protestors. Godric, well dressed as he is, goes unnoticed as he walks through the front lobby and into a sofa area, now watching the protest safely away from the ruckus.

"Hello. Can you put me through to Inspector Abley, please? Well, can you tell him that Elizabeth Green is in trouble? Yes, he will know what it is about. Yes, Elizabeth Green. She's been arrested. I presume she'll be heading into Parkside shortly. In one of your police vans. Up at the Science Park. Yes, yes. I think he'll want to know." As he hangs up Godric can see Elizabeth's head disappear into a police van full of protestors.

Looking down from the window above, Dr Eruna smiles and waves at Elizabeth just before the final door slams shut and the police bang it as a signal for the driver to leave. The police van pulls away as scuffles continue and another van takes its place.

*

The police reception area at Parkside is full of protestors and friends and family of protestors who have turned up to bail them out. Inspector Abley smiles at Elizabeth as she is let go after a caution and he signs as her guarantor. The irony does not escape the other protestors who look at Elizabeth weirdly.

"What? Eruna is an Egit. Remember? That was me. I was there. I'm one of you," Elizabeth says, turning back to them to suggest she earned the stripes on her jumper. Elizabeth and the Inspector then shuffle a little further away from the ensuing commotion as the other van brings in fresh protestors to be charged or cautioned depending on the level of resistance. Inspector Abley holds Elizabeth's arm to stop near the automatic doors. She looks across Parker's Piece at the people walking the diagonal paths, oblivious to each other's lives.

"Oh, and the sand on the floor didn't work. No footprints and more of my grapes have disappeared. Can today get any better?"

"Dr Eruna has taken out an injunction against you, and of course the others."

"What does that mean?"

Inspector Abley smirks.

"You can't go within 500 metres of Labzuu."

"Well, this is topsy-turvy policing if ever I heard it. I mean, he's the one doing illegal things, not me."

"We enforce the law. We don't make it up." Abley laughs a little. "Always thought you were a rebel. What you do in your spare time is no business of mine."

"If a small group of concerned citizens cannot make known their opposition to unscrupulous business practices, peacefully, without getting the firm hand of the law shoved down upon their heads, well then what is the world coming to? I've a good mind to—"

"Don't write a letter Elizabeth."

"Never mind all that. Where's Godric? Did he get arrested?"

"I took Godric home half an hour ago. He managed to keep away from police attention, lucky for him. He wanted to wait here for you, but I said you'd need a hot bath and warm food waiting for you at home when you get back. So he's on it. Come on, my wages will stretch to a coffee on the way. I mean hot chocolate." Abley opens the door for

Elizabeth and continues, "And actually... I think you might be onto something with Dr Eruna. Facts wise we have been looking more closely at his business ventures, and as you say I'm not sure he's run it all past the Kenyan Government. They have been chasing him for answers for some time."

Inspector Abley opens the door for Elizabeth as they both leave for his car.

"There's only one place for dark hot chocolate. Take me there."

The Inspector rolls his eyes, knowing full well Elizabeth has chosen the best place in Cambridge to drink hot chocolate.

44
THE WEDDING

Kara and Rebecca are in wedding outfitters along King Street, for Kara's final fitting. Rebecca picks up an embroidered posy, as Kara speaks.

"Thank you for coming. I'm sorry about the timing of this. I know it's too soon and everything. It's just I want to get things ready my end, all my jobs ticked, you know?"

"It's okay. I remember getting married. Best day of my life."

"This dress makes me look fat." Kara looks at herself in the mirror and waits for Rebecca to protest, but she doesn't. So Kara begins to take off the dress. "Jonathan would kill me if he knew I was putting you through this."

"Then we won't tell him."

"Thank you."

Kara picks up a lace veil and holds it above her head in the mirror.

"What do you think?"

"Soon you'll be a Smythe-Jones. Are you sure you want to?"

"Never been more sure of anything. I love you, Rebecca."

Rebecca, only half interested in this shopping, says,

"You're a foolish girl. Now, come on. Let's go back into town and choose some drippingly expensive diamonds for you to wear too."

*

At Foxes' Haven, a police Constable walks around the back of Professor Elizabeth Green's garden. He has his phone to his ear.

"Yes, Guv. I'm here." The Constable looks down at the sand inside a locked greenhouse in front of him. "No, there are no footsteps in it. I'm here. I'm looking at the sand now." The Constsable listens to his Inspector on the other end of the line. "Yes, I'll stay here for a bit, of course, Sir." The Constable cuts the call and shakes his head. He wonders if this was what he signed up to join the police force for, guarding some lady's greenhouse full of grapes? The Constable looks left and right. He spots a garden chair and walks over to it, turning it to face the greenhouse. He then proceeds to take a sandwich out of his pocket and a soft fizzy drink he bought at the corner shop. He opens the paperbag containing his sandwich and eats, all the while not taking his eyes off the greenhouse, just in case someone steals the prize grapes while his back is turned.

*

Kara, Jonathan and Rebecca are sitting at home. Jonathan gets up and pours himself a stiff whisky, spotting a couple of shopping bags on the floor.

"What've you been up to?"

"Nothing much. Just wandering around," Kara replies.

Rebecca forgets it was a secret.

291

"We tried on dresses. I think it is lovely that you're getting married. Kara looks beautiful in silk. The world shouldn't stop because of my heartbreak."

"What?" Jonathan is shocked.

"We can't show you. It's unlucky," Rebecca replies.

Jonathan looks at Kara in astonishment.

"You think we're still going to get married so soon? Have you lost your senses? We've just had a death in the family."

Rebecca can't believe her brother.

"Jonathan, don't be mean to Kat. This has been her dream. To stay in England."

Kara sighs, angry at Rebecca for revealing their secret when she said she wouldn't. But Kara does not show it.

"We just thought we'd sort the dresses, that's all."

Jonathan knocks back his drink.

"You're not listening to me. I said I wanted to talk with you, but every time I try you're not here."

"What do we need to talk about? Everything's taken care of. You've been sorting it with Katie?"

He gets up and moves away from both of them, with his back to Kara, she knows he is talking to her.

"I wanted to talk about us. Look, there's no easy way of saying this. The wedding's off, for now. And we need to talk, in private. Not now." Jonathan then turns around to see Kara's total devastation.

"What? No, you can't be serious?" She hides her heartbreak.

"I'm not interested in talking about this again. That's final."

Kara looks at Jonathan, gets up and runs out. Jonathan pours himself another drink and downs it in one. After some time he turns to his sister.

"I have to go back to the constituency for a second sitting. More of those local critters want to see me than I could squeeze in earlier."

45
LOSING OUT

Fellows stand drinking sherry and chatting as they glance at the spectacle of the protest on lunchtime TV. They are shocked by the news that Labzuu is being accused of serious double standards, of testing drugs on people abroad which are illegal in this country. The Dean walks in to have an aperitif but notices the frosty looks and small backchat. He knows they are questioning his decision to back Labzuu. Carter spots the Dean and tries to rescue him from their gazes.

"Might I let the kitchen know if you're intending to stay for lunch, Dean? In case you have any special requests?"

Professor Flint thinks again and decides he cannot endure an hour of this.

"Something's come up. I won't be at lunch. Thank you, Carter."

Before the Dean can take his leave, Professor Prins comes over with a sherry.

"This is all very, well, noticeable for the college, Dean.

Are we on the right course here? We gave you our backing. Have we been too hasty?"

"Will you excuse me?"

Professor Prins is surprised by Flint's abrupt departure. Professor Flint is exhaling, trying to calm his nerves. What has he done? Carter also watches the Dean leave, worried for him.

*

The Constable in Professor Elizabeth Green's garden still sits on the chair facing the greenhouse. But on closer inspection, it is clear that his eyes are firmly shut, his head leaning to one side. It is also clear that he is snoring loudly. The thieves of Professor Green's grapes are free to steal again with abandon.

*

Not much later, the Dean and Dr Eruna are eating lunch at the Garden House Hotel restaurant outside on the lawns. Empty starter plates litter their table. The waitress pours Dr Eruna another glass of wine and leaves with some of the empties. Dr Eruna turns to Professor Flint.

"So, you've made me wait until this meal. Are you finished writing, are we celebrating?"

"Yes, I've finished." He gets out the paper and shows it to Dr Eruna. "It didn't come easily. I stayed up all last night writing and rewriting. I got a room here. I can't get any peace in college thanks to you. I'm ashamed of this."

"Don't have a crisis of conscience on me now."

Professor Flint can't bear to look at his lunch guest and instead spits out his words.

"What makes you think you're above the law? That you can play with peoples' lives? I wish I hadn't been such a fool to believe you."

Dr Eruna finds the whole thing amusing. The Dean has

performed his use. Now if he can just get his hands on that paper.

"Calm down. You'll spill your wine."

Percival takes the research paper he has just spent so much time sweating blood over and rips it in two separate pieces.

"I've come to a decision. I didn't want to meet you in my office because I don't want a scene and I don't want your dirty money. Do what you like to me, but I'm not associating the college with material malice at the root of your company."

Dr Eruna tries not to visibly show his utter shock.

"You'll regret this... and if it hasn't escaped your notice, your so-called esteemed college has active murder investigations on not one but two of its Fellows."

"They are treating Susan as a murder?"

Dr Eruna enjoys sticking in the knife.

"According to the lunchtime papers. You really should get with the times."

The Professor is shocked but tries not to lose the thread of his argument. Percival gets up to leave, now convinced that Edward was killed in some way because of Dr Eruna and Labzuu, and he feels directly responsible for asking Edward to look into the company while he was abroad.

"I have my deep suspicions that you're responsible for Edward's death, but tell me not Susan as well."

Dr Eruna gets up at the same time and at the top of his voice says,

"You won't get away with blackmailing me, Professor Flint! No favours for a Fellowship. What an outrageous suggestion. I can't help it if your private research money has dried up. You'll have to find collaboration elsewhere. You have the blood of Edward Wiley on your hands!"

"Dear god man, what are you saying?"

"Don't deny it!" Screams Dr Eruna.

"Shut up I tell you." Professor Flint punches Dr Eruna

in the face. Dr Eruna isn't hit very hard, and there is a moment where Dr Eruna almost laughs at the weakness of the blow. But then seizing the opportunity he calculatingly falls back into the next table and onto the food of those dining. Professor Flint feels devastated and humiliated. He apologises to those sitting at the table. "I'm sorry. Please forgive me. I'm so sorry." Percival Flint tries to pick up some cutlery for the disturbed guests, then hurries out of the dining room.

Inspector Abley and Elizabeth are drinking fine hot chocolate in the foyer as a pianist plays in a bar nearby. They see Flint rush by. Inspector Abley stands and calls back to Elizabeth.

"I will go and see what's going on–"

The Inspector leaves, and shortly afterwards Dr Eruna walks past. Elizabeth mutters under her breath,

"Stop following me, or I'll have to take out a counter-injunction."

*

Rebecca rubs Kara's back as they sit in the apple orchard amongst the wildflowers, and says,

"Do you have to leave if the wedding doesn't take place?"

Kara clings to Rebecca in a frenzy, replying,

"He listens to your every word. If you think we should marry he will. I know it. You and Jonathan are the only family I have. If he won't marry me, then it will be over. I'll have lost everything."

*

Sometime later, Carter walks up the stairs to the Dean's rooms with a tray containing a glass of fine brandy and a selection of cheese and biscuits. He notices the light streaming from under the door. Carter knocks twice but gets no reply from the other side. Finally, he turns the knob, and the old creaky wooden door opens. Carter is at once confused to see the Dean, motionless, sat at his desk. After less than a second he can see that Percival Flint is dead, bolt upright in his swivel chair, hands on his desk not typing, but leaning on the keypad. Carter immediately drops the tray with brandy.

Half an hour later and SOCOs are packed into the Dean's rooms, along with Inspector Abley. The police pathologist, Leedham, is finishing examining the Dean's body. Leedham speaks quietly but matter-of-factly to Inspector Abley.

"If he did take these pills voluntarily – and there is no immediate evidence of force – then there are enough to kill him three times over. Quite a cocktail. But I won't know until I have got him back to the lab."

Wearing crime scene gloves, Abley picks up a collection of pills and bottles.

"Can you say when he died?"

"You know I hate estimating anything Abley, but I will estimate that I'll beat you tomorrow on the course." Carter raises a brow. Abley replies to Leedham.

"So you say, 'bunker' Bill."

Abley looks around the room.

"So come on, give me something to work with here."

Mr Leedham appreciates the pressure Abley is now under, this being the third death associated with the college, and this latest being such an essential member of the establishment. Leedham points to the bottle of vodka on the desk, next to an exquisite paperweight.

"Look, if he drank all of that it wouldn't have taken long. I'd say about two to four hours ago, but I didn't say that okay?"

Carter speaks up.

"If it helps to know, the Dean was not at lunch today. This was unusual, as he tends to take lunch in college most days. His favourite on the menu as well, roast duck, yet he left suddenly."

"Thank you, Sir. If you can give a statement to the Sergeant there, I would be much obliged," Abley replies and points at Sergeant Lemon in the corner. Abley knows that he saw the Dean not more than two or so hours ago with Dr Eruna at the Garden House Hotel, so it must have been recent, and if this is the third murder, the killer is still close. He must get Lemon onto finding Dr Eruna, and quickly.

46
NEARLY CAUGHT

Elizabeth is alone at home, sitting reading at the kitchen table. She takes a large gulp of tea and pores over a book Emily got for her from the library on South African families. It wasn't a text that could ordinarily be taken out, but Elizabeth knows the librarian well, a kind woman who had made a 'special dispensation for her favourite Professor of poisons'. Flicking through the glossary Elizabeth finds a page of interest and turns to read 'Slavery and the Mining Dynasty'. There are twenty pages in this chapter and Elizabeth is so tired that the task feels overwhelming. Pages start to move, words floating up off the page into the air in front of her. She's only slept a gnat's amount since Monday night.

Outside she hears a thump. It must be the greenhouse thief. She gets up and runs out into the garden too quickly, in a frenzy picking up a spade and rushing for the greenhouse door. It is already open. No one is outside. A chair has fallen on its side nearby. Running into the greenhouse, she looks up to see more grapes have gone.

As she leans back to survey the damage, she slips on the sand and lands on her back on the greenhouse path, between the vines and tomatoes. Elizabeth is completely winded and lies there, immobile. Crows caw on the roof above her head.

"I don't know what you're laughing at. You should be warning me when the thief comes."

Elizabeth shouts at the crows and then looks through the open greenhouse door. Despite being unable to get up, and feeling the pain that the grazes on her legs are giving her, Elizabeth cannot escape drinking in the beauty in the garden, so peaceful and quiet – apart from the crows; her foxgloves standing tall, framing the lavender, roses and hydrangeas. Elizabeth picks a tomato and pops it in her mouth. Summer has truly arrived. After five minutes of lying on the floor, Elizabeth becomes not only bored but also a little cold. She tries to stand up but struggles into a sitting position instead. Thankfully not long after this Godric returns home. Noticing the open backdoor but no Elizabeth he walks out into the garden and sees his nanna on the floor inside the greenhouse. Panicking at first, but then seeing she seems in good spirits, Godric hurries over. He is about to tell her that there had been a call from the laboratory but thinks better of it.

"The sand worked then. There are lots of footprints."

Elizabeth throws a look at Godric.

"They're all mine."

"No luck catching the culprit then?"

"No, and they've taken even more grapes. The door was unlocked too. Did you leave it open when you put the sand down?"

Godric looks sheepish.

"I thought I shut it."

"So whoever is taking my grapes could swan in. You might as well have put down a welcome mat." Elizabeth looks up at the beautiful, healthy vine above her head.

"I don't know. I grow these grapes for the family, not

for strangers to eat."

"I thought they were for wine."

"For the family to drink then."

"Come on, up you get."

"Ow, ow." Elizabeth looks at her grazed leg, red with embedded grit. Godric doesn't like the look of it.

"Shall I call the doctor out again?"

"Don't be silly. Nothing a bit of antiseptic won't cure."

He lifts her gently and walks her into the house, putting her on the sofa in the drawing room, sitting with her until she falls asleep. As he looks down at her curls he inherited and her little feet he didn't, he worries. What would she do without him? She doesn't look cut out to cope alone, even though she would never admit it. He thinks about staying with her over the summer, just to keep an eye. He loves Cambridge and knows he could do with the rowing practice he'd get if he extended his time here. He also knows his mother would go nuts if he told her, so he's not going to do that just yet. He certainly does not want to go home.

*

Jonathan is talking to his Whip again, this time on the phone from his constituency rooms in Ely.

"Yes, I said to leave it with me. I'm going to deal with it once I've finished here. Yes. As suspected, small children. Working in the mines, up to twelve hours without a break. The Congo, mid-belt, Angola. We've got photographic evidence. There's no mistake. What a family. I had no idea she was up to her neck in it like this." Jonathan can hear the strain in the Whip's voice as he quietly clips each tone.

"We're so close to announcing your appointment, Jonathan. How will it look? Just sort it, and sort it now. Leave the office. What the hell are you doing wasting your time on constituents?" The more serious the Whip, gets the quieter his voice.

Jonathan is worried and remembers what Rebecca told him. That Elizabeth had heard Edward say 'tip' before he died. She knows. That meddling woman. Edward knew too. He knew the dirty secret. Tip. That's what he was going to tell her. That's what he was trying to tell Elizabeth Green. How long would it be before she worked it all out if she has not already? Jonathan suddenly gets up and snaps out of his thoughts.

"I've got to talk to Kat then I'll find her. I said I would deal with it and I will. Don't worry."

"We're going to give you a big job, Jonathan. Close this down."

"I'm on it." Jonathan gets up to rush out but is met by a door opening and a little old lady coming in and plonking herself down on the chair, ready to offload her complaint to her local MP. Jonathan looks at his constituency assistant, who fills him in.

"There are still six people waiting outside."

"Okay, but that's the lot, then I need to go." Jonathan returns to his desk, trapped for now. "Well then Mrs Draper, what can I do for you?" Jonathan slumps back down in his chair while looking at his watch, and then back at the elderly lady in front of him.

"Well, I'd like to make a complaint about the hairdressers next door to my property. They have put up an awning, and it blocks the light for my little Dickie."

"Excuse me?"

*

At Parkside Police Station, Inspector Abley sits on a chair next to Sergeant Lemon. His shirt sleeves rolled up, Lemon picks at the spots on his arms; a habit Abley has watched him do for years. Abley stares at Lemon to try to stop him, but Lemon is oblivious. On the other side of the table, Dr Eruna shifts uncomfortably in a chair, flanked to one side by a smartly dressed solicitor and another police officer standing by the door. Irritated, Abley continues to drone on in monotone with his questions, a tactic he has often found to successfully wear down the accused in the interview room by simply overwhelming them with boredom.

"Mr Eruna, you were seen publicly rowing with the Dean just hours before his death. We have eleven witnesses who saw you shouting at him, accusing him of all kinds. He was making you cross. Is that when you followed him to his rooms?"

"I didn't."

"Can you tell me what you were rowing about? What's this?" Inspector Abley pulls out the research paper Flint tore in half. Dr Eruna is surprised to see the paper but just shrugs, so Abley continues. "I retrieved it from a bin outside the Garden House Hotel. I saw Professor Flint throw it away after seeing you. There are back-ups on his computer. Very glowing about Labzuu. Why would he rip it up?" The Inspector knows more than he is letting on, but Dr Eruna continues to give nothing away.

"I don't know."

"Are you sure? It's just that Professor Flint made clear his reasons in a letter of resignation we also found on his computer. I wondered if he was sharing those reasons with you over lunch?"

Dr Eruna senses the police know enough to incriminate him.

"Look, we'd just not seen eye to eye on a couple of things. We decided to go our own way, not to collaborate any further."

Abley leans across the table and glares at Dr Eruna.

"That's one way of putting it. Apparently, he could 'no longer live a lie', no longer support your company, and begged his college colleagues for forgiveness for getting so closely into bed with such 'an abhorrent company'. He warned them against you in particular. Why is that?" Abley continues to stare, watching Dr Eruna's every move. Dr Eruna's solicitor looks at him pointedly to keep a tight lip.

"No comment."

"You were peers at the college with Edward and Susan, isn't that right?"

But Dr Eruna throws his hands in the air.

"Now wait a minute. I have nothing to do with their deaths."

Abley pulls out a tissue and blows his nose.

"They all got in your way. One by one, to make a multi-million pound deal with the college, for your company to hit the big time with, what's the word, gravitas, kudos, a huge signpost, isn't it? To have your company backed by a college of such repute. Only both Susan and Edward were dead against it – the college having any involvement. We have found letters on Edward's computer."

"I haven't hurt anyone!" Dr Eruna thumps the table.

A SOCO enters the room and deposits a mobile phone in a plastic bag next to Inspector Abley.

"Edward Wiley's pay-as-you-go, Sir. We retrieved it from the River Cam half an hour ago. We're contacting the telephone company now for records."

"Thank you." Abley turns back to Dr Eruna. "So, Mr Eruna, will we find calls from you to this phone, or perhaps Edward called you from this phone? Interesting he had a pay as you go."

"No. I haven't spoken to Edward Wiley."

Abley frowns. He doesn't believe Dr Eruna for a minute. Surely now that they have the phone and will soon have the evidence it wouldn't be wise to lie.

"Perhaps you're telling him you were going to murder him. Perhaps you were trying to murder Professor Green in the department."

"No."

"You hit Professor Green though didn't you?"

Dr Eruna looks up at the Inspector, and Dr Eruna's

solicitor looks agitated.

"You see, the department has CCTV outside. It caught you going in around the time she was attacked."

Dr Eruna knows he can't deny this.

"I didn't mean to hurt her."

Abley leans into the digital recorder, opening a packet of mints as he does.

"For the record, Mr Eruna has admitted assault on Professor Elizabeth Green." Inspector Abley pops in his mint and sucks. There is a long pause as he thinks of his next question. The solicitor shakes his head. Abley sighs. "So are you going to tell me why?"

Dr Eruna, now red-faced, fiddles with his tie.

"Edward was slandering my company, sending poison to Professor Flint. I just wanted the letter back."

Abley is confused. He can't piece the bits of the puzzle together.

"Go on."

"Flint told me Edward had brought back evidence about things we'd done abroad. I didn't know what to find, what was out there. So I was looking for it, that's all. But when I got there she'd found it before me."

Abley pushes harder, as Dr Eruna unravels in his seat, sweating.

"So you killed Edward, and you tried to kill Professor Green."

Startled, Dr Eruna's eyes dart up to meet Abley's.

"No, I haven't killed anyone. And I wasn't trying to kill her. I pushed her, that's all."

"That's not what the medical report states. You hit her violently on the head, Mr Eruna. I am charging you with grievous bodily harm under the Offences Against the Person's Act against Mrs Elizabeth Green. You do not have to say anything. But it may harm your defence if you do not mention when questioned something that you later rely on in court. Anything you do say may be given in evidence. D'you understand? For the record, this interview is paused at five twenty-three p.m." Dr Eruna nods and drops his head. Abley stands up and turns for the door, throwing a final comment, "Why should we believe anything you say now? This isn't over." And with that Abley leaves the room.

*

Kara has her 'mood' box for the wedding out in the living room and is rummaging through it. All those last-minute things. Lists of replies, seating plans. Rebecca enters the room. Kara looks anxiously at Rebecca and asks,

"Thanks for talking to your brother for me. What did he say?"

Rebecca is tired and could do without this conversation.

"I'm sorry, I tried to talk sense. We had a long chat on the phone. But, I think I made things worse."

Kara picks up some ribbon and twists it tightly around her finger.

"But I thought you were going to help? You promised."

Rebecca sighs,

"I tried all right? He didn't even want to bring it up. He seemed preoccupied with matters there. I had to listen to all this Cabinet appointment apprehension. He said he thinks the wedding's a bad idea and he'll talk to you when he gets back."

Kara pours herself a drink, in denial, but her face cannot hide the cracks.

"No, he doesn't mean it. He's angry. He'll come round."

There is silence from Rebecca. She cannot give Kara false hope. She knows her brother meant what he said, and he is the most stubborn person that she knows – aside from herself.

"He'll come round, won't he?"

"He said you shouldn't even be thinking about a wedding now Edward has just died." Rebecca pauses, not knowing whether to cushion the blow. "That it didn't show a good side to you. I'm sorry."

Kara is now completely panicked. She cannot let this happen. Surely there is something to cling to.

"He wants to stop the wedding just for now though, doesn't he?"

Rebecca feels pushed, she cannot breathe. Won't this selfish woman leave her alone? Hasn't she been listening?

"He doesn't want to marry you, all right!" Rebecca shouts. Kara drops her drink. She stands frozen in the finality of the words. She can't get them out of her head now, they are shouting at her. Just like Rebecca. He does not want to marry her. It has all been for nothing. All the nights alone, all the waiting. This Englishman, her true blue.

Rebecca regrets the force of her delivery. "I'm sorry. Kat, come here." But Kara storms down the garden below the orchard and out along the footpath until Rebecca cannot see her anymore.

47
EVENING GARDEN

Some time later the doorbell rings. Rebecca has remained on the couch, dozing. She stirs and goes to answer thinking maybe Kat will forgive her. Through the spy hole she sees Godric standing against the Talbot, so she opens the door. He smiles at her and shrugs.

"Hello? I thought you were Kat, forgetting her keys. She left in a hurry. You'd better come in."

Godric walks up the steps through the porch and into the hallway, flicking his fringe out of his eyes. He takes the opportunity to look around.

"Are you alone?"

"Yes, why?"

"Oh, just wondered. I was calling on the off chance. You said when Bunny was better she could come round for a cup of tea. She is otherwise engaged at the moment, so I thought, well, why didn't I visit you instead?"

"Lovely." Rebecca walks through into the living room, beckoning Godric to follow.

"See how you are, and all that?" Godric asks, looking

around.

Rebecca wipes her forehead, as it is a sticky night. The doors are open to the garden, and it is already quite dark outside. Godric continues, as he observes all the wedding material and the box on the coffee table.

"You ran off like that from the car. I was worried about you and was in the area. I've been to The Cutter Inn for a pub quiz."

"Did you win?"

Godric smiles again.

"The Quizzicals always win. We're getting a bit of a reputation."

Rebecca looks at her watch. It is already late.

"Oh, well, Um. Would you like something to drink? Tea, coffee, beer?"

"Perhaps a beer? Can we sit outside? I've been indoors all day. Yes, thought I'd come over and tell you they're planning to resume the choir next week. The show must go on… or something like that in the email."

Rebecca's mind is so far from the choir, but she is pleased to see a friendly face.

"I'll put the lights on by the pool. We can sit out there and pretend we're somewhere else in the world. California maybe. I'm always pretending I'm somewhere else at the moment. Kara and Jonathan mean well, but I hate it here."

Rebecca leaves for the kitchen as Godric walks through big garden doors. To his right is a huge swimming pool, perhaps forty or fifty feet up on the terrace with a marble area around it, a bar, tables, sun loungers and a swing chair for bathers to relax. Right in front of him are steps down onto the lawn, framed by two stone statue lions. He wonders how he missed noticing the lions last time. They are seriously imposing. Someone has placed a top hat on one of them, which makes him think there must be some good parties here. He smells the fresh scents from borders and many Mediterranean type pots along the terrace wall. He can see the croquet still set out from when he was here last and manages to avoid a hoop in the twilight.

Rebecca comes out to join him with two beers still in their bottles, and some nuts in a bowl. Godric takes a beer.

"Bottoms' up."

"Down the hatch."

"It's not that strong stuff, is it? Shouldn't really if I'm driving."

"Just have the one then."

The two clink and then pause to drink, enjoying this semi-rural location. It is so quiet in the garden that they can hear the snails munching vegetation. Godric breaks the silence.

"This is a lovely garden. I don't think I noticed before. You know, when you kissed me."

"I was in shock at the time."

"Most people are when they kiss me. But you know I'm—"

Rebecca shakes her head and looks out down the lawn.

"I wasn't sure. But, yes. I shouldn't have. I know."

Godric changes the subject glad she's understood and won't misread his visit for something else.

"So, who's the green-fingered monster in this household?" He breathes in the summer evening air for effect and touches his chest before taking another sip of beer.

"Kara. She's always out here. Growing some plants for her wedding over there. Tends them every day. I think she studied horticulture when she was younger. Tells me it helps her relax. Maybe I should take it up."

Godric looks at the breathtaking borders, which hang in the silvery air, motionless, asleep, waiting for tomorrow to blaze out their colour.

"I do like hostas." Godric points at some peonies. "Great for a dry, sunny spot aren't they?"

Rebecca looks at the peonies, nonchalantly agreeing.

"Yes. They're lovely."

Godric continues to talk to Rebecca about the plants,

observing her.

"And the lavender. It must get watered a lot in this spot. They love loads of water and shade, don't they? Simply shrivel up and die in the sun."

Rebecca looks at the lavender. She strokes it with her hand.

"They do look dry. Maybe I should tell Kara to move them do you think? You seem to know a lot about gardens then?"

Godric smiles. Of course, he knows a lot about gardens. He lives with the queen of botany. He's sure she plays him tapes in his sleep to remember all the names of the plants.

"No, not really. But it can't help but rub off living with Bunny, you know. Sometimes I think she's a gnome that's come to life. Does your brother like gardening? Is that what the two of them have in common?"

Rebecca looks down the end of the garden to the orchard, wondering if Kara will reappear and worries where she has gone. She did not mean to be so harsh, but Kara would not stop.

"Well, he likes being in the garden. He likes to take off his shoes and socks when he comes back from London and put his toes on the grass, but I think that's about the size of it." Rebecca smiles fondly about her brother, then steps back up onto the terrace. Floor lights around the swimming pool illuminate her face as palm trees in four big planters at each corner give the area a tropical feel. Two parasols strung with pretty fairy lights stand beside a small bar with a straw roof. And nestled under the parasols are two little cafe tables with two chairs each, which look like they are set out for supper, having all the crockery, glasses, as well as candles flickering.

"Edward thought the pool and BBQ so passé. He was happy that we didn't have to waste time on the manicured outdoors, what with the college doing all the formal lawns. He said it was the best of both worlds, the beauty with no work necessary." Rebecca pauses. "He liked to sit out in Bene't's Fellow's garden with a cream tea before it got busy."

Godric joins Rebecca on the terrace by the bar.

"Yes, I like that, until it fills up. Can get quite busy in the summer holidays. And I'm with Edward on the whole BBQ thing. Why have another kitchen twenty feet from the one you've got? So Jonathan's out here at the weekends, cutting that grass?"

"Goodness gracious no. Jonathan? Hardly. They hire someone to do that actually. Kara gets him to do the manual labour. I've seen him trim the hedges and cut the grass in the past. Looking a bit long now. Haven't seen him in a while."

"Tell me more."

"Godric, you're wearing me out. I know nothing about gardening. Can we talk about something else?"

"All right." Godric puts down his beer on a table. "Family, why don't we talk about family? My family is so dysfunctional. My mother doesn't talk to my nanna. My sister doesn't talk to my mother. My father doesn't talk to anyone. You know, I think I'm the only normal one in my family, yet I'm the least normal person outside my family that I know." Godric picks up his beer and takes a swig.

"Your nanna is lovely. I'm sure it isn't as bad as that."

Godric raises his eyebrows as if to say she does not know the half of it. He is happy that she is opening up.

"What about yours?"

"My brother is my best friend. Yes, he is. Jonathan and I have always been close. He'd beat up boys at school who were nasty to me, and wanted to beat up the girls too, but his pride stopped him. I know he's a politician and a busy one at that. But he is always there when I need him."

"He sounds like he loves you very much, and also that he loves a scrap."

Rebecca smiles and takes a sip of her beer. It is the first time Godric has seen her smile.

"No, that was when he was younger. He's a law-abiding citizen now."

Godric has Rebecca right where he wants her. He leans towards her, so that he can get closer. He picks out a bit of grass from her hair.

"What about the rest of your family?"

Rebecca likes Godric. She feels safe. He is such a gentleman, and wicked all at the same time. She feels the need to unburden herself.

"We have parents in the Cotswolds and family in Scotland. But the distance stops us being close. We go back on daddy's side. Uncle has a seat in Norfolk. Proper aristocrats, you know, the ones money can't buy and all the rest of it. All very tame really. It doesn't mean anything anymore, being wealthy from an estate."

Godric keeps quiet about the substantial pile his own father owns, instead asking,

"What about Jonathan? Is he looking forward to the wedding?"

Rebecca takes another sip of her beer, the bubbles fizzing as she sets it back down.

"I happen to think that might be off right now."

Godric is surprised. Wasn't Jonathan going to marry that attractive woman? I mean, he was not into women, but if he were, then she surely would have been his type. A party girl, full of bounce, athletic and sexy. He could see that, even if he would not want to touch anything.

"Perhaps Edward's death has caused too many unintended ripples. I'm sure it hasn't been easy looking after me. Maybe they'll patch it up. Would you like a nut?"

Godric takes a few nuts from the bowl and pops them in his mouth.

"At least you have them both to look after you right now. I'm guessing Kara is quite a caring soul."

Rebecca walks over to sit by the pool, then perches on the side and dips her toes in the water.

"She's growing on me, I guess. She'd never really be

one of us though."

"What do you mean?"

Rebecca can see that Godric is upper middle class, intelligent and cultured. Someone who would fit right into an aristocratic circle.

"We're old money. She's new. And, she's a foreigner. Not that I care. I'm just saying, the English aristocracy is a tight circle. You'd be most welcome, Godric." Rebecca continues, "I think Jonathan has always had trouble accepting some of her more brash friends and I'm not sure mummy likes her much."

Godric thinks this a little harsh of Rebecca, watching her face twist with spite makes him immediately think less of her.

"We're all from somewhere, Rebecca."

Rebecca moves her toes about and then turns her head back to Godric, still harsh.

"I sometimes wonder if Jonathan loves her because of her money."

Godric looks around at the gardens and house. They're very comfortable, but not of mansion proportions.

"But you said your family is loaded."

Rebecca flicks her feet causing ripples in the pool.

"No, I mentioned the estate. But death duties of my grandfather almost crippled Pops, and upkeep of the land and property and all the rest of it. You know it eats money."

Godric walks over to join Rebecca by the pool, bringing the beers and nuts. He squats down on the edge but doesn't remove his shoes.

"So, what are we talking then, in terms of Kara's wealth?"

Rebecca sneers.

"Don't you know?"

"Know what?"

"She's a billionaire. I mean a big one. She's always in those society magazines."

Godric picks up a nut and tips his head back and throws to catch it in his mouth. He misses.

"They're on my piles of must-reads at home by my bed." Godric is being sarcastic, and Rebecca knows it. Godric throws another nut and catches it in his mouth.

"They only keep this property to look good for the voters. He makes her stay up here, for the image. You know, it shows they live locally and are normal, not insanely elite and removed. You should see her place in Mayfair. It's like a town. I think her family own a part of Africa the size of England. Not that I'm jealous. I don't care about money. That's probably why in his will Edward made my brother responsible for looking after our money. I literally have nothing. I had no idea."

48
A FRIEND IN NEED

Inspector Abley is standing outside the interview room with a coffee cup in hand. Through the little window in the door, he can see Dr Eruna still sitting inside, looking beaten. Sergeant Lemon walks up to him.

"Sir?"

"Hold him for now. We can decide about bail shortly. I'll speak to his solicitor later."

"You have a call from Professor Green, Sir."

"Thank you Lemon."

Lemon hands Abley the phone, he takes it and listens intently.

"Hi, yes we've got Eruna here." Abley's eyes open wider as he continues to listen to Elizabeth. "But that means. What?" The Inspector can't believe his ears. "Yes. Okay. Don't leave without me. I'll get the blues in on this. Just wait for me there. We can go together. Elizabeth?" Abley looks shocked. He hands Lemon back the phone. "She hung up on me."

Lemon stands stationary. He has more news for the

addled Inspector.

"And we have the call results from Edward Wiley's mobile, Sir."

Lemon hands Abley a document.

"Lemon, can you get a squad car. I want to go over to Elizabeth Green's."

Lemon is flustered, but points to the call sheet for Abley to look at and then hurries to the car park. Abley looks at the phone call sheet and Lemon's notes along the right-hand side. He takes one last glance through the round window at Dr Eruna inside the interview room and then dashes off to pick up his jacket.

49
GIFTS

Elizabeth and Godric are sitting on the sofa in the drawing room. Elizabeth has a blanket over her legs, peppermint tea steaming by her side. She puts the phone down after talking to Inspector Abley and turns to Godric.

"He was saying 'servus tip'. Emily reminded me that servus is the Latin word for name. Though why Edward would speak in Latin goodness only knows. Perhaps it was the poison. But he was saying a family name 'Tip', and I then found this book." Elizabeth points to the huge book of African family dynasties on the coffee table, clearly marked 'Cambridge University Library, do not remove' on its cover. "I've been looking through it. There is a big family in Africa, called Tip. Edward had just got back from Africa. He was warning me about the Tips, you see?"

Elizabeth pulls the book open to a page where she's inserted a marker. There are historical pictures of white men standing in front of mines, and black workers going into the mines, and some young children too. Godric does not understand what she is trying to tell him.

"Are you feeling better after the slip in the greenhouse, Nanna? I'm still happy to do your legwork. I felt quite the detective, talking to Rebecca like that. She had no idea I was trying to glean just how much she knew about plants. Let me tell you. She's a real first class idiot when it came to the basic green finger questions. You were right."

"Did you close the greenhouse?"

Godric nods and continues,

"Interesting that Kara is so wealthy, Bunny. Is that why she's changed her name to Kat, to be less conspicuous?"

Elizabeth has already made up her mind about Rebecca, Kara and Jonathan. Nothing Godric will say from now on will change it. Elizabeth drums her fingers against the open page.

"Maybe she's embarrassed about her wealth. Maybe it doesn't fit with her soon-to-be husband's political career?"

Godric is still in the dark. He screws up his face as he drinks his coffee.

"How could someone in Africa kill Edward? He died here. So did Susan, and the Professor. What is it with the family and mining, Bunny?"

But Elizabeth is in her own world. She doesn't hear Godric now. Almost as if talking to herself she starts to speak.

"I should've known when I saw they both had the same paintings of horses with toothy grins. Susan and Rebecca. They both had scarves with little Scotty dogs on too. Blue scarves. There are coincidences and coincidences. I was blind."

Godric has now lost his grandmother's train of thought. What does she mean scarves and paintings? What can Bunny be talking about?

"I don't follow."

"Edward bought his wife and his mistress the same presents. He always bought two presents. They both had the same Scotty dog scarves. So, what else did he buy them both? Just think, when he came back from Africa. What if he bought them the same presents there too?"

Godric is finding this hard to follow, then remembers the necklace.

"What, you mean the necklace?"

"There had to be more than one necklace because the beads were not missing from Susan's. What if there were two necklace presents to two women he knew? Get the Talbot out. You're driving me to Ely. We need to get to Rebecca. Before we have yet another murder on our hands."

*

Dr Eruna's legal brief walks down the steps of the police station. He stops for a moment, breathes in fresh air and then continues along Warkworth Terrace with its tall houses, heading towards the local pub, the Free Press. They know him well in there, and he hopes to get a pint or two with his friends before he goes home to his empty house. His mother never told him how unpopular he would be as a lawyer, and all the stress attached when she pushed him to work harder at school and get a proper job.

Inside the police station, in a cell, Dr Eruna sits on a hard bed, having failed to get bail and awaits the magistrate in the morning, who will assign the case to Crown Court. This is not how his week was supposed to go. He sits in the dark, without a television, so is unable to see the news bulletin, which has his mug shot against his formal charges of GBH against an esteemed Cambridge Don.

*

Elizabeth and Godric are in the Talbot, racing along a country lane. Godric is driving and glances at Elizabeth.

"Bunny?"

"It took me longer than usual this time. I'm losing it. I hope we're not too late. Faster!"

"Are you sure? I mean, it's the Talbot."

"Just drive!"

Godric looks at her again, and back on the road, with increased determination to get there in time. The Talbot speeds along the lane, passing a car and narrowly missing, continuing rather too quickly.

*

Jonathan is still in his rooms, desperate to leave. His assistant opens the door and Jonathan dreads having to talk to one more constituent in his evening surgery.

"No, I don't care who it is I have to go home. So do they, it is very late!"

"It's the prime minister on the phone."

"Put him through."

50
MANHATTANS

Rebecca is on the terrace. It has grown even darker since Godric was here earlier, but this has not deterred her from remaining outside, as it is an unusually warm night. A sparkly pool and terrace lights illuminate much of the garden and lawn. For the first time since Edward died, she has managed to stop crying every ten minutes and instead feels rather calm. She has just been for a dip in the pool and is now wearing a towel dressing gown, covering her swimming costume. She lies back on a sun lounger and is almost drifting off to sleep, her eyes shut and snuggling under a blanket for warmth. Kara has crept back up the garden and now stands silently over Rebecca. She watches her for a while, and then with some water from a drinks bottle, she drips a little onto Rebecca's face to wake her. Rebecca stirs with a start.

"Oh. You made me jump. What did you do that for?" Rebecca can see the bottle, hanging over her head. Kara shrugs and smiles. Rebecca opens her eyes properly and tries to be friendly, remembering their last encounter and

Kara's distress at the news about the wedding. "I've been for a swim, Kat. I highly recommend it. It's been so hot today. I think I'm ready for bed soon. Where did you go?"

Kara is subdued and shrugs her shoulders.

"Oh, just for a walk. I don't know. I had to get some air. This family is enough to make anyone want to run away and never come back." Kara perches temporarily on another sun lounger adjacent to Rebecca's. She throws down the bottle of water, and it rolls into the pool. She watches it bob for a while, and knock against the side. She has one thing still on her mind. "I don't know. The wedding, eh?"

Rebecca shakes her head, smiles a little, then reaches across to place her hand on Kara's.

"I do understand. It must be devastating. We're both in the wars."

Kara takes Rebecca's hand and holds it between hers close to her chest, causing Rebecca to have to lean towards Kara, the blanket falling off her body. Kara starts to pour out her feelings to Rebecca.

"The thing is, you see, I see you as my sister. I mean, I know we're not related, but I thought we would be, and well, I don't want you to leave here now you've just moved in. I would love it if you'd stay with me, even if Jonathan doesn't. We can live here together. And anyway, I'm sure he was just in a mood when you spoke to him. He has been acting strangely because of the Cabinet reshuffle."

Rebecca can see that Kara is getting her hopes up about Jonathan. She feels awkward and so places her other hand on top of Kara's.

"I'm sorry for telling you what Jonathan said. But he seemed pretty certain, Kat. He doesn't usually change his mind once it's made up. You should know that more than anyone. He's a stubborn old fool. But of course, talk to him."

Kara pulls away, gets up and walks over to the bar. She leans on the bar with her back to Rebecca.

"Why are you determined to upset me? Of course Jonathan wants to marry me. You got the wrong end of the stick."

Rebecca thinks this odd and sits up, covering her legs with a towel robe to try to stop the goosebumps.

"He just phoned me from the car, and he seemed pretty angry actually."

Kara laughs to herself.

"Always phoning you, seeing you. He always puts you first. Why don't I get a call?"

Rebecca points to the table, bemused by Kara's more harsh tone than she recognises.

"You left your phone here for goodness sake. And Kat, how can you say such a thing? It's not my fault you two haven't been getting on."

But Kara twists around and glares harshly at Rebecca.

"Isn't it?"

Rebecca shifts, wrapping herself more in the towel robe, now feeling uncomfortable.

"What do you mean by that?"

Kara turns back round to face the bar, putting ice in a couple of glasses.

"Oh, nothing. I'm just stressed. Why don't we have something strong, eh? I'll mix us up some Manhattans. Something with a kick."

Kara sets about mixing a couple of cocktails, bourbon, sweet vermouth and angostura bitters. There is silence between the two until Kara has finished and pours the drinks into pretty, shallow green cocktail glasses. Rebecca takes hers from Kara and looks at it.

"Ooh, this looks nice. Bit strong for me right now though I think. Thanks anyway."

"Nonsense. You have to join me. Let's cheers. We must have things we can cheer about, eh? To sisters." Kara clinks her glass gently against Rebecca's and then raises the drink to her mouth. As she does someone starts violently banging on the front door and ringing the bell. Rebecca looks at Kara.

"Who on earth?"

"Ignore them. It will be cold callers. We get so many around here. Jonathan has his keys. C'mon, let's make a toast. To you." Kara clinks her glass again on Rebecca's and then raises her glass to her lips and takes a sip. But the banging continues, and Rebecca cannot ignore it. Rebecca gets up, still holding the cocktail, and starts walking to the door.

"I'll see who it is. They seem pretty determined to say hello."

As Rebecca opens the door, Elizabeth comes into the room just as Rebecca puts the drink to her lips.

"Don't drink that!" Elizabeth points at Godric to take the drink and as he does he mouths 'hello again' to Rebecca, then follows his nanna, now cocktail in his hand, through to the terrace.

"What are you doing? Hey?" Rebecca is bemused by the fact that they have waltzed straight in and past her. On the terrace, Kara turns to see Elizabeth coming through the living room and also spots Godric now holding Rebecca's drink. In her panic, as Godric steps outside and gets closer, she tries to grab it off him.

"What are you doing with that?"

As Kara reaches for the drink, Godric accidentally spills the contents in the swimming pool. He then looks at Rebecca.

"Rebecca, come over here."

"What?"

Godric takes Rebecca's hand and pulls her aside, away from Kara. Elizabeth spots the pool pump and turns it off. Kara is angry at Elizabeth.

"What are you doing? That's my pool."

"Preserving evidence, Kara."

Kara spits at Elizabeth, her cheeks aflame with anger.

"Get out of my house! My fiancé will be furious when he gets home."

Elizabeth looks at Kara with calm resolve.

"There is no need to be rude, Kara. It's Kara Tip, not Kat Anderson, isn't it. And, he's not your husband yet, is he? Some people will go to extreme lengths to marry though, won't they? Never thought you were the type. How wrong was I about you."

Rebecca looks confused.

"Kat. Whatever's the matter?"

Kara screams at Rebecca.

"Why couldn't he love me? Even half the amount he loves you? But no, that would be too easy. He saves it all for you, so there's nothing left. You really are a selfish little bitch!"

Jonathan slams the front door and walks in holding two bottles of champagne, and finds Elizabeth, Godric, Kara and Rebecca by the pool.

"I got in!" Jonathan is in a state of euphoria, happy to share his news with everyone and anyone who will listen. He disappears into the kitchen to get some champagne flutes and comes back in. "I'm in the Cabinet. How about that?" Jonathan smiles hugely. "Secretary of State for Justice in the end, not Home Office. Phoned me, didn't want to drag me down to tell me in person because of the circumstances. But it's official. So I don't care what you're talking about, or even that I appear to be celebrating with you, Professor Green. I don't care that you're in my house, or what you think or say. Today is my day. We're having champagne!" Jonathan starts to pour out the champagne and hands the first one to Rebecca. It is only then that he can see Kara's face is red and her eyes watery, and that Rebecca is looking a little upset. "Er, is everything all right here? Someone?"

Elizabeth interrupts, walking towards Rebecca and Godric and away from Kara.

"I think you should ask your fiancée. It may have a bearing on your own news."

Jonathan continues to pour while glancing at Kara.

"Kat?"

Kara starts to pace along the side of the swimming pool, feeling increasingly uncomfortable following Elizabeth's use of the word 'evidence' in relation to the drink. She can't look Rebecca in the eye but manages to glance over to Jonathan.

"Why wouldn't you marry me? Was I so unloveable? I'm pretty aren't I? Faithful? What was it? Do I have to pay for the sins of my father? Is that it?"

Jonathan puts down the champagne bottle and takes a flute of champagne over to Kara, unhappy with the way the conversation is developing.

"What are you talking about?"

"I think you know. I know you've found out."

Jonathan's eyes dart to Elizabeth, Godric, Rebecca and then back to Kara, urging Kara not to spill the beans about Africa.

"You've broken my heart it's true, but now's not the time."

Kara shuns Jonathan's champagne. Instead, she picks up the water bottle bouncing in the pool and starts to peel off the label, pacing again.

"You knew where I came from. That didn't stop you wanting to marry my money."

"Nonsense. What is this?"

"You politicians are all the same. Say one thing, do another."

Jonathan defends himself, drinking the champagne and then pointing a finger at Kara.

"Oh no. Oh no. You can't say I'm complicit in this. You told me nothing about your family."

Rebecca is confused and stands up from her seat.

"Will someone please tell me what's going on?" Rebecca looks at Godric. "First, you grab my drink. And Kat, why are you being so horrid? How could you call me those names when you know I'm your friend?"

Elizabeth interjects.

"Anything to become Mrs Smythe-Jones wasn't it, Kara."

"Get her out, Jonathan. Just get her out. I didn't invite her. She just walked in of her own accord. Isn't that illegal?" Kara implores.

Elizabeth ignores this and continues,

"The notorious African mining company Kara's father runs, to this day, is still using child labour. I say labour, as I believe payment is not involved. Here we call that slavery. Not something Kara has been keen to share. So when I said I liked your dress when I first met you I didn't know your family had blood money. I don't like it anymore."

Kara's face has gone from upset to angry as she spits at Elizabeth.

"What would you know about Africa?"

Elizabeth remains calm, and picks up a pink flamingo cocktail stirrer from a sun lounger and looks at it.

"I like these, Godric." She twirls the flamingo in her fingers then directs her attention back to Kara. "Quite a bit actually. My husband worked there on many occasions, but he helped people rather than sending them to an early grave through torture and slavery abuse."

Jonathan tries to close the conversation down.

"Is this the best time to rake this up? What has been happening here?"

Elizabeth is shocked.

"You knew about this?"

"I had it confirmed yesterday. I still can't believe it, Kat." Jonathan turns to Elizabeth. "But I didn't want it to ruin my day. At least today could be free of this stress."

"Stress? Your fiancée has just tried to kill your sister." Elizabeth replies. Jonathan is startled and drops his drink, which smashes on the marble tiles under his feet. Elizabeth continues. "Be careful of the glass, Godric." Elizabeth hates it when people leave broken glass. She looks at Jonathan. "You should sweep that up. She poisoned Rebecca's drink. Did you have any before we came in, Rebecca?"

Rebecca now looks extremely worried and looks at Kara then at the glass that Godric has placed on the table away from Kara; the contents still in the pool.

"No." Rebecca shakes her head. "No, I didn't drink anything."

Kara is frozen. Her secrets are tumbling out. She leans against the terrace wall, looking down at the floor. Elizabeth continues, lightly treading over the broken glass and now with Jonathan and Rebecca in her sights.

"I have reason to believe that Kara murdered Edward Wiley and Susan Bunt."

Rebecca looks at Elizabeth dumbfounded. As this news sinks in with everyone, Rebecca manages a quiet voice to question Elizabeth's logic.

"But Susan, it was her who cut up my dress. Remember I told you when you came to see me after Edward had been murdered? I told you, she followed me all the time. If anyone killed Edward, Susan did. Out of jealousy," Rebecca replies.

Elizabeth scratches her head with the flamingo stirrer.

"Didn't you say Susan cut up the wrong dress, a dress Jonathan bought you?" Elizabeth looks at Rebecca, continuing, "You were right about the jealousy, but it was Kara who cut up the dress to you from your brother, don't you see? Kara was jealous of your relationship with Jonathan. You told Godric earlier how close you are. It's obvious for all to see. Kara is jealous of you, Rebecca. I half suspect she broke up your black velvet shoes. The ones damaged in the burglary to your college flat after Edward's death. What burglar smashes up a pair of shoes?"

Kara, rushing to Jonathan, pleads with him for his understanding.

"You were always showering her with affection, with presents. Always calling her and checking up to see if she was all right. How do you think that made me feel?"

Jonathan is in such shock. He stands rigid, unresponsive to her grabbing at his arms and chest.

"She's my sister."

Elizabeth continues to press Kara. She knows it is only time and she will have this case wrapped up. What is taking Abley so long?

"Was that a reason for murder?"

Kara answers Elizabeth but still focuses her attention on Jonathan, pleading with him to understand.

"You don't know what it's like to be an outsider every day of your life. With you, going on and on about your precious sister. How you can only come up to Cambridgeshire to do things with Rebecca and Edward. All the joint dinners and holidays with Rebecca while Edward is busy. Nothing for just us, nothing left just for me."

Jonathan in a state, unsure what to do with himself, walks over to the bar and pours himself a large whisky, then swigs it straight down. Elizabeth continues, walking around the front of the pool, aware she has a captive audience for now and must test out her theory, but also that she needs to close this down before Kara does something stupid, especially as she has no backup, and Godric, although handsome, is no fighter.

"You said you didn't know Edward well. That day I walked with you from the punts, but that's not true, is it?"

Jonathan, in disbelief, turns to Kara.

"What have you done? Murder? You must be a stranger to me. Otherwise, nothing makes sense."

"Don't say that," Kara pleads to Jonathan.

Elizabeth hasn't got time for Jonathan's emotions. She needs to keep focused. Get a confession.

"You poisoned Edward because he came back knowing your secret, didn't he?"

Kara twists round now and faces Elizabeth, snarling aggressively,

"What would you know of it? He'd always come across

so kind and nice. But he was so worried about his reputation. Huh, you'd think Jonathan would have more to worry about than Edward, what with him being in the public eye. But no, Edward was paranoid the university would find out about my family, and it would be guilt by association. You think I can stop my father from doing anything? You think I'm responsible for what my family does? No, but Edward. He was too worried about himself."

Elizabeth can't believe the light in which Kara paints her colleague. Elizabeth puts a hand on Godric's shoulder as he sits on a lounger near Rebecca.

"I don't think he was, Kara. You were worried he'd tell Jonathan though, worried Jonathan would call off the wedding."

Kara opens the top of the water bottle in her hands.

"Yes, well. He's done that now, so Edward's won."

Rebecca interjects, at the horror of Kara's words.

"He's dead, how can he have won? You killed my husband?"

Elizabeth leans against the back of the lounger, her hip hurting her from her earlier fall in the greenhouse. Elizabeth's body is reflected in the pool, however, making her look much taller. Kara stares at Elizabeth, almost hypnotically as she throws the water bottle against the wall in anger.

"You can't prove any of it anyway."

Elizabeth sinks her head into her shoulders. She's tired. This is nearly over.

"I'm afraid, Kara, we can. We already have enough evidence in the pool to charge you with attempted murder of Rebecca. You poisoned her drink."

Jonathan looks at Kara closely and can see she is not denying it. He cannot believe his eyes and walks further away from Kara, now almost inside the house, in the hope that it is not real.

"I should call my Whip immediately. We need to close

this down. Get her out of the country."

Unperturbed by Jonathan's train of thought, Elizabeth continues to get the confession she needs for Abley, and so Abley can see she can do this again.

"Edward came back from Africa knowing your secret, didn't he? Your secret of child slavery you'd hidden so well, your secret which would force you back to Africa, an exile from Britain, back to your poisonous family. Jonathan was your ticket to staying in this country – into respectability was he not, Ms Tips? If you could marry him, you could stay here forever. No need for a visa, no awkward questions from the State. Edward was trying to warn me about you, Ms Tips... that's what he was saying. Then I thought: how did you do it? And it suddenly occurred to me that I'd been looking in the wrong place. I'd been ignoring something vital." Elizabeth pauses and looks down, and everyone in the room hangs on her next word. "Rebecca, do you by any chance have a necklace that Edward brought back for you from Africa? One with red and black beads?"

Rebecca looks surprised.

"How did you know he bought me–?"

Elizabeth interrupts.

"Just a hunch. It appears Edward bought you the same presents as Susan on more than one occasion. I saw the photograph of the horse with the gap in his teeth in your drawing room behind the door, near the wellington boots, and then saw the very same painting hanging up at Susan's home. Then there was the neck scarf you both had, with little Scotty dogs?"

Rebecca touches her neck, thinking of the scarf, wondering where it was, and how she could have been so wrong about Edward. She can't believe it all. She gets up to go into the drawing room and comes out with her bag. She opens the clasp and retrieves a necklace, and Godric holds her steady and returns her to her seat. Elizabeth continues talking to Kara.

"So, you took Rebecca's necklace, Kara." Elizabeth looks to Godric. "Godric, can you have a look in the kitchen to see if there is anything that will crush one of these beads?"

"Sure."

Godric walks off to the kitchen. Elizabeth walks over to stand at a table near the bar. She continues to look at Kara.

"Perfect for framing Rebecca. Look, it's loose. Some of the beads are missing. Hey presto, you made it look like Rebecca has taken some beads off and used the poison in those beads to kill Edward for leaving her for Susan."

Jonathan is trying to follow Elizabeth.

"I don't understand. Edward was poisoned?"

Elizabeth explains, matter-of-factly.

"Kara is better at gardening than she will lead you to believe. Quite a whizz with the poisonous plants. Yes, she stole Rebecca's beads to try to frame her. Poison Edward with some of the beads."

Godric comes back with a pestle and mortar for herb crushing.

"This do?"

"Thank you."

Elizabeth puts the pestle down on the patio table and then separates a bead from the others on the necklace. She then crushes it and shows Rebecca and Jonathan.

"What is this?"

Rebecca is upset and confused.

"What are you doing?"

She shoves it under Jonathan's nose.

"How the hell should I know? Dust?"

"You don't know. Why should you? You're not murderers. But Kara knows. It's abrus precatorius and the poison? Abrin. Kara would know, being green fingered, wouldn't you Kara? You paid someone to make sure Edward brought this necklace back with him from Africa, didn't you? You got them to offer it to him in his hotel, as a gift with compliments of the hotel management. All wrapped up classy ready for his wife. You got him to bring back his own murder weapon. Don't deny it. I phoned the hotel manager to ask for some more necklaces, and he told me Edward had asked about some necklaces after a man gave him a complimentary one."

Kara looks agitated and walks backwards to the left of the bar, eyeing a possible getaway through the orchard. She explains her reasoning to Elizabeth as if to prove her own intelligence.

"Rebecca was always whining about Edward. 'Does he love me?' 'I think he's cheating'. It got on my nerves. I thought it would be fitting that it came from a present for her."

Jonathan and Rebecca are completely stunned, watching Kara squirm like a stranger before their eyes.

Elizabeth used to the final denouement with the guilty, is far more concerned about containing Kara's anger while also trying to make sure she admits everything in front of witnesses.

"You saw him earlier, the night he was killed, had drinks with him in The Green Magician. They found your fingerprints on a glass in the dishwasher in the kitchens at that establishment."

Rebecca tries to process this.

"But Edward said he was going to the department and then he would eat nearby… Professor Green?" Rebecca asks.

Elizabeth looks at her watch and then replies,

"Oh, he went to the department, but he left early. We know this because we found traces of the poison in The Green Magician, once we knew what we were looking for."

"From the beads?"

"Yes. You see this," Elizabeth holds up the crushed bead powder, "although it looks fairly innocuous, if ingested it inhibits cell protein synthesis. I'm sorry to have to tell you Rebecca, but it causes multiple organ failure. Usually, after perhaps ten hours it makes it impossible to breathe and often causes people to vomit. Finally, low blood pressure will do it. But you had to make sure it was quicker than that, didn't you Kara?" Kara is staring at Elizabeth with hatred in her eyes. Elizabeth continues, "You had to make sure he didn't tell Rebecca or Jonathan about Africa. So, you put it in a line of cocaine so he'd inhale it, didn't you? Quite handy being his drug dealer."

Kara laughs out loud.

"He was almost my biggest client, nearly." Looking at her fiancé, Jonathan who is licking over his teeth and looks worried that she could so easily have murdered him the same way.

Elizabeth continues,

"Among the statements the police took of those who had eaten at The Green Magician Monday night, one man, who had been at a table with his dog, made a joke that Edward had gone downhill with his women over the night. I found him, and I asked what he meant, and he said Edward had met a very glamorous woman earlier in the night and then she was replaced by a rather frumpy woman later on. So, I just put two and two together. First, he met you, Kara, and then he met Susan Bunt. You had prepared an alibi, to go out with your friends all night after seeing Edward, after poisoning him. Only Edward scuppered your plans, as when he was with you in The Green Magician – after you'd given him cocaine – maybe in such a confident state he revealed all. He told you what he'd found out about you in Africa. He told you that he was going to get away from you and the family for good. He talked to you about his mistress, Susan, and showed you he'd bought a necklace for her."

Rebecca asks Elizabeth,

"So he was with Susan before he died?"

Elizabeth nods.

Rebecca gets up and walks to the edge of the terrace

for some air, now standing in disbelief, with her back to the others. Kara walks behind the bar, she dips down below for a second and then re-emerges and walks out of the bar with some vodka. Elizabeth feels very tired, and her leg is hurting, but she's also very excited, as she knows she has been right about the murders.

"It was the same necklace as Rebecca's," Elizabeth continues, "You'd already poisoned Edward, so you had to get that necklace from Susan, to still frame Rebecca for his death. So it looked like Rebecca's necklace had poisoned Edward and not Susan's. We thought it was Susan's at first, didn't we? No wonder you weren't happy then. I'm not sure who the man was on the bicycle Susan told Inspector Abley about, but I sense because that failed, you took matters into your own hands and followed Susan down an alley to get the beads back from her neck."

Jonathan looks up at his fiancée.

"I don't understand?"

Godric believes he understands and so tries to explain.

"Kara slipped in, in the morning, to Rebecca and Edward's apartments and took Rebecca's necklace to use to poison Edward. To frame Rebecca for Edward's death, and take Rebecca out of the equation too. It was all going to plan. But after she'd poisoned Edward, Kara heard Edward tell her he had another necklace. I guess if there was just one necklace with beads missing and the poison could be traced back to the necklace then all the fingers would point to Rebecca. But with Susan's in the mix, she could be accused instead. The whole point of killing Edward this way was to frame Rebecca, to get her out the way as well to spend more time with Jonathan? To kill Edward and silence him so he couldn't share her dirty secret about child slavery, and get Rebecca locked up and out of Jonathan's life. Is that right Bunny?"

"Exactly."

"Good God." Jonathan cannot believe his ears.

"The police found Susan's necklace, which Edward

grabbed from you. Kara, as you pushed him into the river. He was trying to stop himself from falling in off the bridge. It was a mistake. You didn't want him to have Susan's necklace. You still had it in your hands after taking it from Susan. This was a nightmare. That's what was odd for me when I knew what the poison was, but no beads were missing from Susan's necklace."

Rebecca cannot believe what Elizabeth is saying. She screams at Kara, "You killed him?!"

Godric tries to calm Rebecca on the steps of the terrace, putting his arms around her, seeing his nanna needs to get through this. Elizabeth continues, talking to Kara.

"It had all gone wrong, so you thought you'd better make sure the beads you'd stolen from Rebecca were easy to find by the police, to frame her. Only you kept being interrupted trying to put the beads back as the bedders and Porters were constantly keeping an eye on the rooms to keep the press away. So you engineered a very visible break-in. Only Inspector Abley interrupted you and thought you were clearing up. There was never any man running down the stairs after the so-called 'break-in', was there, Kara? That's when I realised it was you. You broke some black velvet bow dress shoes Rebecca told the police were from Jonathan. A clue too far, as nothing else seemed to be destroyed in the phoney break-in. And Rebecca had her necklace returned."

Jonathan is both upset and curious.

"Tell me it isn't true. Why did you lie to me about your family? I just found out about your father, but you? Didn't you love me?"

"Because you wouldn't have married me. You, with your political aspirations. Married to me?"

Elizabeth can't let herself stop, and will not allow Jonathan to interrupt her flow.

"Trading in children, in Namibia, in the Congo," Elizabeth says, looking at Kara, "Buying them to work in the diamond mines and cocoa fields. Feeding them mud."

Rebecca turns around from facing the garden and looks at Kara from under her brow.

"You are a heartless woman. You have something seriously wrong with you. I thought you were my friend and you do this?"

Kara shouts at Rebecca,

"Oh shut up! I'd have been okay if it hadn't been for your stupid husband!"

Elizabeth continues,

"Edward had found out, and your next problem was that he might tell Susan about it. He had written to Susan about it. It was his insurance policy if something happened. He posted it the night he died. He was worried that you might shut him up before he could tell. Ironically, you had no idea about the letter. But you suspected Edward would have told Susan that night, so you took no chances and poisoned all the drinks in her fridge the next morning while she was out."

Jonathan gasps, but Kara spits back at him,

"Well, you were doing something dodgy with Edward in Africa too. I found the cheque."

"We were planning to fly everyone over to Africa as a holiday for part of our wedding celebrations. Edward had taken some money to find locations and book hotels for everyone. He was returning the remaining money he didn't need—" While Jonathan is finishing his reply, quick as a flash Kara grabs Elizabeth and holds a fruit-slicing knife to her neck, getting the full attention of Godric, Jonathan and Rebecca.

"No one come close. I'm not going down for this."

"Put that down right now!" Godric shouts at Kara, but Kara tightens her grip.

"If anyone comes close I'll cut her throat."

Godric is poised to try to get the knife off Kara, but Kara starts to look behind her and move backwards.

"I'm going to leave, and no one must follow. If you do,

she will get hurt."

"Just let her go. Take me," Godric tries his best to reason with Kara. "I won't hold you back. My nanna is injured, she will be slower."

"Shut up!"

Kara is angry with Godric for trying to interfere, and as she shouts at him, she looks at Elizabeth's hip, as Elizabeth is now buckling under the pressure. As Elizabeth falls and Kara's eyes dip, Godric makes his move and grabs the knife from Kara. As he catches his breath, so Inspector Abley turns up out of nowhere behind them both and catches Elizabeth before she falls to the floor, gently easing her down so she can sit. Kara makes a run for it, but Godric chases her and is joined by Sergeant Lemon who has driven over to the house with Inspector Abley. Everyone watches as they catch and handcuff Kara, her face pressed into the grass.

Abley raises his eyebrows at the open-mouthed Jonathan and Rebecca. He smiles as he addresses them.

"The front door was locked, so I thought I'd come round the back. I see everybody's here. Everything okey-doke?"

Elizabeth, now sitting on the floor looks up at Inspector Abley.

"You might want to arrest Kara Anderson Tip for the murder of Edward Wiley, Susan Bunt and for the attempted murder of Rebecca Wiley tonight – your SOCO may want to sweep the bar for evidence and take samples from the pool. It has abrin in it from a glass. Should be enough to find molecules for evidence."

The Inspector looks quite shocked but listens intently.

"And perhaps another GBH against you too? Think we can do that," he replies.

51
CARDIGAN

Elizabeth and Godric stand by the Talbot Lago on the gravel drive of the new Secretary of State for Justice, Jonathan Smythe-Jones. They do not doubt that this will be the shortest appointment term in history, as when he tries to inform the Prime Minister about what has happened, they are sure his feet will not touch the ground. Jonathan follows Kara out, who is being taken away by two uniformed police officers.

"You have ruined everything! I never want to see you again!" Jonathan is barking at her.

Elizabeth speaks to Godric in hushed tones, "At first I thought it was Jonathan. He was smoking the same menthol cigarettes Edward had in his jacket. But they were Kara's. She must have given him them in the restaurant."

Godric replies,

"Me too. I thought perhaps Jonathan killed Edward to get hold of the family money or something. When he stood to inherit the lot that was suspicious, and then when he learnt that Susan was pregnant, that would possibly mean he wouldn't. As Edward suddenly had an heir."

Elizabeth answers Godric, as she gets out her keys and passes them to him.

"Yes, I can understand that. Rebecca also had quite the motive. Kara made a convincing case as to her jealousy, and I grew suspicious of her, it is true. But the dead campanula on Rebecca's college window ledge, and knowing nothing about plants ruled her out of killing her own husband. As soon as we knew the poison came from plants we knew it wasn't her."

Godric adds to Elizabeth's conclusions.

"And Rebecca told me Kara had sacked her gardener," Godric says.

Elizabeth explains why.

"Kara realised she didn't want anyone to know that she had taken a batch of Oenanthe crocata, or hemlock water dropwort as it is also known, from her garden. The very plant that killed Susan."

Rebecca comes out, and Jonathan holds her tight.

Inspector Abley walks over to Elizabeth.

"Flint was a suicide. He left a note. Dr Eruna is an unsavoury character, but not a murderer apparently, though we have put authorities in contact with the relevant information about the company conduct in Africa. We're also charging him over the assault on you. He admitted hitting you on the head."

"Everything balances out at some point," Elizabeth replies.

"And you were right. Kara paid a friend five thousand pounds to grab the necklace from Susan. Kara told him to put the frighteners on Susan. When we caught up with him tonight, he squawked that he couldn't do it. Said he didn't come forward because she had friends in high places. She'd asked him to break into Susan's and keep an eye on your house, that she had her sights on you, he thinks."

Godric pipes up.

"Oh, the man who was staring at me through a camera

lens. Must have been him."

Abley looks at Elizabeth,

"So, are you glad to be back?"

She smiles. "I never left."

"We have solved all the murders together again."

"No, not quite all, Inspector. You didn't help me solve the great greenhouse grape massacre."

"Oh. Did you find out who did it?"

"Crows. Crows were lifting the window lid themselves and getting in."

"Caw, I bet that must make you angry, what with you liking animals so much."

"On the contrary. How clever they are! They are to be celebrated even more. I shall be phoning the relevant academics so we can add this to the pile of evidence which shows not only how ingenious crows are, but how little we still know about them. Fascinating!"

Abley puts his arm on Elizabeth's.

"Hang on." The Inspector goes to the police car, opens the front door, and retrieves something from the passenger seat. He returns to Elizabeth and gives her Gerald's cardigan. "We have all the evidence we need, thanks to you."

Elizabeth turns and looks at the Talbot. She smells the cardigan. She looks around at the police cars and then gets in the passenger seat next to Godric. She holds the cardigan close as Godric turns on the engine and pulls away. Elizabeth does not look back.

THE END

Thank you very much for reading *Poison*, book one of the series Cambridge Murder Mysteries.

Titles available in the Cambridge Murder Mystery Series:

Book 1: Poison

Book 2: Cursed

Book 3: Blood Moon

Book 4: A Christmas Mystery

Book 5: Valentine's Day – Kiss of Death

Book 6: Coming Soon!

Short Stories in the Cambridge Murder Mystery Series:

Christmas Eve in Grantchester

Green *(available by subscribing to my newsletter)*

Other titles by Charlot King:

Animal Tales: Woof

Animal Tales: Pup

For more information on the other books in the series please do visit www.charlotking.com. If you'd like to follow what Charlot King is up to, you can find her on Twitter: @queencharlot. And, if you enjoyed this book, Charlot would be very grateful for a review on Amazon as well as telling all your friends. Much appreciated. Thanks again, and happy reading!